Also by Amy Shearn

How Far Is the Ocean from Here

The MERMAID *of* BROOKLYN

AMY SHEARN

A TOUCHSTONE BOOK
Published by Simon & Schuster
New York London Toronto Sydney New Delhi

Touchstone
A Division of Simon & Schuster, Inc.
1230 Avenue of the Americas
New York, NY 10020

First Touchstone trade paperback edition April 2013

Manufactured in the United States of America

10 9 8 7 6 5 4 3 2 1

Library of Congress Cataloging-in-Publication Data
Shearn, Amy.
The mermaid of Brooklyn / Amy Shearn.
p. cm.
"A Touchstone book."
1. Stay-at-home mothers—Fiction. 2. Mermaids—Fiction. 3. Depression, Mental—Fiction. 4. Self-realization in women—Fiction. 5. Brooklyn (New York, N.Y.)—Fiction. I. Title.
PS3619.H434M47 2013 813'.6—dc23
2012024927

ISBN 978-1-4516-7828-4
ISBN 978-1-4516-7829-1 (ebook)

For Adam, Harper, and Alton, the loves of my life:
thank you for not being the family in this book

one

Before I died the first time, my husband left me broke and alone with our two tiny children and it made me feel very depressed, etc. It's the same old story: He went to buy cigarettes and never came home. Really. Wouldn't you think you'd want to pack a bag or two, leave a forwarding address? Couldn't he have at least taken the dog? These were the things I wondered in the beginning. Not: was he having an affair, or: was he mixed up in something nefarious, but: I can't believe he wouldn't bring his datebook, his favorite loafers; I can't believe he didn't change the lightbulb in the hallway before deserting us. He knew I couldn't reach that lightbulb. The whole thing was unlike him. Then again, I was the one who died, which was unlike me, too.

I would be lying if I said his leaving wasn't a tiny bit of a relief, at least at first. My initial thought—due mostly to sleep deprivation, the effects of which, as any mother or political prisoner knows, never entirely fade—was that once the girls were in bed, I could ignore the dishes to be done and laundry (still in a compact three-day-old brick from the Laundromat drop-off service) to be put away; I could take a bath and then sleep (until Rose's next feeding) in a big empty bed with pillows mounded up on either side. I wouldn't need to make a grown-up meal for Harry, who annoyingly preferred dishes seasoned with things other than butter, and who inconveniently favored dinner conversation consisting of topics other than whether or not mermaids existed and, if so, whether or not their mommies made them take baths. I would not need to stifle the yawns that he mistook for boredom as he dramatically recounted the undramatic details of his day. I would not need to come up with a compelling excuse to avoid sex and then feel guilt both at the refusal and at the unoriginality of the desire, the undesire.

I know this doesn't make me sound like the nicest wife. But back then I only thought he was late coming home from work. I didn't know he would be gone so very long, that it would take him months and months to battle his way home, as if he were returning from the Crusades and not the Ever So Fresh Candy Company headquarters in Bay Ridge, Brooklyn. It didn't occur to me that nothing would ever be the same.

I forgot and didn't remember for some time that I actually had spoken to him on the evening in question. My days had a habit of bleeding together, and it was often difficult for me to pinpoint whether we had indeed talked a few hours earlier or whether I was remembering the day before. But no, I think it was that night, that fateful night, when, believe it or not, it was raining ominously, a storm of Great Plains–style velocity, unleashed by restless nymphs polluting the city's clouds, must have been, because there was such vindictiveness in the thunder rattling the kitchen window and spooking the imminently spookable baby so that she was wailing into my collarbone as I called Harry's phone, wanting to know if (oh God, so typical) he could pick up some milk, a request that was met with irritation—he didn't see why I couldn't take care of these things without involving him. Betty sat on her booster seat, swinging her legs with a buoyancy that belied her scowl. I looked over just in time to see her open her mouth and hatch a mound of chewed grilled cheese onto the table.

"Jenny?" Harry answered, sounding confused. "Is everything okay?"

"Oh, sure. Just another day in paradise," I said. Rose quieted, distracted by a hank of my hair.

"I miss you," Harry said. "I miss the girls." He sounded sad, or maybe just tired.

"Well, you're in luck," I said. "We're all right here, and we're taking visitors."

"I wuv you, you wuv me," Betty sang to her grilled cheese. The girl had a passion for dairy.

"Shh, baby, please," I said to her, to Rose, to the thunder that grumbled a little farther in the distance now, to the world. "What, Harry? I'm losing you."

"I'm going to stop for cigarettes on my way home," it sounded like he said.

"So you're not quitting, then," I said, having forgotten all about the milk. I would remember only when I poured my dinner bowl of Cheerios at eleven p.m., which I ended up eating with water, as I'd done more times than I cared to admit. Then he was gone. He would stay that way for a while.

When Harry left and I died it was the beginning of a desperately hot summer, a long sun-scorched stretch of days determined to silence doubters of global warming. The sidewalks of Brooklyn baked all around us, Prospect Park an expanse of brownish hay. I had these two babies, and people were always saying that my whole life was ahead of me—nosy grandmothers on the subway tugging at Rose's bootie or boinging Betty's curls, neighborhood eccentrics dispensing unsolicited advice from their bodega-front benches. I nodded and thanked them, or sometimes rolled my eyes.

My life with Harry had begun five years earlier, right around the time I started feeling my biological clock doing the *My Cousin Vinny* thing. I was working an exhausting job at a magazine that I was just starting to realize was not going anywhere: not the magazine, not the job, not me. I was officially Single and Loving It but in reality too tired by the end of the day to do anything more fabulous than drag myself home and watch fabulous amounts of television. (Romantic comedies counted as educational if they were in black and white. "We all go haywire at times, and if we don't, maybe we ought to," I'd mouth along with *The Philadelphia Story*.) I was too old to still have a roommate who called it "cooking" when she added pepper to her ramen; I was too young to retreat to the Midwest, capitulating to a life with many cats. It is annoying to find yourself living a cliché. It is doubly annoying to turn your life upside down only to settle into a fate even more banal than the one you were trying to avoid.

I met Harry on my thirtieth birthday, which I took as an omen. It was a few weeks after September 11, the bad one, and everyone in the city was feeling existentially wigged out, nostalgic for things we'd never noticed before. There was a barbecue on one of the last warm days of the year in someone's closety backyard, morning glory strangling the brick. ("Those vines are lovely," I told my host, trying to be friendly. She'd frowned, confessed, "They're killing *every*thing.") I didn't know these people well, but in those weeks everyone was overly solicitous and given to gallows humor, getting together to consume comfort food and avoid the subjects of death and patriotism in favor of those vaguer favorites, What Was So Great About Our City and The Things That Really Mattered. It smelled like burning rubber in Brooklyn. Every night I dreamed I had children who got lost in my pockets. In other words, it was a dangerous time to meet someone new.

Over by the fence was Harry. He was wearing a leather jacket that was too warm for the weather, which I didn't question at the time. His white shirt gaped open at the collar. I first noticed that triangle of neck. He stood talking to a trio of pretty blondes, and I couldn't hear what he said but all at once, as if choreographed, they threw back their heads and laughed. Here was Harry in one of his—of course I couldn't have known this then—manic highs, characterized by bravado and boisterousness, beloved by all. I thought (ha! ha!), *There is an uncomplicated man.* Having split recently from a morose Bushwick-loft-inhabiting artist, I looked at Harry and my gut said, *I know him. He is happy. He knows* (he knocked back a swig of microbrewed beer, squinted at something over my head, the fire escape maybe) *how to enjoy life.* People are always saying to follow your gut. Unfortunately, as it turns out, my gut is kind of stupid.

You know you're in trouble when you refer to your own relationship as a "whirlwind romance." Harry was fond of this phrase, which to me stank with a rot-sweet whiff of desperation. It's true that it all happened very quickly. There was something deeply flattering about his passion for me, how he had to have me immediately and forever. His professions of affection were always larger than life. Two dozen white roses would greet me at work on a gloomy Monday, to the cooing envy of my coworkers. Or I'd wake on a weekend to a homemade cappuccino, a new pair of golden gladiators (he'd pinpointed my weaknesses), and marching orders—"Get up, get up! We're going on a helicopter tour of the city in an hour!" My therapist posited that Harry was the Un My Father, what with his charisma and spontaneity and vague sheen of hazard.

She called him the Prince of Darkness Charming. She called him James Dean Lite. I called her Not My Therapist Anymore.

Within a year Harry and I were married (he wanted a Vegas wedding but worried it would kill his mother), and I'd traded my Xanax for prenatal omega-3s; a year after our wedding, Betty was born, and not quite two years after that, Rose. I'd been in college longer than I'd known my husband. I'd had a more protracted relationship with my academic adviser than with the father of my children, the man whose DNA I'd chosen to tangle with mine. And now here we were, piled into the crummy two-bedroom rental that was all we could afford in Park Slope, the yuppie neighborhood we clung to because I was afraid to bring my kids anywhere else in the city. Or here I was, anyway. Who knew where Harry was.

When I awoke at three a.m., Rose howling wolfishly at a blackout-curtain-defying streetlamp, Betty standing in the hallway with her hands over her ears, and Harry still wasn't there, it occurred to me to worry.

"Rosie, Rosie." I launched myself from bed, the sheets withed around my legs, only to step squarely on the dog. Oh. The dog. I was perpetually forgetting about the existence of Juniper, Harry's scraggly, immortal mutt. *Our* mutt now, of course. Had I taken her down to pee before bed? There were too many creatures' bodily functions to keep track of. The dog looked up at me mournfully. I apologized, stumbled into our nubbin of a hallway. My legs were stiff, Frankensteiny. I couldn't remember the last time I'd exercised in any way more significant than a walk pushing the stroller around the park, which I hoped counted for something. Every day I promised myself I'd at least stretch out before bed, and every night I was twelve times too tired to even consider it. Anyway, "going to bed" was more like waiting for Rose to relent and then immediately applying myself to my mattress.

Rose had hiked her swaddle up around her neck in a sort of haute couture cowl and was inching across the crib like a demented caterpillar. She stopped howling when she saw me, grinned toothlessly. "All right," I said. "You're very charming." I pulled the swaddling blanket off of her and lifted her out. Betty followed us back into my bed. I didn't bother trying to stop her. I nestled Rose down in the center of the mattress, and she immediately started snorting with the pre-meal enthusiasm of a true Lipkin. I lay down beside her and offered her the boob with the less destroyed nipple. Betty lay down on the other side of Rose.

"Mommy, where Daddy?"

Rose popped off and craned her neck curiously toward Betty.

"Sweetheart, please don't distract the baby," I said as dread gripped the top knob of my spine. Right. Where *was* Daddy? "Daddy's, um, at work."

Betty considered this. "Aren't the lights off?"

Rose latched back on. I closed my eyes and allowed the pull of sleep to drag me under the surface. Sleep was like water, my brain thought, unoriginally. And as with a river, you never stepped into the same sleep twice, it was always a different texture somehow, there was a different current tonight, something roiling in the distance. What was this dream that I—

"Mommy."

Without really waking up, I said, "Yes, honey, the lights are off. He has a flashlight."

"Oh."

Rose stopped nursing to stare up at Betty again. "Please, no talking, Betty," I said, already mostly asleep. I was so tired that it hurt to wake up and fall back asleep. It was like how it used more energy to turn something off and on than it did to— But the thought stopped making sense as I thought it, breaking apart like bread dropped in water. I was dimly aware of Juniper jumping onto the bed and coiling up behind me. Being sandwiched between little bodies this way seemed cozy for about thirty seconds, until my leg wanted to stretch and couldn't. It was another hot night, the mugginess unfazed by the air-conditioning unit lodged in the window, and here we were glued together by sweat and spit-up and dog hair. It was all very glamorous.

When I awoke again—five minutes later? an hour later?—Rose was snoozing with her mouth slightly open around my nipple, milk pooled on her tiny tongue. Betty and Juniper were curled together at the foot of the bed. The room was shadowy, lit by the streetlamp, the lights of night-owl neighbors, the lights of early-rising neighbors, the hazy undark of the city at night. And really, now, where was Harry? Alarm rang through my limbs. I tried to temper it with some Vulcan logic, a technique I'd had to teach myself over and over, every night of my anxiety-laden first year of motherhood. No, no, he wasn't dead in a ditch, that wouldn't make any sense— He had said something . . . Oh. He was going to stop and buy cigarettes. My brain, still half-sleeping like a dolphin's, invented a story: He'd gotten a call from his alcoholic brother, Fred, he'd gone over to comfort him, he'd probably called my cell phone but I hadn't gotten the call because the phone was loitering as usual somewhere deep within the diaper bag. He had ended up spending the night at Fred and Cynthia's place near the office and had texted me so as not to wake up the girls in the miraculous case that one or both of them might be sleeping and when I saw him tomorrow, today, whenever, he would chastise me for not paying more attention to that particular hunk of electronics, which, it was true, I saw more as an emergency distraction device for Betty than as an actual tool for communication. Okay, that made sense. I was drifting back to sleep, so tired that my joints felt jumpy, my skin prickly. I couldn't process whether I'd fallen asleep or else had slept for hours when there was Betty, patting my cheek.

I opened an eye. Rose sprawled out on her back, taking up more room than seemed geometrically possible for a person who weighed twelve pounds. It was a good thing Harry wasn't here, actually. He hated when I let Rose sleep in our bed. "You made me buy that rocking chair for the nursery," he'd say crossly. "I thought that was for nursing. It's not safe to sleep with her in our bed." I had a mature, reasonable response to this, being the excellent wife and mother that I was: I waited for him to turn around, and then I stuck my tongue out at the back of his head.

"Mommy. Cookies?" Betty said experimentally. When I opened both eyes, I saw Juniper behind her, wagging her tail. When Juniper diagnosed me as awake-ish, she leaped up and started pacing around. "No and no," I said to both of them. I probably fell back asleep. "MOMMY," Betty said, patting my cheek harder. Okay, hitting. Smacking my face. Her hand was sticky, somehow, already. It was a lovely way to wake up. It wasn't even light out yet. So, four forty-five, maybe? Juniper jumped up onto the bed, and Rose's eyes popped open.

"Oh God," I said. Every morning I lay in bed thinking, *I cannot possibly do this for one more day*. Then I got up and did it for one more day, every day. All parents did, I told myself. My exhaustion was nothing special. And likewise, the moments in which I managed to cope in a halfway-decent way were not exactly the triumphs of maternal spirit I liked to pretend they were—more like basic competence. "Tell Daddy to take out Juniper," I said.

Betty shook her head. "It's too far."

"What?" I lifted Rose, who belched loudly, looking surprised and pleased, a diminutive frat boy. I hadn't burped her after her last dozy feeding. Another habit Harry hated.

"It's *too far*. Daddy at *work*."

Oh *God*.

Thirty seconds later, I was wearing the same T-shirt and shorts I'd worn the day before; Rose and her diaper, transformed into an anvil of pee, were tucked into the sling; Betty was dressed in her pajamas, a tutu, and pink Crocs her grandmother had gotten her expressly against our wishes; Juniper was harnessed into her leash. The whole happy family clambered out on the street. It was already about eighty degrees out, the world damp and steaming from the night's rain. Day-old spit-up baked on my shirt, emitting a not entirely unpleasant bready odor. The sun was just beginning to rise, a bright sore bleeding over the park. Juniper peed in someone's tree box, irrigating the "Curb your dog" sign. Some days the city seemed almost supernaturally beautiful to me. Then there were days like this, when unforgiving light revealed rats performing acts of daytime derring-do, when everything in sight—a withered crone collecting cans, a paralyzed poodle dragging its hind legs on clanging wheels—looked damaged and deranged. It was garbage day, and stinking boulders of trash punctuated the sidewalk, which reminded me that I hadn't taken down our recycling, a thought that filled me with despair. Betty toddled over to a rank pile, lifted up a diseased-looking teddy bear.

"No!" My voice startled Rose, who started to cry. It was easier to have sympathy for her, I found, than her sister, the toddler terror. Rosie couldn't help it. She was a baby. Her crying was uncomplicated. When Betty turned on the waterworks about one of her complex big-girl issues, like not getting an eighth Dora Band-Aid with which to decorate the dog, my skin curdled with irritation. But the baby I could deal with. I wasn't *that* heartless. Usually.

"Shhh." I swayed back and forth, extracted a pacifier from my pocket, and plugged her mouth. "Betty," I said in the creepy-calm voice of fake parental patience. "Put that down right this second. Haven't you ever read *The Velveteen Rabbit*? Scarlet fever! Bedbugs! Death!"

Betty knitted her brow.

"Drop it!" I said. Juniper stopped walking and looked at me. "Not you."

Betty released her treasure and poutily stuck her thumb in her mouth, the same thumb that, moments before, had been caressing the grimy toy's eyeless socket. I closed my eyes. I'd been awake for two minutes and already felt overwhelmed by the length of the day ahead of me. I was officially over Harry's disappearing act.

After Juniper had crapped a portentously watery crap—"What did you feed her?" I asked Betty, who pretended not to hear—we made our way around the block, dotted with trucks making their deafening morning deliveries to the corner store, the bakery, the bar. We trooped back upstairs. I finally changed Rose's diaper. She grabbed at her crotch, grinning. We went into the main room, a relentlessly cluttered living room with an open kitchen, which had seemed like a good idea before we had kids. ("Perfect for entertaining!" Harry had said when I moved in. Ha!) Betty sat cross-legged next to Juniper's bowl, crunching.

"Oh dear God, what are you eating?" I said, depositing Rose into her bouncy seat. She promptly commenced howling. I picked her up despite the twinge between my shoulder blades. Betty put her hand back into Juniper's food bowl and then froze. "Please do not eat dog food," I said halfheartedly. I searched for my phone in the diaper bag, which seemed to contain everything we owned except diapers. I heard Betty crunching again. Juniper lapped at her water. Betty splashed in Juniper's water. Rose snuffled around at my chest.

I only feel like crying because I am so tired, I told myself. *It's just that my eyes are all dried out.*

No messages on my phone. No missed calls. Staying calm for the sake of the girls took all the energy I had. Which made me mad at Harry—what a jerk, to put me through this, and on such a hot day!—which made me immediately bite the inside of my cheek, hard, to punish myself for thinking such mean thoughts about someone who was maybe missing and in danger, or maybe just a huge fucking jerk, or maybe a huge fucking jerk who was nevertheless missing and in danger.

I called the office (neck prickling, lungs hollowing out), but no one answered. It was too early for anyone to be there in any normal sort of capacity. I pictured Harry asleep in his chair, head cocked back at a terrible angle. Okay. That would make a funny story someday: *He was so tired, because you never slept, Rose, that one night he called to say he was on his way home and then promptly fell asleep in his chair.* Cue Harry rubbing his neck ruefully, as if remembering the pain upon waking.

After all, he had been working a lot of late hours recently. I coped by changing into my pajamas at six p.m. every night and entertaining Betty and myself with elaborate, magical bedtime stories. He was the one missing out, I told myself, on these great bonding whatevers. After all the moments of parenting that, let's be honest, really sucked, I lived for that twilight time when Betty snuggled up and prompted me, "Tell the fishy." Then my oft-mocked master's degree in Russian folklore (it sounded good at the time) got its moment to shine. "Yes," I told Betty, working a comb through a post-bath snarl. "Once there was a fish-woman who lived at the bottom of the river. Every night she came out and danced in the meadow by the light of the moon."

"At the park?" In Betty's two-and-a-half-year-old mind (as in mine), all woodland adventures took place in Prospect Park.

"Yep. In the big field on the way to the carousel. And she would dance and dance. And sometimes climb a tree to brush her hair."

"But only if her mama there."

"Right. Exactly. For safety. And so one night a man walked by . . ." Betty loved when these ghostly mermaids lured children with fruit snacks and Pirate's Booty (hey, water spirits know what little kids like) and especially when they tickled men to death.

"But not *wheely*? She tickle him? But not *wheely*."

"Well . . ." And then would come a tickle to end all tickles. The fish-woman stories had emerged from a fit of overparenting pique, when it was revealed that while babysitting one night Grandma Sylvia had exposed my daughter to Disney's insipid *Little Mermaid* movie, with its teeny-bopper heroine. I'd relented on a lot of the perfect parenting ideals I'd had as a pre-parent, but this was too much. Mermaids had been my favorite figures in the Slavic fairy-tale pantheon, but it was because they were weird and powerful and a little scary, not because they looked great in clamshell bikinis. I admit that I tended to neglect the girls' wardrobes—the cuteness quotient of their coats and dresses not nearly as high as one might expect from a pair of brownstone-Brooklyn babies—and things like clipping their nails and educating them about etiquette or God or non-microwaved cuisine. But simpering female role models and saccharine fairy stories? Come on. I left out the parts about mermaids being the unavenged spirits of suicides, forsaken girls, betrayed brides, unwed mothers-to-be. I figured that stuff could wait at least until pre-K.

Bedtime, sleep. I never would have thought these would someday be my obsessions, occupying such large portions of my daily consciousness. Starting at around four p.m.—the witching hour, when all down the street you could hear children begin to howl like werewolf cubs: my mind clicked with calculations: *If everyone has dinner at four-thirty and then baths at five and then cartoons for Betty during Rosie's bedtime and then assuming Rosie stays asleep for Betty's bedtime, it's possible I'll get some time to sew before Harry gets home*—and I'd start zooming toward bedtime in a maniacally unsoothing manner. The day ended definitively around dusk, and I never left the building after dark, but when your kids are little and wake up all night, you don't ever get to clock out. I fantasized about a sexy eight-hour block of sleep. I salivated while telling Betty the part of *Sleeping Beauty* where the princess snoozes for a century.

Such luxurious lengths of sleep were not to be, not in this lifetime. I remember reading—it must have been soon after Betty's birth, when peaceful nursing sessions mellowed into snuggling naps, when she would snooze on my chest while I browsed child development books (nowadays taking care of one baby sounded so easy, total amateur hour)—that infants need something like twenty hours of sleep a day, and that by four months old they will sleep through the night and take at least two naps a day. Which is how I knew that Rose was an exceptional human destined for great things. Think what an advantage it would be not to need sleep! This was what Harry and I had joked about before we were too tired to joke, when Rose was a squalling kitten balled up in blankets; we assumed this would all be an amusing anecdote someday. "We have here," Harry announced into a rattle, "the parents of the youngest ever Nobel Prize winner, Rose Lipkin, who credits her extraordinary body of work to the extra hours she has to work, as she only sleeps for forty-five minutes a night. Now, tell us, Mr. and Mrs. Lipkin, did Rose ever sleep like a normal person?" And while the old me would have answered in some funny, snappy way, I'm sure, at the time I smiled wearily into Rose's sweet-smelling scalp. Even Betty, who seemed to forget about her little sister's existence for hours at a time, eventually commented on the situation, strutting into the room on chunky toddler legs and pointing and saying, "Baby needs night-night," furrowing her brow in droll fury. Baby needed night-night, indeed.

As a result I was worn down by exhaustion, my edges rounded, like a giant ambulatory pebble. My brain didn't work the way it once had. I felt at all times an instant away from tears. I expended a lot of energy I didn't have convincing myself this was due to being tired. I didn't want to believe that it was, as my well-meaning psychiatrist sister seemed to be hoping, postpartum depression, which she insisted on calling, awfully, "baby blues," as if describing Frank Sinatra's eyes and not a mental health condition. Still, Sarah had called once a week from Seattle since Rose's birth, the way she had with Betty—making small talk before edging up to the subject and finally saying, her voice taking on the queasy sheen of sympathy, "So, how are you *feeling*? Any *baby blues*?"

I knew the answer she was looking for. "No," I'd tell her almost apologetically. "Everything's great. I'm just tired."

"Okay," she'd say, exhaling. "Okay, good. Because after Max was born, I was a wreck, and I didn't feel like I could admit it to anyone—"

"I know, Sarah, I know."

"I hate that you stopped seeing your therapist. I just want to make sure you have someone to talk to."

"Yes. Thanks."

"Okay. The only reason why I mention it is because for someone with your history of depression, it's really common. And there's nothing at all the matter with it. You need to know it doesn't mean you're a bad mother or that you don't adore your kids. Really, did you know that twenty percent of woman experience postpartum depression, which can lead to postpartum psychosis—I mean, of course, not *you*—and especially women who have to go off their depression meds when they have their babies—"

"Yes, I know. Thanks a million for the cheery call, Sare, but I really have to go now. Time to drown the children in the bathtub."

"That's not funny. Jenny. Jenny? I do not like that joke. Jenny?"

Almost five months later, not much had changed except that Betty had taken more of an interest in Rose, so now neither of them slept. I would jerk awake in one odd situation or another—sitting in a kitchen chair while breast pump parts boiled, lying on the baby's blanket surrounded by toys—to find Betty lugging Rose into her lap or the two of them huddled in Rose's crib. "Betty! What did I tell you about the baby—gentle touches! Gentle touches!" I would cry ungently. Betty would stare up at me, green eyes wide, grubby fingers tangled in Rose's scant strands of hair. Or Rose would be about to relent, her eyes rolling shut, as Betty would toddle in with the toy Harry had been entrusted to hide, a plastic meteor pocked with buttons, each triggering a mechanized song more eardrum-busting than the last. Who in the world designed those things? The wardens at Guantánamo Bay?

It wasn't only the sleeping, either. Rose constantly wanted to nurse, but would stay on the breast for about thirty seconds before absentmindedly pulling off. Whenever I put her down, she wailed. "She's spoiled," Harry's mother, Sylvia, said. "You carry her around too much." "Early teething," said a lady on the train. "It's reflux," diagnosed my sister, Sarah, long-distance. The pediatrician shrugged, not unsympathetically. "She's a baby," he said. "They cry."

So you couldn't really blame Harry when he started working later and later into the night. He swore up and down it had nothing to do with me or the girls, that he wanted to be home to help me but things were not looking ever so good at Ever So Fresh and he was needed at the office. "Never go into business with your family," he grimly told Betty one morning as she fed Cheerios to her plastic cash register. She looked at him for a long moment before offering a delicious choking hazard to Rose, who was doing her baby cobra pose on the floor nearby. "Nononono!" We rushed forward in unison. (It was our fault, my mother-in-law informed us, that "no" was Betty's favorite word. Before I'd had kids, I'd never known this was a thing, how you weren't supposed to use the word "no." I still didn't get it. What else could we say to her as she, for example, lurched toward the busy avenue we lived on? *Un-yes?*)

What with the economy, and the recession, and the "crazy food faddists" (according to Sylvia, as if believing candy to be unhealthful were some wrongheaded new idea), sales were down at Ever So Fresh. Harry's year-end bonus had been a bulk-size bag of stale fruit gels, disgusting enough when new and, by the time we encountered them, chewy as sugar-shellacked beef jerky. His brother was busy divorcing his second wife, one of those gently psychotic types who enjoyed visiting Disney World despite being a childless adult, and baby-talked to her houseplants. Therefore, Harry was needed at the office later and later into the night, each night, and sometimes on weekends. Allegedly.

The morning after the epic cigarette run: "You're sure it's only . . . work?" My friend Laura puckered her forehead. She knew Harry was working crazy hours, but I'd left out for now the part about how he'd never come home last night. We'd been putting in extra-long hours of our own at the playground. Laura's husband worked a lot, too. Then again, Laura's husband was a surgeon. Their apartment could have fit four of ours inside, and contained within its original-prewar-detail-adorned depths a washer, dryer, *and* dishwasher, oh whirring objects of my most fervent desire.

Betty and Laura's daughter, Emma, busied themselves palpating an anthill with bendy straws. I squinted at them, pretending to watch them play instead of mentally critiquing the cute-but-slightly-misaligned sailor dress I'd made for Betty. I would never admit to being happy to have girls strictly for the wardrobe options, but I will say that as an amateur seamstress, jacked cotton dresses for unpicky models were sort of my specialty. Betty offered Emma a wood chip, which she sucked on tentatively. I took in a breath to tell Laura about the woodsy snack and then didn't, for some reason.

I stood near the fence, swaying back and forth with Rose sleeping fitfully in her sling. She seemed determined to sleep only when the nap could be of no use to me. I felt the sleepy weight of her body, not looking at her, and for a moment imagined she'd been replaced with a Tereshichka-like wooden block. Checked. Nope, just a regular human, non-imp-from-a-folktale baby. Phew. I wondered if all adults had similar moments of panic caused purely by overactive imaginations. It seemed like a question you couldn't ask without seeming, you know, crazy.

"I mean," Laura said, "Harry's a great guy—I'm sure he wouldn't—but—"

"Oh, please," I said. My bravado sounded forced even to me. I felt close to tears because I was so tired, I told myself as usual, just because I was tired. "Harry hates everyone. He doesn't have any friends. How on earth would he have a girlfriend?"

Laura smiled, sort of. We both knew this wasn't remotely true. He was moody at home with me, but out in public Harry was the life of the party, gregarious and large-hearted. Somehow, everywhere we went, people knew his name.

"They're really super busy at Ever So Fresh," I added. Now

Betty was sampling the wood chips. I again took a breath and then stopped. I had learned to conserve my energy; I only had so much left, and the day was long. Besides, Betty was building immunities. I was pretty sure I'd read that somewhere. A childhood spent nibbling Brooklyn dirt could only result in an iron stomach, right? I pictured a twenty-year-old backpacking Betty impressing her hostel-mates by devouring street food in Indonesia. *You're welcome, grown-up Betty,* I thought. My mother had encouraged quiet play indoors and endless hours of television, had suffered a phobia of dirt so debilitating that I'd never so much as seen a sandbox until I had kids of my own, had taught her girls that trying anything new would bring only trauma. I did what I could to escape her with every parenting move I made.

"Girls!" Laura interrupted. "No eating wood chips!" She turned back to me. In her mirrored sunglasses, I looked overly round and worried. I focused on relaxing my brow and applying a small smile. "Didn't you say business wasn't good there, though?" Laura said. I loved her, I did, but sometimes her attention to detail was exhausting. I closed my eyes and jolted them open. Was it possible to sleep standing up? If I fell asleep standing up, would I fall down? When I fell down, would I stay asleep?

"Well, that's why he's so busy," I said, starting to feel confused.

"Hmm. Okay," said Laura, frowning into the distance. "Emma! No!" she called toward the girls, who looked back at us and retreated farther into the dusky distance beneath the slide. It was one of the curious qualities of our friendship that Laura and I never looked each other in the eye as we spoke. Maybe this was how it was with mothers of small children. When I thought about it, I wasn't exactly sure what Laura looked like, though I knew Emma by heart. Laura and I sat side by side, quietly heckling the park populace like a non-Muppet Statler and Waldorf. "Is he trying to drum up new business? Or something like that?"

"Something like that, yes," I said. "And in the meantime, I get the shitty parts of being a single mother without any of the fun. Like dating. Maybe I should start dating."

"I hear it's not as fun as we remember it."

"I don't remember it being all that much fun, so I probably wouldn't be disappointed."

"I just— I would just watch him, you know? Remember what happened to Jeanie and Jon, is all."

"Geez, Laura. You're a real ray of sunshine." These Park Slopeians we vaguely knew had been the talk of the playground for a few weeks, when Jon absconded with the nanny and Jeanie had to sell their condo at a huge loss. I hardly saw the parallel. If there was a lesson to be learned from them, it was that, hello, when hiring live-in nannies, you went for the overweight grandmotherly type, not the hot recent college grad with an education degree. I mean, didn't everyone already know that? I'd never be able to afford a nanny anyway, let alone a hot one.

Laura didn't respond for so long that I finally looked up, and—oh! Cute Dad. She nudged me. "Stop that," I said.

Sam held the distinction of being the least uncute stay-at-home father we knew, and accordingly had been mythologized as Cute Dad. I think we just needed a Cute Dad in our lives. We saw him nearly every day. We'd once followed him around the entire loop of the park, like giddy preteens. Our shared crush seemed totally innocent to us, but I admit it probably would have struck our husbands as a little creepy, possibly predatory, had they known. "Shh!" Laura giggled. Cute Dad flashed his famous smile as he fast-walked past, trailing his kids on their scooters.

"You're terrible," I told Laura as we watched him disappear into the woods. "The timing of this is highly inappropriate."

"Timing of what? I'm just waving hello to a neighbor."

"And blushing."

"I am not."

But she was. I mean, we both were.

When Harry hadn't shown up or answered his phone by ten a.m., I called Sylvia at her desk, across the office from Harry's. I could practically see her frowning at Harry's empty desk, then picking up her phone gingerly between her flawlessly manicured fingertips. She kept a pencil near the phone for dialing, one of many household items that had been transformed into prosthetics to accommodate her metallic magenta talons.

"Ever So Fresh," she droned, the antithesis of fresh. They had to be the last place of business in New York, perhaps the world, to not have caller ID. Or a receptionist. Sometimes if she was feeling playful, Sylvia imitated a dial-by-name directory, but that was about as technologically savvy as they got. They didn't have a website, not a single sad page with their contact information.

"Sylvia," I said. My voice cracked unexpectedly. I was not used to sharing a great deal of emotion with my friendly but brittle mother-in-law, and here I was, wet-faced, snuffle-nosed. Betty stopped running a crayon over Juniper's back and stared at me. Rose grinned toothlessly from her swing, a plastic contraption that took up half our living room.

"Hello? Hello?" I could hear another phone ringing in the background. Was someone calling Harry? The police, having found his wallet floating in the Hudson? A not-so-secret secret girlfriend? I tried to pull myself together, pressing at my eyes with my fingertips. "Sylvia, it's me, Jenny."

"Hi, dear. What's the matter?"

It was difficult to speak.

"Honey, let me put you on hold." On hold! I sat there, listening to the hold music—an ancient assortment of Rat Pack crooners Harry's father had chosen before he died, nearly three years earlier—feeling more and more depressed. I dabbed my eyes with a burp cloth that smelled of sour milk. "Mommy?" Betty said hesitantly. I shook my head, voiceless. Then Sylvia was back. The other phone had stopped ringing.

"Is it so bad having Harry home for the day?" Sylvia had the lox-y voice of a lifelong smoker, which was enough to annoy me on a day like today: the unhealthy rasp of her stretched-thin voice.

"Home? Sylvia, I haven't seen Harry since yesterday morning."

There was a pause. "You mean he's not home sick?" It was amazing how we'd all figured out ways to explain it—explanations that demanded so much work on our parts! The mental calisthenics! I heard a muffled sound, as if Sylvia had placed a hand over the receiver and started talking to someone else.

"I was hoping he'd—I don't know—fallen asleep at the office. And forgotten to call this morning. I guess. Or something." It sounded incredibly stupid when I said it out loud.

"Wait, what? Jenny. Have you tried his cell?"

"Of course. It goes straight to voice mail."

"Why didn't you call earlier? He could be bleeding to death on a subway platform somewhere!" I had always thought Sylvia was given to histrionics until Betty was born. Then I realized there was nothing crazy about believing your constant vigilance to be the only buffer between your child and the abyss, about feeling sure that you could keep your baby safe by sheer force of anxiety. "Have you called the police?" Hearing her say this made it sink in. Something had gone very wrong with my husband. People didn't just not come home and then not call. Well, okay, Harry did, now and then. But it wasn't something you got used to easily. "Should *I* call the police? Jenny? Hello?"

"I don't know. What if he's—you know. In Atlantic City or something."

A chilly pause. In my panic, I had broken the unspoken Lipkin rule: You don't talk about the Lipkins. Even to the Lipkins. Especially to the Lipkins. You don't talk about Fred's drinking problem. You don't talk about the paterfamilias's obesity, and when he dies of a heart attack, you act like no one ever saw it coming. You don't talk about Harry's obsession with gambling, even when it's painfully obvious, even when he's your own husband and it's your money being frittered away on poker nights and Vegas weekends. It was all very suppressed, very 1950s. Sylvia wasn't going to rescue me, either, or heaven forbid admit that I sort of had a point. That it had sort of happened before. Finally, I said, "Is Fred there? Has he heard from Harry?"

"He's here. He doesn't know anything. We assumed Harry was home sick, or that maybe he'd taken the day to spend with the family. He's been so upset about everything lately, and—"

"About what?" I interrupted.

Sylvia paused. Was it a knowing, considered pause? Or the normal pause of the interrupted? A paranoid queasiness percolated in my gut. "I'm sure he's told you business is bad. And I know you kids are looking to find a bigger place, and it's stressing him out, and that you, you know"—and oh, duh, I got it—"you haven't been feeling well . . ."

"All right," I said. "I didn't know if there was something else. I'm feeling fine, by the way."

"Of course you are, dear."

"I'm just tired. You know? Rose doesn't sleep. It's tiring. Betty, *no*! Do *not* feed boogers to the baby!" I said it a little too loud and right into the phone.

Sylvia paused. "Dear, why don't I come over."

I looked around the apartment. This was not one of those "Oh, ha, sorry it's such a mess" moments. It was dangerously messy. It was call-child-services, doubt-the-mental-health-of-the-mother messy. It was TLC-reality-programming messy. We cohabited with dust bunnies I knew by name, tiles that were actually milk spills. The windowsills were furzed with old-building lead dust. I wouldn't have been surprised to find the jumbled hall closet mobbed by mischievous gnomes. Moments earlier Betty had been sitting on the kitchen floor playing with "ladybugs," a friendly assortment of crumbs and shed paint chips.

"No, no," I said too quickly. A weepy weight welled in my throat. "No, thank you. We have a ton to do today. But—keep me posted."

"If we haven't heard from him by tomorrow, I'm calling the police," said Sylvia. This was a small victory: Her all but admitting that Harry might have gone off to gamble, that there might be a reasonable, unreasonable explanation for everything.

"All right," I said.

"You don't think he might be—"

I pretended not to hear and hung up the phone. When I turned around, Betty's face was screwed up bulldoggishly.

"Wanttoo talk to Grandma!" she wailed.

"No, you don't," I said. "Trust me."

Getting to know Harry after we'd married was interesting, I'll give it that. The gambling problem, for example. Who knew there was such a thing? When we were first together, he'd taken me to hipster poker nights in smoky speakeasies, tucked into warehouse warrens or behind doors hidden in brownstone bookcases. I loved the whole secret-supper-club phenomenon for the retro charm, the sense of in-crowd illicitness, and most of all, for the excuse it gave me to wear high heels too impractical for real life. Besides, Harry looked so cute leaning over in his pressed dress shirt, his hair slicked back like a movie gangster's, calling someone's bluff. I was enjoying myself, infatuated with being infatuated with him. I didn't realize that for Harry, these nights were about the shuffle of cards, the plunking down of dollars. Which is to say, I didn't think about the poker part of things much at all.

Once we were married, I would wake up in the middle of the night and wander into the living room to find him up in front of the computer, his face flickering in the light of an online poker site. I never suspected that this was his intermediary fix, like a junkie trying to take the edge off with drink. When I was eight months pregnant with Betty, he disappeared one Friday, just never got to work, without calling or answering his phone or responding to the dozen texts I sent. I dedicated that Saturday to calling every hospital in New York City, spent Sunday-brunch time hysterically camped out at my local police precinct, scored an exclusive tour of the Kings County morgue to view a baseball team's worth of frozen white men. Needless to say, when he reappeared, rumpled but triumphant, in the meager light of Monday morning (having weekended in Atlantic City and doubled the money we'd received as wedding gifts and had been saving as a down payment for something or other), I was a hormonal mess—relieved, furious, exhausted, overjoyed, threatening murder and/or divorce. "I looked at dead people!" I'd screamed. "You made me look at dead people!" The fight that ensued caused both our upstairs and downstairs neighbors to call 311 on us. (No one thought to knock on the door to make sure the shattering plates weren't meeting skin—thanks, Brooklyn!) Still. You wouldn't think this of yourself—I know I didn't—but it so happens that it's easier to forgive when your wrongdoer (contrite, begging your pardon, crying for the first time in your presence) has suddenly become twenty thousand dollars richer and apologizes with a weekend at a SoHo spa. It sounds shallow, I know, but hold judgment until you've had a Thai herbal rub applied to your extremely pregnant belly.

So here was this man I'd married, revealing himself to me as we formed our family together. A gambling problem! Either he was really good at hiding it or my powers of denial were superhero strength, because by the time I understood the severity of his sickness, our lives were so entangled that it became my problem, too. I remember wishing (and then immediately taking it back, pretending not to have thought it) that he could have had a health problem instead—something I could feel sorry for him about, something we could try to survive together. The gambling thing was embarrassing. It was something I'd never heard of, which made it feel somehow weirder than something like plain old alcoholism.

Once, before I knew better, I mentioned it to his mother. She was so offended, I feared I'd caused irreparable damage to my standing among the Lipkins. Which I had. I'd been unintentionally offending my in-laws ever since I'd arrived on the scene and their mistrust of me—an overeducated gentile from Minnesota—metastasized when I refused the ridiculous job Sylvia offered me when Harry and I were first married.

The thing was, I actually loved my job as an editor at a home-decor magazine in Midtown. What was so confusing was that I'd thought it was something Harry liked about me—that I had a career, that I had ambitions, that I was, modesty aside, a really good editor. I worked long hours, sure, but I was happy there in my tweed skirt, biting a pencil (a prop, as I typed away) in the buzz and flicker of my cubicle at nine p.m., ordering in sushi on the company card and trying to sift the various pieces of interviews and research and background material into a story that read smoothly, that illuminated the photography, that expressed its meaning and humor and good taste in a breezy but not too breezy manner, that people would read, admittedly, on the toilet (but that was hardly the point, now, was it?).

My job held no allure for the Lipkins. They'd never heard of my magazine and had only a fuzzy concept of what it was I did. (I once overheard Sylvia at a family Passover seder describe me as a "sort of a newspaper columnist.") So when we'd been married a month, they banded together, decided that I would be happier writing advertising copy, managing contracts, and answering phones at Ever So Fresh. It had been a whole *thing*. I was horrified at the thought and even more horrified that Harry, the stranger I had married, would think I would want to do such a thing. I loved my job. I complained about it constantly, but there was no denying the thrill of excitement I got every time I walked into the cavernous lobby of my fancy building near Times Square. I spent a lot of time getting dressed in the morning, blow-drying my hair, de-scuffing my oversize, overpriced handbag, selecting my shoes.

Sometimes I think what I liked most about working was the shoes. I had always been on the shrimpy end of the spectrum and, in adulthood, had topped out at barely five feet tall on tiptoes, with a size-four foot. In New York this was weird enough, but back home in Minnesota, land of big-boned Scandinavians, it had been downright freakish. My whole life, large-limbed friends had gasped at my feet and told me how lucky I was, but in truth there is nothing so great about having to special-order every single pair of shoes you own. As a result, my shoes were stupidly expensive and carefully chosen. A cobbler's sample here, a ballet slipper there, perhaps in a pinch a child's extra-large patent-leather party shoe. Working had given me an excuse to collect more variety in footwear than I'd ever had in my life. I'd spring out of the shower and pace in front of my tiny closet with its tidy racks of shoes. The evilly pretty sling-backs (Marni, snakeskin) I blew my first paycheck on? The buttery calf-skin boot brought back from a friend visiting Japan (that mythical land where an elf like me wore a medium)? The Manolo Blahnik d'Orsays (feathered, like the bird-human hybrid feet of a sirin) presented by Harry, flying high from a big win at poker? I had shoes no one back home had heard of. I minced through the city like a salaried Cinderella.

Harry found it all faintly ridiculous. It *was* all faintly ridiculous, but I didn't care. I'd call and apologize for missing dinner when I had a housewares store opening or cocktail party to go to (in the stalky, sparkly stilettos I kept stowed under my desk) or when I was just mooning around the office, waiting to sign off on a proof during the crazy monthly close. I would take home each issue as soon as the glossy tablets arrived, and show Harry—"This is the architect profile I edited, God, that guy was a douchebag"—and he would flip through it with very mild interest.

One night—I was drunk, admittedly, from too much champagne at a going-away party for a coworker—Harry finally said, "It's just that you're so smart, Jenny. You should be writing for *The New Yorker* or working on a book or something." I'd reeled. "What's that supposed to mean?" It stung because I knew the magazine was idiotic, I knew it took over my life in an idiotic way, and also because it implied that I had the ultimate choice in the matter, as if I could say, *Hey, ya know, that sounds great, I think I'll start as the features editors of* Time *next week!* I busted my hump all month, endured tirades from the fascist editor in chief, worked and reworked stories and spreads endlessly, all for a wage slightly higher than a waitress's and far less than a stripper's. But I was a good editor. I knew I was a good editor. And I'd had the job (complete with business cards and a line on the masthead) only a few years, having suffered though several horrid assistant positions to get to where I was. I certainly didn't need Harry saying, "There's hardly any *words* in it." I knew that. Obviously, I knew that.

The magazine folded while I was on maternity leave with Betty. I never got to clear off my desk. It was what was happening. Even my bookish friends took to saying things like "Well, we all know print's dead!" and then laughing nervously, like they'd gotten away with some outrageous joke. So in that way, the working/not-working conundrum decided itself for me, and for a while things were fine. I was home with the girls, which was its own kind of interesting. Though I could never say it to Harry, there was so much he missed during the day. I knew my babies. I knew every inch of them, every predilection, every habit, every experience they'd ever had. I saw Betty's giddy joy when she took her first drunken steps; I memorized Rose's constellation of recurring diaper rash.

Still, it took a leap of faith not to think about what I would end up doing once they went off to school—getting into, one prayed, G&T, which in our strange new world meant not an alcoholic beverage but the much less refreshing Gifted & Talented public school program. When I did think about my future, I became immediately nauseated, headachey, heavy with fatigue. I was either harboring some serious self-doubt or had hepatitis B. It was the same life crisis everyone I knew was having, the same conversation all Park Slope moms shared around the swing set. *But my production company! My teaching degree! My doctorate!* Blah, blah. My work had been kind of my deal. It was who I *was*. And now? I dreaded meeting new people and facing the inevitable What Do You Do?: "Oh, this," I would say sheepishly, gesturing toward my sweaty offspring. Or else: "Nothing." Nothing. How I would have loved a day to do nothing, to lie perfectly still on the couch and stare at the television.

I would have to do something eventually—we couldn't afford for me not to be working, not financially and certainly not mental-healthily—but all my work up until now had earned me a whole lot of experience in a field that barely existed anymore, that might have vanished by the time my kids were in school. Well, I'd gotten that sweet master's in Russian folklore that I was still paying for, from the small liberal arts college in St. Paul where I'd puttered around before gathering up the nerve to move to New York. So! That was sure to come in handy amid recession and growing unemployment.

In the meantime, I stayed at home with the girls and sewed and baked cookies (and then, unfortunately, ate the cookies) and went to a lot of sing-alongs and story times. It was a pleasant enough life crisis. I admit there were plenty of times when I was walking with the girls at seven a.m., trying to convince Rose to take a morning nap because she'd already been up for hours, and I'd see women going to work, hurrying toward the subway in skirts and heels, and I'd feel a pang of—something. At least, as Sylvia was always reminding me in a tone I knew was meant to be conciliatory but which struck me as foreboding, there was always a place for me at Ever So Fresh. Jesus. I didn't know exactly what I wanted out of life, or even who I was, but one thing I did know was that I didn't want to end up in that stuffy Bay Ridge office with my in-laws, selling jelly rings in bulk to grocery stores and bars. And they sensed it. The Lipkins knew. They knew me for the superficial snob that I was.

Meanwhile, my own family could not have been farther away while on the same continent—my pathologically busy sister, Sarah, all the way in Seattle, my travel-averse parents marooned in the Midwest. Every time I spoke with my mother, she said something like "Gosh, it sure does kill me to be so far from those sweet grandbabies of mine," so I'd been calling her less and less frequently to avoid the guilt trip. My pre-baby friends in New York were magazine people who had visited with flowers and impractical gifts—dry-clean-only onesies that buttoned up the back, gorgeous picture books for clean-fingered six-year-olds—when Betty was born, and most of whom I hadn't seen since. I didn't have a job or my own money; I couldn't see past my own nose, really. And now I was alone with a toddler and a colicky infant, and it was hot, and I was tired, and Harry was gone.

two

By early afternoon Laura and I had reunited at our usual playground bench, Betty and Emma tiptoeing toward the sprinkler and then boomeranging back, screaming. I couldn't tell whether I loved or hated how, for little kids, every mood—happiness, sadness, hunger, boredom—inspired top-volume shrieks. Rose rubbed her eyes crankily in the sling. I gazed at all the grouchy nannies on the benches opposite, rocking strollers back and forth, ignoring their screaming charges as they motormouthed into their cell phones like auctioneers. It would be nice not to care. It would be nice to let Rose howl in a stroller, as she would do, since she hated the stroller. Until she was born, I hadn't known it was an option for babies to hate strollers. I looked down at her just as she horked a glob of spit-up directly down my sweaty cleavage. Refreshing. "Girls, careful!" shouted Laura as they skittered in their plastic shoes across wet pavement.

No matter how dark I was feeling, a trip to the park did always seem to help. We, like all the Brooklyn families I knew, essentially lived in Prospect Park, our shared backyard, our landscaped Garden of Eden. There was enough wildness here to keep us human: stands of trees, fields of flowers, snaking woodland paths lined by drug-dealer sentries. My brain had lost its ability to picture a forest engineered by deities other than Olmsted and Vaux, waterfalls that didn't get shut off when the city needed to conserve water. The dreamy names helped, too: Lullwater Trail; Nethermead Meadow. I wouldn't have been surprised to learn that the tagged trees cackled at night and reached their spindly limbs toward lost children, or that urban ornithologists spotted the occasional firebird on their weekend walks, or that witches homesteaded in the historic cabin preserved in the park's innards.

It was a big place, after all, with unknown depths: 580-some acres of sculpted nature as artificial as the cobalt-blue daisies they sold at the bodega and every bit as irresistible. Those glinting ponds, the antique carousel corralling antic carnival beasts, the capacious flower-dotted meadows, the ice rink and the horse trails, and all the way at the other edge, the Parisian roundabout lassoing Grand Army Plaza and the beaux arts central library (which, for as long as I could remember, had been shrouded in a facade-repairing net like an ill-conceived Christo installation). I was a sucker for the park's crumbling foot paths and shady culverts lined by ancient benches, relics of times when Edith Wharton-y pairs promenaded in too many clothes, whispering beneath their parasols of flouting New York society's honor codes.

I think my obsession with the park, with our whole neighborhood, had something to do with the dream of Brooklyn that had beckoned in my brain long before I'd ever seen the real thing—some vague seed planted by *Sesame Street* or maybe *The Cosby Show,* pollinated by books about urbane city kids who got lost in museums and caused trouble at prep school, nurtured by tales of beatniks and bohemians, until, in that perfect hothouse of a midwestern girl who'd never been anywhere, there bloomed this vision of New York City as It, as Everything, as The Only Place to Go. The concurrence of *Sex and the City* fever and my own supposedly glam career-gal days calcified my NYC chauvinism.

Though people made fun of the stroller-clogged yuppie enclave where I'd settled, Park Slope was, aesthetically speaking, my fantasy Brooklyn: leafy streets lined by brownstones with jewel-box gardens, the main avenues dotted with mom-and-pop shops and restaurants and cafés. I loved how old everything was. I loved how the bluestone sidewalks smelled after a summer rain; I loved the song of the pigeons cooing in neoclassical eaves. I loved how I had come here and started my adult life just like that, with no one I knew around to remind me of the person I used to be, or who they thought I was. That is to say, I was new enough to the city that it seemed largely imagined, like a place where anything could happen.

So no matter how cramped our apartment got, we clung to it because of its proximity to the wide world of the park. I figured with all the hassles of city life—the lugging of children up stairs and on subways, the yin-yanged plagues of tourists and trash in the summer and cabin fever and household mice in the winter, the endless laps driving around looking for parking, the gritty air, not to mention the confused but constant sense that everyone was either doing much, much better than you or else was, like, homeless—we might as well get the good parts, too. Here was a good part: sitting beside a friend in the shade on a hot summer day. Hailing a woman pushing a brick of ice around in a shopping cart to stop and concoct a crimson shaved ice. The children racing around the playground amid a picture-book-diverse swirl of other kids. And knowing that if, at a moment's notice, we were struck by a desire for Thai food or a handmade wooden baby rattle or an obscure volume of poetry, we could probably have them delivered to us there on the bench.

"I'm so tired," Laura said.

"Me, too." It was an exchange we shared about thirty times a day, like songbirds trading musical phrases. Here was something else I loved about city life, when I managed to remember to appreciate it: Laura. Not Laura, exactly, although she was a reliable and convenient friend; we'd grown closer recently, as most of my mom friends had gotten swept away in the "second kid, gotta move" migration. I loved how, whenever I left my house, I was bound to meet some mother of small children, how there was this community of parents—a sometimes bitchy, competitive community, sure, but a real community. I couldn't imagine what I would do in some Minnesota suburb like the one where I'd grown up, where everyone drove everywhere and housewives were truly alone all day, unless they arranged to meet at the mall. There may have been a lot of assholes in my neighborhood, but at least they were *around*.

"Is Harry working late tonight, too?"

I laughed out loud, surprising both of us. "Actually, he never came home last night." Some dream city life I'd turned out to lead, mired in domestic muck.

Laura raised her eyebrows. "What?"

My brain was too soggy to pretend. My eyes welled up. I looked away. "Yeah."

"And why was that?"

"Didn't say. I mean, I haven't spoken to him yet. I mean, I can't get ahold of him."

Laura raised her eyebrows even higher. I was tempted to warn her that her face would stick that way, but it kind of already had. "Oh, Jenny." I knew what she was thinking, and while I understood why, I still didn't think he was having an affair. It just seemed so . . . normal. Too normal. Or maybe too horrible. At least a gambling binge was nothing personal. It was expensive and demoralizing, but it didn't implicate me, my personal failings, my waning attractiveness. At least I didn't think it did.

"Well, actually, he did call"—Rose started squalling, and I stood up to sway, a baby-soothing automaton—"and said he was stopping for cigarettes on the way home. Around seven. Last night."

"And?"

"And nothing. That was the last I heard from him," I said, pressing at the quiver in my cheeks. "God, could it be any hotter? What do you think it is, like, a hundred degrees?"

Emma stood on one of the jets of the fountain, leaping off and squealing when the water shot out. I wanted to feel that filthy city water on the bottoms of my feet. In that moment I wanted nothing more than to trade places with Betty. I wouldn't stand off to the side, frowning at my friend that way. I would lie down along the jets, letting the sewer-warmed water pound at my back. I would play and play and play and then go home and lie on the bed, fun-weary and sun-soaked, and look out the window and be bored, and then someone would make me dinner and bathe me and read me stories as I fell asleep. It sounded like heaven.

"Aren't you worried? What if something happened to him at the store? Or on the train?"

"I don't know." I was annoyed that I'd said anything at all. It made it real, which I wasn't quite ready for. I didn't want to find out he was having an affair and have to acknowledge the chest pains I suffered every time Laura suggested, weirdly hopefully, that he might be. I definitely didn't want to know if something terrible had happened to him, if he was expensively languishing in some ER somewhere with amnesia or a gunshot wound.

Depressingly enough, the best option was that he'd once again taken our down payment and was slapping it down on an Atlantic City poker table, charming a busload of retirees. The thing was, he often had a lot of luck. It was both the best and worst part of the whole situation. When he came home from a poker night with an extra thousand dollars or two for me, telling me to get something nice, do something fun with the girls, what could I do? I had to not act too happy about it, though it was always like a ray of light bleeding through the gray wool of everyday life. As soon as I ordered in a lavish meal of sushi, or signed Betty up for a stupidly expensive toddler music class, or hired a babysitter for a few hours and went and sat by myself somewhere and did nothing, I was complicit, like the greedy peasant wife in a fairy tale whose husband makes a deal with a devil so they can eat roast goose. And I wasn't quite big enough, or good enough at being poor, to refuse his money because I didn't approve of where it came from, to go back to eating gruel. "When the girls are old enough to understand, you have to stop this," I'd say, sitting at the computer desk in our bedroom, ordering an inappropriately gorgeous roll of damask or oil-slick-shiny patent-leather boots that cost about the same as a week of day care. He'd flash that smile of his and say, "You worry too much, you know that?"

"Maybe you should call the police? Or something?" Laura said.

"Uch, yes. Possibly. I think his mother did, or is going to," I said, swaying, rubbing Rose's back through the fabric of the sling. "Can we talk about something else?"

"That's just so weird. Harry, what are you doing?" Laura sighed. "Isn't it weird how little you can know a person? How you can think you know a person more than you know yourself, how you can think you know everything about them and then it turns out you don't?"

"That's not changing the subject. I'm not that dumb."

"Actually, it *was* changing the subject."

"Are you talking about Will? What kind of secret life could Will possibly have? He's so . . . nice."

Laura shook her head, said, "Never mind," and called to the girls, "Hey, no throwing sticks! You'll take someone's eye out." Then she looked at me grimly. "Never thought I'd say that one."

Rose emitted an angry squeak, as if in response. Poor Rose. I didn't want to think of her as a tiny, red-faced enemy. I wanted us to be on the same side. I wanted to make it all okay. She often seemed to me like an extension of my own body; I picked over her like a monkey, which, since becoming a mother, I felt I had become or reverted to; I wore her in a sling while watching Betty on the playground, picking golden curls of wax out of her ears or flaking shingles of cradle cap off her scalp. (Now that Betty could smack my hand away when I tried to pick her boogers or spit-finger her cheek, I had to focus my unquenchable grooming energies on Rose.) I slept with her attached to my breast. I looked into her eyes, sometimes the only thing that calmed her fits of colic, and studied her corneas, trying to determine exactly what color her grayish-greenish-brownish eyes were.

I'm sure I was this way with Betty, too, probably more so, but it was hard to remember now that she was a little person with opinions and the ability to sass. Betty was such a happy baby that I secretly congratulated myself. People—strangers!—on the subway, in the C-Town supermarket, would compliment me on what a calm and competent new mom I was. I would smile and say, "Oh, it's just that she's easy," not believing myself at all, suspecting that I was a natural, that my own competence made Betty feel at ease, that my love was enough, that it infiltrated her every cell with sanguine grace. Was I the same mother with Rose? What had I forgotten to do? What was I missing? Because I often felt like she already couldn't stand me; no waiting until tweendom for her! Standing on the playground, I rubbed her tiny back, feeling each articulated knob of her spine, and I closed my eyes and tried to think to her: *I am here, and I love you, and my love will protect you. My love is a huge white light surrounding you. Everything will always be okay because I love you so incredibly much. You can feel my love, and it makes you know everything is okay.* I have to admit that a lot of times I was also thinking, *Shut up, shut up, shut up, please shut UP already would you PLEASE.* When I opened my eyes I saw she had hurled her pacifier into the dirt and was sticking her bottom lip out. There it quivered, and there (*But you are surrounded by this vast halo of love!*) she began to cry.

I paced back and forth. Laura handed me a fresh pacifier—she always had a clean stock of the eco-friendly, good-for-your-gums kind, even though Emma had mostly outgrown them—which I deposited in Rose's mouth. It sat there on her vibrating tongue for a while, only slightly muffling her cries. I sighed, took it out, resisted the urge to suck on it myself. I could have used some self-soothing, as the lingo had it. I promised myself a glass of wine and some time at my sewing machine at the end of the night, hours and hours from now. "Anyway, I'm sure there's some completely normal explanation," I said over Rose, rubbing my temples. "Maybe he fell asleep somewhere. No one is getting much sleep at our house. If I had a quiet moment, I'm sure I would conk out."

Laura lowered her brow. "Hm."

I shrugged, mad at Laura for not offering the sensible explanation that would make it all okay, or maybe for not having a disappearing husband herself, for suspecting Harry of having an affair, for having only her one sweet girl to deal with and still having the gall to claim she was tired sometimes or busy. Fucking Laura. How hard could her life possibly be? She had a dishwasher!

I focused on the girls over by the fountain. Some big boys had arrived on the scene—a handful of parentless seven- or eight-year-old Latino kids in baggy hip-hop shorts. They shoved each other recklessly in and out of the water. Laura and I stiffened, our hackles up. "Girls, please be careful!" Laura called out. Emma craned her head to look at her mother. I studied Betty's small back in her striped sundress and hot-pink sandals, her dark curls in messy pigtails. My girl. I missed the days of just the two of us. *My little love,* I thought at her, willing her to get the message. *My girls, I will protect you with this insane animal love I have for you. You will always be loved.* I rubbed Rose's back (she was quieting down, hiccuping, her face splotchy and red) and closed my eyes, and that was when I heard Laura gasp and scream, "Emma!" and leave the bench, running. Shit.

Laura had realized what was happening before Emma, who was still looking around, stunned. Only when Emma saw the blood speckling her arm did the long silent inhale of breath come, and then the high-pitched wail. The arm was ratcheted at a crazy, wrong angle. Rose blinked in surprise, looking around to find the source of the competing scream. I hurried over. Betty threw herself onto my leg, weeping, as if she, too, had fallen. The big boys scattered, spooked by the scene, probably thinking we'd somehow find a way to blame them, which we would, despite ourselves. It was one of those unspoken, awful things about life in the city. The boys were obviously from the other side of the park, where the playgrounds were scruffier and the dogs meaner and the kids louder and significantly less white, and we knew it and they knew it, and we never would have admitted to noticing, but then when one of the girls fell, we—even I, though this was not how I thought of myself in any way—blamed them, as if they themselves had imported free-floating violence over from the projects, like a flu virus.

Laura lifted Emma—who in all likelihood had slipped on the wet pavement; whose stupid idea was it to have a fountain in the concrete playground, anyway?—and held her, rocking her back and forth. When Laura looked at me, her face was pale. We all had terrible playground moments every day; we all witnessed our children taking lethal-looking plunges from poorly designed equipment, sucked in our breath, and told ourselves to stay calm, ordered them to dust it off, pretended our hearts weren't racing. But this was different, as if the fears of every parent on every playground had chosen to swarm and materialize. "Jenny," Laura said quietly, "I think her arm might be b-r-o-k-e-n." I was bad at that spelling-out-loud thing. It took me a minute to register the word as I watched Emma wail into her mother's collarbone. The angle of her wrist turned my stomach. "Oh Jesus," I said. "Oh God. Want to take my car? Wait, I have no idea where the car is parked. Okay. Okay, 911." I said it as calmly as a person can say it. Now all three of our girls were wailing, moms and kids and nannies circling like concerned vultures. A mom I knew vaguely from some story time or another thrust a pink cell phone in front of me, then took it back. "I'll call," she said, looking warily at the screaming bundle attached to my chest.

Just like that, a day could take a turn. A two-year-old girl could step the wrong way on a poorly designed fountain's raised spigot, and suddenly, life went eerie slo-mo; objects and people took on a sickly sheen; the entire landscape, so familiar I hardly saw it anymore, looked new, shimmery with danger. A group of bystanders made everything cinematic. Betty buried her face in my leg, and I stood there dumbly, my finger in Rose's mouth. Laura shot me a harried look, and I knew my wailing girls were making it worse but couldn't figure out what an appropriate response might be. Emma had stopped crying, which for some reason was terrifying. She lay collapsed against her mother's chest, moaning quietly. An ambulance barreled down the park's paved path, thanks to the competent mom with the pink phone, who was now shooing away the tiny gawkers. She was good, this mom! I tried to give her a grateful look, but just then Rose grabbed a fistful of my hair like a little bookie owed a lot of money.

So we couldn't protect them with love alone: It was a thought I had almost every day in one way or another. The paramedics (my mind took a moment to notice how bizarrely hot they were, these young, fit men) scurried Emma into the ambulance with the automatic efficiency of ants. Emma! This tiny creature, broken, at the mercy of trained strangers! Laura stayed admirably collected throughout the whole affair, whispering with the paramedics while keeping a cool hand on Emma's forehead. Our eyes met, and I waved as if they were leaving on a trip. *Bon voyage! Don't forget to write!*

"She was *cwying* and *cwying*," Betty kept saying on the walk home. My first thought was to call Harry with a report. It wouldn't feel real until I had told him, until he bore witness—I typically called him throughout the day to run the day's insanity by another adult. "Well, sounds like everyone's okay now," he'd say. "You're a good friend to have helped out." Or that's what I would call hoping he'd say. Usually, he was busy and distracted as I spoke to him, so there was a delay before his responses, as if he were a correspondent reporting digitally from Karbala; when he did respond, it would be in the form of some non sequitur like "Oh, did you pick up my dry cleaning?" and I'd stare off into the distances of the messy apartment and get preemptively mad for when he came home, looked around wearily, and said, "What do you do all day, anyway?"

But of course he wasn't at his desk. The cell phone went straight to voice mail. Oh, that's *right*—he'd disappeared, or left me, or been murdered, or was making some extravagant statement or another that I was unable to process. He was gone, and Laura and Emma were gone, and all I could think was, numbly, *Now what are we going to do?*

Just when I'd thought nothing could get worse, it did. We were out of dog food. Betty pointed it out to me when we got home from being dragged by Juniper down the block for her evening constitutional. I slumped into a mysteriously damp kitchen chair. It honestly felt like the end of the world. *I can't do this. I can't do this with Harry, and I certainly can't do it without him.* You'd think I would have gotten used to myself by this point in my life, how a little thing like the absence of dog food could shake me loose, send me bobbing along bummed-out riptides. Rose was squirming around on her play mat, contented for once, batting at a plush giraffe with a rakish grin. I peered out the window. I could see the corner store from here. I would be gone for a minute, maybe, tops. Rose wasn't rolling much, really . . . no, no. Not today. Today had proved itself to be unlucky enough already. I felt terrible for even being tempted. I squinted at the open cabinets. Rice cereal? Goldfish crackers? What was that humped in the corner—a molded lump of wheat bread? Juniper leaped dangerously close to Rose's head. I would have to remember to move the play mat before anyone came over. No one could know I'd put my baby anywhere near this floor—studded with ancient crumbs, patterned in black spots fused to the plastic tile like gum on a subway platform.

"Juniper! Want some Cheerios?" I said. Juniper cocked her head at me, the only mannerism of hers that looked halfway intelligent.

"Mommy," said Betty, and when I turned my head, I started—she was standing on a chair, so close to me that our faces were touching, which made her giggle. "Won't Joomper get a tummy-ache?" It was true. Last time I'd tried to fake her out with a ham sandwich in lieu of kibble, we'd all woken up to a rancid volcano of vomit, right in the center of the Oriental rug Sylvia had loaned us.

And so, into the sling went Rosie, into one rain boot and one ruby slipper went Betty, and we headed downstairs once again. The last time I'd seen my sister, Sarah, she'd said, "Wow, Jenny, your calves look amazing." I had laughed: all those fucking stairs. It was the one selling point of the loathsome fourth-floor walk-up. My middle may have been soft and bulbous, my breasts alternately cartoonishly large and sadly deflated depending on where we were in a feeding cycle, my hips wide in a way that seemed unlikely to subside anytime soon, but at least my calves were amazing.

Unfortunately, I was also starting to resemble a baobab tree, especially on days when I didn't get around to washing (okay, or brushing) my thick, curly hair, which had been transformed by the relentlessly steamy summer into a caricature of itself. I'd always prided myself on not being obsessed by my body or weight, with being healthy but eating a cupcake now and then, with not agonizing over magazine spreads like the girls I worked with, who sat around admiring the models' gaunt cheeks. I'd always scoffed at actresses who claimed their boob jobs had been about improving their self-esteem. But I had to admit, feeling so frumpy all the time was starting to get to me. I was reaching the age where a little bit of obsession over my personal appearance might not be such a bad thing. My clothes did nothing to help. My look, if I had a look, said, "I'm about to do yoga," but I wasn't about to do yoga. No, there was no excuse for the elastic-waisted pants and T-shirts that were somehow both too large and too small. Where I lived, you couldn't even comfortably employ the new-mom defense, surrounded as I was by women who wore eyeliner home from the hospital—or, excuse me, the birthing center. The very sight of my feet depressed me: the toenails scabbed over with ancient burgundy polish and cracked as a Renaissance fresco; the thinning rubber flip-flops I'd trimmed with a pair of scissors to make fit. Saddest of all, I'd tried—what a joke—a "quick and easy" hairstyle I'd seen in a magazine borrowed from the library, and gotten interrupted before I could perfect the effortless look, so my hair was incoherently gathered in a half-braided updo that was part Audrey Hepburn, part squirrel's nest.

Naturally, there he was at the bodega. Cute Dad.

He wasn't remotely my type. I wasn't sure he was that cute. Water in a desert was what he was, a pin-up poster in a prison. But he was *around*. And he was really sweet to his kids, and his daughter was really sweet to Betty and Emma, and he was just so . . . nice. And—he ducked his head as he waved—he was *shy*. "Hi, Jenny." I didn't mean to, but I grinned. My limbs shot through with something. What on earth had we needed from the store? Betty meandered down the narrow aisle, bopping her stuffed monkey's head on each dusty can and jar.

"Oh. Sam. Hi." Harry, Emma, everything that had happened in the past twenty-four hours conspired to jar me loose, to make me forget how to be normal. "Hey. What's going on with how you are?" *What?*

The thing was, he was a touch soft around the middle. His attire was all that was terrible about Brooklyn dad-dom: baggy cargo shorts, a T-shirt advertising his kids' tony private school, Crocs. Crocs! And messy too-long hair at an age when too-long hair was no longer in any way appropriate. And the biggest darkest eyes I'd ever seen, fringed with ridiculous Minnie Mouse–pretty lashes. And a scar on his left cheek that deepened the dimple. Overall, he was quite teddy bear-ish. But so *nice*. And artsy! I'd seen him clacking away on his laptop in the coffee shop on weekends when his wife was home to watch the kids, and when I'd asked him about it once, he'd revealed that he was writing a screenplay. When I'd mentioned this to Harry, he'd snorted dismissively. "You're kidding. A white guy in Brooklyn who sits in a café writing a screenplay? How *amazing.*" But I liked that Sam had this project, this creative inner life. When Harry came home from work, he flipped on the TV and swore at sporting events. It didn't seem so terrible to me that someone should spend his free time making something. And Sam's wife, whom I saw around the neighborhood on the weekends, was sort of grouchy and not very pretty, which made me love him even more. She was a lawyer who worked in some way that managed to benefit minorities while making her family rich enough to own a co-op on the park and send their kids to St. Ann's. The *artsy* fancy private school.

I even loved their kids, Maude and George, both adorable and brown-eyed like their dad, and so sweet and polite that you could tell Sam and Juliet were really good parents. I guess I was sort of in love with the whole family—the calm, happy way they lumbered down the sidewalk in a pack while I watched, not as creepily as it sounds, from the living room window. I was in love with six-year-old George and his guitar case. I was in love with four-year-old Maude and her obsession with ladybugs. It was the way you knew people in the city—I'd seen them around when they were little and before my kids were born, and over the years I'd seen them so many times that eventually we all somehow knew one another without ever introducing ourselves. I experienced a jolt of happiness when I saw them take off on their bikes, Maude and Sam perched on a bicycle made for two, George pedaling along furiously on his Huffy. I imagined they were going to the farmers' market to carefully select vegetables they would all make into a delicious and well-planned dinner. Kale! Endive! Rutabaga! This was a family that feared no produce! I was sure their lives were purer and tidier and lovelier than mine because of Sam and his intense sincerity, his glowing kindness.

"I'm doing well"—of course he was!—"and you? Getting any better?"

Any better? Was it that obvious? Did my erstwhile Upper East Side therapist use my face on her business cards or something? But Sam was winking at Rose. "Oh, her? Not really. I think we went straight from colic to teething." I tried to say it lightly, shrugging off the juicy heat that swelled beneath my eye sockets. Betty appeared at my elbow with a can of sardines. She held it out in both hands, like a precious *milagro*. "I *wheely* want this," she said, her voice tinged with insistence.

Sam smiled and knelt down. "You like sardines, too? I didn't know that! I love how slimy they are."

Betty peered dubiously at the tin, which featured a yellow crown that I guessed had been the appeal. A can of princess power. "Um, *yes*."

"I love those little fishies," Sam said. "I love how they squish and crunch between your teeth."

Betty frowned. "Be wight back," she said, holding the tin between two fingers.

Sam rose, laughing. *I love you,* I thought accidentally. Harry would have just roared at her to put the tin back. He didn't believe in parenting sleight-of-hand. He felt that children ought to obey their parents because their parents were their parents. It was an attitude that, while not unreasonable, seemed to me to come from not spending very much time with children.

"How's Harry?" said Sam. "Still working such long hours?" People brushed past us in the tiny market. Nearby at the counter, a squat woman in a housedress was meticulously ordering scratch cards. "And a cherry," she said. "Wait, two cherries. And one little luck."

"Yeah," I said. The phrase "one little luck" echoed in my head. It was all anyone needed, wasn't it? One little luck. Although if Harry knew what was good for him, he was hooking up with a huge, voluptuous beast's worth of luck. "Looooong hours. Very long."

I realized then that I wouldn't tell anyone besides Laura that Harry had gone missing unless it became absolutely necessary. It was embarrassing to admit that I didn't know where my husband was, that I had married someone who would leave his wife and kids alone for a day, a week, who knew how long, that I was the kind of woman you would leave. It would be even worse to have to explain why my demeanor was one of long-suffering irritation rather than the alerting-the-authorities hysteria you'd expect of a loving wife, of a wife pretending to be a loving wife. What could I say? *Oh, Harry's run off somewhere, but it's okay because he does this every once in a while. He's probably gambling away our life savings, ha! Oh, well, it usually only takes a few days for him to find his way back!* Like a puppy with a cracked homing instinct. "Really long hours," I added.

Sam studied me. His expression revealed something to me about my expression, something I didn't like. I turned away. "Well, we better pick up a few hundred more tins of sardines."

He hefted a box of butter in his large, clean hand and smiled. "Sounds like a delicious dinner."

I looked over my shoulder and said, "Jealous?" immediately blushing to the roots of my hair and diving into the ice cream aisle. I was so bad at whatever I was trying to do. Sam laughed politely behind me. I listened to his banter with the man who owned the store. He even remembered the names of the man's many similarly named children—Hassan and Bashem and Bassam and so on. God, he was good. Then the doors tinkled and he disappeared.

We had all just had our bath—it was so much easier to do it that way, and besides, I was sure all the kid pee was great for my complexion—when the phone rang. Sylvia. "I'm calling the police."

"Hi. Fine, and you?" I said. Betty had added a tutu to her pj's and now presented me with a stack of about fourteen books. I shook my head and held up three fingers. She slumped away, dropping books as she went. Sorry, downstairs neighbors. I shifted my weight, tousling Rose's hair with her hooded towel.

"Something about it just feels weird." Sylvia lowered her voice, though she was in her own home. "Jenny, he took a thousand dollars out of the company account yesterday."

I covered the receiver, as if she would hear my smile. Okay! This meant he was *somewhere,* as I'd suspected, and not loitering corpsily in the Gowanus Canal. A gambling binge was good. It was identifiable. It was finite. And that he'd taken money from Ever So Fresh and not our slender savings account, for once! A secret candle of relief flickered beneath my breastbone.

The last dregs of sun spilled into the living room. It was a mellow, flattering light, one that camouflaged the clots of dog hair in the corners, the dull spots on the wooden floor's tired varnish. The kitchen mess had begun to migrate into the living room. Whenever Harry was gone for a few days, the apartment annoyingly proved his theory that he was the one who cleaned up. Pieces of Betty's Peter Rabbit plate set and piles of Cheerios colonized every surface. Even Juniper was sick of eating floor Cheerios. Beneath the mess, it was possible to see how we once envisioned the room, how we'd imagined our lives would be: Harry's framed vintage travel posters, my books and magazines in color-coded grids on the bookshelves, a black-and-white wedding photograph of us looking thin and young and like someone's parents before they were parents. On the mantel of the nonworking fireplace sat a snow globe from Atlantic City. I took the snow globe and went over to the kitchen, cradling Rose in her towel burrito. The trash under the sink was full, but I pressed the globe into it, anyway. "He's only been gone since yesterday. I doubt they'll do anything."

Someone said a muffled something on Sylvia's end of the line. "His brother says he thinks he knows where to find him," Sylvia translated.

"Fred's there?" I asked. Betty padded over again, this time with a phone-book-sized children's encyclopedia. I shook my head and mouthed, "Three short books." Her posture, walking away, was that of a shamed politician, chastised but defiant. She disappeared into the girls' room.

"Cynthia kicked him out. He's living here now." I could hear Fred's protest. "Tempo*rar*ily, he wants me to say."

"Let me talk to Fred," I said.

My mouth-breathing brother-in-law exhaled moistly on the line. "I'm just here to keep Mom company. She's really worried about Harry." Fred sounded like he'd already been drinking. What a pair they made. The television screamed in the background. Sylvia was the last person in the world who videotaped things, but she did it every day, taped her favorite soaps and then watched them in the evenings, frowning as she fast-forwarded the commercials with what she called the "clicker." There was a pause. Fred went on, "What if someone forced him to take that money out at gunpoint or something, my mother is asking. Ma, please, it's not exactly unheard of for Harry to do something like this. Ma!" They were arguing offstage.

Rose had tired of wearing only a towel and started whimpering, rubbing her eyes. I went into my bedroom, the phone pinched between my ear and shoulder, and laid her down on the unmade bed, trying to fasten her diaper without losing the phone. "I mean, we pretty much know where he is, right? I'm not saying it doesn't suck, but I also feel like we're going to see a very contrite Harry in a few days." And maybe a very rich Harry, I didn't say. Obviously, it was wrong to indulge this kind of fantasy. Obviously, this was what got

Harry into trouble in the first place. But you never knew, was all. Sometimes it worked out. We were finally getting close to being able to afford a bigger place. One little luck could put us over the top. One little friendly sprite enchanting Harry's hand in exchange for otherworldly favors or maybe his free drink tokens. You never knew.

"Yeah, I don't know. Ma's bugging out."

"Does she know something we don't?"

There was a pause. *Fred,* I wanted to say, *I can't hear you shrugging.* Rose had rolled to her side and discovered a corner of the sheet that she busily tried stuffing in her mouth. I watched her, honestly unable to remember the last time I'd washed the sheets. It could not have been before she was born. It just couldn't have. At last Fred said, "I say we give it a few days, see what happens. I feel like he'll come back on his own."

"Yeah, me, too." Betty crawled onto the bed, shifting the mattress and rolling Rose onto her stomach, which surprised her and inspired a gale of tears. Betty perched on top of my pillows and primly spread out three of the longest storybooks she owned. Juniper leaped up beside her and started licking her own butt with long, wet slurps. Betty found this hilarious. I lifted Rose and bounced her. "I gotta go."

"Sure. Hey, Jenny, you're okay, right? I mean, I know—"

"Why does everyone keep asking me that? God, I'm fine," I said more testily than I meant to.

"Nothing. No reason. I just mean—if you're feeling, you know—" *If he says "crazy,"* I thought, *I'm hanging up.* "Uh, overwhelmed or whatever. You know. Cynthia would love to take the girls for the day, I'm sure, sometime. Heaven knows she doesn't have a fuckin' job right now."

Fred's soon-to-be-ex-wife was the sort of woman who called kittens "babies" and babies "kittens." *He* couldn't even stand her, and he'd married her. "Gee, that's a nice offer."

"Well, you don't have to be like *that,*" Fred said. "I was just trying to help."

I hung up and immediately lost the phone somewhere on the cluttered bedside table. Rose was snuffling around at my shirt, and Betty was impatiently tapping at the god-awful *Little Mermaid* book Sylvia had bought her twice despite our protests. I sighed. Bedtime.

Once the girls were asleep, I knew my duty as a halfway decent friend was to call Laura to check on poor Emma, but I could not muster it. It was as if I didn't want to risk contamination by getting any closer to her bad luck, and I'm sure she felt the same way about me; she wasn't terribly secretive about thinking my marriage doomed. In this way, our friendship had its limits.

Besides, all I wanted was this: to be settled at the sewing machine with a glass (okay, mug) of wine, a bolt of corduroy, and a pattern for a simple one-piece rag doll. If there were a thing in the world that made me unadulteratedly happy, it was sewing. My seamstress grandmother had taught me when I was a kid, and as soon as I'd conceived, my inner crafty housewife had emerged out of some dormant hormone bundle. Every spare moment I had I spent sewing for my brewing baby: clothes and blankets and pillows and too-elaborate dolls. Our kitchen table was usually lost beneath my hulking hand-me-down Viking and some piles of mismatched fabrics. Harry found this more annoying than anything else. It had not occurred to me, let alone to him, that I was good at this and that it might be useful in some way. Then it was just another way I made things more difficult than they needed to be.

I closed my eyes to breathe deeply and enjoy the moment of peace, the small tremor of anticipation, the promise of an hour or two to do something uninterrupted. Immediately, Fred texted that

I should call. It was tempting to ignore the text, but if I did, Sylvia would call the home phone, and in the time it took me to find the damn thing, everyone would wake up, so, reluctantly, I did. "They won't do anything," Sylvia answered the phone.

"Why am I not surprised?"

"Why are you so *casual*? Jenny, your husband is *missing*! They said we can put up posters of his face if we want, or drop off his *dental* records to help identify a *body* if it comes into the *morgue*!" I could hear Fred in the background, or maybe it was the soaps. I yawned, collapsing onto the couch, letting Betty's affable Raggedy Ann hold the remote. *Access Hollywood* flickered soundlessly through a scrim of fingerprints, the Barbie-doll host trying to look solemn. Red-carpet footage of an actress flashed across the screen, then a paparazzi shot of the same actress with her kids, looking tousled and tired and much better than I did on my best day. Then a still photo of a hospital with a well-known psych ward.

"I don't have his dental records," I said.

"That's not the point! I mean, he's not dead!"

"Well, right. Exactly. He'll be back in a few days, Sylvia, don't worry. We all know he's done this before."

"And no *wonder*, since you seem to care so little!"

Fred was saying, *"Ma!"*

Oh? And what about the last time he disappeared and I did all that running around for nothing? I wanted to say, but a yawn preempted it. It wasn't that I didn't get it. It was a mother's prerogative to freak the fuck out every time her son didn't answer his phone. I felt for her, I did. I even appreciated how her terror allowed me to be the calm one.

"Jenny? Are you there? Listen, can you believe this—they said, 'Well, ma'am, it's not illegal to disappear.' They said, 'It may be inconvenient, but not illegal.' Do you believe that?"

I did believe it. "It *is* awfully inconvenient."

There was a pause. "I really don't understand you sometimes, dear." Sylvia sounded almost soft. Then, back to her regular brisk self, "So, unless we think he's in danger or kidnapped or murdered or something, they're not much interested. They were halfway interested when they thought he was a child, but when I told them how old he was, there went that. As if a mother doesn't mind her child missing as much when he's forty as when he's four. I mean!"

"Thirty-nine," I said.

"Pardon?"

"He was thirty-nine. I mean, he *is* thirty-nine." Juniper scooted by, rubbing her butt on the carpet, a look of great consternation puckering her brow.

Sylvia could not possibly have sighed louder. It was like a windstorm in a receiver. "Just—just call if you hear anything. Can you do that, dear?"

"Of course," I said. "Don't worry." I believed myself, too. Here was what I had to go with: *He's fine. He'll be back. And then everyone will get to be mad instead of worried.*

"Right," said Sylvia. I turned off the television and sat back down at the sewing machine just in time to hear Rose start to wail.

I probably should have seen it coming: his departure; my death. Harry came home from work cursing his brother, cursing his mother, cursing clients who kept them in business whom he'd known since he was a boy. This was the way it always started, and if I'd been paying more attention, I might have felt the twinge in my elbow joints, like an arthritic predictor of storms ahead. He was getting antsy. Everything made him jittery. "I'm leaving that place," he was saying for the millionth time, drinking whiskey out of a sippy cup we'd lost all the complicated straws for, his hands spread out on the sticky table, his thumbs tapping. I was doing the dishes, annoyed that he wasn't offering to help and thinking only of that. This was the night before he left or maybe the night before that. "I gotta get out."

"Yeah?" I said, not that nicely. The sink was soppy with cereal bits and not enough suds. I kept forgetting to buy dish soap.

"I don't know what I'm doing with my life. Ever So Fresh is going nowhere. All I'm doing is prolonging the drawn-out demise of what my father created. It's not—it's not what I'm meant for." Harry was staring at the wall. His loosened tie looked dangerously nooselike.

"Not what you're meant for, eh?" Here was an attitude I blamed on Sylvia. She had always been convinced her boys were special, destined for greatness. His whole life, because of his charm and good looks and bravado, people had led Harry to believe he was something, a star, a noble creature. As much as I loved him, even in the dazzle of those first days, he was just a guy. A good guy, but—a guy.

Now he looked at me. "You know what? Never mind. I can't talk to you when you're like this."

I didn't turn around. "Me? When *I'm* like this? When I'm like *what,* Harry?"

"You don't believe in me. You would rather I stay in a job that—"

"Look," and now I whirled around, wielding a dripping spatula, my comically ineffective weapon. "Do you think anyone is happy a hundred percent of the time? Life's tough, baby. That's just how it is."

"Oh," he said quietly, as if talking to a tiny scuba diver deep in his drink. "I see. So from someone who drinks lattes on the playground all day, that's very nice. I should keep slaving away selling fucking *candy* because you don't want your pretty little life to get shaken up."

"My pretty little life? Really?" I was gesturing wildly with the spatula, Jackson Pollock-ing the kitchen with spatters of sudsy water. "You think this is how I envisioned things turning out? Stuck home all day with two screaming children in a shoe box because we can't afford more because you—"

"Don't say it, Jenny. You just—just watch what you say."

It was hard for me to look at him when we fought like this. His whole being was transformed, the man I loved possessed by someone so ugly, so dark and twisted, that he was rendered unrecognizable. I pushed because I couldn't help myself, because I was tired and annoyed that there wasn't enough soap and that Rose would surely wake up in a few minutes, and I got up in his face, and hating myself, I said, "People work, Harry. Men work. It's not the hugest tragedy in the world, you know."

"*I* work. You—" He was looking at me like a blind man. It was impossible to find him in his eyes.

"I what. I *what*. You think this is easy? You know, the work I'm doing is actual work with intrinsic value, you know, even if I'm not getting paid," I said, quoting some women's magazine he apparently didn't read.

"Great," he said. "Let's pay our rent with some of that intrinsic value this month."

For a moment I saw myself through his eyes: squat and plump and disheveled, wearing a too-loose nursing bra and a stained tank top, angry and flushed and nostril-flaring and hair-flying, waving around a spatula deformed from when I left it too close to the stove's flame. That afternoon we'd strolled through the park, Rose staring at the sun in the leaves, Betty chattering happily. Betty and I had shared an ice cream cone. It *was* easy sometimes. It was literally fun and games. I liked it usually, and I hated that I felt like I had to be unhappy in order for it to count as important, and I hated that Harry felt like he shouldn't have to work, like everything should be handed to him, and I hated the city for being full of people who *did* have everything handed to them. I hated that this was our life, that this was our conversation, that this was the world we were creating for our children. I felt rotten, soggy and black inside, like falling-apart bread from the back of the fridge.

Harry sat there tapping his thumbnail on the side of his cup, his leg bouncing, not looking at me. *I wouldn't look at me if I were him, either,* I thought, and without warning, I started to cry.

"Oh, *please,*" he said. "That's so unfair. You make everything about you."

Only later did it become clear to me that our problems were excruciatingly average. We both felt, like everyone does, underappreciated and put upon. But at the time I knew only my own feelings, or rather, I didn't know them well enough. That night I dropped the spatula in the sink and went to lie down on the bed.

It was a miracle that one or both of the girls hadn't woken up. You could breathe the wrong way and Rose would start yodeling, but here we were shouting at each other while the babies dozed fitfully a few feet away. I closed my eyes in the brilliant dark of our bedroom, trying to remember when things had been different, when we'd appreciated each other and been kind.

It was hard to remember a perfect time. Harry had always been tempestuous, and it's possible that he would have said the same of me. In good moments he was magnanimous and sweet and charming, expansive and warm; in good moments I couldn't, sometimes, believe my luck. How was it that this man loved me? But you never knew when a good moment would sour, when his brow would lower and everything would darken.

Maybe if we'd talked more that night, maybe if I'd had sex with him before Rose woke up screaming for her eleven o'clock feeding, maybe if I'd been able to be a little nicer, to dredge up an ounce of sympathy, to recall, in the way of the married, what it is that once made this man so irresistible to me, to remember that we were two people who once were strangers who, for some reason, decided to become less strange (and thus, more strange) to each other, who chose to become a family. But all of that is a lot of work, the kind of work that, like pushing myself to sweat on the elliptical machine, I was not cut out for. There were certain challenges I was cut out for. Reading a long, difficult book: I seemed to remember that I once was good at that. Editing an unruly article about historically accurate building renovations, okay. Sewing a baby dress without a pattern, sure. But willpower, or maybe I mean patience, or maybe I mean compassion—it was tough for me. Anyway, whatever it was I should have done, I obviously had not done. And now our lives had become a baroque mess I'd need a miracle to escape. I mean, fix.

three

By the second day, Harry's absence had taken up residence in the apartment, a deadbeat roommate in an invisibility cloak who never took a turn doing the dishes or walking the dog. A waft of his scent beneath Juniper napping on the nest of his coiled sweater, a residue of shaved stubble gunking up the bathroom sink, his running shoes taking up an aggressive amount of space on the shoe rack in the closet. I was beginning to realize how many things he normally did around the house, even with him working such long hours. Our household was, after all, a decently oiled machine, but it worked only when Harry was there to reach the glasses in the high kitchen cabinet, to take the meticulously sorted recycling down to the street, to read books to Betty before bed while Rose nursed like her life depended on it. What made me feel like I was drowning was not wondering where he was but realizing there was a mouse carcass mummifying in the trap beneath the sink and no one but me to disinter it. The worst was Betty, who kept saying mournfully, "Daddy's *still* at work? *Still?*"

"Yes, honey. He's on a business trip. So we won't see him for—a little while. You'll just have to wait." Here she was, looking to me for some explanation for this strange occurrence, for some information about the world. As always, my response was cruelly incomplete.

At an unsettlingly early hour in the morning, the buzzer rang. We all stopped what we were doing. Betty looked at me questioningly. "Gwoceries?" she guessed. "Chinese food?" Rose dropped the rattle she'd been turning over in her hands and scrunched up her face. "Uh, hello?" I called into the pointless intercom. An energetic exclamation of static replied. I pushed the button to unlock the front door. Meter reader, UPS man, Jehovah's Witness, jewel thief. I guess my heart lightened a little. Maybe it was Harry. Having lost his keys. With some story of mischief and hijinks that would explain it all, perhaps a souvenir. Or, more likely, someone for one of the neighbors, confused by our doorbell's cryptic arrangement of buttons, numbers, and names. I had practically forgotten about it when, nearly a minute later, the apartment door opened. "Jenny?"

Sweet Jesus. Sylvia. I cast a panicked look around the apartment. The sink contained a bulbous moonscape of plastic plates and sippy cups, the kitchen table glossy with a sealant of juice. Every toy that had ever been invented, sold, resold at a stoop sale, or abandoned at the park by a thoughtless child with an unvigilant nanny congregated on the living room floor—a good distraction from the weeks' worth of crud stiffening the rug. I am not exaggerating when I say there were tumbleweeds of dog hair. I could smell milk rotting somewhere but had not been able to ascertain the source. Betty sat under the overturned toy bin, still in her pajamas, which she had also worn the day before and the night before that, eating her breakfast. Rose was trying her darnedest to roll directly beneath the couch. When Juniper heard the door creak open, she leaped over Rose and threw herself at Sylvia as if they were long-lost lovers.

Sylvia, perfectly turned out in a tidy jogging suit, gasped and staggered back. "Oh God, this dog."

"Juniper! Juniper!" I impotently waved a rectangle of graham cracker. "Here. Come *here*." I lunged forward and grabbed the scruff of her neck. When Juniper was stashed in my bedroom, scratching at the door and whimpering pathetically, Sylvia stepped all the way into the apartment. "Sorry, Sylvia. I wasn't expecting you."

"Clearly," she said, jabbing her nails into her stiff hairdo, as if even Juniper's attentions could shake loose a shellacked strand. Sylvia's silvery helmet of hair reminded me of the antique taxidermy at the American Museum of Natural History, resembling something living but only distantly. She'd had her boys later in life, and Harry was a little older than I; more than once I'd accidentally referred to her as his grandmother. The few times she'd met my parents, it had gotten even more confusing; she was a New York City seventy-five and my mother a Minnesota fifty-five, which netted out to be about the same.

"Gwamma!" Betty erupted from beneath the upturned bin, spilling her bowl of Froot Loops dangerously close to Rose's head.

Sylvia received the embrace without removing her steely eyes from me. "Why was she eating cereal under a trash can?"

"It's a toy bin," I said, as if this explained anything.

"I see." Sylvia patted Betty's back. "Okay, dear, hello. And where's our little Rosie?" Betty looked around, as if having been alerted to the presence of another child. "Wosie?" she said vaguely.

I took this as my cue to step over and lift the baby, who was only halfway under the couch. "She's getting good at rolling."

"How wonderful."

I handed Rose to Sylvia and hefted my sewing machine off the table and onto the floor. "Can I offer you some coffee or something?" I swept the table ineffectually with my cupped hand.

Sylvia kissed Rose's drooly mouth and then handed her back and began to roll up her sleeves. "No, dear, thank you. Betty, honey, if you're finished with breakfast, then why don't you put your toys in the toy bin? Show Grandma how many toys you can put in there."

"WOTS!" Betty leaped into action.

"Okay, to be clear, she wouldn't do that if it were me asking," I said, watching Sylvia dab at the spilled milk on the rug with a wet paper towel. The cereal had stained the milk a gruesome pink. Betty's entire digestive tract was probably dyed the same color. "You don't have to do that."

Sylvia reached beneath the sink to throw away the paper towel and the handful of soggy loops. Without taking her eyes off me, she washed her hands and began to run water over the sticky mound of dishes. "It's my pleasure, Jenny. Is everything okay?" The sympathy in her voice made me cringe. "I mean, I know you don't like to talk about this, but do you think you, I don't know. Need to. *See* someone?"

I studied Rose's fingers. Rose studied my mouth as if lip-reading. "Hey," I said, as if that were an answer. "Tell me your house never got crazy when the boys were little." She didn't respond. It probably hadn't. Fred and Harry were seven years apart and not exactly little at the same time. On the days Sylvia had gone into Ever So Fresh, her mother had come over to watch them. On the days Sylvia was home, Harry had told me, she cleaned the house herself—the same tidy home in Bay Ridge that was spotless whenever we visited. She didn't play with the kids or arrange playdates or take them to the playground or toddler tumbling classes or baby swim lessons—and she took no pains to hide how ridiculous she found our child-rearing philosophies—but her house was always immaculate. And so was her hair.

"Of course, dear. Why don't you sit and relax a minute? I'm happy to do this. Fred is holding down the fort at the office today." How reassuring. Sylvia made a face at the squeeze bottle of hand soap teetering suicidally at the sink's edge. "That's dish soap," I lied. She nodded and commenced to wash the dishes more thoroughly than I ever had, quickly and with those inch-long nails, all while talking to me over her shoulder.

"So they want to know if he's endangered."

I bounced Rose on my knee and squinted out the window. The thuggish squirrel that patrolled our fire escape stood with its claws dug into the screen, looking in at me. I swear we maintained eye contact for a good five seconds. I blinked first. He vanished. "Endangered? Like a panda bear?"

"No, like, *in* danger. The police will investigate the disappearance of an adult if he is believed to be endangered. Or if the disappearance was involuntary." The words clamped on to my skull like a large, cold hand. Honestly, it was a possibility I hadn't allowed for. I kept telling myself he was off being irresponsible, which was annoying but survivable. I knew how to be annoyed with Harry. I didn't know how to be afraid for him.

I couldn't think of any decent response, so I said, "When you said you were going to wait to see what happened today before you contacted the police, I guess I thought you meant, like, this afternoon. Or after, you know, nine a.m."

Sylvia held a delicate china teacup over the sink and let it drip before wiping it efficiently with a clean dish towel she'd produced from somewhere, possibly her palm, like Spider-Man. So I had used every coffee mug and started in on our wedding china. So what? "Or if we think he was kidnapped," she said.

Betty skidded across the wood floor. "Okay! Toys in the bucket! Wantto see?"

Sylvia peered over the counter into the living room. "What about those puzzle pieces?" Betty skittered off, miraculously into the game. Sylvia lowered her voice, turning off the water, running a damp sponge across the counter: "Or if he had any dangerous enemies." I was annoyed at her cleaning and at the same time so thankful. I knew I should stop her; I was aware that it was humiliating. But at the same time, the dishes were clean. I studied Rose's scalp, telling myself I was too busy with her cradle cap to worry about anything else. I flaked off a particularly satisfying clump. She murmured in protest, and I sniffed her sour milk breath. Intoxicating.

"I don't know, Sylvia. I mean, I don't think he had any enemies."

Sylvia froze. "What did you say?"

"What?"

She finished wiping off her hands deliberately, took a tiny sweatshirt off the other kitchen chair, folded it, and sat down. "You said 'had.' Past tense."

"No, I didn't. I said 'has.' I don't think he has any enemies." I ignored the warble in my voice, the crying-fit tell.

Sylvia looked at me hard. "Okay," she said finally. "So I'm asking. Jenny. Do we think this was voluntary?"

I tipped my head back. The last thing I wanted was to cry. "God, it is so hot in here. Isn't it? How hot is it today?"

"Jenny."

"Sylvia. What do you want me to say? I mean, no, I don't think he was kidnapped. Of course not. Right? Jesus. I feel like I've already said this a million times. I think he's just off—you know. Blowing off steam. It's only been two nights. I mean, is there something you're not telling me about? Actually, wait, seriously. Is there something I don't know? I guess he could have enemies. When I think about it. Someone he owed money to? I don't know. Jesus."

"Okay, dear, now don't panic—"

"I'm not panicking," I interrupted in panicky protest.

Sylvia clicked her nails on the table as if calling me to order. "I don't know anything you don't. I'm just asking. Fred thinks if he's gone a week, we should hire a private investigator. But I don't like the idea of some stranger knowing all our family business."

"Hm."

Betty was back at my elbow like a witch's familiar. The mischievous look on her face made me nervous. "Oh, Gwaaaamaaaa," she singsonged. "I'm fiiiinished!" We turned around to look at the living room. Everything that a two-and-a-half-year-old was capable of lifting had been piled atop the toy bin: throw pillows, blankets, the remote control, an unread paperback on sleep training, a scented candle, the last sad potted plant to survive the children. A glint of something that was probably my keys. A few loose diapers she had fished from the diaper bag. Betty waited for us to see what she had done and then threw herself onto the floor with exaggerated laughter. I had to admit, the living room did look better for it. We all watched the potted plant—a money tree, ha, picked up on an ambitious outing to Sunset Park, forty blocks south, for dim sum and exotic produce a year or two earlier—slide, settle, slide some more, and then catapult off the top of the pile, greens down, onto the rug. "Why do I even have a rug?" I wondered aloud.

"Because I gave it to you," Sylvia said, sounding sad.

"Oh. That's right. Um, thanks."

Sylvia wanted me to go out, to get groceries or get my "hair done," as she said—as if I had ever had my hair done in my life. I wasn't sure what she meant, how that worked. Did you stroll into the salon and say, "Do my hair, please"? Did she mean I should get it cut or something else? Blown straight or spun up in curlers and devoured by a dryer resembling a space shuttle? Maybe I should go stand by the sink and "do" my hair all off with the shears I used to cut up chicken. Then it would be done, all right!

"Go ahead, Jenny. I don't have to be to the office until noon. You know I'm happy to watch the girls. You poor thing, with

Harry gone and all. Go on." I was annoyed by the suggestion that I couldn't handle what I obviously couldn't handle. I was annoyed that I didn't have any pumped milk in the fridge to leave for Rose ("Oh, that's right, I keep forgetting you're still *breast*-feeding," Sylvia said every time she saw me, as if I were the first person in the history of the world to nurse a young baby, as if it were some wacky idea I'd come up with myself out of pure perversion), so I couldn't go far. But I did desperately want to leave the apartment, so I scooped up as much laundry as I could carry into a big blue IKEA bag and spent a blissful hour and a half in the Laundromat down the street, staring into a take-out cup of coffee that seemed to always stay full, an enchanted goblet with a plastic lid.

By the time I got home, Betty was perched on the couch, hypnotized by a strictly forbidden non-PBS cartoon, Rose was sleeping in her crib huffing the ragged, snuffly breathing of a long cry's aftermath, and the apartment reeked of bleach. It was as if a domovoi had escaped from a Slavic folk story to help with the household chores. The thought made me chuckle—such household spirits appeared as small hairy beasts with tails and horns, so I pictured Sylvia in this form, rocking her tracksuit and careful hair—but my chuckle was oddly timed and strange-sounding and earned a sharp look from Sylvia. Anyway, where had she found bleach? All I had were ineffective sprays in bottles with trees on the labels. For the rest of the day, after Sylvia left, I found evidence of her in unexpected places—the bed had been made despite Juniper's occupation of the bedroom, there were no dog hairs in the tub of margarine. Had she really cleaned out the margarine? How were her fingers so nimble, complicated as they were by those impressive claws? And how had this orderly creature produced my emotional mess of a husband? Maybe by being such a slob, I would produce two girls who rebelled by having firm grasps on reality and organized billfolds. Maybe, just maybe, some good would come out of my perpetual confusion. Or anyway, this was what I had to tell myself over and over again.

There's nothing that sends a person from brain-tingling joy to tapped-out despair as often as parenting young children. That night at five p.m., as on pretty much every day at five p.m., an evil demon possessed Betty, and together they tore through the apartment, methodically getting into every single thing she knew she wasn't supposed to—oven, toilet, dresser drawer, outlet, dresser drawer, toilet, oven—like a palindrome of misbehavior. After a tearful time-out, she disappeared and then padded out of my closet in a pair of pumps that cost more than the copay for her birth. Telling myself she was trying to push my buttons did nothing to prevent those buttons from being pushed. How I longed to have a temper tantrum right back at her! What a luxury it would be to hurl myself to the floor and kick and wail—or at least to be able to turn her over to her other parent, home from work and brimming with kid love!

After Betty's bedtime, as I was congratulating myself on not throttling her, Rose picked up where her sister had left off by screaming so lustily that our downstairs neighbor thumped on the floor with a broom handle. Helpful. Then Betty locked us out of the girls' bedroom, pushing the rocker against the door and refusing to come out or admit the squalling infant. Even Juniper slunk away to sleep on the couch like a disgraced husband. I am not exaggerating when I say I tried everything there is to try with a crying baby. I changed her bone-dry, factory-fresh diaper. I sang her every lullaby I'd ever heard, with a few Christmas carols and aged TV jingles thrown in for good measure. I nursed. I rocked. I walked. I swayed. I put her down. I picked her up. She wailed until she was hoarse. My brain thought without ceasing, *Oh my God will you please SHUT UP baby I love you but SHUT UP SHUT UP!* By midnight I understood why the hospital made you sign a form after you gave birth promising you wouldn't shake your baby. Two hours into a crying jag, a vigorous shaking honestly doesn't seem like that bad an option. I sent text messages to Harry that I was pretty sure he wasn't getting: "Pls come home Harry pls come home." Finally, I lay down next to Rose on the bed and sobbed, and in that manner we fought our way to sleep.

four

Sylvia took to coming over every other day or so. It was the most I'd seen her in, well, ever, and it was simultaneously a relief and a pain. One steamy day she tired of circling for parking and ordered me into her car. I sat behind the wheel, confused by my moment of freedom, watching the familiar street transformed by the frame of the windshield. After a few seconds (and a honk; someone else wanted my double-parked hydrant spot), my autopilot kicked in and I drove to the new Fairway in the gently gentrifying, cobbled, and sea-stained neighborhood of Red Hook. I walked slowly up and down the grocery store's aisles, holding a paper cup of coffee, my iPod blaring music I liked in high school, music I knew was cheesy, that Harry had always made fun of, but that reminded me of some nascent part of myself, some innocence I'd had no idea was innocence at the time. Morrissey, the Replacements, the Pixies. Soul Asylum, dear God. The songs sounded like dispatches from another world: grungy and crackly and distorted, luxuriantly whiny. Now that I actually had something to be upset about, their angst seemed vestigial. I missed Harry, I hated Harry, I loved Harry; I was embarrassed, I was stunned, I was at sea. My anger wasn't enough to dull over the layer of pure anguish, like snow camouflaging ice; I could hardly walk without slipping on a patch of unseen sadness and losing footing.

I tried to focus on the task at hand, which I was pretty sure was how people dealt with such things. I bought the groceries. Grocery shopping without the girls was almost too easy. Where was the challenge when no one was lunging from the unsanitary shopping-cart seat, straining to yank anything shiny or remotely pinkish from the shelves, reaching out for the hair of everyone who passed by, begging for fruit snacks or any package with a happy-looking animal on it? As a result, it took me much longer than usual. I examined each apple, avocado, mango, pear like a scientist evaluating an alien specimen. I browsed through ingredients. I constructed a ziggurat of canned goods in my cart. I stopped at the café in back and bought a sandwich and sat outside, staring into the inviting blue blur of the harbor, at the barges piled high with pallets in *Princess and the Pea* mattress stacks, the sailboats with their peaked caps like friendly gnomes, everything just so, sparkling in the incessant sunlight. There was the Statue of Liberty with her silent wave, an old acquaintance reluctantly admitting to having spotted me in a crowd.

I found myself stuck there by the edge of the bay, frozen goods melting in my cart left behind in the store. The water looked delicious. I could see how fishermen in folk tales were always doing things like trading their firstborn in order to commiserate with water nymphs. It looked so damn refreshing. I was thirsty all the time, between the heat and the nursing and the coffee, so much so that I stood there and thought, *The only way I will ever not be thirsty is to leap in that water, to feel its scummy smoothness covering my head.* I often had this feeling when standing at the edge of a precipice, by a crease of shore or on an elevated bridge, and on this day I was afraid I would do it, leap right in. My brain said things to me like

Then Harry will be sorry! and *The girls would really be better off without you. It's no good to have a crazy mother.* And I would say things to my brain like *I'm not crazy.* And my brain would say, *Fine, then sad. You can't say that you aren't sad.* And I would say, *Why shouldn't I be sad? My husband has left me!* And my brain would scoff at me like a snotty teenager and tell me to buck up. Then I would turn up my iPod in an attempt to drown out the whole stupid conversation, and sit back down like a totally normal person and finish my sandwich, and make a concerted effort to think totally normal things like *This is a good sandwich. I enjoy the pesto* and, thinking of pesto, would throw out my paper plate and return to my cart and continue the expedition. *Pesto, pesto, pesto.*

I knew what Sylvia was getting at with all the volunteered child care. I knew that she was trying to help me keep an even keel. Despite all our differences, she was the person in my life who came closest to understanding my situation, which was a weird thing to realize. She knew Harry. She knew what it was like to take care of small children. She knew that you could tell yourself you had it easy—that, thank God, your children were healthy, and that you didn't have to work nights at a donut shop or cleaning houses or whatever actual single mothers did, and what if you had to live in the projects and had a deadbeat boyfriend who beat you, and what about pioneer women who had to do all this plus make their own soap and eat salt pork!—but really you were thinking that everyone around you seemed to have it so much easier, the well-groomed ladies who stayed home and still had nannies so they could work on business plans for vanity projects like benefits or boutiques or just get lunches and manicures and things, ladies whose stupid kids would have every advantage that yours wouldn't, when obviously yours were much more deserving. Sylvia probably also knew—did she? could she possibly?—about those moments when you looked at the sun glinting on the water like light on the crown of a child's head, and all your courage left you and you thought, *Me? Somebody's mother? Two somebodies' mother? I can't do that. I can't do that. I can't.* Wait, maybe she didn't. Maybe these were not normal mother thoughts at all. I kept them to myself, just in case.

Anyway, it was nice of her to watch the girls, it really was. "Free day care!" Laura exclaimed when I mentioned it. "That's, like, from another dimension." I tried to focus on feeling appreciative, but in those days it was hard for anything to pierce the gray blanket draped over me. Every evening Betty stood by the front door, opening it at random intervals. She didn't say, and didn't have to, that she was waiting for her daddy to come home.

"Oh," said Sylvia before leaving one sultry afternoon. Harry had been gone about a week. That morning I heard Betty informing Emma that Daddy was at Coney Island, stuck on the teacups ride. I kind of wished she were right. That would show him. "I meant to tell you," Sylvia continued, biting her lip. A flicker of uncertainty was out of character. I braced myself.

"Oh?" I said.

"Harry took his bag."

"His bag?"

She nodded. "He kept an overnight bag in the closet at work."

"An overnight bag?" I was reduced to repeating phrases like a toddler learning to talk. "Why?"

"I don't know. I never asked. One time, a while ago, like months ago, I was looking for something and opened it. It was packed. I thought maybe you guys were planning a vacation. Anyway, I meant to ask him about it, but I never did."

"And now it's gone."

"Yes. I mean, at least we know that wherever he is, he has some clean underwear. Right?"

Betty skidded by on her stocking feet. "Onionware!" she shrieked.

"Okay," I said. "Well, thank you for telling me." We were calm as could be, as if discussing the purchase of paper towels and not proof that my husband had been planning for months the abandonment of his family. *What a dick* was all my brain offered. *Seriously. Dick.* Also, for some reason, I thought: *Oh, our fucking car.* In all the weirdness, I had forgotten to move it for street cleaning, a chore I was used to leaving for Harry, so it was surely adorned with one of those cruelly expensive, heart-stoppingly orange tickets, a sticker plastered to the back window passive-aggressively announcing that "because of this vehicle, the street could not be properly cleaned," impossible to remove, like a scarlet letter from the Department of Transportation. The city was obviously conspiring to crush my soul. I wanted to think about where Harry had gone, to review any clues I may have missed, honestly I did, but in the meantime, I had to deal with the car.

Only, when I walked by the spot where the car had been, where I thought it had been, where I was pretty sure it had been, Rose in the sling, Betty in the stroller, Juniper lunging for a squirrel and jolting me and the baby and tangling her leash in the stroller wheels, the car was gone. I blinked at the irritatingly cute Mini Cooper in its place, nestled between bumpers, snuggled up close to the curb. Perhaps there was another reality in which my life was aesthetically perfect and this was my car (in this other life, I always used cloth napkins, adorned my table with fresh-cut flowers, and even my crying fits were sort of soft-focus and Garboesque); perhaps a momentary super-string-twitching had confused the two? It was always possible that I was remembering the wrong spot, remembering where I had parked the week before, or the week before that, but no, fuck all, Harry had taken the car. I turned our ungainly craft around and began the quest toward home. Fine. At least it was one less thing to worry about. Or really, more realistically, one less chore to manage in my here-and-now life, even if it was also one more thing to worry about Harry messing up.

Harry. Once we had lain in bed together, a soft summer breeze blowing the curtains in the window, and I had closed my eyes as he stroked my skin and I hadn't known where I ended and where he began; we had been one dozy, loving creature. Now I found it impossible to imagine what on earth he could possibly be thinking. At this point, even if he came back, even if he were back when we returned from our walk, there would be something that could never heal, a third-degree burn scarring our marriage.

He wasn't back. He was somewhere, driving down the open road with all the windows down, maybe, or shivering in an over-air-conditioned casino on some Indian reservation. I pictured our humble Honda, disfigured from its life parked on the street, sitting out there alone in a sunny lot somewhere, and I felt immeasurably sad.

Then Juniper lunged toward a lady's perky Pekingese. I hadn't seen the other dog coming down the narrow sidewalk and so hadn't proactively reined in the beast. The leash shot out, upsetting the stroller so that Betty was flung backward and began screaming, jerking my arm so that Rose was jolted and she, too, began screaming. Juniper bayed at the rodent of a dog, scrabbling her paws, while the woman gathered the furball up in her arms and shot me a horrified look. "What the fuck is your problem?" I barked at her. It was a deeply silly question. I mean, there was only one thing I knew about her, and it was what her problem was. She rolled her eyes at me and said only "Oh, *Jesus,*" which was about the most infuriating response imaginable, and walked away. I examined Rose first—she was already over it, staring with great interest at the woofing Juniper. Then I hurriedly righted the stroller and yanked the leash in with all my might. Juniper regained her senses, cowering, tail tucked under her butt. It was too late. I grabbed her nose and smacked her side as hard as I could without jiggling the baby. "You fucking dog," I hissed into her watery eyes. "I am going to take you to the fucking butcher, you hear me?" Rage pumped through my veins. My hands shook. Why did the world hate me? Why was I so incompetent? Why was the dog such an asshole?

I wrapped the leash around my fist and peeked at a sniffling Betty. "I'm so sorry, sweetie," I said. "Are you okay?"

She crossed her arms over her chest. "No!" she said, obviously fine. "Bad doggie!" She twisted around and wept into the back of the stroller. I felt like the worst mother in the world.

"Yes, true. Bad doggie. I'm so sorry, and I'm sure Juniper is, too." My heart was racing with adrenaline and anxiety and grief at the thought of the girls getting hurt and humiliation at the ugly scene which I could only hope no one I knew had witnessed. You never knew, out there on the street. I pictured people watching from their windows, tsking their tongues at the way I smacked Juniper when she stopped in front of me. *But you don't understand,* I wanted to say to them, *this dog is being an asshole! And she's not even really my dog! It's not my fault! None if this is my fault!* Unless it was. But I wasn't going to think about that just yet.

I was still, then, dumb enough for moments of hope. When my phone rang and the caller ID read "Unknown Number," I pressed it to my ear in a fervor. But no, it was my mother, calling from a new cell phone she'd just acquired at a mall kiosk. "How *are* you?" she trilled, live from Edina. I love my parents, I do, but they unironically worship *A Prairie Home Companion* and shop for clothes at Costco and call things "salad" when the main ingredient is mayonnaise. And they're really nice. I mean, we just don't have that much in common. "How is the weather there? It's terrible here." I mouthed the words along with her. Every conversation with someone from Minnesota begins this way. It's basically a salutation.

"Hot," I said, switching Rose to the other boob. Betty ran into the kitchen to show me a large comet of a booger balanced on her forefinger. I widened my eyes and nodded in appreciation before swiping it into Rose's burp cloth.

"Yes, that's what Sylvia said. So what's new? How are the girls? How's Harry?"

"Oh, you know. Fine. Wait—Sylvia? You talked to Sylvia?" Rose popped off, and milk trickled down her chin and my shirt. I jostled her into a floppy sitting position and closed my eyes. "Why are you asking when you already know?"

"Honey. Is everything all right?"

"No, Mom, everything is really shitty, okay?" Here came the tears. God, I was just so tired. "Harry took off, as you already know, so I don't see why you had to call, but okay, there it is, he's gone. And no, there's nothing I haven't told Sylvia that I'm going to tell you now. I don't know why he went or where. He's just gone."

There was a long pause. My mother had given birth to me, squalling and naked; she had changed my diapers and sung me to sleep. Why should we now pretend to be polite acquaintances? Why couldn't we say what was on our minds? It worried me, my reaction to my mother, Harry's to his: the hackles, the sighs. I didn't want it to happen to me and my girls, and I couldn't see how to prevent it. In fact, I could have drafted them a list of things to hate about me, in case they needed help. After the pause had gone on long enough to suck the air out of the phone, out of my head, out of my apartment, my mother said, "Oh, sweetheart," and I forgave her. More than anything, I wanted her to come hug me and tell me everything would be all right. And then immediately leave.

"I'm so sorry," she said, "I just— I didn't know what to say. I don't know what to say. I can't believe he would do this to you." What made it worse was my parents had never really liked Harry. I don't think I was imagining the "I told you so" hitchhiking along in her dulcet tones. "Your father is beside himself." Sure. I could see my father beside himself—sitting in his suburban office-park office in his cheap suit and tie, staring into his World's Best Grandpa mug, looking exactly as he did when overcome with joy. He was about as emotional as a walnut.

My throat was constricting. "Mom, I have to go take out the dog. She looks like she's trying out for the circus." It wasn't even a lie. Juniper had positioned herself in front of the door and was leaping straight into the air, trampolining off the scuffed wood floor.

"Well, sweetheart, you let us know what's going on, okay? If you need to talk to anyone or, you know, go back on your medication—if you need some extra money or anything—just tell me. I'll come there and help with the girls, you know I'd be happy to."

Oh God. The mercenary! Trying to take advantage of my pain and humiliation in order to finagle a grandchild visit out of it! Just what I needed: a visitor who hated walking, feared the subway, and obsessed over how Brooklyn restaurants were all too small and stingy with portions ("I thought you said Apple*bee*'s," my mother had once said in thinly veiled dismay as we were being seated at a new slow-food bistro called, confusingly, rudely, Applewood). "No, no. Thanks. But no. I'll let you know if I hear anything. We're fine. Thank you."

"Well, okey-dokey," said my mother, clearly disappointed. I could almost see her taking her blindingly white walking shoes out of her wheeled suitcase. When she hung up the phone, it felt weirdly final, as if I would never hear her voice again, as if I'd never had parents at all.

⁓

He had been gone two weeks when I got the postcard. A postcard! He couldn't even be bothered with an entire letter. It made me feel exposed and quivery; I imagined the inside of some dusty mailbox reading the note and mocking me. The whole thing was as predictable as it was surreal—the postmark claiming Nevada and the image on the card, of all things in the world, depicting the Coney Island Mermaid Parade with its greasy-looking, scantily clad women frozen in midsummer revelry on the scuzzy boardwalk, the ocean peaked merenguishly in the background. *Really, Harry? This was the postcard you wanted to send me?* Then again, I doubt he'd thought about it that much. Maybe he hadn't even looked at it. He was doing things hastily these days, this much we knew.

"J," he'd scratched out in his cramped hand. It was dead-giveaway leftie handwriting. I couldn't believe I once found it adorable. How could I possibly have cared? In retrospect, the minutia of new love was so exhausting. "I want you to know some things: I'll be back. I swear that I will. And I'm really, really sorry. I am. I just have some things I need to figure out. I know I don't deserve you. Have my mother help out with anything you need. I'll be back soon. I hope you can forgive me. My love to the girls. H."

I read it over three times there in the vestibule of our building. Betty had unsteadily climbed halfway up the treacherous staircase before I came to my senses and hurried after her. What I really wanted was to punch the metal mailbox in its stupid keyhole-eyed face. How dare that smug compartment spit such a note at me? I stomped up the stairs, mad at the mailman, mad at the inventor of the postcard, mad at the designer of the postage stamp. After the girls were in bed, I read the card about eighty times more, like an errant student cramming for an exam. I wish I could report that I did something dramatic and destructive with it—tore it up, set it on fire, ate it so that I could shit it out. Instead, feeling like I should cry but pressing my lips together instead, I climbed on top of a chair, reached up to the top bookshelf, and stuck it into our wedding keepsake box. Bouquet, guest book, postcard from the road. There was my marriage, preserved for the future.

I would have this thought a dozen more times in my life, and each time it would zing throughout my skull with the electricity of a real revelation. But it was true, wasn't it, how you came to hate the very aspects of a person you first fell in love with? In most cases, I'm sure "hate" was too strong a word—Laura complaining about Will's workaholic behaviors she once admired; Sarah bitching about how *nice* her husband was to everyone all the time. But with Harry's twin demons, compulsiveness and impulsiveness, I think "hate" was exactly the right word. I wanted to hunt him down and wring his neck. More than that, I wanted him never to have done this thing to us at all.

I didn't look at the card again, and I didn't receive another one, and—I know this is unforgivable—I didn't tell Harry's family about it. But in the worst moments of the months that followed, I thought of it up in that box like a kind of talisman. The card meant that he was alive and he would be found when he was ready to be found. The card meant that I wasn't to look for him or imagine him dead in some accident or pester the police. My work for now was to survive.

Fred found out how much a private investigator would cost and decided to wait a bit longer. "I have a really good feeling," I kept saying to him, to Sylvia—they surely thought I was insane or else guilty of an expertly concealed murder. "I'm sure he's okay! And I'm sure he'll be back when he's ready." It would have made things easier to tell them about the postcard, in case Harry didn't think to send them one, too, which apparently, he hadn't. But I couldn't. I wanted the card to be mine and mine alone. To tell the truth, none of us had expected his return would take that long. Another week or two, we gave it, until he won big enough or his money ran out. For once it was hugely fortuitous that Harry was employed by his family; despite their own financial woes, Sylvia assured me that Harry's paycheck would keep appearing in our bank account. Less his sales commission, which was often most of our income, but it was something. In the meantime, I became a subject-avoiding ninja, backflipping and shimmy-footing around the edges of conversations. Laura was the only non-Lipkin who knew what was going on. His friends were not my friends—they were hardly even *his* friends—so in his absence, we had no contact. My day-to-day acquaintances were used to not seeing Harry when things got busy at Ever So Fresh, so they were easily deferred with vague apologies. I got used to our new Harry-less existence the way you get used to a new puppy or getting your period. For a week or two it seemed like nothing would ever be the same; I would jolt awake and feel normal for a few seconds and then remember with a great ca-chunk of dread. I told myself that worse things had happened to people. I tried to believe myself. Soon enough it was just life. I dragged myself through the days, trying not to think very much or, especially, to feel anything.

five

Sometimes I think that we are a secret tribe—because in saner times, I know that I'm not alone, it's why they invented antidepressants, for heaven's sake—living life perched on the edge of the abyss. For those of us in this tribe, it's a matter of circumstance. Here is the half-assed version of chaos theory that I privately use to explain my moods, which always feel as though they have been pressed down on me from without rather than bubbling up from within: Somewhere a breeze gusts, a window slams, a feather falls, and eventually, this confluence collides with an unfortunate conversation or a passing thought. If all this happens to happen to a person like me, and that person is in possession of prescriptions or a pistol or a precipice, that person might—poof!—disappear. If the feather never fell, if that person weren't alone with a length of rope when the dark mood swarmed and massed, everything might be different. I know I'm getting gruesome. All I mean to say is that I don't believe, especially after what I've been through, that our fates are sealed, that some people are destined to be suicides, or that even suicides always have compelling reasons to do what they do. I mean, this is true. I know it for a fact. I remember.

The day I died, it was hot, just unbelievably way too hot, the kind of hot that made everyone creep around like sloths in sandals, attempting to cool themselves with makeshift fans—folded take-out menus, MetroCards, hands—and saying to each other, "Hot enough for ya?" because their brains were too melted to say anything less idiotic. It was hot enough. It was hot enough for anyone. The sky was the unwholesome color of singed laundry. Even Juniper just panted down the block, peed, and then begged to go back upstairs, where the window air-conditioning units leaked intentions of coolness. Betty went limp in the middle of the street, melted into a whiny version of herself. Rose stuck to me. None of us had slept. During a midnight fit, the baby's razor-like fingernail had gouged a long scrape down my neck that stung when my sweat welled into it. The day before, I'd run into Nell, the annoyingly perfect mom about town, who was weathering the weather with her customary grace and who said, "Oh, *dear*. I heard Harry's been MIA for weeks. *Jenny.* You poor *thing*! I'm *so sor*ry. You must be worried *sick*." Had it been that long already? Her hair was pulled away from her face in a movie-star-fresh swirl. Her sunglasses obscured her eyes. I wondered who had told her. I didn't see why Nell of all people should get to glory in my misfortune. It also seemed to signal that this misfortune was real enough for people to know about. That it was here to stay, part of me. *Jenny, you know, short, a little chubby, curly hair, husband disappeared?*

What makes a person snap? In movies and books, it's always something particular—a big emotional blowup, a letter received, a sign acknowledged—but in real life, things are never so simple. For me it wasn't. It's not that I was abused as a child and then something reminded me of that. It's not that I learned, reading through his old e-mails or snooping in boxes, that Harry had a girlfriend or a boyfriend or some other double life besides the one I already knew about. It was hot, and I was tired, and I hadn't been eating well—grazing on Betty's leftover kid food, and then, starved from a marathon nursing session, binging on sad combinations: freezer-burned ice cream, peanut-butter tortillas, rice with ketchup. I was drained. I was post-drained. I was empty. Maybe most important, the logistics were right. There were a few bottles of pumped breast milk in the fridge. I'd gone grocery shopping the day before, and the crowded kitchen shelves were Tetrised with Betty's favorites: mac and cheese, Cheerios, cinnamon grahams. I didn't have any errands to do. And I had a babysitter. For a woman in my state, a free afternoon was a dangerous proposition.

I had the thought in the morning, first thing, as I lay there more exhausted than when I'd lain down for the night. *I don't want to do this anymore.* I dismissed it and peeled myself from the bed. Moments later Betty marched over while I was nursing Rose and smacked the baby's leg. "Betty!" I said. She looked just like Harry when she was mad.

"No milk for the baby," she said. When I was pregnant with Rose, I'd braced myself for a bit of sibling rivalry, but sometimes it was ridiculous. I understood Betty not wanting the baby to drool on her toys, but the baby wasn't allowed to drool on me, either?

"Sweetie, the baby needs her milk." Also, where did a two-and-a-half-year-old get off being such a grouch for no reason? "I think you woke up on the wrong side of your big-girl bed," I told her.

Betty frowned at Rose, who beamed back at her—and there, in a nutshell, was the relationship between sisters. Jeez. I thought of Sarah, how, when we were little, I had adored her with a passion she recoiled from like a plague. Betty stamped her foot. "No! This is *my* mommy," she said, trying to climb up on my lap, elbowing the baby out of the way.

"Hey, hey, now. Relax. Gentle with your sister."

"No," she said, still frowning. She sat on my knee, arms crossed. I adjusted Rose into what my lactation consultant called a football hold (as if I'd known how you hold a football before breast-feeding class), nestling her on a nearby throw pillow so she could finish nursing. Juniper came up sniffing to investigate. It was getting awfully crowded but sort of sweet, I was thinking, until Betty smacked the baby again, this time right on her soft-spotted little skull and as hard as she could. I shot up, lifting Rose and upsetting Betty and Juniper, who both tumbled to the floor. "No!" I cried. "Do *not* hit the baby!" Rose, her meal interrupted, started crying, and the dog began to leap around, excited by the chaos.

Betty gathered an assortment of developmentally appropriate blocks—I realized that all those responsibly crafted wooden toys from Sweden were just thinly disguised bludgeons—and hurled them at Rose one by one, aiming for her head. "But! I! Hate! The! BAAAAABBBBYYYYY!" she screamed. I sent down a silent apology to our neighbors as Betty pounded the hardwood. And then I stood in the middle of the apartment, Betty wailing, Rose wailing, the dog howling. Just stood there. I guess it could have seemed funny, but at the time it didn't. It really, really didn't. It felt like a nightmare. A nightmarishly boring nightmare. It was awful to have the thoughts I was having, to wonder if I'd made a huge life-level mistake by having a second baby, by having any babies at all, if everyone would be better off without me. I would never admit to anyone how I stood there and stared. A better mother—any mother—would have come up with some way to calm Betty or reprimand her or *something*. But I watched her like she was a stranger. She *was* a stranger. She wailed and shrieked, transformed into an ugly, pug-faced little monster. It's awful, and I don't want to admit that I did it, but I did, I screamed, "Betty! Shut UP! JUST SHUT THE FUCK UP FOR ONCE!"

I almost think the "for once" was the worst part—implying as it did that this was one in a long line of her incredibly annoying behaviors. I know that distinction is lost on a toddler, but I felt rotten the instant I shouted it, my anger escalating rather than diminishing as my voice rose, and I felt even worse when Betty stopped and blinked and stared at me and then started bawling, as did Rose. Great. I knelt down, beckoned Betty close, guiltily soothed her, promising everything was really okay, okay, okay, like a maternal Ike Turner.

In the afternoon Sylvia came over to watch the girls. Rose had started to cry every time I left the room, so we had to do these sneaky exits. "Look at this, Rosie!" Sylvia shrilled with manic cheeriness. "Watch Betty," I said. "Don't let her murder the baby." Sylvia nodded, waving me away without looking at me, rattling a wooden contraption the opposite direction from the door. I waved at Rose's tiny back, at Betty and Sylvia, who both ignored me. These stealth goodbyes made me feel jumpy and superstitious, but they were better than having the baby's screams chase me all the way down the stairs. I closed the door, and then I was gone.

It was the hottest part of the hottest day of the hottest summer in the world. I rode the subway just to be in motion. I stared straight ahead of myself, trying to evince a sense of purpose. It felt important that the other people on the train thought I had somewhere to go. And then I did. I did have somewhere to go. I switched trains at Jay Street and got onto the A, which I never took. Being on the A made me feel like an entirely different sort of person, the sort of person who took the A, whoever that was—me but with a limestone in Brooklyn Heights, meeting a friend at some pretentiously unpretentious restaurant that had been ours alone until it got written up in the *Times,* or maybe a harried single mother toting too many plastic bags, maneuvering her way downtown. I got off at High Street. Here was a whole new landscape. I could see Harry's point. There was something delicious in escaping, in that moment of losing oneself in a crowd. These people didn't know I had two small children whom I had failed at sleep training, that my apartment was a mess, that I was worried about money, that I was worried about my future, that I was the kind of woman whose husband left her. I was just a thirtysomething person in a sundress and crooked sunglasses and non sequitur shoes.

I'd dug into my working-days shoe stash and chosen, to go with my spit-up-stained shift, my favorite pair of all time, footwear so fantastic I was almost afraid of them, dreamlike slippers that fit my midget feet as if they had been made with me and only me in mind. In a fit of inspiration or maybe desperation, I had slipped off my molting flip-flops and left them nestled in the box where usually these heels slept like twin Sleeping Beauties in a tissue-stuffed coffin: ruby-red satin and calfskin leather, with a crystal-crusted flower that perched like an engagement ring on my dirty toes. These shoes were perilously precious to me, literally priceless, and so beloved that I never wore them.

They'd been prototypes sent to one of the fashion magazines in the building and arriving in a mangled box with labels rendered illegible by a rain-soaked city tour in a bike messenger's satchel. The market editor who found the box weeping on her desk had wanted to use the mysterious slippers in a shoot—everyone who saw them fell in love—but even the most dogged interns couldn't track down any details on who had made them or where they had come from. I was friendly with the editor, and I once (drunkenly, goofily) gushed about her at some party to a woman who turned out to be her boss, so she had a soft spot for me. Also, none of the other girls at the magazine could wedge their big stepsister feet into the diminutive things, even though every last one tried. In the end she interofficed them my way, much to my unending mystification.

They were truly shoes that made you believe in the power of shoes, once-upon-a-time pumps that transformed you the second you put them on, with soles that made the city sidewalks sound sweeter, heels that clicked along beneath you with the spritely optimism of Dorothy's ruby slippers, hand-crafted vamps that lifted you up toward the you that you wanted to be. They made you believe the story of *The Red Shoes,* made it seem totally reasonable that the right footwear could make you so vain it would break your brain, that you would eventually have to cut off your own feet because you couldn't stop dancing. Wearing them, I could have been anyone. I could ride to Grand Central and take a train anywhere and be a whole new me, a better someone. I could start fresh. But these were crazy thoughts, I reminded myself, and I was too practical to be crazy. I was Jenny Lipkin, dependable friend. Jenny Lipkin, average wife. Jenny Lipkin, passable mother.

I walked as if in a movie; the streets passed me by on camera dollies, as if they they were moving and I was standing still. Was it just the shoes? No, things had felt this way for some time. Harry's leaving had transformed me into a kid in the family-vacation backseat. I was no longer doing the driving but kicking the seat in front of me, sullenly watching the world smear by, waiting to find out where I was headed. There was a movie theater that Harry and I had gone to once or twice. There was the all-night diner with the wan waitress trapped in a terrarium of perpetual daylight. There was a row of ornate brownstones, like an illustrator's idea of Brooklyn. There was the bridge. The bridge! I was drawn to it, mothily.

It was always weirdly difficult to find the footpath's start, but there, in an unassuming corner of the small pigeon-noisy park, was the handwritten sign, charmingly unofficial, as if written by some tree elf in the parks department. I started up the incline to the bridge. My lungs swelled with the exhilaration of a moment of freedom. It was exciting to be doing something alone. It reminded me of the anticipatory pleasure of sitting down at the sewing machine, about to lose myself in the rhythm of stitches, or of being a little kid and being allowed to walk to a friend's house by myself. Trees leaned forward, their kindly faces visible to me for the first time. A butterfly landed on my shoulder for a cartoonish instant. My magical shoes were not cut out for such a long walk. The bones in my feet began to twinge, quietly at first, like an overture.

It's hard to remember exactly what I was thinking as I climbed up to the bridge and first saw the city view rise like a cat's back arching in panic. It would make sense that I was thinking of Harry. Things had started to surface, things I had willfully ignored for so long that I could now barely convince myself they were real—for example, an odd frequency of text messages that he'd received in the past few months. And when I had once accidentally reached for his phone (identical to mine), it was snatched away with an accusation of snooping, I recalled. His mood had been strange, jumpy and defensive and restless. A gambling binge had seemed inevitable, though full-scale go-out-for-smokes-and-never-come-home family desertion had not. Still, I blamed myself. How could I not? It was like Wile E. Coyote looking down and realizing he'd run off the cliff into the air, and then, the spell broken, sinking into nothingness.

I guess I'd been running on air, and that day I looked down.

The bridge's walkway was strangely underpopulated, probably because it was the middle of the afternoon on a blazing weekday. The pavement simmered. A bedraggled-looking posse of tourists ambled by, bowlegged from more walking than they were used to, slugging back overpriced bottles of water. Manhattan's skyline leered, a grinful of broken teeth; the river shone too brightly to look at. Because I was going crazy, the brilliant sun angered me—what kind of place was this, that there weren't trees to soak up all that heat? Cars growled beneath the walkway, and the whole bridge vibrated. I stood at the edge, my hands on the rail, which burned my palms. When had the city turned on me? I remembered a night when Harry and I were first together, when we were bored in the airless apartment and decided to walk across the bridge, and we had stood with our arms around each other and the city had seemed warm and humming and alive with twinkle lights, as homey and pleasant as a Christmas tree, and an excitement had thrummed up my spine and I had pressed against Harry's side and closed my eyes and thought, *I am alive. I am alive*—and the sheer strange truth of it had made my fingertips tingle. At least I tried to remember it. It seemed impossibly distant, that kind of feeling. A flutter overheard: a glowing red firebird, conspicuous in a swarm of seagulls, leered down at me, dropping a feather into the river. A bad omen, signaling a dangerous quest, but also a mythical creature. I elected to ignore it. I turned my head toward Brooklyn, toward the warehouse with the giant letters spelling WATCHTOWER, and this too seemed like a sign of something. But no one was watching. There was no one around. I slipped off my shoes, to my aching arches' relief.

A phalanx of Japanese tourists was headed my way from the Manhattan side of the river, following a white-gloved tour guide who toted a red balloon. It was all wrong, the symbol of childhood harnessed into such a dreary task. I pressed the heels of my hands into my eyes. For once I wasn't crying; just beat. Just—beat. I hadn't planned on doing it. Even during my craziest moments, I had never been one to plot ways to off myself, and if I had, it would have been something housewifely and painless, like pills, or maybe a Drano daiquiri. I never even thought of jumping until the instant before I actually did. I wasn't thinking of anything in particular as I set down my shoes and climbed up onto the guardrail. I was thinking only of weightlessness, of being alone in the air, of not having to think anymore. The water winked. I thought, *Well, there you go, I could be free of everything.* I could have sworn the river beckoned, something swirling beneath the surface and hissing to me and me alone, an eerie *Here, here, here.*

Someone shouted, far down the bridge—you couldn't ever have a minute to yourself, it was awful!—and involuntarily, I turned. What I saw was: my shoes. Those gorgeous shoes sitting there side by side, patent, patient, like kids waiting to be rescued. And I thought, *Fuck if I want someone taking those shoes.* They were *my* shoes, and it had not been easy to get them, and I would never have shoes as lovely ever again. The crystal petals shone, frozen flowers fallen victim to an early chill. Something about seeing those shoes reminded me of my whole sad little life, of all the things I liked about being alive. A cup of coffee. A thicket of herbs at the farmers' market. Coming up from a subway station and feeling a pocket of city assemble around me. The soothing tread of my sewing machine huffing along a seam. The pattern the sun made trickling down through leaves at our favorite spot in the park. And—the girls. My girls. It was as if I'd been shocked back to life, as if someone had zapped me with those dog-brush-shaped things paramedics placed on chests in TV shows. *Clear!* My girls! I saw not my life flashing before my eyes but the world flashing on without me—Sylvia giving the girls dinner when I didn't come home and letting Betty eat some processed junk, giving Rose her bath but making the water too cold and using the wrong soap. I loved bath time. I wanted to rub the sponge over Rose's shining belly and dance the rubber ducky around until it made her laugh. Sylvia wouldn't do it right. And I wanted to see these girls grow. I wanted to know the women they would become. How I loved those girls, with such a gorgeous ache in my chest! How spoiled I was, in the grand scheme of things—how lovely my life! And I didn't want to die, of course I didn't want to die, not *really,* only somehow that hadn't registered for a minute, but now it did, and I was going to climb back down and put on my beautiful shoes and run home and hug the children and possibly even the dog—to be alive! what a gift! what a blessing, if I'd believed in that kind of thing!—but I lost my balance. I slipped over the edge, seeing myself fall in slow motion. And what happened then was, I died.

six

Dying wasn't at all how I thought it would be. The fall was not like flying, it was just like falling. I closed my eyes and thought, *No, no, no,* and hugged my arms across my chest and tried to not be falling. My girls! My life! Harry, even! Then the water opened and swallowed me down.

Well, shit, I thought. *Now I've done it. Now I'm dead.* How annoying was that? Honestly, I could not do one single thing right. I floated there, somewhere, berating myself. When, after a minute, nothing else had happened, I opened my eyes, first one, then the other, waited for them to focus on the sand and cartilagey strands of tide-spun trash, and then I was a goony, gape-jawed tourist, there at the bottom of the East River. Who knew it was like *this*? My dress and loosened hair floated around me with seaweedy grace. The river floor glittered with seashells and glass bits and the lacy sculptures of spines stripped clean. Light refracted down from the upstairs world, illuminating a school of small fish like a handful of fairy dust. Weedy roses bent in the watery breeze. It was *nice* down there. It was *wonderful.* At the ends of my limbs, my toes and fingers looked far away and beautiful. In that moment I forgot all about dry land, about my angst coming down, the shoes, the girls, everything. I could have stayed in that silent, enchanted world forever, and I would have, too, but the water above me whooshed, warm as a bath, and something blocked the trickle of light and I looked up and there she was.

Her eyes were entirely black, which for some reason did not immediately strike me as being alarming. A cape of sea-dark hair the length of her body billowed behind her. She was naked from the waist up, her breasts buoyant in the water, her torso forties-starlet curvy, and from the waist down—I'm not kidding—she had a golden fishtail with which she muscled her way around. I know how it sounds. I *know*. But let me stress that at the time this seemed totally unsurprising. There was something soothing about her, nurturing in a slightly aloof, sex-kittenish way. She smiled as if we'd known each other our whole lives and swam close, somehow managing to swing her hips as she moved, winding her long, pointed fingertips into my hair. I closed my eyes and let her.

Obviously, I should have known better, but it is one of the defining characteristics of those moments when you should know better that you don't. It was only on the way home, sitting on the over-air-conditioned A train and shivering into the extra-large "I Heart NYC" sweatshirt I'd bought from a street vendor to go over my besmirched sundress, that things started to come together. Only then did I remember what I had, in another life, written an entire master's thesis on: that ghostly mermaid of Slavic folklore, the rusalka.

Nothing like the cheery princesses that obsessed Betty and the rest of the pre-preschool set, these were the restive spirits of abandoned wives and illegitimate mothers who threw themselves into bodies of water; the angry souls of women without a place in the world. They were as oversexed and lonely as housewives in cheesy romances, and accordingly, they swam around braiding each other's hair and gossiping until sailors dropped into the drink.

Then they swam to the unfortunate men and seduced them, kissing them until they drowned, not understanding that the fellows wouldn't be able to breathe once they joined them underwater. But who knew they could migrate all the way from the Baltic Sea! New York really *was* a melting pot. The thought made me laugh out loud there on the A train, garnering the suspicious stares generally reserved for shoeless people screaming into transistor radios. A discovery: Riding the subway after you've died is very much like it is when you're alive.

Underwater, the rusalka seemed like a long-lost friend. When she held me, when our hair twisted together, when our skin touched, I was able to relax for the first time in a long time. Her thoughts entered my head, unbidden: *I am going to take care of you. You are not going to suffer anymore.* I believed her. It was impossible not to. I didn't think that she might have unfinished business of her own, some ulterior motive for saving my life. Taking my life. Whatever it was. She was saying what I needed someone to say. She took my face in her hands and looked at me with those large black eyes and kissed me, sucking oxygen out of my lungs and blowing in her own aggressive essence.

And then I wasn't Jenny Lipkin anymore. It's difficult to explain how it happened, how I knew it was happening. I understood, I understand, that no one would ever believe me, that I had misunderstood what rusalkas did, what they could do. The physical creature before me had disappeared, but I felt her burning along my airways, bubbling through my veins. The old Jenny Lipkin stayed guttering in the tide like sloughed-off skin. I was one of them now, I knew it somehow, just as I'd known the thoughts the rusalka was projecting to me. I felt her there, in me, even when I kicked my way up to the surface, headed for the Brooklyn shore, a better swimmer than I'd ever been in my life, navigating the oily isles of floating trash, greeting minnows as if they were friendly neighborhood eccentrics, the evening air sandpapery against my skin.

I know I should have been troubled to find that the mysterious being was living in my body like a bossy parasite. But it was clear to me that by taking over, she had allowed me to live, and it seemed like an okay deal at the time, particularly since I had decided I did in fact want to live. What kind of melodramatic ninny drowns herself? Anyway, I felt terrific all of a sudden. I felt *alive.*

I dragged myself onto the shore, skipped past the staring tourists and ferrymen. After her sodden decades of aquatic real estate, the rusalka was excited to be on land, and therefore so was I. The cacophony of sirens and car horns was jaunty as a Gilbert and Sullivan show tune; a rat skittering along the shore glinted with a dapper sheen. Who knew the world was so brilliant?

I tried to ask all the normal getting-to-know-your-new-spirit questions: where she had come from, how she had come to be, well, a mermaid. She had no patience for this. Bubeleh, *please, it's "rusalka." I don't like "mermaid." It sounds silly, like a unicorn or something. Anyway, thanks to you, I'm not even a rusalka anymore. I'm you, us, Jenny Lipkin, a lady with legs and lungs and all of it. Right? So,* nu, *let's go. Show me where we live,* ordered the rusalka. I didn't hear her voice so much as know it. "Okay!" I couldn't wait to get there, overwhelmed as I was with gratitude, so happy to be alive and strolling toward the subway in my—how had she done it?—favorite shoes. In rescuing me, she had even remembered to save the slippers from their precarious perch on the bridge, had placed them beside my wallet and keys and phone in a little line on the shore. I loved her.

There are so many things I want to do here, she told me, giddy as a child. I didn't blame her. At her bidding, I felt drunk with glee. Even the grungy train, packed with humorless commuters, seemed magical. I was gloriously tired, like after a day at the beach, my limbs loosened and full of sun. I couldn't wait for her to meet Betty and Rose, even though I knew that wasn't what she meant. She wanted to see the city in an upbeat montage. She wanted a romantic-comedy interlude. Enough with sorrow and longing. She wanted to go to the top of the Empire State Building and ride the French carousel in Midtown and wander through the Central Park Ramble; she wanted to stare down the white whale at the Natural History museum and get caught in the rain at the Cloisters and try on funny hats at a Times Square street vendor's stand. She wanted to crash the Mermaid Parade at Coney Island and correct everyone. She wanted to drink cocktails at outdoor cafés and flirt with men. She wanted to do more than flirt, she wanted to fuck. She wanted to do all the things a long-dead person would want to do. And so, suddenly, did I.

seven

"Have you done something different with your hair?" Sylvia greeted me, the new me, us. A pause. The longest heartbeat. She knew. It was real. I was caught. I was crazy—"unfit" was how they said it if you were a parent, and it was true, I just didn't *fit*—and they were going to take my children away, and here it came, thundering close, the end of everything.

Then, mumbling within like the dulled voice of a snowstorm: *You might as well stop with the guilt and the suffering and the wah-wah-wah. Nobody knows anything because there's nothing to know. We look good is all. That's all she's saying. I mean you. You look good! You look, what is it . . . refreshed. Relax, why don't you?* I'm sure it doesn't say anything good about my mental state that I found it reassuring to hear this voice in my head. But hey, it's not easy to go on as if nothing has happened when you've contemplated suicide, died, been possessed by a spirit, and brought back to life, only to be home by dinnertime. I appreciated the help. How was it that Sylvia couldn't tell? How was it that nobody noticed? Even the dog only snuffled at my hand, none the wiser. Did this kind of thing happen all the time to all sorts of people without anyone knowing?

Listen, Jenny, hello: I give you permission to be happy. You may cease all the depressive moping and enjoy life. Starting . . . now. So I laughed, gathering Rose in my arms, leaning over to accept a passionate leg hug from Betty—my girls, my girls, what a joy it was to squeeze those little monsters!—then straightened up to survey the tidy kitchen, the neat living room. For the first time I looked at Sylvia's cleaning job and felt not shame that I hadn't been able to keep things this clean myself but vague amusement at what manifested itself to me as Sylvia's OCD. *What's with this woman, anyway? Doesn't she have anything better to do than persecute dust bunnies?* "You missed a spot," I said, trying to sound breezy and, you know, normal.

Sylvia frowned. "Where?"

"I'm kidding. Thank you so much, Sylvia. I'm sure you have a lot of work to do at the office." I didn't even sound like myself, not just what I was saying but my actual voice, which seemed lower, richer, with a brassy pitch like a bell. I was sure I wore the whole story on my skin like a corny tattoo: bridge; mermaid. I couldn't help feeling nervous. But the rusalka whispered, an encouraging hiss beneath my skull, *Don't you know,* bubeleh*? That's how it is with secrets. A surprise party, an affair. You think the world has changed and that everything is so obvious. But believe me, no one knows. No one even suspects.*

I came to enjoy hearing the rusalka's abrasive interruptions, like the friendly thumps of a pregnancy, but like that other sort of inhabitation, it took some getting used to. I knew it was impossible, that what had happened to me couldn't have happened to me. And yet.

Sylvia started to say, "Oh, I can stay for din—" And the rusalka hissed, *Oh no, please, this woman. She tires me. Enough!* I turned to Betty, who was whirling around in circles and watching her skirt billow, energized by some private engine of joy, or perhaps smuggled-in Ever So Freshness, and said, "Say, 'Bye-bye, Grandma!'" I felt jumpy and exhilarated, caffeinated by near-death. "Bye-bye, Grandma!" Betty hollered. *Bye-bye!* We smiled as we waved. Sylvia gave me a funny look, but she gathered her things and left to the notes of our antic "Bye-bye" chorus.

I stood in the hallway, Rose perched lightly on one hip—I actually felt physically stronger than I had that morning—and surveyed the apartment. I was embarrassed for the rusalka, for my new self, to see it, embarrassed that she either knew or would soon know about Harry, about how I was a woman to be pitied, about how I wasn't someone with an imperfect marriage so much as someone who was married to imperfection. I didn't want her to get the impression that the girls didn't have a father, that he had abandoned us, that this was where and how we lived. And yet here we were. Here was our temporary situation that had somehow become permanent. It was as if I'd been distracted for months, maybe years, as if I hadn't gotten to the real part yet but believed I would someday.

"Dinner, Mommy?" crooned Betty.

Ordinarily, I would plop Rose in the bouncy seat and prepare some sort of pseudo-healthy convenience food—tofu pups, Amy's frozen mac and cheese—conjured up out of a mix of laziness and guilt. But tonight I didn't feel like it. The rusalka nagged in my brain: *Honey, I'm starving. You know how long I've been a watery specter? You know what the food is like down there? I want to try human food. I want to taste something delicious. What's good around here? Just no kelp, please.* "We're ordering a pizza," I said. So there. Betty bugged her eyes out and then shrieked, "YAYYY!" galloping around the apartment. I never ordered in. It was a favorite indulgence of Harry's but one I always felt bad about, what with the expense and the ease and the inevitable waste, so we ended up ordering Harry's favorites and never mine. Forget it. I let the guilty tightness go, like the unwanted thoughts I was never able to release when commanded to in yoga. *Whoooosh.* "With spinach and garlic," I added, "because that's how I like it." Betty wrinkled her nose, but when it came, she wolfed down her slice happily.

And that was the first act of my new life. Ordering pizza.

Hey, you have to start somewhere.

I introduced the rusalka to the kids, the dog. After bedtime, she ran us a bath. *I need a little hydrating. Old habits die hard, isn't that what they say?* I didn't know how to talk to her. I whispered, there in the echo chamber of tile and mildew, which felt goofy, but I wasn't sure whether she could hear me unless I said the words out loud. "That's what they say," I whispered. "They do. Someone does." We lay there, I lay there, my hair seaweedy in the lukewarm water. The water felt better to me than water ever had. I wiggled my toes around, or maybe she did. It was disconcerting, the sense that my body had the capability to move without me. *So? What are we doing here?*

Oh, right. I explained about Harry as best as I could. Then I moved on to my own questions. "And you? Got tired of the whole 'unresting spirit' thing?" It was your average, everyday getting-to-know-you kind of talk. And where are you from? And how long have you been dead? "What was it—what made you do it? I do know a little bit about your kind. An unloyal husband? An illegitimate baby?"

But she was offended. *What? What kind of thing is this you ask me? What's with you?*

"Jeez. Sorry. I figured since you—since we—" Since we what?

Since she had possessed me? Saved my life? Compelled me to jump in the first place? It was a tricky relationship to define.

Bubbe, *please. Let's focus here. I have some ideas. But first we're going to need some money.* Ah. Wasn't that always the way?

In the morning we embarked on a mind-numbing round of errands, which, I'm sorry, is what you get when you possess a stay-at-home mom. I walked briskly, propelled by this chatty new force within. Every now and then my knees would buckle. I think she was trying to do the walking part herself, relearning in my legs. I understood her desire, though I wasn't in love with the idea of lurching down Seventh Avenue in a perpetual palsy. These were, I admit, unusual times.

We eventually made it to the bank. I'd realized that, humiliatingly, I didn't know the password to access our accounts online. How had I let Harry take over? I wouldn't have imagined myself this way, but here I was, a housewife who never saw my own bills or bank statements, who was made anxious at the thought of handling anything by herself. The more I considered these things, the more my sadness festered into a hot irritation. I found myself wondering not what had I done to Harry or what he had done to me but, um, how were our 401(k) investments doing? Did we pay our car insurance monthly or annually? Had we ever started the 529 college plans we said we would? I hadn't always been this way. Once I had lived alone, traveled alone, balanced my checkbook—in some distant alternate reality a half decade in the past—and now I needed to access that part of myself. Today. In the fluorescent buzz of the bank, while Betty whined in her stroller and Rose whined in her sling, I transferred most of our down-payment-fund savings account into my old personal checking account, which had been dwindling down to cobwebby dregs and which I hoped Harry did not realize he had access to. We would live off of this while he was gone. If he never came back, the plan would need to be reassessed—a contingency that, like the cost of three-bedroom apartments in our neighborhood, I could stay sane only by ignoring.

Now for some housecleaning. And I don't mean that crazy-cuckoo-Sylvia-lady kind of cleaning. I mean, let's get ready to live. At home I cleared off the answering machine, including all the aging messages containing only an ominous click of disconnection—a well-trained mistress, or a weirdly considerate bookie, or perhaps a string of disappointed telemarketers. I clicked through every file on Harry's computer, searching for clues and finding only a disconcertingly large stash of pornography ("Psh," Laura said dismissively when I called her in a weirded-out panic, "completely normal. As long as there are no animals involved, I wouldn't worry."). The rusalka was a believer in feng shui. Harry's stuff had to go. I spent a sleepless night clearing off his cluttered desk that hulked in a corner of our bedroom and emptying his side of our cramped closet. It called up all the ruthlessness I'd learned from living in New York apartments. Sentiment was for the suburbs. We didn't have the space.

The next time Sylvia came over, I asked her to take everything and store the body-sized duffels in her basement, saying it was all too painful to look at. Surprisingly, she agreed. That was the thing about being a little crazy sometimes. People were really accommodating when they were afraid of being responsible for an episode.

That afternoon I sold Harry's television for cheap on Craigslist, unloading it to an incredulous and psyched college student who changed my hall lightbulb on his way out. Betty wept when the boy came to take the TV away. "Elmo?" she said mournfully. "Wiggles?" The rusalka barked out orders, a spectral director. *Don't think.* I took off my wedding band and the jelly-bean-sized engagement diamond, wrapped them in a wad of Kleenex, and stuck them in the top drawer of my nightstand. *He is the one who left.*

That wasn't the worst of it. How can I explain myself? I was in the mood for betrayal. After the television ran off, I called Fred. "I need you to come pick up Juniper."

He was driving somewhere, cursing at traffic. "Jenny? Hello? Why, what's wrong with the dog?"

"Nothing. She's a great dog. You like dogs, don't you?"

"Well, yeah," he said suspiciously. "What's going on over there?"

"I just can't do this all on my own. It's ridiculous. She's Harry's dog, anyway."

Betty was watching me, alarmed. I turned away from her.

"Jenny, I'm staying with my mother. You know she won't let that dog in the house."

"If no one picks Juniper up by tomorrow afternoon, I'm taking her to the pound," I said. Betty stood with her hands in fists, emitting a shriek of cartoony distress. I covered the phone and whispered, "Not *really*! Stop shouting, honey, please!" Fred's voice pixilated robotically, and I hung up. Juniper ran over as if I'd whistled for her (not that she ever came when someone actually wanted her) and rested her slobbery head on my knee. I patted her muzzle and stood up. My heart pulsed with pain once, twice, thrice. Then I closed my eyes, shook my head, and the pain fizzled and dissipated, leaving behind a sense of calm, like an existential Alka-Seltzer.

By the next day, Juniper was gone—Fred made Cynthia take her—and I found myself staring at the crusty length of the kitchen floor where her food and water dishes had been overturned so many times. Harry and I once used our sweet treatment of the dog as evidence of our good-parent potential, so the implications of shipping off the animal to my almost-ex-sister-in-law were uncomfortable at best. I tried not to think about it. Anyway, whenever I got too sad, I remembered walking the dog with the babies, squatting to scoop up runny poops into bags that, once filled, inevitably revealed previously invisible holes. Forget it. I felt like a general: I had to be strategic. I had to wear emotional blinders, focus only on what was ahead of me, or all would be lost.

My life baffled the rusalka. She was unimpressed by the children but extremely amused by the microwave. She loved my cell phone so much that I found myself flipping it open and closed and staring into the lit screen way too often, garnering strange looks from fellow adults. Like any visitor from another realm, she marveled at the diversity of people in the city and the speed of the cars and the height of the buildings. She especially loved the bridges, so that we had to visit the harbor-side park down in DUMBO again and again, just to be beneath the Manhattan and Brooklyn bridges, which crossed over our heads like the gestures of a giant priest.

The rusalka did not like how the noise from the street invited itself into the bedroom at night. She hated taking showers, begging me to linger in impossible baths instead. She disapproved of what she saw as my overinvolvement with my kids, finding my treatment of Rose particularly annoying. *You run like a chicken with no head every time that baby peeps,* she hissed one night after I'd tried to put Rose down in her crib for the billionth time.

"What am I supposed to do? Wait for her to submit a request form? She's a baby."

Yes, and you're her mother. You need to teach her.

"Teach her what, exactly?" I was pacing around the living room, muttering to myself, jostling Rose in a not-very-nurturing way. "Psychology? Long division?" I was too strung out to be comforting; even I knew this. "SHH! SHH!" I whisper-screamed into Rose's pink face.

To sleep.

"Right, right, right. How easy. Harry was saying the same thing before he left. Hard-core cry-it-out. Let the baby shriek until she's so depressed, she goes to sleep while all that sadness seeps into her cells. Great idea. Do you have any idea how it feels to me when she cries? It's like I'm being stabbed in the heart again and again. It's not exactly relaxing."

Oy, what's with you? Depressed, are you crazy? She's not depressed. She's a baby. Babies cry. You know what? Forget it. Let me handle this.

I felt as if I could be described only in the kind of hacky cliché I'd once so delighted in editing out of magazine pieces: my eyes roving wildly, my hair snaking around my face. "You make it sound like it's my fault she doesn't sleep. That makes me feel even worse, you know."

You're doing that to yourself. Just trust me. I had lots of brothers and sisters. I had lots of babies. I know what I'm doing.

And then she was behind the controls, moving us dreamily into the bedroom, rocking Rose, who insisted on ignoring these soothing entreaties. Betty roused, and I told her to go sleep in the big bed. "Smart. Sleep-train one kid, sleep-derail the other."

Relax, will you? It'll be like this a couple of nights, and then they'll both be asleep all night in the same quiet room. For millions of years, babies are born, they cry, they figure it out, they sleep. You are not the first person to have such miserable struggles. Why do you think the Virgin Mary looks so sleepy in all those paintings? Trust me.

I didn't have any other choice. We placed the squalling babe down in the crib (was Rosie comforted by the fact that the sheets were made of responsibly harvested organic cotton? no, no, she was not) and then floated back out into the living room. The baby screamed as if her life depended on it. Maybe it did. "I can't do this. That's my infant daughter in there. My whole body is telling me to go back in and scoop her up." Well, not my whole body, exactly. A stolid new sector was sitting my bottom firmly on the couch, where I stayed. Not because I wanted to or had come to terms with the whole parenting-philosophy concept but because I physically could not get up. I struggled to, but the rusalka was stronger than I was. I spent a solid hour there, glued to my seat like Odysseus lashed to the mast, while the baby siren-sang in the other room. It was torture, it truly was, but in the end, I hate to admit, she was right. By the next night it took twenty minutes, and the next night five. I ignored the poor thing throughout the night, too, and before I knew it, the rusalka had my sleepless wonder snoozing until dawn. This was a bona fide miracle, better than spinning hay into a barnful of gold. Soon I was starting to feel rested, which made me feel like I was returning to myself. It's a testament to how sleep-deprived I'd been, and to how dreadful it is to be that sleep-deprived, that I felt I owed the rusalka everything, anything she wanted.

And then came a night when both girls went to sleep quickly and I found myself in a dogless, dustless apartment, unexhausted at eight p.m., a glorious stretch of free hours ahead. Dying and then undying was one thing, but this! This was ecstasy! I settled down at the unsticky kitchen table with my sewing machine and a glass of wine, buoyant with joy.

What's this?

"This is what I really love. The mutter of the foot across the fabric. The neat X'ing of thread."

Sewing? You're kidding me. I used to have to sew all day. I was the oldest sister, so, you know, I had to make all the younger kids' clothes. Tuesday was sewing day. Then Wednesday was darning day. Feh! I hated it. You modern girls don't know how good you have it.

"Really? But it's so satisfying. What's better than holding up a dress you've made that turned out just right? I don't get to do it as often as I would like."

Right. I can think of a lot of things that feel better than that. Almost anything, really. Where I'm from, that's just another chore.

"The bottom of the river?"

I mean originally.

"And where is that again?"

She ignored me, started humming instead. And so, to the mermaid's ancient lullabies, I sewed.

eight

I've found that living through your own personal drama—like falling in love, like having a baby, like being left by one's husband—has the result of making a person feel extraordinarily unoriginal. You think: *But how amazing/awful this is! How intangible this joy/pain and how distinct and how difficult to express!* Then you hear a corny song on the radio or remember a scene from a romantic comedy you always dismissed, and you realize that everyone goes through the exact same thing, feels the exact same way, that it seems every bit as singular and surreal to each of them, and that others have managed to express it after all. That you're not the first person in the world to experience something unpleasant and try to weather it with slavish devotion to daily routines. Bedtime rituals, diaper-change ablutions, the communion of mealtime. "You just keep going," I kept remembering my mother saying when my aunt lost a quick and catastrophic battle with breast cancer. "You just *do*." Instead of making me feel better, like part of a community of the brokenhearted, it made me immeasurably bored with myself. Selfish even in misery, I wanted my feelings for my own.

Predictably enough, after I died, I devoted myself to business as usual. Why should a long day feel any longer than it had before?

From the postcard (which sometimes seemed to glow in its hiding place in my apartment, like a paper telltale heart), I knew that Harry was okay somewhere, that I had permission to be wounded but not worried, which was sort of my resting state, anyway. My job, as the rusalka reminded me, was to get from one day to the next.

Just be, *just get on with your life. You have to be strong for your kids if not for yourself. You have to start acting like a halfway normal person.*

"A halfway normal person who came back from the dead possessed by a mermaid spirit?"

You know what I mean.

I would tell myself that Harry would be home late and put it out of my mind, pretend he was leaving the next morning before I was awake. The rusalka approved. Naturally, she didn't miss him. How could she? She didn't know what there was to miss. *So,* nu*? What do we do here when we aren't moping around all day? When I was alive, we didn't have this time to mooch around and feel sad. We had things to do. So? Here we are. What do we do?*

Because I lived in white-person Brooklyn, an important part of my post-abandonment routine turned out to be doing a lot of yoga. I made fun of myself as I was getting the girls ready for the trek to the Y, apologizing to the rusalka—"I know, I know. Oh, the hardships! Only mom-baby yoga can save my soul!"—but I have to admit that as soon as I dropped off Betty in the babysitting room and took Rose into the baby-yoga class, I could feel something unclenching. *Why should you apologize for this? You exhaust me. Just stop with the thinking so much already. I give you permission. In fact, I order you, how's that.*

Maybe it was being in a quiet room with gleaming wood floors, other mothers cooing at their gurgling grubs, or maybe it was the moments alone with my baby in a world governed by her big sister.

Maybe it was the mere fact of doing something physical, paying attention for a few moments at a time to my limbs, the rare instants of balancing. I noticed that for the first few days after I died, my body acted strangely, responding slowly to my commands. Maybe it was mad at me for not exercising, for eating so many cookies, for trying to kill it. For letting in this strange force that occasionally, without warning, twirled me around in a pirouette or steered me toward water, any water, sprinklers, kiddie pools, other people's beverages, because for all her talk about helping me to be normal again, the rusalka sure had me doing some weird things. In those first days and weeks of my new life, these yoga sessions were the times when I felt united with my body, less like warring triplets—flesh, Jenny, rusalka—and more like a powerful new kind of creature.

It had been a long time since I'd done something, in the parlance of ladies' magazines and the blogs of more competent mothers, *for me*. What with all the procreating and nursing I'd been up to lately, it had been years since I'd had my body to myself. Including relationships in which sex was regularly expected, it had been at least a couple of decades. It was exhausting, all that being needed, the friendly parasitism, the amorous symbiosis. For years I'd had the strange feeling of living slightly to the side of myself, connected to my body by a few tenuous threads. *It's all the thinking. Entirely too much thinking.*

"Just breathe with your babies," murmured the purple-clad yoga instructor. "Clear your mind." As soon as she said it, the worst thoughts imaginable surfaced, rubber duckies of doubt. Were they mine? The rusalka's? These were scary moments, when she was new and I wasn't used to sorting out my thoughts and desires from hers, when I couldn't tell. *Maybe Harry has another woman. Maybe he has another family. Does the other woman know about me? Does she pity me? I think I could stand his straying but not her pity. He probably says the things all cheating men say: "My wife is crazy, but I'm stuck." It's true in this case, but still, they all say it, don't they? Sure their wives are crazy—they're being cheated on and lied to. That would make anyone crazy, wouldn't it?* "And now let's chant *om*, creating a soothing vibration for our babies and ourselves." *Or maybe he really is dead. No, I think I'd know if he were dead. I'd have a feeling. So maybe he's lost everything. Maybe he's been taken prisoner by Mafiosi he owes money to. Maybe they'll be coming for us next.* "Now let's sing 'I'm a Little Teapot'!" *He'll be back in a few days. He's done this before. He has a problem. But he has to stop. This is no good for kids to live through. And it's not my fault. Maybe a little, but mostly not. We'll work it out when he gets back. After I kill him.* "Tip me over and pour me out!"

I glanced at Rose, gumming an unfamiliar teether, and then stole an upside-down look around the room while creaking myself into a mangy downward dog. For an instant I was sure each of the other mothers in the room was weathering a similar internal tempest. The super-together mom whose baby was always better dressed than I'd ever been in my adult life, the frazzled-looking sweatball in a stained T-shirt who shushed her child with a slightly hysterical "SH! SH! SH!," the beautiful black lesbian everyone was always trying to befriend in a sick kind of friendship-affirmative-action way. All of these women had some trouble you wouldn't suspect from the outside. Didn't they? *Let me share some wisdom,* bubeleh, *from the great beyond: It's true. Everyone has something. No matter how perfect their lives seem. Everyone.*

These were women I knew slightly from the neighborhood—I knew their children's names but not their own—women with whom I would have weirdly intimate conversations at the drop of a hat. After yoga was over, we all mooned around, slowly gathering our various baby toys and accoutrements, making excuses to talk to each other about infant sleep patterns or our various bodily ailments, discussing cracked nipples and lingering hemorrhoids, chatting breezily about how we'd lost our identities as if it were all an experience as shared as weather. How we missed our old bodies. How we missed our old relationships. How we missed sleeping and reading newspapers and having uninterrupted meals and going to the bathroom by ourselves, resources we'd never known were exhaustible, had never thought to appreciate. Ever since Betty was born, I'd found I possessed a limitless fascination for these conversations, that if I went a few days without finding some other mom to bitch to, I started to feel as if I would completely lose it. Even when Harry had been around, it wasn't like he was living the same life I was. Another unoriginal problem, I'd learned from chatting with neighborhood moms. It wasn't that our new planets, populated by sippy cups and tiny socks, were so terrible. It was that our husbands didn't live there, and interstellar travel can be a bitch.

After yoga, I found Betty hoarding the toy daddies from the babysitting-room dollhouse; managed to drag her away from her game (what a novelty it was for her not to have to share with Rose for an hour! what a horror it was for a two-year-old to have to share, being a tiny walking id after all!); and convinced myself I had the energy to stop at the grocery store. Every step I took down the sweating stink of the street, Rose plastered to my chest, Betty kicking her feet in the stroller, I told myself, *What a normal day! Just walking to the store! Harry will be home tonight! Maybe he will be home for bedtime! Maybe he will tell me to go take the night off and get myself a manicure and read stupid magazines somewhere air-conditioned! I bet that will happen tonight!* I was almost able to convince myself for moments at a time, gritting my teeth into a simian grin. The rusalka broke in: *Throughout time, mothers have been coming up with ways to get through the days. Since the very first mother spent the very first day with small children. Someday your prince will come, or however you want to do it. Whatever works, dear. Whatever works.*

I reminded myself of the educational value of shopping trips, chirping at the girls as I wedged groceries into the stroller basket. "How many apples do I have? What color are these apples? Betty, what's one apple plus one apple?" I sounded psychotic. The flickering of a damaged fluorescent bulb threatened to unhinge me completely; the jangly Muzak grew spikes that jammed into my eardrums as we made our way past a demented-looking lobster clawing at the side of its tank. But I could do this. I could. I could think about dinner, I could pretend I'd need dinner for Harry, too, I could select ingredients and pay for them and arrange them in the stroller basket, I could buy Betty a sticker from the gumball machine on the way out, and I could smile at a familiar mom on the sidewalk. Somehow it helped to have the rusalka reminding me in her slightly cranky way that this was nothing new, that my everyday struggles held within them an echo of the legendary, that maybe if mothers had time to write, all the old epic poems would be about trips to the grocery store instead of wars.

Once we arrived at our building, I stood at the bottom of the stairway, panting, gathering my strength. What a dull daily Everest. One of my more grating neighbors, an older woman who had lived in the building since the beginning of time and paid about $12.50 a month in rent, waved from the landing, a useless Sherpa. "Gosh, you all look hot! Is it still so hot out? I haven't been out! I was hoping someone would go out and pick up milk for me!"

"I bet you were," I grumbled under my breath before propping my mouth back up into a neighborly smile. "It sure is hot out there today! Hotter than ever!" I freed Betty from her strapped-in perch and gathered up the hugely heavy shopping bags in one hand while abusing the stroller into a folded position with the other. Rose started to fuss in the carrier, licking hungrily at my clavicle. I tried to balance out the grocery weight on either side of me. "Betty, no way. I know what you are thinking."

Betty nodded, holding out her hands. "Carry! Carry!"

"No way, ladypants! You are walking! March!"

"Those little legs must get so tired on all those stairs," called out Mrs. Second Floor.

"I assume you mean mine," I said. Somehow the rusalka made even this easier, lent me strength enough to bound up the stairs, to repel the sticky heat.

"Aren't you a hoot!" said Mrs. Second Floor.

"Must be," I said. She didn't move over, and I practically knocked her down with my bunch of bags.

"Oh, I sure hope that little girl doesn't fall! Isn't that baby too hot in there? Can she breathe in there? What is she doing right now? Is she licking you?"

"Yeah, seems that way!" I said. "Babies! Crazy! See you later!"

I stood in the doorway for a moment as Betty scampered inside. "I need to start drinking more milk," I said to nobody in particular. "Maybe take a multivitamin." As in an actual vitamin for adults, not a gummy vite swiped from Betty. I needed to be stronger than I was to live the life I was living. I could manage to feel fine for an hour or two at a time, and then it would slip away from me, like an unpracticed foreign language.

Oy, no, we're not doing that. Jenny, you are strong. We are strong! You've given birth. Twice. How much harder is that than doing errands and entertaining kids on a miserable day, no? There was something about having her there, even when she was annoying me by sounding like my mother ("Why so glum? Just turn that frown upside down!"), that did make me feel stronger. She was right. I could do this. I settled Rose on the floor and managed to make a game of putting everything away and then cleaning the whole kitchen, singing a song I'd never heard. The baby napped, I parked Betty in front of a DVD on the laptop, and I was so invigorated by my twenty uninterrupted minutes mangling a hem at the sewing machine that, believe it or not, in the afternoon I launched us all out into the world again. Into shoes, into sling, down the stairs, into the stroller, down the stairs, down the street. Betty would have been happy at the playground, but I didn't have it in me—the chasing, the tumbling, the constant near-death experiences. Instead, we shoved off for story time at the grand Central Library, starting the long walk a little too late, so that the whole time I was moving as quickly as I could through the soupy air, anxious about whether I'd be able to get a ticket. Oh, the sophisticated joys of urban parenting! Within a block, I'd glamorously sweated through my T-shirt.

I don't know if it's this way everywhere, or a special perk of being a suburban expat, but I found myself every day evaluating the pros and cons of where I lived, as if it were a decision to be made over and over rather than simply the way things were. I doubt my mother ever asked herself whether she was doing her children a disservice by rearing us in White Bread, MN, a few miles from where she'd grown up. Everyone knew it was Good for Families there, regardless of whether it was, and there's no underestimating the comfort of common knowledge. Meanwhile (I pushed the stroller into the park, choosing the inner path shaded by trees, where you could pretend you were in the woods), my parents, whose concept of New York had been forged in the seedy chaos of the seventies, were sure I was dooming my children to playgroups of druggies and prostitutes, teaching them to read using unwholesome scrawls of graffiti. It didn't matter how many times I told them that the brownstones on the park sold for millions. They'd squint down leafy Prospect Park West and shrug. "If they're not worried about being mugged by junkies, than neither am I!" my mother would concede cheerfully, clutching her purse as we strolled by the exquisitely rehabbed home of a famous local novelist.

There was a break in the foliage and we were out in the Long Meadow, delicious as an enormous bowl of sunshine, unleashed dogs bounding around like friendly spirits, kites dotting the sky on a mission to make everything look bucolic. The view always reminded me of some freewheeling city-park experience in London or Paris that I wasn't sure I'd ever had. The view made me think how ridiculous it would be to be dead. How ridiculous that anyone was dead and how unlikely it seemed. I didn't believe in it anymore, in death, and like a child, I ignored it entirely.

At this point in my life, I'd gotten good at dismissing people I didn't agree with. It was one of our best talents, Harry and I, mocking the opinions of others. But still it nagged now and then, my parents' urban anxieties, my own. Maybe it was true that my children faced more daily danger here than they would elsewhere. Maybe it was a crime against childhood that Betty was never allowed to be simultaneously outdoors and unsupervised. It was possible that having to hurry to obtain a ticket for story time made it less fun. There would be a line; there would be a rush of nannies; they would run out of stickers.

Soon we'd reached Grand Army Plaza and its terrifying traffic circle which itself felt like a shield against outsiders: If you can't handle almost getting run over by a livery car, you don't deserve to get to our library. I hurried over the cobbled sidewalks where the farmers' market taunted me on the weekends, populated with happy families. With Harry working so much lately, I was already well versed in the customs of the lonely, knew to avoid family spots on weekends when grinning pairs of parents flaunted their coupledom, the ease of tag-team child wrangling. What I needed to fuel me through my days were the bad times, the prickly moments, help to hate Harry and not miss him—not the time he had taken over a street performer's failing marionette show to Betty's delight and the crowd's admiration. Or seeing him across the busy market and for an instant not recognizing him and thinking, *What a handsome guy,* and the happy jolt of realizing he was mine. The afternoon when I was miserably pregnant with Betty and he'd bought me the hugest bunch of flowers imaginable, but I'd been so annoyed at the thought of having to carry the prickly bouquet home that he'd given it to a couple of old ladies from the nearby rest home and replaced it with a much more welcome chocolate-dip cone from the ice cream truck. I closed my eyes, shook my head, the way they do in movies: Scat, memory. *You, dear, are a mess. I'm telling you, just forget about him. Try. It would seem he has forgotten about you.*

We made it to the library in time to score the last ticket. I dumped Betty out of the stroller, nudging her into the grim story-time chamber, and then plopped onto a chair, unhinging Rose and turning her around so she could experience our hard-won reward: a librarian mumbling *Goodnight Moon* in a moist, windowless room. It was truly a wonder that such a majestic building, its facade complete with columns and sweeping staircases, could conceal within such crummy warrens. In this way, it was like the city itself. So much of its sparkle was on the outside—the glitter of the skyline on rare cab rides across the bridge (my last one had been on the way to the hospital to deliver Rose, and I had been in no mood to appreciate the view)—while the places where we spent our time were smaller and grittier than would have been imaginable elsewhere.

For all my crankiness, I did feel something in me loosening, opening, expanding, just like I had in baby yoga. It seemed I could relax only when I was with the girls doing something silly and little kid-ish, when my anxieties about what kind of mother I was and what kind of life they were leading were allayed for an hour or so because I knew we were somewhere appropriate, doing something they enjoyed. There was some sort of equation that I think we were all trying to decode: How many hours a day did we have to actively cultivate the children's senses of wonder before we earned a few hours to ignore them? Betty wandered into the center of the rug, befriending a stricken-looking boy. There were usually other mothers and sometimes even a friendly nanny with whom I could share mindless banter. The librarian pressed play on a rattly boom box (she couldn't be bothered to sing a song), and Betty joined in on a flamboyant round of "The Wheels on the Bus."

Watching her shimmying around, bus-wheeling her arms, I felt such love for her that I thought I would burst. I never would have imagined it, the love I had for my kids. I closed my eyes. In my old life, this would have been a moment for crying or accidentally falling asleep. Now the rusalka rose within and provided an image of me transforming into some sort of maternal gorgon with a laser-beam gaze, capable of protecting my children from anything. I could shield these small people from quotidian dangers, from the sadness of a broken family, from the eyes of the world. I could! Whatever was happening with Harry, I had to make it all look okay, to protect Betty and Rose from the pity of outsiders. The world we lived in was inhabited by perfect families—successful parents with interesting careers and famous friends, beautiful children who played piano and knew how to ski. Even people's pets were better than ours, well-trained thoroughbreds with urbane social skills. Maybe I couldn't give my kids the advantage of wealth, which safeguarded you from anything, or the super-bohemian artsiness that lifted you above conventional expectations, or the born-and-bred New Yorker toughness that nullified all questioning, but I could love them, and I could try to show them what I loved about the world, and I could make them at least feel like everything was okay, even when it clearly wasn't. I could take them to goddamned story time, and we could have fun, goddammit. *Yes. You get it. Good, Jenny, you're learning! I knew you weren't hopeless.*

I took a deep breath and opened my eyes and joined in "The Hokey Pokey," singing along with the children, the librarian, the rusalka, the world, "That's what it's all about."

nine

Conveniently, or maybe I mean crucially, the rusalka made it possible for me to let Harry's problem, whatever his fucking problem was, be Harry's problem. Well, okay, she forced me to. She had other things on her mind, and her mind was on my mind. She loved to be out in the hot, flat, sunny world. She loved eating things. Unsurprisingly, she loved water—swimming, dashing through the sprinklers at the playground with the shrieking kids, taking long baths. At thirty-four and three quarters, I found it strange to become this new kind of person: the kind drawn to aquatics; the sort of woman who lounged languidly in her own body, feeling, thinking all the time of sex, of flesh, of touching, reaching out to hug people on greeting, mastering the cheek kiss, even (I'd always been so stymied by those European pecks!); above all, to be, in this new way, not fully alone in my body. Then again, it was strange of me to die and to be saved by a spirit. I couldn't be too picky.

Above all, my mermaid loved shoes. She wanted to see them lined up in the bedroom, the fantastic ones only. She made me throw out my ruined flip-flops, the decaying gym sneakers. She wanted to be told the story of each stalky heel, each spiky boot.

Every morning she picked out a more amazing pair. "But we're only going to the sing-along." *Oh? Is there a rule at singing time that you can't wear those patent Chanel flats?* "With jean cutoffs?" *Is there?* She would compel me from within, slipping foot into ill-conceived slipper like one of those twelve enchanted sleep-dancing fools. It fit every time. We would admire our tiny feet—even legs were a novelty to her—and then patter out into the hallway, the street, the world, half blinded by leather and vanity.

Which explains why I wore ridiculous sandals, impractically strappy and audaciously high-heeled, as I milled about, bright and early, alone and never alone, Rose in the sling, Betty in the stroller, not quite knowing where to go or what to do. With Laura and Emma broken and stuck at home, my morning lacked structure. Betty had cruelly dropped her nap, which meant there was way too much day ahead of us, an endless desert of time. Even factory workers get coffee breaks. I saw a leg extend from the stroller and kick like a tiny Rockette's. "Wanta cupcake," the leg announced. "Fine," I said, surprising all of us. *What's a cupcake? Finally, we do something that sounds fun.* We turned around and headed for the tiny bakery on Eighth Avenue. A cupcake. Some coffee. We could do this. Here was another day we could conquer, fueled by processed sugar and caffeine, which I'd recently read reacted in the brain the same as crack, a fact I ought to have found alarming but instead rather liked.

The small round tables at the Two Little Red Hens bakery were perpetually covered in a spread of newspapers that I never saw anyone touch but that always looked just read, as if each section had been vivisected by a crew of news surgeons. Ah, the newspaper—I remembered it, sort of. Betty unhygienically plastered herself to the pastry case, pointing at each sprinkle-speckled cupcake and muttering under her breath, an inquisitor of icing.

Sitting at the table in the nook by the window with the basket of books was Cute Dad Sam and his daughter, Maude. Their heads were almost touching, bent over a picture book and a shared oatmeal cookie. I dreaded the moment when he'd look up and smile, the goony way I would wave and then look away. Why did I have to act so awkwardly, perpetually the ugly girl being asked to dance?

Weeeellllllllllll.

Oh, stop.

Now, this is interesting. This is interesting. *Now we are talking, my dear.*

We are not talking. Stop talking. We are talking about nothing. This is just a person I know. A parent in the neighborhood.

Riiiiiiiight.

When it happened, when he saw me, the rusalka took over—my back straightened, my mouth pouted into a smile that was pointed but not overly friendly, eye contact was brief but intense. It was like a three-second tutorial in flirtation. So *that* was how you did it.

"Hey, Jenny," said Sam. He was one of those people who always said your name when greeting you. I couldn't tell whether I loved this or hated it.

"Hello, Sam," I said. One of my nipples started leaking. Hot.

"What kind of milk?" the girl behind the counter interrupted. Milk? Had she seen my leak already? Oh, *milk*. It was a tiny shop. We could have reached out and all held hands—Sam, me, the bakery girl. I looked at her. For a weird instant, I wanted her life. She was maybe twenty-five, with a vaguely artistic air that made me think she was probably slinging coffee and cake to support an oil-painting habit or a burgeoning crafts business—ironic quilts, maybe, or hip totes screen-printed with owls. I imagined her apartment was an airy loft shared with aspiring filmmakers in a marginal neighborhood that offered a few cool bars and maybe a recently opened fancy cheese shop but bad public schools and library branches without story times. They probably drank mixed drinks from thrift-store glasses on their roof and complained about their stupid day jobs and all looked wonderful doing it. At this particular moment in her life, the girl looked, if not happy, at least lovely in a way she would probably acknowledge only later in life—her hair glinting in a tousled ponytail, a small stud glittering among the freckles on her nose, a pert vintage dress beneath her apron. She probably had the time and energy for things like bike trips to Rockaway Beach, bathing suit under shorts; she probably went to art openings and flirted with handsome men who would make terrible fathers. Maybe if I reached out and held her hand, we would trade lives, like in a corny movie.

"Um, skim," I said finally. I hated when they asked. I wanted whole milk, but I wanted it without asking for it, and I couldn't bring myself to say "whole" in front of Sam. It seemed too vulgar.

"Anything else?" The girl, just a bakery employee again, shot a dismayed look at Betty, who was flattening her nostrils against the glass in front of a vanilla cupcake covered in a riot of sprinkles.

I nodded at the cupcake. "That one."

"We missed you at the playground yesterday afternoon," Sam said. The rusalka thrilled at every exchange. She burbled girlishly: *He missed you, eh? Look how he looks at you. I think we could have some fun with this, Jenny. I think you've been holding out on me.* I struggled to tamp her down, to ignore her voice like just another bad idea vaporing around my brain.

It was true that we almost always saw him in the afternoons, after he'd picked up his kids from their fancy school in Brooklyn Heights. (I once looked up the school's "2's and 3's" preschool program online and suffered a heart palpitation—the tuition was more per year than I had paid for my in-state undergraduate degree.) Laura and I completely devolved when Sam showed up. Cool-headed Laura would immediately apply lip gloss, which was often how I knew he'd been spotted. "What? My lips are dry," she always said. Because sad as it was, Sam was the highlight of the three p.m. playground shift change, when most of the nannies began to wheel their infant charges home, when the big kids who had been in school all day arrived with their motley assortment of part-time babysitters and flexibly employed parents. But really, we weren't as hysterical as all that. It was just that there were days when Sam was the only adult male either of us spoke to. We couldn't help it if our biology betrayed us. We bloomed, deranged daylilies.

"Oh," I said, maneuvering Betty out of the way of the next customer. "Yeah. We went to story time. So edifying. And by that I mean air-conditioned."

"That sounds great," Sam said. "I always forget about actual activities. You moms are good. Real good." I could hardly look at his eyes. Maybe it was that they were so large and dark. Maybe they were the reason I felt he was so kind, so open, so interested in me and me alone, which was the secret feeling I had whenever we spoke. The rusalka was getting the wrong idea. It was nothing personal between me and Cute Dad. It was only that all the neighborhood moms were contractually obligated to find him adorable, though he wasn't—he was soft and a little galumphing and utterly unstylish. But he was *there*. And so were those enormous near-black eyes, and the sense that he was really looking at you, really wanting to hear what you had to say. It was the sad fact of our married lives that our husbands were not particularly interested in what we had to say. Whether Cute Dad was interested or whether it was the circumference of his pupils that lent him the appearance of being so (clearly, Laura and I had spent way too much time analyzing this particular topic), it was enough. I couldn't decide whether our obsession was pathetic or totally reasonable. Probably both.

We exchanged see-you-arounds, and Betty inserted herself back in the stroller, and I plugged my coffee into the stroller's cupholder (one of many inventions I thought ridiculous before having kids and now found indispensable) and walked down the sidewalk, maneuvering over the familiar cracks and tree-root eruptions, an unearned lightness heating my chest.

Whenever I saw Sam, I thought of his wife or, rather, of her absence. Working moms! What mysteries they were to me! When I did talk to the working moms I knew, we would have these tennis matches of conversations that went something like "I don't know how you do it!" "I don't know how *you* do it!" "No, no, I don't know how *you* do it!" Which was all any mother wanted to be told, the thing our husbands would never say, the thing we all wished people thought of us. Here were the magic words, the key to unlock any woman's heart: "Gosh, you do SO MUCH, and no one really APPRECIATES it!"

Unfortunately for my stay-at-home sanity, when I remembered working life, I tended to conveniently forget about long hours or the editor in chief's propensity for public humiliation or disastrous pitch meetings or botched interviews or miserable photo shoots. Years after the fact, it was all a highlight reel of satisfying moments, good stories, fat paychecks, meeting people at parties and telling them what I did and having them respond, "Oooh!" Working had been a fairyland of free lunches, unsticky surfaces, magical creatures who never required diaper changes and cried only occasionally and then quietly in the bathroom, trying to hide it. I remembered the monthly moment when the issue arrived in glossy, string-bound stacks and each of us would pick up a copy to flip through, self-consciously groaning over how this shoot had been mismanaged or that spread looked bad, like skinny girls moaning about looking fat. I could still feel the tiny thrill every time I saw my name in print beside the stories I'd edited. I loved walking by newsstands and recognizing the familiar face of our newest cover. Even after years on the job, I wanted to stop everyone I saw reading our magazine on the subway or in the park and say, "I made that, you know!"

Now I found myself daydreaming about the clean, air-conditioned quiet of conference rooms, about drinking entire cups of coffee rather than finding them hours later, their surfaces corroded with curdled milk. I recalled only a handful of days, the exciting assignments, those wonderful (and few) moments when it all clicked and I clacked away at the keyboard in a kind of dream. I would think at odd times of a particular afternoon in a bucolic English-style garden in the Hamptons, interviewing a designer about her eco-friendly home, and how a pair of rabbits had tumbled through the brush like a children's-book illustration come to life. Or a Fashion Week party in a circus-bright Bryant Park tent, wearing a borrowed cocktail dress and too-large Givenchy stilettos and therefore walking as oddly as a child shuffling in dress-up shoes, scribbling notes like the ace reporter in a studio picture.

When I really thought about it, if I really thought about it, I could admit to myself that working life was pretty repetitive, and I had to keep this in mind now, when my new repetitions—feed baby, wipe face, change diaper, pick up toys, feed toddler, wipe face, change diaper, pick up toys—threatened to erode what was left of my brain. It's not like working was all parties and bunny rabbits: wake to alarm, try to remember whether you were likely to see your boss that day and dress accordingly, wedge yourself on the subway, jockey for a seat, read the *Times* folded into the space-saving origami it took you years to master, buy coffee and maybe an egg on a roll from the cart in front of the building, greet the security guard, fish for your ID, race for the closing elevator doors. Realize you've chosen entirely the wrong thing to wear, consider this miserably as you ride to your floor. Sit at desk, turn on computer, check messages, sigh. Work and tell yourself you're going to take a lunch break today instead of picking at a cafeteria salad while hunched over your keyboard, gossip with a coworker in the kitchen, refill your paper coffee cup with the sludgy brew of free stuff, go to a meeting, note what everyone's wearing, pitch article ideas, have one provisionally okayed and the rest humiliatingly killed, walk back to your desk complaining to a coworker in a blasé manner meant to mask your humiliation, pick at a cafeteria salad while hunched over your keyboard, stay later in the evening than you'd intended. Go home, read the rest of the *Times* even though it feels like old news by now because the headlines are familiar from a day on the Internet, try to think of something you might have energy left over to do once you get home and walk the dog, frantic with pent-up pee, and eat takeout hunched over your keyboard. Go to bed later than you'd intended. Wake up. Repeat.

After all, it's not like I'd loved every instant or every person I worked with. Actually, I couldn't stand most of them. I often relived the moment I'd encountered the scrawny editor in chief stalking down a hallway and explaining to the creative director, "Here's my new thing: I just don't eat during the week." The creative director had nodded thoughtfully and then asked, "What if you have an event?" It hadn't been the first question that came to my mind. "Just push it around your plate with a fork." "Genius." Everything was genius around there. *It's a NOUN,* I wanted to scream. I was often so annoyed, I could hardly speak. I mean, I was still *me*.

And who was that, anyway? It had been a while since I'd known how to answer that question. It had been a while since anyone had asked. When Betty was a newborn, other mothers would ask when I was going back to work and what that work might be, but at this point I had the unmistakable look of a lifer. Now if people wanted to know anything, it was what my husband did, and that was only if anyone asked about me at all. They almost never did.

What intensified this feeling of me-less-ness was that with Laura stuck in the apartment with her damaged child, sense of guilt, and suspicion that she would be ostracized for her playground carelessness, I was forced to socialize with the dreaded Other Mothers. These were ladies I half knew from the Y or story time, people I would never be friendly with at all if we hadn't happened to procreate around the same time, acquaintances who had no idea there had ever been any other version of me and didn't much care to find out. Out of sheer desperation, I found myself at the big playground at Third Street. I was decidedly a South Slope mom and felt self-consciously grubby alongside the North Slope moms, who were more of the "I never thought I'd leave Manhattan, but it turns out it's possible to live in Brooklyn and still be fabulous, wheeee!" school than the "We like this neighborhood because there are trees" sort of midwestern expats I tended to associate with. As much as I claimed to love big-city life, I essentially lived in a small town. In fact, I couldn't remember the last time I'd left town. Er, the neighborhood. Er, my corner of it.

I stood there on the playground, squinting at the fringe of trees that were almost too green to look at. It hurt my head: the aggressive summer sun, the exaggerated green. Betty reached for the moon in a big-girl swing, high on sugar. I thought I had a stomachache. I didn't know yet that this stirring in my gut was the rusalka was getting bored, that she was about to lash out by making me say something reckless.

"Don't you ever feel like a terrible mother?" It was typical playground banter: Nell, the perfect mom with the un-spit-upped-on sundress and movie-star sunglasses carelessly headbanding her reddish hair around her face; Nell, with the high-tech and weirdly clean stroller and the diaper bag that would go with an evening gown. Obviously, her perfect Sophie was over there helping a smaller child climb on the playground equipment. Nell, your average put-her-stellar-career-on-hold-not-that-it-matters-because-her-husband-is-a-rich-stockbroker-or-something mom with her flawless brownstone complete with gracious backyard garden, with her baby-sign-language classes and nuanced understanding of preschools; Nell, who lost the baby weight by the time she'd left the hospital (I knew this for a fact, since I'd had both prenatal and mom-baby yoga with her when Betty was born); obviously, Nell would lean back elegantly on the bench, squinting toward blond Sophie in her white sundress, and say, as if admitting something, when clearly, it was a trap, "Don't you?"

Oy gevalt, these ladies are terrible. Terrible! What are we doing here? Where is the cute dad?

Stop. These are my friends. Sort of.

You stop. What, you think I don't know your every thought, each hidden desire? Please.

We all nodded knowingly. It was too hot for anything else. I missed Laura. I stared down at Rose, snoozing in the sling with her sunhat drooped on her chest, like an old man siesta-ing away another afternoon of retirement. *I suck at this,* I thought miserably to the rusalka, who didn't answer. The conversation, the socializing, the being-this-kind-of-mom. I wanted to sit alone in a backyard somewhere and let the kids eat dirt. Maybe when Harry returned, he would have won a bunch of money and we could buy a house in New Jersey and go to the mall and eat processed foods and not be judged constantly because our toddler wasn't learning Mandarin. Maybe everything would be easier somewhere else. I felt the gray wool pulling over me. The longer he was gone—the days seemed to multiply rather than add—the more certain I felt Harry had been all that made life in Brooklyn doable for me, life at all. *God, I miss him,* I almost let myself admit.

You only think you do. Enough with the hysterics already. And no crying.

Julie, mother of fertility-drug twins Aidan and Isabelle, nodded a strand of hair loose from her graying ponytail. (I was the youngest mom of the bunch, which my midwestern friends, whose kids were in grade school by the time I met Harry, found hilarious.) "Oh my God, yes. Sleep training, potty training—it's all been such a disaster. I never knew it would be so *hard,* did you?" Of course. Julie was so tightly wound, it was difficult to imagine her body hosting a pregnancy at all. She had the twins on a nap schedule as reliable as a German train table. I'd seen her lose her mind completely when Aidan ate a fruit snack from another toddler's palm. I could only imagine that whatever twins-induced chaos she had not been able to control offended her deeply.

Evelyn waved her hand as if fanning a fire ignited on the tip of her pointed nose. "No, no. Julie—you're fine. We're all fine. I don't think we should be so hard on ourselves." Obviously. Evelyn was a hot mess of a mother—ass baboonish with baby weight and still clad in drawstring pants at three in the afternoon. She was always missing at least one crucial element from her diaper bag. I suspected that was the only reason she had for being friendly with me—our kids were the same age, so if Gus needed a tiny diaper or Charlie lacked an age-appropriate toy or snack, she could come sidling over with an apologetic smile that more or less gave you permission to be impatient with her. It had been no surprise when I met her banker husband and found him to be something of a brute.

I stared into the distances of the playground, the glare of sun prisming off the slides, the constant whirl of kids kicking up dust. Mothers and nannies called to their children—"Cassiopeia!" "Scorsese!"—a chorus of unfortunate displays of creativity. The other day I'd met a toddler named Curly. "Curly *what*?" I'd said, feeling like my mother. "Just Curly," the mom had explained placidly. I couldn't stop myself. "Like the *Stooge*?" There were days when our neighborhood made me want to slam my head against a historically accurately restored brick wall. Around and around the kids ran, in their orthopedically sound footwear, their skinny arms smothered in all-natural sunscreen with astronomical SPF, half of them wearing helmets for no perceivable reason.

Nell smiled a crescent moon of teeth implying Evelyn had admitted to failure, which had been the point of the inquisition to start with. Then she turned on me. "What about you, Jenny? You seem like you've got everything together—do you ever feel like a bad mommy?"

Everything about the question was annoying. The insincere compliment slipped in to disarm me (no one in her right mind would think I had everything together), the shift into cutesy-mommy talk, the fact that it came from Nell, who, let's face it, fed Sophie only organic, locally grown produce (the kid was snacking on edamame while the rest of our kids inhaled Day-Glo goldfish crackers) but also always had an immaculate pedicure that couldn't have been ecologically sound. But like I said, it was hot, and I was tired, so as I lazily watched Betty threaten Sophie with a large stick, I said, "Yes, I do."

"Oh, Jenny!" Julie cooed. "But why?"

The rusalka reared her head and said, "Because last week I almost killed myself."

Evelyn gasped, but Nell just nodded. "Oh, I *know*," she said. "All those hot, sticky days? Me, too. We were *climbing* the *walls*."

The other moms smiled. I didn't. "No, I mean *really*."

Nell punctuated her face with a backslash and changed the subject.

Oh, Jenny, said the rusalka, *I liked that. This is fun, you know this?* She chuckled all the way home.

ten

*"Listen," said Laura, "you have a guilt-stricken mother-in-*law willing to babysit for free. I have a toddler rendered insomniac by her itchy cast. We need to go for a drink." It was probably the last thing I needed, but she was awfully persistent when she made up her mind about something, and the rusalka loved the idea. It was both what annoyed me about Laura and what kept our friendship alive, her tendency toward lines like "Where have you been?" and "Why haven't you called?" and the ever unanswerable "What are you doing tomorrow?"—which was always a trick. "Oh, us, too!" would be the answer, or "We'll join you" or "In that case, hang out with us." I'd never quite understood why someone like Laura—so universally liked, so socially competent—wanted to be friends with someone like me, the original Debbie Downer. But she'd decided it would be so, and her inexplicable affection rendered me powerless to resist.

There we were, decked out in clean dresses and cute flats (they would have been sandals if we were normal New York ladies with recent pedicures), sweet-smelling strands of our recently washed hair floating into the sticky lip gloss we'd forgotten how to manage, having scored an outdoor table at the wine bar equidistant from each of our homes—an even six blocks and one avenue for each (the real reason Laura had become my best friend; when I had kids, I'd pretty much broken up with all acquaintances living off the F line)—and feeling completely entitled to take up the table all night. I hadn't been outside after dark in ages. It had been months since I'd seen a row of streetlamps glowing like giants' torches, or groups of giggling girls heading off to dance their shoes to bits; I couldn't get over how many people were out and about post-bedtime. We staked out our table, nursed a bottle of white wine, watched livery cars Indy 500 down the avenue, said hello to familiar families passing by every five minutes or so. "Remind me never to bring my secret lover here," Laura said, shaking her head after Nell and her husband stopped to chat over the flowerpot barrier.

"No way," I said, helping myself to a disgusting portion of fries and European-so-therefore-not-disgusting mayonnaise. "It's perfect. Out in the open like this, no one would ever suspect. Very 'Purloined Letter.'" *You're thinking what I'm thinking, I know you are. The cute dad and you. Don't you pooh-pooh me! We're going to have some fun, whether you like it or not.*

After a half hour, we'd exhausted the first round of complaints about our children, lists of adorable things these same children had done, and bitchy gossip. I confided that Betty had bitten a child at the Y day care and been asked not to come back. Laura confided that she'd overheard some moms talking about how Emma's accident had been due to her own negligence. Here we were, the outcasts of the outer boroughs. I took a deep breath and watched a swarm of gnats shrouding the nearest streetlamp like a mobile lampshade. I knew what was coming. More wine, please. Would I tell her about the rusalka? Of course not. I could never tell anyone, and I had to remember that. It was a dead-giveaway crazy-lady thing to admit to, and no matter how wine-buzzy and friend-cozy I was feeling, it had to stay inside. *Oh, so now you're ashamed of me? What's this? Just you wait. You see what I can do for you. I'm even better than you know.*

"So." Laura leaned forward. "No word, I'm guessing?"

"Oh, I didn't tell you?" I waved my hand. "He's back! He just got lost on his way home. You know what it's like when they reroute the trains. Two weeks' delay is pretty much the norm. Fucking Metro Transit."

"You can joke all you want, but I know you're hurting."

"Oh, no. You're still watching *Dr. Phil,* aren't you? Laura, I'm telling you this as your friend, you've got to stop."

She allowed a patronizing smile and poured me more wine. But she didn't answer. I was terrible with conversation lulls. If she could hold out long enough, I would crack, and she knew it. I pursed my lips, held my breath. "I'm going to pump and dump when I get home," I said, knocking back my glass. "I swear." She nodded. Flustered, unable to stop, I burst out, "I feel like I should start mixing lunchtime cocktails and smoking a lot. Don't you think? This whole Harry thing seems very throwback to me. Doesn't it? Men aren't allowed to do this kind of thing anymore. Are they? Were they ever? Anyway, I feel it would help me. Some tranquilizers, maybe. I could become a total fifties housewife. Wait, maybe I mean sixties. My history is not great. Whenever it was that you could park the kids in front of the TV and get all blotto but manage to look polished and together and everyone would think everything was okay and no one would talk about how your husband kept leaving you or whatever."

Laura allowed a self-satisfied smile. Of course she was smug; her nontorture interrogation techniques had worked. "You should try acupuncture."

"See? I was born into the wrong era. That sounds so annoying to me. I'd much rather just sulk in a Manhattan. Not in *the* Manhattan, though. Too expensive."

"Or a therapist. You could try a therapist."

"Oh God. What's the point? Trust me, I saw a shrink for years. Why do I want to pay a babysitter so I can go sit in some office, reveal how pathetic my life is, and then weep? That doesn't sound fun."

"It's not supposed to be fun. It's supposed to be helpful."

"You know what would be helpful? A cleaning lady."

"I hear that. Or maybe a houseboy."

"Hmm, I don't know if I could deal with a man right now. A sympathetic hairdresser is probably about as much as I can handle."

"Anyway, you would weep and then maybe, you know, go further. Get to the bottom of things. With the therapist, I mean."

"Can it be a houseboy/therapist?" I sighed, accidentally blowing out the twinkly tea light on our table. "I'm pretty sure I know what's at the bottom of things. I'm pretty sure I'm sort of bummed out because my husband—" I couldn't finish.

Laura reached out and rubbed my arm. "I know. I'm sorry. I'm so sorry." We stared out into the street. On the corner opposite glowed another restaurant with outdoor tables corralled outside. I watched two ladies about our age chatting and laughing. Maybe if we went across the street for our next round, everything would be different. Somehow our lives would veer down alternate, superior paths. We'd chosen wrong tonight, that's all it was! But no, we ordered more wine and more snacks and settled into our uncomfortable designery folding chairs. "Hey," Laura said brightly, "maybe we should smoke cigarettes! Would that be fun? That might be fun!"

"Sounds expensive."

"True. And kind of gross, probably. We'd smell. Will would kill me."

"You know what we should do. We should go to a real bar, one of those dark places down on Fifth Avenue with an indie-rock jukebox and everything, and flirt with boys. Make them buy us drinks and stuff." The rusalka liked this idea. She churned around until I felt carbonated.

"Totally," said Laura, grinning. Of course we wouldn't. We'd order more fancy fare here, and besides, we could tell ourselves we were cute moms all we wanted, but once we found ourselves beside actual twentysomething girls, we would remember how slack our skin had gotten, how uncool our hair, how droopy our boobs, how lame our banter, how wrong our jukebox picks. Plus, I had this weird feeling that although it would be fun to be flirted with right now, even the total barroom creepers wouldn't approach me. It wasn't that I was so horrifyingly deformed or anything, I just knew that I probably stank of sadness, an inner rot people can sense and want to avoid. I'd been a depressive long enough to know that people steered clear when you were being a bummer. It was like how animals could tell when you were having your period. People's mood-preservation instincts kicked in, and they kept their distance. *Oh, please. I don't like this droopy wah-wah attitude you've got, not one bit.*

I'd fallen silent, studying my wineglass intently, as if I'd noticed a shiny engagement ring drowned at its bottom, trying to block out the rusalka's voice. I knew I wasn't being good company. I knew I should rise out of my wallowy sadness, peek out from behind my trauma blinders, provide some interesting conversation. At least ask Laura about her life. If only there were some way to express to her how truly grateful I was for her sympathy and kindness and patience. *I hate me, too,* I wanted to tell her. But I knew it wouldn't come out how I wanted it to, thankful and commiserating; it would sound whiny and needy and strange. I reached over to pour her more wine, hoping she could read in this gesture all the feeling I meant to express and couldn't.

"Do Arabian nomads get depressed? Papua New Guineans? Is this just me getting too into the neurotic New Yorker thing? I read once that tribal African women didn't get menstrual cramps, and that meant it was all in our heads or something. Do you think this is like that?" *Yes.*

Laura daintily dissected a mussel. I'd been eating all the fries, and she'd been eating all the mussels. "I don't think that's the point. It's not like you're feeling whiny for no reason. I mean, Jenny, your husband—"

"I know." I didn't want her to say it.

". . . disappeared."

"I remember."

"That would put anyone in a certain—you know. Funk. I mean, what do you do? How long do you wait? It's not like you can take off and hunt him down yourself."

"No kidding. I can hardly run an errand."

"What do you tell your kids? Your family?"

"Trust me, Laura, I know what sucks about it."

"Sorry. No, you're right. Sorry." As much as she tried, Laura didn't get it. How could she? I was sure she never felt this way—drowning, unable to surface. Even if something awful happened with Will, I knew she would be able to deal. She wouldn't wonder whether she was fit to care for children, capable of maintaining her daily existence. She would chin up and face the music and whatever else annoyingly cheery people like my mother thought sad people like me should do instead of sulking our way into psych wards.

Laura cleared her throat and tried again. "I'm just— I don't know how you're dealing with it so well."

"Am I?" I laughed. "I'm drunk right now. That's helping." *Also, I have a mermaid,* I was glad I didn't say.

We clinked glasses, laughing, and, as if we'd made an unspoken compact, veered back toward our usual conversation topics. How annoying so-and-so was, how rich so-and-so was, so-and-so was getting divorced, so-and-so had been caught cheating. Also, real estate. Also, alternate-side parking. And Cute Dad, of course our conversations always took a turn toward the Cute Dad cul-de-sac. *Yes! Finally. Now we go find him, right? Make a real night of it.* Laura was sauced enough to say, "How can his wife stand it? He's around all these lonely women all day!"

"I'm sure she doesn't think of it that way."

"She *should*! He's so flirty, too! Don't you think? Doesn't everyone want to jump his bones?"

"Laura!" She was really very drunk. So was I. I surveyed the other tables to assess our eavesdroppers. As if everyone knew who Cute Dad might be, or cared. "I think everyone's too tired and sweaty all the time to think about anything like that," I lied.

"Oh, stop!" She rolled her eyes. "It's me you're talking to here. Don't be such a prude."

"Okay, missy! Time for you to go home! You are getting salacious, my friend."

Laura laughed but obediently signaled for the check. She would pay and I would pretend to protest and insist I would get the next one although I never would and we both knew it. "Maybe you're right," she said, giggling.

"Maybe Will is going to get laid tonight."

She cocked her head. "He's probably asleep in front of the news."

"Hot," I said.

"It's true," she said, plunking down Will's gold card. "My Prince Charming."

It took all the remaining energy I had to pretend not to be drunk as Sylvia briefed me on the evening's diaper contents and bedtime-stalling techniques. I considered pumping my winy milk, I really did. I even spread out the pump parts and stared at them. But I was feeling kind of all right for once, and ending the night bovinely nipple-shielded did not exactly appeal. I wandered into the girls' room to check on them. All day I could be desperate for a moment alone, and then once I was away for an hour or two, I'd hunger for a sniff of their hair, long for a grabby, sticky hug.

The room was Sylvia-tidy, lit by an owl night-light and cracks of streetlight breaking and entering past the edges of the blackout curtains. On one side, Rosie kitten-snored in her crib, her paper-crane mobile spinning gently in the breeze from the air conditioner. Sylvia, goddamn her, had tucked a teddy bear and blanket into the crib. She refused to accept that nowadays you weren't supposed to put anything in babies' beds except the babies, preferring to believe I denied Rose blankets and pillows and lovies out of sheer cold-heartedness. I fished out the danger bear and dropped it onto the glider, hissing, "Stay away, murderer!"

On the other side of the room, Betty turned over in her toddler bed. "Mommy?" she whispered. Shit. My feelings of missing the kids hadn't extended so far as wanting any extra duties for the night past ruffling sleeping heads. I knelt by her bed. "Hi, baby," I whispered.

Betty sat up. "Not a baby," she whispered back. "Big girl."

I stroked her curls and eased her back down into her pillows. "Of course, Bets. Sorry. You are my big girl." This had been an important distinction lately. All distinctions had been important lately. No one had ever warned me how *conservative* small children were.

Betty trampolined back up, this time clutching to my arms. "Big hug, Mommy. Big, big hug. Monster hug."

I smiled. "Monster hug! Yes!" I squeezed her tiny body close. She rested her head on my shoulder and I stroked her wing bones.

"Mommy," she said, finally resting back on her pillow, dark lashes fluttering closed despite her best efforts. "Mommy, Gwamma said you come back and you come back."

"Of course I came back, honey. I was just with Laura. You know I'll always come back."

"No going wif Daddy?"

Cue heart: crack in two. "Oh, sweetie, sweetie, sweetie." I wedged myself beside her in her Thumbelina bed, holding her close, breathing in her bready sleeping smell. "Of course not. I'll always come back. You know that. And Daddy will come back, too. I prom— I think he really will. We love you, my babe—my big girl." She was already asleep again, but I lay there for a long time, studying her face, sweetened with sleep.

Harry had once accused me of loving the kids more than I loved him. On one hand, it was a perfectly ridiculous thing to say. There was no comparison. It was like having to deny preferring one child to the other—impossible and preposterous and inevitably guilt-inducing, particularly when you knew your answer was the wrong one. "Of course I have a favorite! Whichever one of you isn't crying at the moment."

Because there was something about the accusation that couldn't be completely ignored, something about the feeling that couldn't be explained. A certain surge zipped through my veins during moments such as these. It was like being in love, like those first heady days with Harry, but also it wasn't. It felt more like a narcotic working through my body—more complete, less pleasurable in a way, though more entire. It worried me. I'd never panicked about loving Harry, never worried that I couldn't take care of him or that I was damaging his life by simply existing in it (although in retrospect, maybe I should have). With my children, everything felt so fraught. There was so much to do for them, so much to protect them from, that my days were suffused with shaky moments, times when I wondered whether they wouldn't be better off without me, with someone else altogether. And now they didn't even have their father. Oh, these girls. Who had let me have children, anyway? Why wasn't there a test or something, a gauge of fitness? It had been more difficult to register for Mommy and Me swim class.

I woke up an hour later, stiffened into a parenthesis, and uncreaked myself gradually, sneaking away without disturbing the cozy beasts. I knew I was feeling overly emotional from drink and sleepiness, but I couldn't bear to leave the room. I stood in the doorway for a long time, frozen by a pair of undersize Medusas.

Lately, as Betty had gotten more independent and we—I mean *I* now, I guess—started to think about things like school, it had occurred to me that this whole having-children situation was essentially a process of unspooling. Once Betty had been so close to me that her feet had gotten stuck in my ribs. We lived literally tethered. And then she was born and screamed if she wasn't being nursed or held. But with each day, she unspooled a little farther away—rolling over, eating food, sitting, walking, screaming, "Go away, Mommy!"—the crimson thread connecting us unraveling more and more as she wandered out into the woods of the world. I had to remind myself of this, of how, even though I hadn't had a moment to myself in years, and even my bowel movements were observed and commented upon by my tiny Greek chorus, before I knew it, they would be off on the other side of the woods and I would long to tug on that crimson tether and call them tumbling home.

eleven

It was disconcerting to feel the way I was feeling—*happy* and strong and capable not only of leaning over to pick a slug of gummed bagel off the ground but even of such a Herculean task as taking the kids on the train somewhere. Harry's departure meant he'd had the last word on everything. I didn't have all the pieces of the story; I couldn't guess at the trajectory. Was I mad—a scorned lover left for some bimbo or, even worse, someone just like me? Was I a widow in mourning? The shamed victim of some crazy hoax? Was I a feel-good news story about to happen? ("And he reappeared months later," anchorman Pat Kiernan would confide to NY1's viewing public, his boyish charm adding a certain sparkle to the tale, "his mysterious amnesia cured!") I couldn't figure out whether I was supposed to be frantically searching for Harry or adapting to my new single life. Enough time had passed that a simple gambling binge was probably out of the question. *Pretty sorry state of affairs. Your most optimistic fantasy is that he's lost too much money and is ashamed to come home. He sounds like quite a catch. Your mother must be so proud.* "Unhelpful," I told the rusalka at times like these. "I thought you were supposed to be helpful." No response to that.

Strangely enough, most things were exactly the same. Daily life. Story time. Sing-alongs. Complicated trips to the C-Town supermarket or the kid-friendly (make that kid-swarmed) Tea Lounge. There we were in the park with Laura and Emma, who slouched in the dirt scratching at her arm beneath her hot-pink cast while Laura implored her to stop and Betty ran around us in circles, blowing bubbles with soapy solution that was probably full of toxins but looked so darn shimmery and innocent. Anyway, I was sure organic chocolate-milk boxes counteracted detergent inhalation. Rose lay on her front on the blanket, trying to scootch herself forward and seemingly in a better mood all around thanks to this new project. The heat had abated a little. The viscous air pressed around us but had lessened, loosened. The park made its summer music—Caribbean nannies shouting into cell phones, Hasidic tweens cheering each other on through softball games in suit pants, thumping Reggaeton music heartbeating its way through the trees from some distant noisy barbecue. And the coos of children—Rose's determined oofs and squeals, Betty's unmelodic humming, Emma's soft grumbling. I stretched out in the grass, arms above my head, like a girl in a movie about the summer that changes everything. I was happy to be alive. We both were.

The feeling of sun on skin! The gleam of dragonflies! The smell of grass and dirt!

"I know. I know!"

Laura peered at me over her froofy Frapuccino-wannabe iced coffee. We sucked them down all summer, investing most of our disposable income into plastic cups that were repurposed as sandbox toys, sometimes before we were quite finished with the fattening totally-not-milkshakes within. I'd gotten mine chocolatey, with whipped cream. It was no good, coating my teeth in a sweater of sweetness with every sip, but I was compelled from within to try things I never would have tried before, even things as small as different flavors. Laura said dryly, "Nice shoes."

I looked over at my Jayne Mansfield-y wedges and smiled, closed my eyes. "Hmm? Oh, thanks." The rusalka had spied them in my closet and ordered me to don them immediately. They *were* nice. They were also ridiculous—it was a miracle I hadn't broken my neck and died all over again on the way to the park—but *really* nice. Laura paused. "You're in a good mood today."

"Am I?" Was I different? Had I changed? Through my eyelids, the sun was a bloodred clot. I opened my eyes. I once read that because they had not yet accumulated all the tiny scratches and scrapes of an adult's corneas, newborns' eyes saw the world with almost unbearable brightness, and that felt like what was happening to me. The sky looked as white and meaningful as the palm of a hand. Everything I saw—a ferny tuft of mosquitoes, a cloud in the shape of a meringue—made me glad I hadn't died. What a stupid idea! Who would want to *die*?

"You are. Did you hear from Harry or something?"

I shook my head and rolled onto my stomach, watching my hand automatically pull a thicket of grass from Rose's fist and reposition her on the blanket, enjoying Laura's puzzlement.

"Did you find a suitcase of money?"

I laughed.

"Did Cute Dad ask you to the prom?"

I propped myself up on one elbow. When the rusalka and I shared a feeling, it was as if a chime reverberated in my breastbone. "Laura. I need you to tell me something, and I need you to be perfectly honest. Do you think Cute Dad is even really that cute?"

Laura shrugged. "Of course he is. Otherwise how would he have gotten his name?"

"Good point."

Emma and Betty were squatting by a jumble of tree roots, digging "potties" with sticks, pretending to poop in them, and then screaming with laughter. It was all going beautifully, though I was preparing myself for Betty to stab Emma in the eyeball. She'd been acting out at every opportunity, biting and pushing and grabbing and kicking, generally operating as if I were one large button to be pushed.

"I feel like they're going to remember their childhood as if they lived in a forest. All they do is play with sticks. Such sophisticated city kids." Laura picked up Rose and airplaned her overhead. Rose giggled, drooling onto Laura's sunglasses.

"I hope so. Sometimes I worry that the city is kind of stunting their growth. Or at least the apartment. Nowhere to roam, you know?" I paused. "Do you think it's okay? For kids to grow up in the city? I mean really okay? Or are we just being selfish?"

Laura held Rose in the air and gave me a look. "Um, hello, *I* grew up in the city. I like to think I turned out okay."

I lowered my sunglasses over my eyes. "You call this okay?"

"Ha, ha."

"I mean, look at you. You're not even practicing as a lawyer anymore." She shot me an unamused look. "Okay, I'm kidding. But—you know what I mean. That was different. You're an only child, your parents had money. They were from here, too. They knew how to do it. They knew the right schools to send you to, when it was okay for you to ride the subway alone, all that specialized stuff. You had a country house. I think you need a country house to raise kids here, in all good conscience. Don't you? Am I missing something?"

"Jenny, it's okay. It's not like my growth was stunted because I didn't have my own personal swing set or spend my teenage years driving to the mall."

"I object to your characterization of a suburban childhood."

"Oh? What am I leaving out? The great cultural advantage of the all-you-can-eat Old Country Buffet?"

"Don't you dare talk about the Old Country Buffet!"

What could I say about my childhood that would explain it to Laura? It was a childhood. I was a child. It was fine. I guess it was weird how little of it I remembered—particularly now that I knew what long days my mother must have weathered, the millions of minute decisions she'd had to try to make correctly, how many hours my sister and I had to be entertained, how many meals eaten, rules taught, boo-boos kissed—and what was there to remember? We drew in chalk on the driveway with the neighbor kids. The street was tree-lined, the sidewalk strewn with sleeping bicycles. Sarah made me stay out of her room. Once my mother burned the roast and Dad went out to get a bucket of Kentucky Fried Chicken—an especially fond memory. I lay on the cool floor in the basement and looked at books while Mom yelled at me to go outside and play, which I never did because the grass in our yard struck me as offensively scratchy and I despised bugs. I pretended to be a mermaid in the tub. So what? We lived on a cul-de-sac in a manufactured subdivision that was an imitation of other, better cul-de-sacs and subdivisions. The streets were named for the construction workers' wives—Lisa Lane, Barbara Boulevard. Did that make my present state any easier for me to understand? When I took Harry and the kids home for holidays, Dad told stories about family vacations I'd ruined by being morose about one thing or another. My parents seemed to have condensed the years into a few recycled stories that all sounded slightly off, making Sarah and me eye each other. "Sarah didn't notice when her cat ran away?" I'd echo, shaking my head. "That doesn't sound like me," Sarah would say.

I was tense and irritable on these visits right up until the moment we were about to leave, when I was flooded with sitcom-y sap, loaded with love.

I couldn't recall any moments of bonding with my father, or any inkling of a sense that he'd processed me as a being any more specific than "younger daughter." That was something Sarah always wanted to talk about—how our parents didn't seem to *know* us—but I couldn't see the point. Did we really *know* them? Did they really *know* each other? Our mother was constantly telling us how our father loved mashed potatoes, but at family dinners, I watched him flatten them with his fork without eating, like a six-year-old. How was it she'd never noticed?

Still, I bristled at Laura's comments. They seemed uncharitable, coming from someone who was so effortlessly a part of something I was trying so desperately to access. "Well, you know, there's the little matter of having your own space as a kid. A room to put a 'keep out' sign on, where you can hide from your siblings."

"Hmm, yeah, sounds great."

No, no. I jumped a little. *Don't even start with that. I lived in the country. It was a bore, full of small-minded peasants. You think it's so great? You want to sleep on hay? You want chickens in your living room? Well, not me, so you can just stop that all right now.*

That was a long time ago.

Oh? I didn't realize you knew so much about it. Never remind a lady of her age, Jenny. Anyway, the answer is no. We stay in Brooklyn. I've been hearing about it for years, and now I want to live it for myself. Why do you think I'm here? I didn't save your life to be bored back to death with dreams of Jersey.

Fine, fine, fine. Just stop distracting me. You make me look crazy when you do that. I was dimly aware that when the rusalka started chatting, I stopped whatever I was doing and cocked my head, like someone getting a transmission from a headset. Laura was frowning at me. Then she waved in my direction.

"Sorry. Hello, I'm here. I'm just out of it today."

"What? I'm not waving at you, silly."

I rolled to my other side, my skirt falling over my thighs, my hair springing absurdly from its bun. Had my thighs always looked so, well, good? The sunlight mellowed over my skin in a particularly flattering way. I stared, hypnotized by the thought that possibly someone could look at me and find me sexy. It had been a long time since I'd thought of myself that way. Maybe ever.

There he is.

For there he was, Cute Dad, strolling down the path, Maude's hand in his. He *was* actually cute. I was sure of it today. *But what is this ponytail? On a man? What is this?*

Shut up. I was aware that I had never fully rebuttoned the neckline of my loose shirtdress after nursing Rose last.

It's fine. Leave it.

I was not so far gone that I didn't sit up, though, and straighten things a bit. "Hello! Sam!" I called. "Maudie! Come join us!"

I ignored the look Laura shot me. Maude ran up the hill and over to Betty and Emma, immediately changing their game. "What is *this*? Don't you want to play *house*?" she said, imperious with big-girl bossiness. They stared up at her with open mouths.

Sam approached us cautiously. "Hi, Jenny. Hi, Laura."

"We won't bite!" I called out. I turned back toward Laura, who mouthed, "Slut!" But she was laughing. "What has gotten into you?" she hissed.

"You wouldn't believe me if I told you," I whispered back, sucking down a gulp of the tongue-lacerating slush we were calling coffee. I had ordered a large this time. My membranes buzzed with a sugary giddiness.

After a moment of hesitation, Sam perched at the edge of our not quite large enough picnic blanket, closer to Laura than to me. Rose rolled over on her back and blinked at him before reaching out and beginning to inchworm toward him. We were all starved for male companionship.

"So how's big-kid life?" Laura said. She was sitting in what we always called, whether we were talking to the girls or not, crisscross applesauce, her spine gym-teacher straight. She was obviously uncomfortable, but I didn't care. This was the luxury of my new life. I just didn't care. Sam had never joined us before. We had chatted by the swing set, or at the bakery, or at the Y after swimming lessons, but he had never crossed the blanket divide. It was a park-clique coup. We were straight out of a teen movie: the scrappy outsiders who, against all odds, score the attention of the boy who—well, the only boy. We were Molly Ringwalds with stretch marks instead of shoulder pads.

"Pretty good, pretty good. George loves camp."

"He's going to Park Slope Day Camp?" Laura had an amazing memory for other people's business. If you happened to mention that it was your mother's birthday, the next year your mother would receive a birthday e-mail from Laura hours before you got it together to call. It was extremely annoying.

"Mm-hm. Loves it. Maude is going to the mini-session, mornings only. She loves it, too."

Oh, no. Is this Cute Dad boring? He better not be boring, I'm telling you, bubeleh, *I will boot him right off this blanket.*

"What about you two? How are your summers going?" Sam looked enormous on the edge of the blanket. Rose had scooted near him and was patting his shoe. He grinned down at her. We forgave him his boringness. He was just so *nice*.

"Oh, fine. I mean, you know." Laura sort of nodded at me. I hated her.

"Yeah, other than my husband leaving me, mine's been awesome," I said. Better for me to say it than her. Better to get it all out in the open. Let it all hang out. I sucked down some crushed ice and chewed it as if my life depended on it, and maybe it did. Sometimes I had to focus on something for a second, something small and tangible—the collapse of ice shards between my teeth, the horizon line of treetops wavering like oversteamed broccoli—and then wait for the rest of the world to refocus around the one thing. A baby. A pair of shoes. Sometimes you needed one thing.

I looked over at Sam, who was nodding with a weird half-smile frozen on his lips. "Yeah, I heard about that. So sorry." Where were people fucking *hearing* about it? The Park Slope Parents message board? *Je*sus. "How are you holding up?"

I picked up Rose, who had started puffing out her bottom lip in a way I knew all too well. I stood up to sway with her, so that I was awkwardly looking down at Sam and Laura and willing Sam not to notice the downy surface of my unshaved calf. "Oh, fine. You know. It's very odd. Well, actually, yes, not fine, really, because it's all so odd."

So coy. Just get it out so we can all get over it and move on to something more interesting.

No, I'm already saying too much.

Well, it's too late now. You've already begun. Look at them. They're waiting. Just say it. Go ahead, then.

It *was* too much, I could tell from Laura's face. *Dial it back, Jenny.* But sometimes once you started, it was hard to stop. Anyway, I liked Sam. I really, really did. And I wanted him to get his information about me from me and not the weird yenta-y grapevine. Plus, as much as I loved Laura, I suspected she was my leak—after all, we gossiped constantly, so why should I be surprised if I was sometimes her subject? I figured I might as well tell her, too, so that maybe a more accurate version of my story could virus through the neighborhood. If I was so interesting. Which, apparently, I was.

I cleared my throat.

So go for it already.

Fine. I am.

So say it already.

I am. *Let me speak!* "The deal is that, I, well—" I stole a look at Betty, who sat on a bumped root while Maude braided her hair and Emma watched. Start again. Begin. Go. "The deal is that . . . I mean . . . no one really knows what the deal is. I mean, he didn't leave me for another woman or anything. Not that I know of, that is. He just— He went to buy cigarettes one night and hasn't come home yet." I laughed despite myself. It sounded so ridiculous. It *was* so ridiculous. "But the thing is, he's taken off before. He's a compulsive gambler—it's a real thing, it really is, a big problem, lots of people have it, it's an addiction like alcoholism—and he goes on these binges. If that's what this is, it's the longest he's been gone. So anyway, I don't think it's, like, foul play or anything. If you're wondering why I don't seem that worried. I mean, I'm worried, of course. The thing with the compulsive gambling is that it really is a disease, you know? I've read about it. It has something to do with serotonin levels in the brain. Anyway, so what I'm saying is I don't think that he's abandoned us, exactly. But he may have. He may be really, really gone. But probably not. So, there you go. That's the truth, the whole truth, accept no imitations, et cetera."

Sam blinked. Laura blinked. The rusalka and I, we threw back my head and laughed. "I'm sorry!" I burst out. "I know, I don't mean to make you feel uncomfortable. Don't feel uncomfortable. It's really okay. I mean, every marriage has its problems, right?"

I sat Rose down on the blanket. She had the slumped posture of a man you wouldn't want to end up next to on the train. She beamed up at us. Sam offered her a hand. She took his finger and, tentatively, took it in her mouth and started gnawing on it. We all laughed, relieved to break the tension. My surge of bravado left me, and I felt exactly like you do in the dream where you realize you've come to school naked.

"It's true," said Sam. Aha. He was so nice that he would even sell out his own wife to make me feel momentarily better. He smiled at me. He had those eyes that gave new meaning to the phrase "puppy-dog eyes." Now and then something happens that reveals, with startling clarity, the complete truth of a certain cliché, and here was one of those happenings. Love at first sight, puppy-dog eyes. Like, as in, eyes that rearrange something in your chest cavity. As in, seriously as irresistibly cute and open and innocent as a goddamned puppy dog.

"I blame those anti-smoking groups," said Laura. "They make it so darn hard to find cigarettes anywhere these days."

Sam laughed. I hated Laura for winning his laugh. Our eyes met, mine and Sam's, and I looked down at the blanket, and I think he did, too. We all quickly cast around for a new subject, something we could all get into, complaining about the exorbitant cost of preschool, about real estate, about whether or not they used pesticides in the park, about anything but me and Harry.

Then Emma gave us something to talk about: She screamed, because Betty had bitten her good arm. We rushed over, we scolded, we soothed. A biter! Who would have thought? It was the worst kind of kid-on-kid violence—it drew blood, it freaked everyone out, it caused people to ask if your child was disturbed about something. And did I mention it drew blood? I put her in a pointless, misunderstood time-out under a tree, for lack of knowing what else to do. Sam escaped, Emma cried in Laura's lap. Apologies were coaxed. Halved grapes were eaten. I was lucky Laura was so understanding and encouraged Emma to be, too. Half an hour later, all was well again, and the girls had gone back to collaborating on a pile of stirred-up dirt by the tree trunk. I fantasized about leaving the girls there with Laura and sneaking a nap in a grove somewhere. I fantasized about sleeping for days.

I didn't forgive Laura until later in the day, when we were walking the long track that looped around the park, Emma snoozing in her stroller and Betty toddling alongside hers, wanting to push it and then veering it right into the woods, making us move at a monkish pace. Rose turned red, staring at me with an intensity that could only mean she was taking an enormous poop, and then she sighed, nestled down into what she'd made, and fell asleep. The sling felt heavy and damp but fine, I'd take it. If my girls ever napped at the same time, it would be an absolute, no-exaggeration, makes-you-believe-in-God miracle.

So we were walking, and Nell passed us by, effortlessly sprinting in a spandex number I wouldn't wear lying down, pushing Sophie in a jogging stroller. She stopped to run in place at us. "Oh, hi, girls!"

"Hey, Nell," we answered in flat unison.

"Beautiful day, isn't it? Great news—Sophie got accepted into Poly Prep! I'm just ecstatic! After all the interviews and everything, you know, it's just such a relief! What about your girls? I hope some of Soph's buddies will be joining her at preschool!"

"Nell," I said before I could stop myself—*Don't think, just say it, she deserves it, oy, what a pill*—"it *is* a beautiful day. Don't ruin it for us."

She laughed, surprised. "Oh, Jenny, you are too funny!"

I ignored Laura's warning look. "I'm not being funny. Why don't you just jog on, lady? Leave us masses to our plebian pleasures!" She laughed again, but there was a stricken look in her eyes, and she was still there, so I said, "Personally, I'm going to get some Baby Einstein DVDs and call it a day. Preschool's for the weak!"

Nell was scarcely able to stifle her gasp. Laura contributed a strangled giggle. She was about to say something, probably by the way of apology, when Nell waved her hand. "You are too funny!" she said again, uncertainly. She waved an exaggerated baby-wave, wiggling her perfect manicure at us, and took off down the track. "See you girls at Wee Sing!"

Laura watched her shrink away and said, shaking her head, "Look at her butt. It doesn't even move." Then she turned to me. "You're insane."

I shrugged. *I'm not the crazy one,* I wanted to say. *It's my mermaid spirit.* I went with: "She deserves it. What an asshole."

I could see Laura's mood undulating behind her face. She decided on amusement, thankfully, and after we had walked a few moments in silence—after Betty had climbed into her stroller and busied herself with a crinkly bag of fruit snacks, and we'd picked up our pace, listening to our breathing and the rattle of leaves and the distant music of the carousel—Laura said, "I want to tell you something."

Ugh, here we go. Sometimes I'm so tired of women. Aren't you? Here comes some confession, a cathartic cry. Give me a stoic man any day. Actually, do. Soon, preferably.

Oh, stop. We love Laura.

Hmm. If you say so.

Laura took a deep breath, not looking at me. "This is something I've never told anyone."

I nodded. "About Will?" I prompted. I knew it. He had always seemed way too perfect. Maybe he wasn't working late all those nights, saving lives. Maybe there was a reason Laura constantly suspected Harry of an affair. Maybe—

"What? No. About me."

Now I really was curious. "Oh. What is it?"

Laura looked embarrassed. "It's not that exciting. I just— I've— It's so silly."

She looked at me. Her eyes were a deep olive green, flecked with gold. Had I ever truly seen them before? Her expression was so strange that my mind raced. She was having an affair. She was terminally ill. She was secretly in love with someone—Cute Dad! Nell! Me! "I've been sneaking out of the apartment at night when Emma and Will are asleep."

"And?"

"And going to Donuts."

"Donuts? The greasy spoon on Seventh? This is your big confession? And what, you get the corn-beef hash? Jeez, Laura, who cares?"

"Well—I talk to people. I mean, I interview people. I've been recording them. I just pick people and ask them about their lives. I don't know why. There are the weirdest people there in the middle of the night. Or sometimes the most boring people. Which is weird in itself. Immigrants with PhDs who work crappy night shifts. Homeless schizophrenics bubbling with conspiracy theories. Nurses from Methodist, still wearing their scrubs with Betty Boop or whatever on them. Chatty insomniacs. I just— I don't know why I'm doing it. I just like it."

For an instant I was disappointed that I hadn't elicited some juicier confession. But in a way, it was sort of a shocking thing to hear. I guess I did think I knew everything about Laura. It was weird to think she had a secret life, even if it was a harmless project that took place for a few hours a night, even though—especially though—it was nothing sordid. Laura! Who would have thought?

"Will doesn't know. He's a sound sleeper. And the thing is, I don't want him to know. At this point, he would be upset to learn I've been doing something without telling him. Don't you think? Even though it's nothing . . . bad, you know? Also, I like having a secret project. I know it's silly, but—it's mine. You know?" I watched Laura as she spoke, and I realized two things, or rather, the rusalka narrated in my head: *One: You have been thinking about no one but yourself and your own problems for months now. Why is it some big-time shock to learn that your friend has something—anything—going on? Of course she does. Doesn't everyone? Don't we all have our own private things happening, bubbling to the surface only when the kids go to bed, when the men aren't looking?* For Laura, it turned out, it was something solid, pleasantly concrete, which made sense, given her tidy personality. Of course Laura had a project, an organized and productive way to rebel, a secret inner world that injured no one.

And two, look at her. I did. Laura, in the coins of light tinkling down through the trees, in the soft summer air, her hair in a loose ponytail, the collar of her white oxford shirt slightly damp from sweat, Laura, leaning over to check on Emma in the stroller, was beautiful. When had it happened? Had she always been this way, and I was looking at her only now?

But she was waiting for my response. There was a certain beseeching quality to her silence that I recognized from something, from someone, from myself, like when I would say something to Harry, present some idea (Let's go out to brunch! Let's move to France!) and breathlessly wait for him to shit on it or maybe, possibly, but probably not, approve. I looked my friend in the eyes for once. The rusalka breathed to me what to say. "Laura," I said. "That's amazing. I want to hear some of it."

She rolled her eyes. "It's not amazing. It's stupid. And I feel so guilty—like if I can't sleep, I should spend that time cleaning the apartment or doing laundry or making a quilt. I don't know. Something."

Tell her. Tell her this is nothing to feel guilty about. Be a friend. It's not so hard.

"You have nothing to feel guilty about."

"What if Emma wakes up and I'm not there? What if Will does?"

"So tell Will. He won't be upset. Why should he be?"

"I should stop, anyway. I've been staying longer and longer, until I'm so tired I can hardly see straight. If Emma drops her nap, I'm done for!" She gestured dramatically, only half-joking.

The rusalka had perked up—a weird feeling, a jittery jolt of energy. She ordered me, *Tell her this. Repeat after me.* "Don't downplay what you are doing. I'm serious. Don't be self-deprecating. What you're doing obviously means something to you. Why shouldn't it mean something to others, too? You're making a documentary about the nocturnal life of a neighborhood! That's something a lot of people would be interested in."

Laura shook her head. "It's nothing. You haven't heard the recordings. I haven't even heard them all yet. I just meant—"

I interrupted. "It's something. I'm sure it's something. Hey, doesn't Julie's husband work for NPR?"

"No. I mean, he does, but Jenny, no. It's nothing like that."

"Why not? All I'm saying is—" What was I saying? It came from within, without me. "There's no reason why you couldn't be making something people would care about. You're a creative person, and you have good taste, and there is no reason to believe that what you're making isn't worthwhile."

Laura opened and closed her mouth a few times, like a fish. Then she turned to me and smiled helplessly. "Thanks for the vote of confidence. I mean it. I don't— Don't tell anyone yet. Let me listen to everything and try to do some editing and see if there's anything there. It may be nothing."

"Fair enough. But you admit that it may be something?"

She paused. "It's possible."

Laura had become a less suggestive version of my high school boyfriend: People thought of us as a unit, and we assumed without confirming that every day would involve each other. We even spoke in the slack-jawed idiom of teenage paramours: "Wanna hang out?" "Yeah, that'd be cool." "Whaddya wanna do?" "I dunno. Whatever." There was an unspoken ambition toward more, a shared suspicion that we weren't made for each other, but since we had found each other and were both available, we should continue the ceaseless hangouts. So the next morning, I camped out on a blanket in our usual spot in the park, by the curve in the path where the trash cans stood sentry, haloed with obese bees—ah, nature. I hadn't told Laura where we would be or when, and she hadn't told me when, if ever, they planned to leave the house, but we knew the drill by now, how to find each other when the need to see another adult became unignorable.

Today, however, my rusalka had had it. *Don't you ever leave this neighborhood?*

Rose sat, leaning on her hands like a tripod, staring off into the heat-hazy distances. Betty was force-feeding her stuffed bunny acorns and telling it softly, "Eat scones!" I was just happy no one was crying. It hadn't occurred to me to want more from a day. *What do you mean? We walked to the other side of the park yesterday. And why would we live in this neighborhood if we wanted to be somewhere else?*

Oh, please. I had no idea you people were so provincial. Isn't there a whole city out there?

Ugh, the stroller on the train, and the diaper bag, and Betty needs to be home at noon to nap, and . . .

She had no patience for this, and soon we were packing everything up. How was it that we had been camped out for under an hour and had spread out so completely? Toys and books and diapers and Betty's snack container and a Hansel and Gretel trail of Cheerios zigzagging across the blanket, which itself was tie-dyed with grass stains, spit-up, apple juice, probably pee, who knew what else.

In the last few weeks, Betty had mastered a very teenagerly withering glare, and she lasered it toward me now. "Where going?" She had the bunny in one hand and a palmful of acorn-scones in the other.

"The Met." *The Met? Do you have any idea how long that train ride is? What about nap time? What about—* "It's a big art museum in the city. It's about time we get some of this fabled culture I hear so much about this city having to offer. And I don't mean spending an hour at Barnes and Noble." Jesus.

I have to admit that despite the dread churning up in my chest like a wave of pregnancy heartburn, and despite the extended hassle of prepping the stroller and strapping in the squirmy toddler and settling the baby into the carrier and begging reluctant passersby to help me lug the stroller up and down the dungeony subway steps and entertaining the kids throughout the bizarrely long ride, it was the best afternoon I'd had in a long time. Betty ran through the armor room, saying excitedly, uncomprehendingly, "Knighttime, Mommy! Knighttime!" Rose sobbed and then nursed in the Temple of Dendur, rallying to gaze intently at the Tiffany stained glass. I could have sworn I could feel my brain opening, twisting toward paintings, like a rose slow-motion-blooming on a Nova program. I did have a moment when I saw myself in the reflection of a framed photograph and remembered what a mess I was and wished myself not in a cuter outfit but simply back home among other messy mothers—but it did feel good to be out in the city. Betty and I shared a stupidly expensive snack in the museum café, where the cute boy working behind the counter smiled at Rose and then at me and awakened some warmth in my limbs—so pathetic—out of mere simple politeness. It didn't take much these days, did it?

Rose took exception to the modern-art galleries—everyone's a critic—and we beat a hasty retreat out into the heat and blare of the street. Betty refused to get back in the stroller, galloping up and down the steps. "Watch me, Mommy!" It was one of those summer days when the city seems animated by a large benevolent force: The pillars at the museum's entrance seemed to bend and wave; taxicabs swarmed down the street like huge, happy bumblebees. I wouldn't have been surprised if the skyscrapers fringing Central Park had begun to sing and sway in time. *See, didn't I tell you?* And there it was—an ebullient fetus of happiness, kicking me from within. Happiness! What a lightness it was, what a peculiar energy it gave you. How strange, the way you could live without it and hardly notice its absence.

We stopped in Central Park so the rusalka could see it, and so I could change Rose's diaper and nurse again before the train ride home and Betty could chase some fancy Manhattan pigeons around for a change before being strapped back in the stroller. It was the big sister of Prospect Park—neater, with prettier and more carefully considered flower beds, more shapely fake lakes, greener grass. Even the birds seemed cleaner. It was a city park dressed up to meet visitors, and today we were the visitors. Betty and I shared a hot dog from a vendor. "Mommy! This hot dog is SO GOOD!"

Betty said rapturously. The poor kid was used to boiled tofu pups. Rose fell asleep strapped to my chest, and a nice businessman carried the stroller down the stairs to the subway platform. I couldn't remember when I'd been so happy, electrified by a peculiar zinging, my mind cleared like a nose after a cold's last sneeze. I felt like taking an antihistamine-commercial deep breath, sighing luxuriantly. "AHHHH!"

In the days and weeks that followed, the rusalka had us on the move. *How dare you be bored in this city? You can travel the world in an afternoon! We're getting dim sum in Chinatown for lunch and lasagna in Little Italy for dinner.* The girls and I went to museums and parks we'd never seen. I found myself trying foods I had never heard of. We marched in the Coney Island Mermaid Parade, the rusalka snorting at all the body-paint scales and Halloween costume fish tails. We dragged Laura and Emma to Brighton Beach, where the rusalka seemed especially happy, compelling me to slurp down ice-cold borscht while Laura watched in horror. "What's gotten into you?" she demanded. "You seem so, like, normal lately. Happy or something."

"Do I?" I said as we strolled the boardwalk, the girls skipping among the fat Russian men stuffed into hanky-sized swimsuits, grandmothers looking greasy and brown as rotisserie chickens. "Well, good. I guess I'm just feeling a little better." It was true. I was. It was as if I'd begun to remember about the world as the rusalka rushed forward to see it; as if, like her, I was seeing everything for the first time.

twelve

All of which was very well and good, except that, as Sylvia reminded me frequently, there was no word from Harry. I was worried. It would have been heartless not to worry. But the rusalka wanted me to stop, and when she wanted something, she had ways of being very convincing. She didn't care a whit about Harry. She thought I was a fool to pine over him. *What, he was such a prince? Let's move on, sweetie.*

She somehow dredged up my worst memories, excavating from my mind the most miserable moments with Harry: the fights, the gruesome scenes, the protracted fits of bickering. The party at the Village town house of some snooty friends of his where he'd said, "Oh, Jenny's from the Midwest. She's practically part cow." We'd all laughed into the fondue. How funny! How sophisticated we were, that we could be so cruel to each other! Sweating it out later in the subway station at West Fourth Street, I'd said, "Part *cow,* Harry? What the fuck." He'd exploded. "Why are you always trying to pick fights? It's like you're only happy if I'm unhappy." "Oh, I'm sorry! I didn't realize calling me a cow was such an important part of your happiness!" The A train rumbled overhead, so we shouted louder, attracting the attention of everyone standing around. It was awful, awful.

Or the night he came home drunk and said, "You're ugly when you nag." "What nagging?" I'd said, genuinely surprised. "I just asked where you were. You said you'd be home five hours ago." And he'd waved at me on his way to the bedroom as I slid his gelled hunk of casserole into the trash, playing the part of put-upon movie housewife.

Or the weekend in Atlantic City, before we were married, when I woke up on the beach, sunburned and dazed, to see that he'd abandoned his towel next to me. I'd found him a few hours later in a Wild West–themed casino, down three hundred bucks and flirting with the sad-eyed blonde dealing cards.

I knew he couldn't have been as mean as all that. I once loved him so much, I'd felt a physical ache in my chest. When we were first together, I'd gone to my doctor, asking about the frequent sudden pains—that's how much I loved him. I loved him so much my doctor was worried and ordered a scan. I remember wondering what she'd find. An enlarged valentine-shaped heart, thumping like a cartoon's, bleeding its outline through my shirt? Nothing. She found nothing. Obviously. But this feeling, it was like trying to remember a smell. I could recall only its effects and not the feeling itself.

Oh, please, was the rusalka's response. *We are over this. Onward, my dear. The man is gone. His loss. All I want to know is: What's next?*

I have to admit that a large percentage of my brain devoted itself to worrying about money, namely my lack thereof, and about taking care of the girls despite this inconvenient poverty. The rusalka whispered, *Don't be silly. You can make money. You can make money with your sewing.*

How? That's not going to work.

Such an attitude! It works, of course it works. I'll show you how.

Somehow, she did. It started with Evelyn, at the place where all important deals were negotiated, in Park Slope, anyway: on the playground. We were pushing our babies slowly, slowly, on the baby swings, vaguely aware of our older kids plopped in the center of the sandbox. Gus loved the swing, squealing and bouncing. Rose hunched in hers, glowering at me. Evelyn sighed. "I have to go to this event for Darren's work. A fund-raiser thing. And I would be excited about it—you know, a fancy night out on the town without the kids—but I have nothing to wear. And I'm not exaggerating. Nothing. None of my clothes from when I was working fit." She nodded at Gus as if to indicate why. We were all fatter and exhausted by trying to act like we didn't care.

I yawned, bored. It was one of those days that stretched out before me, the distance between the present moment and the girls' bedtime seeming to lengthen as the day wore on rather than diminishing. I squinted at Betty and Charlie, playing nicely together for once, even if they were sculpting a disturbingly phallic sand castle. Sometimes I thought I had the kind of brain that had no right being near kids. The other day at the Y play space, I'd heard a mom call out, "NO LICKING BALLS!" and I'd almost lost it completely. It was terrible. I'm not saying it wasn't terrible.

Evelyn went on, her voice the bleating blah-blah of a parent in *Peanuts. Her ability to drone on is astounding. Poor Darren! It's like she's determined to be a bore.* "Mm-hm," I said, taking mercy on Rose and lifting her out of the swing. She was happier on my hip, tugging at my hair. "Mm-hm . . . Yeah . . . Wait, what?"

Evelyn looked taken aback, as if startled to remember she was talking to someone. "Oh. Have you seen the one I'm talking about? It's this really pretty, really simple gray shift dress. Silk, I think. At that little boutique on Seventh and Fourteenth or Fifteenth, I think, where everything's so pretty you can't stand it? I was just saying, the stupid dress is eight hundred dollars, and I'm sure if I could sew at all, it would be the easiest thing in the world to make. But I can't sew a button. Not that the dress has anything as complicated as a button! Anyway, I can't spend that kind of money right now."

I tapped her on the arm, a gesture so unlike me that we were both a little startled. "Buy the dress."

"Yeah, right. No, I don't mean like *Oh, I shouldn't* can't afford it. I mean like I don't have the money. Even our credit card is maxed out from our apartment renovations. We have a beautiful kitchen and no money."

Oh, boo-freaking-hoo.

She's a spoiled idiot, obviously, but that's hardly the point. Think, Jenny, think!

"No, I mean, buy it and give it to me."

Evelyn barked a terrifying laugh.

"No, no. Listen to me. I can sew. I used to be really good. I think I'm really good now again, or I could be. What I mean is, bring the dress and I'll make you a copy. Then you can return it."

Evelyn stopped pushing Gus's swing, causing him to squeal in protest. "Are you serious?"

"Evelyn, I'm always serious."

"You are not."

"Okay, but I am now. I can do this. Just pay me back for the fabric and maybe fifty dollars for the time it'll take. When's the event?"

"Next Friday." Evelyn sounded dubious.

It took me a weirdly long time to compute in my head. Math! "Today is Thursday. I think. Okay, so, buy the dress tomorrow and I'll have it finished by Monday."

"You're serious?"

"I told you. I'm always serious."

The conversation was cut short by a shriek piercing the muggy air. Used to ignoring kid sounds, I didn't even look. Then Evelyn was extracting Gus from his swing and hurrying toward the sandbox, where my darling Betty had just mistaken Charlie for a chicken nugget in a sunhat. Evelyn was understanding. Charlie was not. Betty grinned psychotically, and I swear I saw blood in her teeth. Just what I needed. As if a normal two-year-old weren't difficult enough, mine had to go and turn vampire.

The next day Sylvia came to watch the girls so I could ride the F train into the city and prowl the garment district in search of gray silk. It was stunningly hot. I sweated into my calfskin sandals, crossing narrow side streets kept dusk-dark by office towers. Squat Latino men my height and three times as muscular yanked overladen carts over broken sidewalks, in and out of delivery docks the size of modest suburban driveways. Hasidic men hurried in pairs toward the kosher deli. Here and there, neon steam undulated above neon bowls of ramen, advertising lunch spots, but mostly, the storefront windows were bright with rolls of fabric. I felt foreign, wobbly, as if my legs were new and not quite my own.

So here *is New York! I like this place, I do.* I'd taken her to one of Manhattan's last remaining sordid corners. Peep-show theaters lit the avenue with kinetic rainbow signs; a man in a filthy trench coat exited the parole station and promptly commenced peeing onto a Dumpster. I started like an out-of-towner when a hunchbacked hag with knobby, chickeny legs staggered out from an alleyway, offering me an enchanted treat, wait, no, mumbling about a conspiracy and holding out a hand for change. I gathered myself and ignored her, strode on. Despite my nerves, I felt elated to be there, to be anywhere, to walk down the street alone, carrying only a small handbag and on a non-baby-related mission. It was almost as if—could it be?—I had my own life.

I walked quickly down the shrouded side streets, passing by the stores devoted to wholesale and the cheap shops offering bolts of leopard-print polyester, hot-pink rickrack, and stiff, sparkling lace. Spandex World. Cloths 4 U. Finally, I found a decent shop and spent half an hour or so in a kind of tactile ecstasy—fondling linens and silks, holding samples up to the window to examine the colors, testing the weave with a gentle tug, rubbing a peachy satin to my lips and remembering how I first loved fabrics, like this, as a child in my mother's closet, sniffing and softly gumming the hems of her few fancy dresses. I spent four times as much as I would have had Harry been around to frown at the credit card bill. And I found the most perfect, swingy, pearly, dove-gray silk for Evelyn's dress. I was going to make that dumpy woman the belle of the ball.

Rose, the new rusalka-trained Rose, went to sleep easily that night. But Betty was feeling rambunctious. I suspected Sylvia had given her juice, because of course there was no reason to listen to me when I asked her not to. What did I know about these kids, anyway? In the hyperactive whirlwind of evening, picture books were browsed through and then flung at the wall, a raucous tea party ended badly when Emma the tiger bit Emma the bunny. I motioned for Betty to come out of the bedroom, where she was kicking her blankets on the floor and heartbreakingly moaning, "Daddddyyyy . . . my daddddyyyy," and less heartbreakingly, "My arrrrmmmm is broooookkkkkennnn." Her eyes wide in disbelief, she followed me into the hallway. I pointed to the couch. She padded over cautiously, a small specter in her ballerina nightgown. I opened my laptop and popped in a *Dora the Explorer* DVD. Betty's eyes widened. This was so out of the ordinary that she didn't have the proper structure in her brain to even comprehend what was happening. "You may quietly watch, but Mommy has some work to do. And if you wake up the baby, I am sending you to live with Grandma. So you must be quiet."

Betty nodded and sat down, trying to hide her grin. "Mommy?"

"Yes?"

"Where I will sleep at Gwamma's?"

"I'm kidding, sweetheart. You won't really go to live with Grandma. Just please please please don't wake up Rosie. Please just be quiet and watch *Dora*."

She nodded. I turned toward the kitchen table. "Mommy?"

"Yes, baby?"

"Can I sing with Dowa?"

She crouched on the couch, peering into the laptop's moony screen as if it were a mystic oracle. The expression on her face, the crinkle of her dark brows, looked so much like Harry that I almost lost it completely. I took a deep breath, gathered up whatever I had inside—*This is not so bad, any of it. How lucky you are, when you think about the big picture*—and went over to kiss her black curls. "Yes, sweetheart. Sing very quietly, though. Whisper-sing."

"Okay, Mommy," she whispered.

The hardest part of making the dress was getting the kitchen table clean enough to lay down the delicate silk. What *was* all that grit? The dollops of crusted dinner bits, the spatters of sticky something—so she *had* given Betty juice, the traitor—the driblets of salad dressing that I could blame, much to my dismay, on no one but myself. It was one of the many luxuries of marriage that I had been tabulating since Harry's disappearance, having someone to blame things on; unless Rose had developed a predilection for roughage, this mess had to be mine. After a hot and heavy session of scrubbing, I was ready. I fed the sewing machine a spool of silver thread. I laid out the dress Evelyn had brought over, carefully unfolding the tissue paper, spreading it over the two extra kitchen chairs like a precious shed skin.

I spent the next few hours draping muslin over the dress form that had been serving as an anthropomorphic coat rack for longer than I cared to admit. My grandmother's tricks were all coming back to me—she'd given me lessons along with the ancient Viking sewing machine the summer I was thirteen, friendless, and looking for a pastime. In a kind of trance, I pinned the fabric into place, consulting the original now and then, and before I knew it, hours had passed and I was creating and then trueing the pattern. My fingers flew over the fabric as if enchanted, moving much more quickly than they should have after so many years of relative disuse.

I didn't even notice when Betty closed the laptop and tiptoed off. I remembered her existence (some mother, I know) only when I crawled into bed to nurse Rose back to sleep after she woke up around three, and I found Betty curled up in a nest of my pillows. For a brief, painful instant I missed Juniper's sweet, slobbery presence, her furry warmth. And then, with a more painful pang socking my stomach, I missed Harry. I missed Harry so much, so deeply, curled up there in what was once our bed, with Rose suckling at my breast, my breast that once was more than just food, with Betty curled at my back, her sleeping fingers coiling into my hair, my hair that Harry had always said he loved, no matter how unruly it got—I missed my husband so much I thought I would die of it. My chest went hollow, and as Rose began to doze off, I saw in the dim light a few of my tears dampening her brow. The rusalka, with all her bluster and bravado, seemed to have left me. Left me? Had she ever been there? Or had she just been a stressed-out housewife's imaginary friend, a nice way for me to convince myself that I was a little less alone? I cried that night, there between my children. *It is only because I am so tired,* I told myself. *It's just that I need to sleep.*

I did feel better in the morning, even when Rose woke at five, even when Betty began bounding around begging for juice. I stumbled out of the bedroom in my underwear and stopped in my tracks. I had been very sleepy by the time I went to bed, so it was possible I didn't remember. I mean, it must have been that: I was too tired to remember exactly all I had done. There was no other explanation. No other explanation for the finished, perfect dress (which should have taken me at least eight more hours), finished with French seams and all hung, neatly ironed, on a pretty padded hanger (propped on a hook usually reserved for my singed oven mitts). No other explanation for the tidied kitchen, the original dress folded and returned to its paper bag, the sewing machine closed back in its case and returned to its corner, replaced with a coffee cup and a bowl of dry cereal for Betty. Her Snoopy spoon lay sweetly on a folded cloth napkin. The coffeemaker dinged. Had I suddenly remembered, in my exhaustion, how to program the damn thing like Harry used to do? I must have, because it was full of fresh coffee, and the whole apartment smelled like a Folgers commercial.

Betty stood in front of the dress, reaching out a hand. Then she looked at me. "No touching?" she guessed. I nodded, stroking Rose's peachy cheek. *You did it. That dress looks perfect!*

There you are. But I don't even remember finishing it. How did you . . . ?

I don't know what you could mean. Now call Evelyn.

Evelyn, once I had convinced her that the copy was really a copy, actually hugged me. "Jenny! You are a genius!" She insisted on paying me for the fabric and two hundred dollars extra. "It's the very least I can do. Are you kidding? This is beautiful! Better than the original!"

I had to admit, it was. It was kind of a shame to waste such a dress on frumpy, frazzled Evelyn, but in a way, it felt just right. I made her try it on, and when she came out of the bedroom, she was barely recognizable. The color was perfect on her, made her creepily translucent skin look like porcelain, invited her watery blue eyes to introduce themselves. It hung beautifully on her body, making her weight resemble curves and not just pregnancy detritus. Even Betty stopped playing to stare. Rose bounced on my hip, batting at my chin.

"All right, then!" I said, trying unsuccessfully to hide my excitement. "Tell your friends!"

I took Evelyn's envelope of cash, and for a few hours I felt like a rock star. I was gleeful at bath time, singing "Rubber Ducky" with operatic gusto (the rusalka harmonizing in my head), and patient at bedtime, even when, as I was sneaking out of the room, avoiding the familiar land mines of creaky floorboards, Betty sat straight up in her toddler bed and said, "Want to say night-night to Daddy." I shushed her and peered over at Rose, slowly, as if my turning my head too quickly might wake her, but she was snoring quietly in the crib, a pacifier dangling out of the corner of her mouth like a nonchalant cowboy's cigarette. I tiptoed back over to Betty and sat on the edge of her bed, and she nestled comfortably against me as I stroked her dark mass of curls. "I know, sweetheart," I whispered. I hadn't decided how long I could keep up this business-trip business, but every day I put off the decision longer. It wasn't like kids had the best concept of time, and besides, I told myself, he would be back soon, and when they grew up, they would never remember a thing about it. Reassuring myself, though, was starting to sour, to fill me with, instead of relief, a squicky dread.

Dread? Of course. You're starting to live your own life. Forget him.

Forget him? Are you crazy? I kind of planned on spending the rest of my life with him, you know.

That was your old life.

Seriously, shut up. Just shut up.

Soon Betty was asleep again, and I shimmied out from under her, arranging her miniature frame on the pillows, pulling her blanket up to her pointed chin. Tiptoed back out of the room and took about thirty seconds to pull the door unsqueakingly shut, then cleared a space at the cluttered kitchen table, poured a glass of wine, opened my envelope of money from Evelyn, sat there, and smiled.

The fizz of joy lasted for about three minutes, because then I did something very reckless. I flipped over an envelope, and with a stinking Sharpie and the calculator on my phone, I did some math. I added up our monthly expenses, including the credit card bill minimum payments. In the opposite column, I wrote down Harry's base salary. We'd never lived off just this salary. Even in lean times he had some sales, and the commission, though it varied throughout the year, bumped up his salary to a supporting-a-family-in-Brooklyn-with-liberal-help-from-credit-cards-and-gambling-windfalls wage. But the salary itself. I am not exaggerating when I say my heart skipped a beat. No wonder he was always so stressed out about sales. No wonder he couldn't resist the poker table.

Oh.

Fuck.

"This isn't going to work," I said to my sewing machine. It wasn't going to work. I had our down-payment fund to sponge off of, though the thought of emptying that was depressing, to say the least. Who knew how long he would be gone? Sylvia had offered to subsidize Betty's preschool, but before I knew it, I'd have to worry about Rose going, too, or not going, and there were the bills, and our huge credit card debt, and my student loans, and at any given moment Harry could, from wherever he might be, siphon off our bank account. And then there were whatever gambling debts he might have accrued that I had no idea about. I broke out into a sweat, my heart kicking at my throat. Miserable. It was just so miserable. If he stayed away—why, I would need to go back to work full-time, and leave the girls with Sylvia or some random babysitter, and what work did I think I was "going back" to? All my magazine contacts were out of work, too, or going to work at websites, and I was so tech-incompetent that I wasn't sure what the Myspace thing everyone was talking about even was. Fucking money. Fucking New York and our bloated rent. Fucking Harry. Fuck, fuck, fuck.

What are you talking about? Jenny, you've got your sewing. There are others like Evelyn. If you could make a dress a week . . .

How can I make a dress a week? I know four people. And two of them are babies.

That's not true. You spend a lot of time feeling sorry for yourself, you know that?

Excuse me? She was nervy, but this was too much. *Listen, you existential parasite. If you don't like it, why don't you pick someone else to haunt?*

It was an odd feeling to have her angry with me, sort of like extreme indigestion, or the end of pregnancy when someone is constantly palpating your ribs from within. I downed some more wine, hoping to calm her, us, me. *This is absurd.* "This is absurd," I said out loud. "You can't be mad at me."

Me, a parasite? I saved your life!

Okay, okay. I'm sorry. I just . . . I think I'm allowed to feel a little sorry for myself. I'm all alone.

All alone? Jenny, please. What about me, hello? I'm here! And listen, your mother-in-law watches your kids three days a week for free. You have more friends in the neighborhood than I had in my whole earthly life. Excuse me, but if you saw what life was for us then . . . My mother was illiterate and had nine kids and no heat or running water. She had to make her own soap, Jenny. From lard. You don't even like cutting open packages of chicken breasts.

So?

So your life's not that bad. You've hit a rough spot. Buck up. It's hard to be a mother. It's hard to be a person. *You need a little money. So make a little money.* Nu, *so, what's so difficult?*

It was impossibly exhausting, like trying to argue with Betty when she really wanted to wear her rain boots into the bath. "Fine. I'll give it a shot. It's not going to work, but fine. I guess I can always borrow some money from my parents. God, how humiliating."

You're not going to have to. Trust me.

You're annoying sometimes, you know that?

So are you.

Gee, thanks.

Nu? *Do you have anything else to say to me?*

I'm sorry. Sorry I called you a parasite.

And?

Um. Thanks for saving my life. Or whatever.

You're welcome. By the way, you might as well discontinue your cable, since you're not using it, and get Sylvia to buy your groceries at Costco. You could probably save a couple hundred bucks a month that way.

All this, and financial advice, too? I was starting to think that jumping off the Brooklyn Bridge was the best thing to ever happen to me.

Until word of my dress magic spread, I never realized how much of a nonentity I'd considered myself. I slunk through the rarified world of Brooklyn yuppie parenting like a mousy high school girl, neither popular nor unpopular, following just enough of the rules to stay unseen. As in high school, there was an unspoken undercurrent of competition that I secretly wanted to be a part of and couldn't hack. There were too many exceptional people here. Laura thought this was why we liked it, and she was probably right, but it was also why Brooklyn made me crazy at times. Every day I met some mom who was beautiful and stylish, patient and kind with her well-behaved and well-dressed kids, and was also a successful conceptual artist/Internet entrepreneur/Emmy Award–winning television writer/locavore caterer/homeopathic dog masseuse/*something* amazing, and usually the owner of some mystifyingly great bit of real estate besides. It always struck me as funny when I read some article or another about how Park Slope moms were slobs, but it all depended on whether you were coming from Manhattan or Minnesota. Whenever I was back home, I felt a bit stunned by the widespread politeness, lack of worldly ambition, and acceptance of sweatpants.

A few days after Evelyn wore her dress to the party, things started changing for me. First Julie ran up to me at the playground and reported that she'd seen Evelyn's dress and it was too beautiful for words and I should go into business or at least post on Park Slope Parents. "I had no idea you were so *talented*!" she gushed. I know it was meant as a compliment, but I couldn't help responding with a bitter laugh. *Like it comes as such an earth-shattering shock that I of all people have some talent! Like she knows me so well and was so sure I was just this total schlub!*

Relax. This can only be good for business.

What business?

Just wait.

Then it was Mary, a mom I had befriended strictly because her apartment was actually worse than mine. Hey, sometimes you needed a playdate in a dim, tenementy one-bedroom stuffed with particleboard furniture for a bit of perspective. Mary cornered me at the riotous Barnes & Noble kids' section where we'd decamped to soak in the air-conditioning on a particularly unforgiving day. I nodded, trying to keep track of Betty as she pillaged the Elmo books. "Everyone's talking about the gorgeous dress you made!" she cooed, as if I'd discovered the cure for cancer or the secret to finding affordable co-ops. She was one of those ladies who was so sickeningly nice that it made me nervous. I half suspected that she was at all times an instant away from wiping the smile off her face and telling me what was really on her mind. Mary. She never whined about not having money or about sharing a bedroom with a two-year-old; she seemed to be genuinely and completely in love with her husband and kid. In other words, she was sort of hard to like.

"Oh!" I said. "Uh, thank you!"

"You are *too* good! Do you do stuff for little kids, too? Because I'm looking for something really special for Sydney to wear when she's the flower girl at my cousin's wedding . . ."

If I'd ever doubted what a small town I lived in, that was all over. Suddenly, everyone wanted to talk to me, everyone wanted to place an order, and I don't think I was imagining a change in the way people regarded me. I was the woman whose husband had disappeared, yes, in the land of storybook marriages (divorced people and single moms were supposed to flee to Manhattan or, if they were poor, to Queens), but more than that, I was the magical seamstress with quick fingers who would make you look hot while saving you money, and honestly, what was better than that? I was able to forget about the mess of my life for whole minutes at a time.

See, Harry? I'm not so useless after all. You probably thought I'd just disintegrate into salty little tear bits when you left, but look at me now.

You know what? Here's a game for us. Don't think about Harry for, I don't know, half of every day. It's not doing you any good.

That's a lot easier than it sounds. Haven't you ever been in love?

You're not in love. You're married. And you're pissed off, not love-struck.

What are you, anyway, some sort of built-in shrink?

Convenient, no? Now, Jenny. About this Cute Dad.

Oh, no, no, no.

But I was beginning to learn that she didn't have to listen to me, and thus, like a sly toddler learning the loopholes, she usually didn't.

thirteen

I probably shouldn't have been surprised that the rusalka was more obsessed with Cute Dad than I ever had been with my low-octane, largely symbolic crush. But there were lots of other things I needed to be thinking about. Fred kept bringing up the idea of a private investigator. "Something's just not right," he said. "He's never been gone for so long. I have a bad feeling." I knew, and I know, that I should have told Fred about the postcard, about the gift of reduced worry Harry had offered, but the rusalka kept me from sharing the news that Harry was on an ill-timed soul-searching mission, less in danger than he was inconsiderate. *Feh, we both know Harry could have sent them a card, too, if he really cared to spare them the heartache. Maybe he wanted them to suffer.*

Fred was worried sick, Fred couldn't sleep at night. "Also, Juniper is licking her butt a lot, any ideas?" I could hardly concentrate on what he was saying because I'd just gotten the electricity bill, and those air-conditioner window units must have been on more than I'd thought. The total made my eyes cross. Though that was nothing compared with Betty deciding she didn't like to go on the potty that much after all, preferring to remove her own dirty diapers and finger-paint with poop like a mentally ill monkey, which I found a particularly unpleasant form of rebellion and which of course coordinated with Rose's resurgence of fussiness and, one morning, a razor-sharp sliver of white on her bottom gum. "Teething? Right now? Are you kidding me?" I asked her as she gnawed furiously on a frozen bagel. And so, naturally, this was when the rusalka began her hissing in my skull. *Sex. I want to have sex.*

You're kidding, right? You can stop that right there. I'm sort of preoccupied, in case you haven't noticed, and honestly, tired of bodily secretions.

Do you have any idea how long I was swimming around with a goddamn fishtail? Jenny, enough is enough.

Well, maybe you shouldn't have come back as someone whose husband is missing. Honestly, my most fervent fantasies these days are of not being touched at all. Of sleeping for hours and hours. So yeah, I don't know how I can help you with that one.

Yes, you do.

No. I don't.

Sam. What about Sam.

"Nothing about Sam. Nothing. That's— You're crazy, you know that?"

Am I? You're the one walking down the street talking to yourself.

Damn her. But she wanted what she wanted, and what she wanted, I wanted. It was like being possessed by a sex-starved demon or a teenage boy. I was constantly horny. I had never been that way my whole life. I don't think I'd ever uttered the word "horny"—it always struck me as so ugly and uncouth and *male*. In my former life, sex had been pleasant but not something I ever obsessed over. I had never done things like gone nude under long skirts so I could feel something, anything, everything; watching men in the street or the park or the Laundromat and wondering what they would be like, picturing them naked; touching myself under the cover of a bubble bath late at night. It was insane! I found it vaguely embarrassing, not to mention incredibly inconvenient. I blamed it all on her.

Very Minnesotan of you. Very Puritan. You Americans.

Shut up. I have responsibilities, you know. I do put some stock in being faithful to my husband.

Oh? Right, because he's been so faithful to you.

I—you—we don't know that. As far as we know, yes, he has been. We don't know anything. Innocent until proven guilty.

Like I said. You Americans.

That has nothing to do with anything. I love Harry.

Of course.

In this weird, overheated state, I was learning some things, things that probably would have been helpful to learn years earlier. Such as: People liked to be flirted with. Even if you weren't much to look at, almost anyone was happy for the attention. How had I gotten through so much of my life without learning how to flirt? The new boy at the bakery across the street was disarmed when I complimented his latte-making skills. "No, *really*," I said, smiling, looking him in the eye. It wasn't what I was saying but the way I said things—I mean, *obviously*, but it felt like a revelation—and here he was, practically blushing. And I was wearing a baby in a pouch on my front, and my toddler was dumping the basket of picture books on the floor, and I hadn't showered, and my greasy curls were swirled up in a natty bun. He was one of those people who I figured was about my age until I realized I was probably ten or fifteen years older than he was, that he was wearing a Nirvana shirt not because he'd seen them in concert but because it had struck him as an ironic retro find. But I touched his arm and said, "Seriously. The way you steam the milk! You should get an award or something!" and then I could feel it turn on like a switch, feel him opening slightly toward me and saying, "Well, it *is* my life's work," and we both laughed. It reminded me of something, or maybe of someone, the way it drew people to you, the way you knew you could then make them do things for you: "Oh, shoot, I don't have any cash. I know this is below your credit card minimum . . ." "Oh, please, don't worry about it. You know what, it's on the house."

I walked out into the press of sunshine, the avenue twinkling with sunflares in shop windows, the nail salons and bodegas transformed into ornaments, the flock of pigeons lunging toward an old man's sprinkling of birdseed, the bus rumbling by like a large hungry beast, my daughter by my side humming to herself, and the happiness of having flirted, having been flirted with, the hope it aroused in my coffee-gurgling gut, followed us down the block like a sweet smell until we reached the corner and I realized who it reminded me of. Harry. It was Harry who was good at that. He could get anything from anyone because he had that magical ability to reach inside and flip them on—acquaintances' beautiful wives, grouchy postal workers, me. God. Maybe I had been a fool all along. Maybe it had been ridiculous (as a few of my girlfriends had suggested when we met) to think that a man who had flirted and dated and slept around and charmed the world for decades would stop cold because of one woman, and not even some spectacular sexpot but plain old Jenny. Maybe it was obvious to everyone but me.

I dropped my perfect latte in the trash can on the corner. Easier to do when you hadn't paid for it. It was too hot for coffee, anyway. "What we are doing today?" Betty said, spinning in circles while we waited for the light to change. I held on to her shoulder to stop the spinning. Enough with the ceaseless joy already.

"I don't know," I said. "Nothing." Oh God, what a long day stretched ahead with nothing to do. We walked around aimlessly for a few blocks, and just as Betty started to get whiny, I was struck with inspiration. "The Y. We're going to the Y for open gym." Betty managed to grimace and light up at the same time. She really was her father's daughter.

Forget preschools and their various well-thought-out philosophies, forget guided-creativity play workshops and bilingual music classes and underwater toddler Latin lessons, here was the hot spot for the under-four set. For a few hours each morning, the stinking, sweat-soaked gym at the Y was padded in big cushy mats like an enormous lunatic asylum cell, with a couple of germ-infused plastic play sets thrown in for good measure, so that the toddlers of the neighborhood could run around and go berserk. I balanced Rose on my hip and watched Betty race toward the collapsible tunnel. I scanned the parents clumped into small groups, all looking in different directions to make sure their kids weren't licking anything too disgusting. I didn't see anyone I knew and felt a flicker of disappointment that made me wonder what I had been expecting. I had just squatted down, releasing Rose to push herself up on all fours and practice her almost-crawling rocking, feeling my capris poof out behind me to reveal an awkward stretch of underwear and butt crack, when—

"Jenny!"

I squinted up at him. The dank atmosphere of the gym called to my attention the semicircles of sweat beneath my armpits and breasts. "Oh! Hi, Sam!"

He waved at Maude, who was directing smaller kids down the slide. "She's too old for this, but she said she wanted to come."

"That's sweet," I said, not really caring. What was more boring than other people's kids?

Cute Dad plopped down on the mat beside me. It's difficult to explain what happened next. I thought I heard a loud *hhhhhhhhhh,* so loud that I looked around at first, thinking a ventilation system had coughed to life, before realizing it was her, the rusalka emitting an annoyed sigh with a sharp, guttural edge. And then she took over. That was when I realized she had been holding back all along, humoring me by letting me think I was in charge, that she was content to stay a nattering voice in my head, a hedonistic Jiminy Cricket. Had I really thought she would be content, having saved my life and returned from the dead, with art museums and new iced-coffee flavors? She shook my head—I shook her head—we shook our head—and sat up straighter and beamed at Sam. "She's a lovely child. You're such a good dad."

"Well, I don't think I can exactly take all the credit, but thank you." He smiled, got on all fours, play-growling at Rose, who giggled, delighted.

Nice ass! Look at that!

Please. Please stop this. Look where we are, for heaven's sake, this is about the least appropriate place in the world for—

For what? Will you just shut up for a second and let me drive?

"So, Sam. How are you?"

He looked up, his dark eyes twinkling in the glinty gym light. "Oh, I'm fine. And you?"

"No, I mean, *really*. How are you *really*?"

His smile was cautious, as if I'd urged him to jump into the pool, saying I'd be in right behind him. "Are we at that stage?" he said. And—there it was. Something had switched. Strange how that worked. It was nothing you could anticipate, but once it happened, there it was and, at the risk of sounding like the tot-yoga teacher, all the energy between us changed. "Don't you just want me to say 'Fine'?" His eyes crinkled, pushing his smile toward the precipice of laughter.

"You could. If you're really fine."

Sam rocked back on his knees and sat up. Our eyes met, and then we scanned the gym for our girls, located them, ascertained their safety, and looked at each other again. "I mean, I'm really fine in the polite-conversation way."

"So am I. But in the real way, I am definitely not fine."

Sam sighed, still smiling. We all smiled too much, as if trying to convince the world we were that good at what we were doing, that everything was fine, fine, fine. "Yeah, me, neither."

"Is everything okay with Juliet?"

His smile dimmed. "No, not really." He paused. "Any word from Harry?"

"No."

"I'm sorry."

"It can get lonely inside a marriage."

He stared at me. I stared back. I couldn't remember the last time I'd looked for so long into anyone's eyes, besides maybe my children's. It felt hugely risky, baldly flirtatious. We studied each other's faces. *Listen, you. This is nothing new. All anyone wants is to be known. To have somebody know you, to have somebody be interested.*

Sam looked away. "Juliet's annoyed with me for working on my screenplay instead of looking for a job. She thinks it's a waste of time. It probably is. Maude starts pre-K in the fall, and that's when we always said I'd go back to work. But I have no idea what to do, and I've been out of work for so long now, and everyone says there's no work, anyway. I think she's sick of having a deadbeat husband. Why wouldn't she be? And I still don't know what I want to be when I grow up, and I'm afraid of wasting my life doing something stupid, and it's scary." Our eyes met again. "Too much?"

"Not at all. Believe me, I understand. You have no idea how much I understand." And there was a tender smile and, Jesus, a hand squeeze.

I know, I know. Just a hand squeeze. Hardly enough to shock a sixth-grader on a mom-chaperoned first date. Afterward I couldn't remember who had reached out for whom, only that our hands met, our palms pressed together. The hair all over my body stood up, a heat squiggled between my legs, a flush lit my flesh. The truth was that no matter how innocent a hand squeeze sounds, we both pulled away as if electric-shocked and looked around, because we didn't want anyone to have seen, because it wasn't the kind of thing you would want Juliet to somehow hear about, so it couldn't have been all that innocent, now, could it? It was not something the old me would have thought to do or would have known how to pull off.

Just then a shriek pierced through the air, and the rusalka disappeared as quickly as she'd whooshed in. Betty. It took me a second to scan the crowded gym and locate her. I stood, scooping up the baby, and jogged over to the plastic slide, where Betty sat on the floor, wailing. "Sweetheart, sweetheart," I said, pulling her close. The whole time I berated myself: My daughter was hurt because I wasn't paying attention! It was every mother's greatest fear, and for the millionth time I had proved—this time by flirting with Cute Dad so intensely that I'd practically gone blind—that I was a terrible parent. Betty pushed away and rubbed her wet eyes. "What happened, baby?" I cooed, overly nice, as if to make up for my negligence. Here came Sam, Maude at his side, concerned and friendly. Sam and I exchanged guilty, freighted glances.

Betty sobbed, "I . . . fell . . . my arm! My arm!" and pulled away from me, examining her knees and elbows for bruises. Another mom leaned in. "I saw what happened. She just tripped. I think she's okay." I smiled gratefully and said, "Her friend broke her arm, and she's super-jealous." My voice sounded different—unsultry—my own again. "I think she's hoping for a pink cast." The other mom nodded good-naturedly. Sam helped Betty to her feet, and we all automatically headed out of the gym toward the stroller parking.

"We should be going, too," Sam said, half to Maude, half to me.

Both Betty and Rose were crankily rubbing their eyes. "We might get a good nap out of this," I said. Voilà—we were innocent parents again, just doing our parenty thing, passionately desiring, if nothing else, a lengthy afternoon nap.

"I think my crush on Cute Dad is kind of like herpes," I told Laura. We were spread out on a couple of bedsheets in the park, waiting for the sky to darken so the Fourth of July fireworks could erupt. Laura laughed. "Oh?"

It was too late for the girls to be out, but Laura's husband was in emergency surgery—and, uh, so was mine?—and it was cooler outside than in our stuffy apartments. Rose had fallen asleep in the sling, so I laid her down in it like a miniature hammock. Emma was lying on her back on the sheet, flipping through a picture book and neatly eating raspberries, the picture of a perfect child. Betty was wired from being up late and was behaving as if she were possessed, running around and shaking her head and shrieking, attracting the glares of grown-ups gathered around citronella candles and clandestine bottles of wine. She had befriended a towheaded five-year-old, and they were leaping after fireflies, trying to trap them in an empty jelly jar. "Come on, people," I muttered at the nearest grumpy faces—two of the approximately seventeen childless people in Park Slope, who made a sport of hating us breeders—"you don't find that even mildly cute?" To me they looked like childhood incarnate, scruffy and wild and beautiful. Betty had been such a savage lately that it was a relief to see her channeling her energy into an activity that didn't draw blood.

"And were you planning on explaining that romantic sentiment?"

I blinked at Laura. Then I lay back, kicking off the vintage Givenchy Mary Janes I'd found at a thrift store on my last trip back home. The shoes, combined with an uncharacteristic swipe of crimson lipstick, had me channeling a film-noir vixen, despite the unassuming bag of a dress they were paired with. A sliver of moon scored the side of the sky, an informative celestial chalk mark. I closed my eyes, enjoying the coolish breeze on my skin. It occurred to me that I was enjoying my own *skin*—perfectly comfortable for once, the extra baby weight feeling for a moment like an extra curve, desirable even. "Ah, yes, my herpes crush. Well, it's mostly dormant. It's not like I think about him a lot, not extracurricularly, if you know what I mean. But then I see him and he smiles or asks how I am or something and—*bam*—total red, blistering, itching flare-up."

"Wow," said Laura, jabbing her straw in her bubble tea. "Romantic." Despite spending most of our days together for the past few years, we managed to mostly bitch about how underappreciated we were by our husbands and trade detailed anecdotes no one else in the world wanted to hear, like about our children's bowel movements and sleep patterns. Since Harry had left, though, I'd found myself confiding in her more and more, really talking about my goddamn feelings, like some sort of guidance counselor or movie sidekick. Poor Laura!

I sat up, squinting at Betty's jumping figure. "Do you think I'm terrible? I mean, God, it sounds terrible. My husband disappears and I'm like, oh, whatever, and start crushing on Cute Dad, because he's around. Don't answer. I know. It's terrible."

Oh, stop that. You deserve happiness. Some romance. Everyone does. Life's too short, blah, blah. You have to think about you.

"But maybe I already do that too much. You know?"

Laura raised her eyebrows. "What?"

Oh, cripes. I rubbed my face. "Sorry, nothing."

"Oookay. No, of course I don't think you're terrible. You're—confused. And lonely. And—but it *is* just a crush, right? I mean, we all know that Sam is happily married. Right? I mean, I want you to be happy, and I know it probably sounds like a kind of adventure; I mean, the thought is exciting, but you wouldn't really—"

"Of course not. I think."

I didn't say what I wanted to say, what *she* wanted me to say, which was that Sam's so-called happy marriage wasn't my problem. I had plenty of my own problems to worry about. It probably happened all the time, trysts sparked on the tot lot, but the goody-two-shoes in me couldn't quite believe it. Did people *really* do that? Even though it was *wrong*? Didn't they feel *bad*? The sky was stained a deep indigo. It wouldn't be long until the fireworks. A few feeble stars appeared, pinpricks of light. I looked at Laura, but she was avoiding my eyes. "Well, it's true that he's married," I said.

Laura paused. "And so are you."

I nodded. "As far as I know."

"This must be really hard for you." Laura leaned forward, squeezing my arm. Part of me wanted to crawl into her lap and weep like a baby. I nodded, biting my lip. "You poor thing. I can't even imagine how lonely and sad and confused you must be. But believe me when I say Sam is not the answer. Besides, Brooklyn is a small town, you know that, none of us has any secrets. It would just be so not worth it. So not fun."

"It might be a little fun."

I wanted her to laugh, in cahoots with my borrowed evil side, but she frowned. Maybe I needed to cultivate some new friends. Maybe Evelyn or Julie would giggle and tacitly approve of misdeeds and make it all feel more fun, less like a big bummer of an ethics conundrum. Laura opened her mouth as if to speak, but then Betty came tumbling onto the blanket, breathing hard. "Mommy," she said, panting, "we ran . . . soooo . . . fast."

"I saw," I lied. "Good job." I'd read somewhere that you weren't supposed to say "good job" to your kids, but I couldn't remember why. Oh, well. It wasn't like unmitigated praise was the only thing between me and the Mother of the Year award. I pulled her sweaty body into my lap and stroked her hair, which she tolerated for two seconds before scootching over to see what Emma was doing. Laura produced from somewhere a farm-animal puzzle the girls were exceedingly fond of. I put on my thin sweater, more because my shoulders were tired of the air than because of any actual chill, and peeked in at Rose, who really did look like an angel sometimes. I was feeling defensive and distant from my friend. My brain roiled with unnecessarily bitchy comebacks: *I'm sorry that everyone's life isn't picture-perfect, you self-satisfied doctor's wife, maybe someday things will go awry for you and you'll understand* . . . But then Laura volunteered to walk the restless girls over to the ice cream stand, which I knew was a peace offering, and it calmed me somewhat. She wasn't trying to be mean or judgmental. She was just trying to be real, to tell me something I needed to know.

Plus, she had given me a few rare moments alone, a few moments to watch the sky darken and my neighbors arrange themselves in the meadow, to take a deep breath, to stretch out for a second, to watch, oh God, Sam and his family troop over the grass. His wife and kids didn't acknowledge me, but Sam waved in the dimming light, and I could have been imagining it, but he seemed happy to see me. Predictably, I blushed—good thing it was almost dark—and waved, and thought, *Stop that.*

Then my crew was back and the girls settled into our laps and the fireworks began. Miraculously, the first twinkly spray of lights woke Rose but didn't startle her, so I scooped her out of the sling and nestled her in my lap beside Betty, who reached out and held her baby sister's tiny hand (instead of pinching her side, for once), and I held my girls close to me and closed my eyes and smelled their sweet smells of baby shampoo and scalp and fresh air, and listened to the twitchy crackle of lights in the sky, and felt so close to whole that I almost expected to see Harry sitting beside me when I opened my eyes. "Just kidding!" he would say, or "Surprise!" or "Here I am! I won a million dollars! I'm so sorry, I can explain everything!" No, but there was Laura, and she smiled at me, and the whole park was pink, then purple, then bright white.

We waited afterward to let the crowd thin before packing up the scattered picnic and the sleepy girls into strollers and walking slowly home. "Sometimes I wish I were a nun," Laura said suddenly.

I laughed. "Because you love Jesus so much?"

"Right. I just mean—I have days when I think I would like to take a vow of silence and walk around in some beautiful stone building on a mountaintop and be alone."

"I think you're thinking of monks."

She tilted her head. "Oh. Hmm. Maybe."

"And/or," I said, navigating the stroller over a cavernous sidewalk crack, "a trip to the Cloisters. We could do that, you know. You just have to get on the A train and keep going up forever."

"You know what I mean."

"I do know." Even though Laura had sort of been on my nerves all day, now that we were near my building, I slowed my pace, not wanting to say goodbye, or maybe dreading bumping the stroller up all the front steps to the stoop. "I think the weirdest things, too, sometimes."

"Weirder than wanting to be a nun?"

"Hmm, maybe. Like"—I didn't mean to say it, but somehow the message didn't get to my brain fast enough, and my stupid mouth said, quietly, in case Betty was awake and listening (*Just say it, just get it out*)—"sometimes I wish Harry had died." It sounded even worse than I expected, and I hastily added, "I mean, not *really,* of course not. But at least then I would have some closure. I would know what happened, I wouldn't have to be mad at him. But I don't mean what I just said. You know that, right?"

We were in front of my building. Laura stopped walking and hugged me. We had been friends for almost four years, since we'd met in our ob-gyn's waiting room, and there had been plenty of days when I'd seen her (and liked her) more than my own husband, but I didn't think we'd ever hugged. Laura had such sweetness in her. She was good in a way that I was not. There was no denying it. She never had those moments, I was sure, when it all seemed like too much, when she felt unequal to the task of living, of caring for the people she was meant to care for. She squeezed my arms and said, "Oh, honey, I know," and something about the way she called me "honey," about the warmth in her voice and the sadness in her eyes just got me. A tear rolled down my face. "He'll be back," Laura said, as if she knew anything about it. "Don't worry. How could he not? He'll be back." *Okay. She doesn't have any idea what she's talking about, but okay, I get that she's trying to be nice. Want to go try to find Sam now?*

I shook my head. "Sorry. I'm just—really tired."

"I know. Do you want some help with the stroller?"

I refused automatically, waved goodbye, then kicked Betty out of her seat so she could sullenly stamp up the stairs while I heaved the thing up each step, counting the able-bodied men who passed by on the sidewalk without offering to help. The lack of chivalry bothered me less now that the rusalka had made me stronger, but it irked me on principle: There were seven steps up to the front door and one, two, three, four and a half men if you included a teenager. Once inside, I jammed the stroller beside the neighbors' mob of clammed-up Maclarens loitering beneath the stairs, scooped Rose out, waking her despite my attempts at gentleness, and willed myself up the steps to our apartment, praying for an easy bedtime and a couple minutes alone to sew. I usually didn't think there was a God, but I figured if there were, he/she could probably relate to needing some time to oneself.

We were, where else, on the playground when Nell materialized by my elbow. I jumped. "What are you, a ninja?" Laura shot me a warning look that I pretended not to see.

Nell shrieked with laughter so exaggerated, I started again. "Oh, you are too funny!" I was not. She wanted something.

Sophie cautiously approached the sandbox crew: Betty, Emma, and a pair of twins we knew from the Y. Nell called out, "Careful of your dress, honey!" Sophie looked down miserably at her starchy petal-colored pinafore.

I sat down on the bench, lifting my shirt for Rose. "Sorry, can't talk, Nell, nursing. The baby gets too distracted." Rose peered up at me as if to prove my point before latching on, her eyes fluttering back in milky bliss. Happiness buzzed through me. It was part hormones, okay, probably mostly hormones, but also the unique satisfaction of being able to fulfill her needs so easily, so completely. The baby part was hard in its own ways, but there was something so pure about my relationship with Rose, untainted by the small-scale power struggles I had every day with Betty. So far I was the solution to all of Rose's problems. It was exhausting, but it was beautiful.

"So. I saw the dress you made for Evelyn." Nell sat beside me, suddenly solicitous. Rose popped off to stare at her. Years of breast-feeding had inured me to the weirdness of boob flashing in public. *Hello, Nell, here is my nipple.* Nell waved her perfect pale manicure and shushed herself. Rose went back to nursing. Nell whispered, "Breathtaking."

"My boob?"

"Oh, you! No, the dress! I can't even believe it! How can I get you to make me one?"

I shot a quick look at Laura, who was raising her eyebrows and nodding toward the playground entrance. I followed her gaze. Cute Dad was on the move. "Okay, Rosie, you done? You're done." I re-assembled my shirt. The baby looked perturbed but not overly so, distracting herself with a length of my hair. "What kind of dress do you want?"

"Well, there is this Alice + Olivia dress I've had my eye on—"

"Okay. Bring it to me. I'll take your measurements when you come. Keep the receipt and you can return it afterward. When do you need it by?"

"Oh! Whenever. I just want it."

"Can do, Nelly." I patted her arm. "My pleasure. I'll get back to you on my fee."

Cute Dad was standing near Laura, smiling at something she was saying. I felt inappropriately ruffled, flaring with unearned jealousy. I could hardly stand to look at him. *It's supposed to be fun to have a crush. Don't take everything so seriously.*

I found myself hoisting Rose onto my hip and abandoning my new best friend Nell, sidling up to the chatting pair. When I reached them, though, I could think of nothing more clever to say than "Hi."

"Hi," said Laura, leaving off the "you idiot."

Sam smiled. "Hi, Jenny. How are you?"

This was all I wanted. Someone to say "Hi, how are you?" Someone to smile at me. A male someone.

"Rose seems cheerier. How's she been?" He watched my eyes as if searching for something misplaced in my pupils.

"Good! Thank you! Much better. Yeah, it's weird." I shrugged, flushing. Could I possibly be stupider and more boring? *Anyway, we're both married. We're just friends. Who am I trying to impress, right?*

Oh, please. He's adorable. Meanwhile, Harry is missing these leaps and bounds in the baby's life. It all happens so fast, he should know by now, and yet he takes off, and Sam is the main man in your life. Certainly in terms of—

Okay, fine. Just flirt, then. I don't want to hear the analysis.

Sam nodded. "Ah, babies. They have mysterious ways, don't they? I remember Maude was like that, too—just so fussy all the time, no matter what we tried, and then not at all." Laura excused herself without either of us fully noticing. "Man, so, isn't it awful?"

"Yeah. Wait, what? Isn't what awful?"

"The thing in London? The terrorist attacks?"

I rubbed my face. You'd think I'd get used to being such a douchebag, but no, it still took me by surprise, my own ability to miss everything. "What? I'm terrible. Your saying this makes me realize I haven't seen or heard the news at all in . . . I don't know. Since, like, 2002, maybe?"

But Sam, sweet Cute Dad, he laughed. "I'll tell you enough so you don't embarrass yourself."

While he told me what was happening ("across the pond," as he put it, a phrase that had always made me cringe but now sounded adorable), I realized he was telling me about a terrible thing in a very gentle, almost apologetic way. That he was trying not to upset me, as if upsetting me would be the worst part of a subway bombing. I kept trying not to feel in love with him, and it kept not working.

Don't fight this. Live this.

Shut up.

You know I won't.

So now the subway's scary again.

Everything's scary. Life is scary. Next!

"How is your screenplay going?" I took advantage of a lull in conversation to change the subject. What was this, junior high? What would I say next, "Gee, I made you a mix tape"? "Could you fill out this note and check off if you a) like me or b) like me-like me"? It was as if I were on a mission to sound idiotic.

But Sam lit up. "Oh! The screenplay's terrible." He laughed. "Thank you for asking. That's—it's very sweet of you to ask. Bad. It's so bad. I reread it all the other night and—yeah. Bad. New heights of banality."

I don't think I was imagining it. His eyes twinkled, they really actually twinkled. And that smile. He was so easy to talk to. Easy for me to talk to. And something about the way he looked at me. Maybe it wasn't him at all. Maybe it was being paid attention to, flirted with a little. ("Love the scarf," he said, laughing at the burp cloth bunched like a vomity corsage at my shoulder. "I was feeling fancy today," I answered, blushing.) The rusalka took notice, seeped into the conversation like water in parched dirt. *I'm considering this time spent getting friendly as an investment, I'll have you know*. She could be so calculating, worse than a man.

"I won't ask you that awful question, 'What's it about?'" I said.

"Oh, good," he said, smiling. "I hate that question. For one thing, I don't have an answer, and for another, whenever I try, it sounds so incredibly stupid that I'm tempted to trash the whole thing and start taking night classes in air-conditioning repair."

I laughed. "You might be on to something there. Then you could come talk to my air conditioner about why it sounds like it has emphysema." And *he* laughed. Was it possible that I was being funny? Emboldened, flushing, I said, "I admit, I do want to know something about it. The screenplay, I mean. So maybe I will ask . . . what are your influences? God, I sound like Terry Gross. You know what I mean, though, like, what movies do you love?"

Sam looked away, rubbing at his stubbly cheek. "Aw, jeez. That question's bad, too."

"It *is*? Oh, dear. I'm sorry."

"No, not like that, I just mean—my answer to that question is also slightly humiliating."

"Oooh, now I really am intrigued. Do tell. I hope it's something scandalous. Wait till all the neighborhood yentas find out you're into hard-core goat porn. Or wait, worse—musicals."

He laughed again. "All right, now, don't get all excited. It's just—ah—well. Old romantic comedies. You know, movies that straight men are supposed to loathe. Chick flicks, I guess, if you're feeling uncharitable. Especially the old studio ones. Katharine Hepburn, Cary Grant, Jimmy Stewart. The black-and-white screwballs where everyone has a weird vaguely English accent for some reason and says witty things all day and no one so much as kisses until the end."

"Oh, *please,*" I said. "Are you kidding me?"

"I'm afraid not."

"That's like a joke answer. That's like a 'I had my sympathetic sister write my online dating profile so chicks will dig me' answer. Like the 'perfect guy who loves kittens and your grandmother and just wants to cook for you and then snuggle' answer. I don't believe you at all. Tell me what you were really going to say."

Sam shrugged, lifting his pawlike hands. "What can I say? I love kittens."

"Shut up." I hurled a handful of grass at him. "So what's your favorite?"

"Kitten?"

"Movie!"

"Now that I've come out, I might as well finish confessing my sins. Er, have you ever seen *The Shop Around the Corner*?"

"The one *You've Got Mail* is based on? I'll do you one better—I admit to liking *You've Got Mail*. Corny, isn't it?" I probably don't need to say that Harry found these movies profoundly boring and unforgivably sappy.

Sam grinned. "Oh, man, I love that movie! Both of them, but the original especially. I want to write something like that—something funny and sad, about people who are in love and don't even know it."

I felt as if my face had been zapped with liquid nitrogen, freezing my smile like a wart. My brain abandoned me, so I robotically quoted the movie, which I owned and had watched way too many times to be healthy. "'You know, people seldom go to the trouble of scratching the surface of things to find the inner truth.'"

Sam straightened and, perfectly affecting the prissy manner of Margaret Sullavan, answered, "'Well, I really wouldn't care to scratch your surface, Mr. Kralik, because I know exactly what I'd find. Instead of a heart, a handbag. Instead of a soul, a suitcase. And instead of an intellect, a cigarette lighter . . . which doesn't work.'"

There was the truth of me, wasn't it? Instead of having a soul, I was occupied by pairs of shoes and a cranky water spirit, hardly human at all. "Wow. You really are sick. You know the whole thing. Disgusting. By the way, I would prefer if you would always refer to me as Mr. Kralik from now on," I said.

He laughed. We talked for so long, it was ridiculous. Rose snoozed in the carrier, face damply nestled into my T-shirt, and most of our friends had left, and Betty and Maude were loitering in the shade of the slide, listlessly playing a dusty game of shanty-town-house. Who knew what we talked about. He asked questions. He laughed at my lame jokes. I stared at his hands, large and clean and knotty in a way that made him seem older than I had thought. What did we know about each other? But that was what I loved: the current of conversation between two people who like each other but do not know each other well. It was just so easy: "Oh, you have a twin?" (Why was it always such a weird surprise to learn this about someone?) "And where does he live?" "She, actually . . ." She! A lady twin! Who knew?

I felt interesting around him, and it's so silly, but I felt pretty. Embarrassing to admit even to myself how, in this day and age, after all I had been through, as the married mother of two children, I just wanted someone to make me feel pretty. All he had to do was to look at me. Somewhere along the line, I mentioned my sewing, my burgeoning business, such as it was, and his eyes twinkled and he said, "Oh! Perfect! I'm placing an order right now. There is this blouse Juliet loved but didn't want to spend the money on—" Who-liet? Oh! Right! I hoped my smile didn't look as faded as it felt. Still, as I told myself, it's not like I thought Cute Dad and I were about to ravage each other there on the rubbery playground floor. We were a couple of bored adults trying to remember how to flirt. Er, talk. Just talking. Like me and Laura, like Julie and Nell. Just parents. Chatting. And smiling. Now and then.

Sartorially speaking, there were some new ground rules. I didn't want to do only copies of boutique dresses; it felt weird to take money from local business run by ladies we sort of knew (and disliked, since they obviously had rich husbands or they wouldn't be able to run their expensive storefronts with the gleaming floors and Spartan rows of overly pretty clothing). Out of respect for independent designers, I decided I would copy their dresses only for very special occasions (by which I meant a really large amount of cash). The clothes should come from Macy's or Bloomingdale's or someplace like that. I would be paid for the fabric and an additional fee, which I'd adjust based on how fancy the mom in question's stroller was. A tricked-out Bugaboo like Nell's got charged two fifty—a fraction of what the dress would cost from a store. Luckily for me, simplicity was in that summer, and the dresses were usually easy to make. Sometimes I got caught on a collar or ruffle, but I always faked my way out. Also luckily for me, these were urban ladies, stalled career people, and while some of them had cultivated a hipstery craftiness, it was largely limited to the cutesy and impractical—knitting knotty scarves, baking the occasional cupcake—so few of them could tell the difference between a perfectly serged hem and drank-some-wine-while-sewing-and-got-a-little-sloppy slip stitch. Within a few weeks, I had more business than I should have been able to handle, except that I was somehow able to drape, pattern, cut, sew, and finish the most complex of dresses in a matter of hours. Somehow.

I remembered enough from my graduate thesis on the intersections of Slavic folklore and Russian literature (which, I wished I could gloat to my parents, was finally proving itself useful) to know that this kind of thing never came for free. You might get the impossible pile of kasha miraculously sorted overnight by a mouse before Baba Yaga came back, but the mouse inevitably wanted a piece of the action. Even enchanted creatures turned out to be mercenaries. Therefore, I wasn't terribly surprised when, after a couple of weeks, she set out her demands one night.

And so, this dress will be finished in the morning.

Of course. Thank you. I don't know how I ever can thank you enough.

You're happy these days, aren't you, Jenny? You feel more confident, nu*? The sewing is going well? You're feeling less frustrated with the kids and less scared at the prospect of being alone? And you're looking lovely, if I may say so?*

She was never this nice. It reminded me of talking to Nell; I felt sure of being trapped but too sleepy to parse it. *Uh, yeah. I do feel much better these days. And the sewing is great. Everyone's impressed that I'm able to accomplish so much so quickly. Like I said. Thank you.* I pushed my chair back and went into the bathroom to get ready for bed, as if she couldn't follow me everywhere.

I'm glad, dear. I'm glad you're feeling better.

Well, spit it out. I spat out my toothpaste. *What is it?*

Bubeleh, *you know that I have certain, ah, physical needs. Having been, you know, dormant for so long. I'm trying to help you out, you know this. Keeping the demons at bay, yes? In return, I need you to help me. I think I've said it before. I think I've been pretty clear. I need you to let me use your body.*

As if she weren't another demon to keep at bay. I splashed water on my face, feeling her twinge of pleasure at the dampness. I was tired and annoyed. *Honestly, if I'm still going to be pestered for sex, then what's the good of not having a husband? I never asked you to come here, you know.*

Didn't you?

It's just sort of unfair, what you're asking me to do. I'm *the one who's going to have to live with the consequences, you know.*

I'm asking to be nice. I don't have to ask. You owe me my due. Besides, I have friends you don't ever want to meet. Ever heard of Koshchey the Deathless?

Now you're threatening me? What, are you going to call up some ancient Slavic vampire just to mess with me? Give me a break.

I am *giving you a break, actually. That's what I'm saying.*

In the end, there was no arguing with her. I did want the sewing business to work out and I did want to make some money and I did want to become a better seamstress, to effortlessly produce dresses without patterns while other stay-at-home moms were falling asleep in front of the television. I did want to keep feeling this way, sane and balanced, confident and capable and entirely unsuicidal. It was an extremely nice way to feel, and as the summer passed with no word from Harry, I was becoming more and more afraid of slipping back into sadness. To be honest, it's not like I disagreed with her all that much, about Sam, that is, about how a woman deserved some excitement in her life even if she was a wife and mother—which was how the rusalka always seemed to couch it, as if it would be some great triumph of the spirit were I to tumble into bed with my hot neighbor. Maybe I'd read too many novels, seen too many romantic comedies. The truth was that she was going to get what she wanted so that I could get what I wanted. It was the way these things worked, after all, and I'd probably known that from the start.

fourteen

"You were such a happy baby." A *favorite bon mot of my* mother's, peppering our conversations almost as frequently as her signature quip, "So, guess who died?" There was no response to either, as I should have learned by now but hadn't quite.

"I'm not unhappy, Mom." I had the phone pinched between ear and shoulder while stirring a pot of macaroni with a wooden spoon and pouring a speck of apple juice into a cup of water for Betty. She eyed it suspiciously and wandered off, nearly tripping over Rose, who was sitting, more steadily today than yesterday, on a blanket in the middle of the floor, gnawing on the ear of one Betty's eighty-seven stuffed bunnies. "I'm fine. I'm actually doing really well. You know, considering." I *was* happy, that was the thing, but for once my circumstances—the husband situation—seemed to require unhappiness, a psychic black armband out of propriety, if not true feeling. I had to make an effort not to seem too happy, even though sometimes I walked down the street smiling for no reason, sometimes I laughed out loud from free-floating good spirits. It was a problem I'd never encountered before.

"Oh, of course, honey, I didn't mean anything by it. How could you be happy, with all you're going through."

"But I'm not— The weird thing is, I feel fine. That's what I'm saying. I kind of am—you know." I couldn't bring myself to say it, like a slur so shocking I couldn't even utter the word. *Happy.*

She wasn't interested in listening. She just wanted to say what she wanted to say. I rummaged in the fridge for margarine and milk. Yet another gourmet supper for the littlest Lipkins. "Everywhere I went, people would comment on what a happy baby you were. Your sister was always a sourpuss. But you, all smiles. It didn't matter where we went or who we were with." It was hard to imagine my mother and me as a team, toodling around the suburban streets together, like Betty and me now—holding hands, watching each other pee, sharing snacks. Hard to imagine my mother as the person I ran to in distress, as the legs I held on to while learning to walk. I couldn't believe we'd ever been that way, which made me sad. I hoped Betty and Rose would never feel as wary toward me, the weird lady guarding the repository of questionable tales of their youth, full of anecdotes that didn't sound like them or like anything that might have happened to them. The tub of margarine had a dog hair in it. All at once I was worried I might weep.

"No one's happy all the time, honey. There's no shame in it."

"Okay, Mom. What are you getting at, exactly?"

"Getting at? Nothing, nothing! I'm happy. I am." I hadn't realized that *her* happiness was in question. No wonder she'd been asking. People were always pretending they were talking about you when they were really, almost exclusively, talking about themselves. When I thought about it, I realized I probably did this, too, but I reserved the right to be annoyed by it, anyway. "Jenny, I want to tell you something."

Dear God. What is with all confessions lately? I braced myself. "Oh? Everything okay? Is Dad okay? Oh, man, are you and Dad okay?"

"Of course! Of course! I mean, your father. It's so hard to tell. But I— Jenny, I'm going to go on a trip."

"What?" I took the phone away from my ear and stared at it. "Mom?"

I could *hear* the woman beaming. "I've been saving. A little bit out of every paycheck." Oh, *dear*. It was enough to break your heart. My mother had been working as the receptionist at a dentist's office since I was in high school. She always spoke of the job with great pride, but it was a depressing affair. Lots of blousy outfits and paperwork, fluorescent lights, paper-cut fingers, kids with fluoride-rinse spittle flecking their faces. Half her conversations, especially when she'd just started there, began, "Well, Dr. *Olson* says . . ." For a second I thought she was about to tell me what Sarah and I had always joked about with grossed-out gallows humor—that she was in love with the white-fingered, fiftysomething redhead, oh he of the elegant cavity filling (ew); that they'd been having a secret romance of tepid snuggling for years.

"I asked your father to come with me, and he looked at me like my hair was on fire. No surprise there! You know we haven't taken a vacation since we all went to Canada together?" I did. I had been sixteen, Sarah eighteen, and neither of us in any mood for family fly-fishing. The trip was an epic disaster, rarely spoken of—so exquisite in its horrors that the stories still had not gained the tragedy-plus-time patina of humor. "So," my mother continued, "I bought my ticket, and I'm going next month."

"Really! And where are you going?"

"Egypt."

I'd taken a sip of cold coffee, mummified with old milk, and now I almost choked. "Egypt? The one with the pyramids?"

My mother chortled, delighted with herself. "That's the one, kiddo!"

"Seriously?"

"I'm going on a seniors' tour. My girlfriend Beverly's coming, too! The bus picks you up at the airport, and they make all the arrangements and everything. They even provide meals, so you don't wind up having to eat anything crazy. We're going to see the pyramids and the Sphinx and all of it."

A squall erupted from the living room, where Betty had wrenched the stuffed bunny from Rose's grip. "MY bunny!" she said angrily when she saw me looking. She embarked on a trail of tears around the room, clutching things to her chest, chanting, "Mine! Mine! Mine!" I turned around. Maybe if I pretended not to have seen anything, the situation would resolve itself. "Mom, how can you go to freaking *Africa*?" *Right when I need you,* I didn't say, because it didn't make any sense.

"Africa? I guess it is Africa! Egypt doesn't seem like Africa, though, does it?"

"I don't know. You'll have to tell me."

"Honey, don't be upset. You told me not to come there. And I just—I just have to go somewhere." In a lower voice, "Your father is driving me nuts. I don't think he's spoken a word all month."

"How long will you be gone?" I spooned the macaroni into two plastic dishes. Sometimes I got so sick of plastic things. I suffered a momentary pang of desire for china plates, silver flatware, linen napkins, an elegant adult life I'd never had.

"Three weeks."

"Three weeks! Mom! What about Dad? What about your job?"

"Oh, I have plenty of vacation days saved up. They can get a temporary girl for a few weeks. And even though Dr. Olson says"—I rolled my eyes automatically—"they can't manage without me, well, honey, to tell you the truth, I'm so sick of that place, I could spit." Sick of it! This did not gel with my idea of my placid mother, chatting with people at work, stopping by the Hy-Vee on the way home for a pound of beef to cook for my dad, settling into their overstuffed sectional in the evening to watch four hours of prime-time network television a night. For an instant I tried to picture her face and couldn't. I should have been proud and excited for her, and I was, I promise I was, but the bratty teenager who leased some space in my brain couldn't stop keening, *But that should be* me*! I should get an adventure! She won't even appreciate it!*

Jenny, my dear, grow up. Can you imagine how bored this woman must be? This is a great thing for her. A great thing for someone you love can't hurt you.

Oh? What about Harry's current great thing? That's hurting me. It's hurting me a lot.

I seriously doubt that whatever he's doing right now is a great thing. I doubt he's having a whole lot of fun. And I think you know that, too.

Rose was propelling yet another bunny toward her mouth when Betty yanked it from her. There went the pouty lower lip, here came the tremble. I held the phone away from my face. "Betty, you have not played with that bunny in ages. You know you don't really care about it."

"What, honey?"

"Sorry, Mom, not you. The girls are fighting—" Rose erupted into wails. I hurried over to scoop her up. Betty stood still until her face had completely flushed, like she was filling up in preparation, and then—lights, camera, action—performed her famous patented boneless-break-dance tantrum.

I could hardly hear my mother anymore. "They can't possibly be as bad as you and Sarah were! You two. I always said you would fight over the cat box if I gave it to one of you."

"I know. You've mentioned that. Betty! Give it back!"

Betty clutched the bunny to her face, ignoring Rose's sobs. "Baby shares wif me."

Oh, the sharing. It was so complicated to explain. Betty had to share with Rosie, with Emma, with all the other kids, but wasn't allowed to take things from them . . . ? I got tangled up myself when I tried to clarify. Not that anyone ever said it was a good idea to try to reason with a two-and-a-half-year-old, but when she was the person you talked to most, it was hard to resist the temptation.

"Look, Mom, I have to go."

"First tell me the news. Any updates from Harry?"

"*Mom.* What is he, a reporter? No. There is no update. There is no news. Obviously, I would have mentioned something like that." A flicker—should I mention the postcard? Part of me wanted to defend Harry to my parents. I thought what he'd done was life-level crummy, but I didn't want my mother to think so; I didn't want her to think of me as married to some jerk. *He sent a postcard,* I imagined myself saying, *and he told me he just needed to sort some things out and he'd be back soon, so it's really all okay.* It sounded idiotic even to me. A postcard. What a jerk.

I didn't say anything. I plunked Rose into her bouncy seat and grabbed the bunny, throwing it, for lack of inspiration, into the fridge with the margarine. Now Betty stamped her foot. "Mommy, nooooo!"

"So what are you having for dinner? I think I'll make a meat loaf for your father."

"I have to go. I'll call you later, okay?"

"That sounds good. We're just having the most humid night here, I can't believe it."

"Okay, Mom."

"Oh, honey, I wanted to ask, ah— So have you— I know you were off your medication because of the baby, and I'm wondering now, ah, just with everyone happening, if you've—"

The woman left me no choice. I had to hang up on her. Also, Egypt! It's possible I'd never been so annoyed with my mother in my entire life. Obviously, I had to call my sister. If there was ever an argument for the value of siblings, it was a moment like this. (Meanwhile, Betty was showing each of her toys to Rose, one by one, then shaking her head and taking each away from the baby's bewildered grasping fingers. I was sure I hadn't made her this way. Right? She was just at that age? Right?)

"You're kidding," Sarah said. "Egypt? The woman has never left the country. She thinks ketchup is spicy."

It really was good to have a sister sometimes. As usual, we reviewed annoyingly provincial things our mother had done while visiting our urban homes, then moved on to ridiculous things we'd been fed or encouraged to do as children. When Betty was born, I'd been flooded by love for my mother—everything she'd done for us! now I understood how difficult motherhood was! how no one ever appreciated all the little things you did!—but that initial outburst had mellowed. Sarah and I slipped comfortably into our well-worn litany of complaints, ignoring our own futures as someone's complained-about mother. "I remember her saying 'Go watch TV' so she could clean," Sarah said, as if recalling an episode of nightmarish abuse. "I *know,*" I said, stepping over the pile of cookware, matte with fingerprints, that had been appropriated for Betty's spaceship. "And then remember how we argued over what to watch too much, so they got us each a TV for our room? How sick was that?"

Sarah laughed. "You say that now, but it was pretty amazing at the time."

"True. Lonely, though. I think I didn't want to watch whatever it was so much as I wanted to fight."

"You always did like fighting."

I chose to ignore that. Even while we were laughing over our past as squabbling sisters, Sarah had the ability to raise my hackles with a single word. It always happened just as I was feeling warm and close to her: She would say just the thing to upset me. As in "So how are you *feeling*?"

I rolled my eyes. Ugh, still?

You modern girls think too much. I never in my life analyzed my relationship with my siblings so much. What's to analyze? She's your sister.

"I'm fine, Sarah," I said testily. "Everything's fine."

"Really? That's great." She paused. I could hear Max shrieking in the background. "Any word from—"

"No. Hey, I should go get these girls ready for bed."

"Okay. But you know, if you ever need to talk—"

"Yep. 'Night."

Oh, my perfect sister. Kind and compassionate, sensitive, worried about how everyone was feeling, all the time with the *feeling*. She had always been an unfair kind of sister to have, beautiful and blond—we hardly looked related—and smart and well behaved and well liked. Now she was a couples therapist, of all things, which made it impossible to speak to her of Harry even before this most recent episode. She was always recommending books with titles like *Learning to Feel, Learning to Love.* Learning Not to Barf at Touchy-Feely BS, that was the one I needed. Her perfect husband even had the audacity to be rich in an unobnoxious way. After all these years, with all these miles between us, I could hardly stand to talk to her most of the time. *Has it ever occurred to you that Sarah might have some secrets of her own? That even Sarah might think she's too good for her life and not good enough for her life, that even Sarah wants to visit Egypt, so to speak?*

No, not Sarah. Seriously, believe me, her life is perfect.

Hmm.

You don't know her.

Hmm.

I thought about my mother and my sister all night as I squinted at the flounces on the flower-girl dress I was finishing. My initial peevish reaction of feeling put upon by anyone else's happiness (a personality flaw I knew was as unbecoming as it was unhelpful) had dissipated with the soothing repetitions of work and the rusalka's mutterings.

After all, it's not their fault that Harry's gone, that New York's expensive, that the girls are at tricky ages, that you're tired.

I know that. I guess I do. It has nothing to do with them.

It does, because they are concerned about you. Because they care about you. Not because they want to gloat at your troubles or make you feel worse. Jesus, Jenny, I never knew anyone who had such a hard time with every last little thing. You think too much. Just let me help you.

Like that, I was suddenly able to remember how I loved these people, how it was true that it didn't hurt me to be happy for them. I know it probably should have started to come naturally to me when I was about fifteen, but I don't know, maybe being able to empathize with your family was part of that final adolescent growth spurt that had skipped over me, leaving me short and bitter. The next day, uncharacteristically, or maybe characteristically, I called them back. "I think that's really, really wonderful, Mom. I think you're going to have an amazing time, and I can't wait to hear all about it." Even though my voice sounded a little fake to me, oversugared like a coffee destroyed by flavored syrup, my mother sounded genuinely touched and promised to send the girls postcards with exotic stamps. "Thanks for your concern, Sarah," I said in my next call, trying not to sound customer-servicey. "Sorry if I get defensive. The whole Harry situation is hard for me to even acknowledge." Why did it feel so artificial to say something sincere?

Still, I felt better, a little lighter, a little taller, a little brighter. Maybe there was hope for me after all.

Then there was the other side of the family, my ties to whom I felt unraveling the longer Harry was gone. I headed down to the Ever So Fresh offices in Bay Ridge, a Brooklyn neighborhood I hadn't visited in a little over a lifetime. Since my last life, actually. Sylvia, who apparently had become a psychiatrist without our knowing, informed me that I'd stayed away because being there was too painful. Maybe she was right. But I had never liked the place, and I was reminded why as I approached, the girls tucked into the fancy new double stroller I'd purchased with my first haul of dress money. This was real Brooklyn, Italian Brooklyn, where men in wife-beaters smoked cigarillos on stoops, listening to transistor radios as if transported from the pre-iPod past; ladies with big hair and bigger nails leaned out windows and screamed unbeautiful arias to one another; kids leaped in the tidal spray of an open fire hydrant. The ice cream truck that tinkled by sold only soft-serve cones, no sugar-free fruit ices, like in Park Slope. It was picturesque, but I always felt like an outsider, as if my ten years in New York were nothing but a tourist's stopover. People who lived here had lived here forever, and their parents had lived here forever; they viewed Manhattan as a suspect foreign country; they knew Harry from when he was this high. Harry hated it, and in his rebellious adulthood he'd migrated some subway stops north, which was about the length of Sylvia's apron strings.

Yes, the neighborhood itself was charming, even with all the American flags and conservative bumper stickers and preponderance of sweatshirts, but it would take an astigmatic squinting to see any charm in Ever So Fresh. The blocky storefront was marked above the door with smallish jade-green letters reading EVER SO

FRESH CANDY CO in an unintentionally retro font. The long blinds were almost always drawn, lending the place a vaguely nefarious look. The front door opened right into the narrow, carpeted office—Sylvia's desk to the left, Fred's to the right, and beyond, Harry's abandoned mess. Here they made calls (or, lately, didn't), fielded orders (or, lately, didn't), and arranged the personalized gift baskets that people in the neighborhood still ordered out of kindness or perhaps an earnest desire for tooth-cracking peanut brittle interred in neon cellophane. Easter was usually a big time, but here it was, late July, and a hutch of bunny-themed baskets still huddled on one of the shelves. The whole office reeked of resignation, like a sick person who takes to housecoats and daytime television.

The room ended in a door with glass panes like a detective's office in an old movie, and behind this door was the factory. A few years earlier, Fred had done the math and realized how much cheaper it would be to outsource the actual candy and nut-mix production to a larger distributor somewhere in the distances of Queens, and the factory workers (that is, Juana, Felicidad, and Carlos) had been let go, the equipment left fallow like ancient ruins. The factory once was a bustling place, I was told, full in the summers and over Christmas breaks with local students—"the girls," Sylvia called them, as in "There's Marla! She was one of our best girls. Hi, honey, how's your grandbaby?"

Something about the abandoned factory made me immeasurably sad. It wasn't just that the company had gone from being Harry's father's successful brainchild to a weird abstraction; they now neither made nor sold candy but *distributed* it in a way that seemed kind of futile and doomed. It was simply the place itself, the machines ghosted in cloths like furniture in a haunted house, the faded smell of cocoa and butter laced with grease and dust, like a necrophilic truffle.

But here we were, having what Fred was Cosbyishly calling a family meeting. I wheeled in the girls while Sylvia watched from her desk. "Oh, honey, do you want help with the door?" she asked once I was in. An instant later, Fred arrived, preceded by a familiar scrabbling of claws. "Joomper!" Betty squealed. It was weird to see the dog straining at someone else's lead. I thought I might die of guilt. Fred struggled with the beast. "No jumping!" he cried as Juniper stood on her hind legs and waggled her front paws at Betty like a rampaging horse. "Cynthia thought you might like to see her," he said to me, shrugging. I detected an evil smirk behind his eyes.

Betty and Juniper rolled around on the floor, and Sylvia bounced Rose like the freaking grandmother of the year as Fred called our meeting to order. "Do you know what today is?"

I slumped in the aerodynamic office chair and stretched out a leg, examining my golden gladiator sandal. "Your birthday?" I guessed.

Fred gave me a dirty look. "No, Jenny. It is not my birthday, although it was two weeks ago, thank you for remembering. No, today marks two months. My brother, Harry, has been missing for two months."

"God, really? Is that true?"

Sylvia nodded meaningfully at me. There was some implication here, and while I didn't understand exactly what it was, I knew I didn't appreciate it. Even the way Fred had said "my brother, Harry"—*his* brother, as if Harry weren't also my husband, the father of my children, as if *my* Harry weren't also missing.

"Without a word," Sylvia confirmed.

"That *we* know of, anyway," Fred said, nodding at his mother.

Now would have been a good time to mention it. The postcard. To help a mother worrying for her child, a brother sick over his sibling. Above all, let's be honest, to make me seem like less of a monster. I could say it now and fix things in this small way: "You know why I'm haven't lost it completely?"

You don't want to do that.

Don't I? Why not?

There's something we haven't really acknowledged, you and I, my dear, which is that as long as Harry has left without a trace, you have permission to be crazy with anger, senseless with grief. You know what I am saying, don't you? He's the wrong one. And that gives you permission to do, well, anything. You understand me, bubeleh. *I know you know.*

Then Fred said, "You'd think his wife would be the first one to hire an investigator, to be calling the police every day. I'm not going to lie, Jenny, I think your whole deal is a little weird right now. How you're just . . . going on with life." He didn't look at me while he spoke. His mannerisms were enough like Harry's to make me dislike him. And the rusalka, she hated him. *What is with this guy? Somebody has to stand up for you. Come on,* bubbe, *do I have to do everything around here?*

She kind of did. I was in the newlyweddish habit of being ruthless with my own family but overly polite with my in-laws, and if we were going to get through, I would need some backup. "Listen," I said, or she said, or we said. "You listen, and you listen well. Good. You listen good." I flushed and continued: "Harry is the one who left me. He is the one who left his two young children." I was aware that Betty's ears had perked up in her extremely unsubtle little-kid way. She was frozen under a desk, a bunny in a field. I lowered my voice and leaned in. "He could be leading a whole double life. I mean, he probably is. We all know he's a gambler. We all know he's a flirt. What if he has another family? We all know he's left for days at a time before. We all know he 'works late' an awful lot for the third in command of a failing family business." Fred uttered a sound of protest. Juniper ran over to him, thumping her stupid silky head in his lap. "I haven't done anything wrong. If anyone should be heartbroken, it's me."

Sylvia faced Rose toward me like a tiny interrogator. "Then why aren't you?"

I stood, sending the chair stuttering backward. "And what exactly do you know about it? How do you know how I feel? What, you need me to cry in front of you? Would you feel better if I drank? If I had a nervous breakdown? How about if I threw myself off a bridge, would that help?"

"Jenny, please," Sylvia said. "Betty, sweetheart, why don't you go pick an Easter basket and open it?" I glowered after Betty's back, skipping toward the shelf. Great. Just what that kid needed, an overdose of petrified gumdrops.

"Don't 'Jenny, please' me. Look, what do you two want? To find Harry? That's what I want, too. So what are we talking about here? Just spit it out so that we can get home for nap time." It was hard to sound tough when planning around naps. "You want to hire a private investigator? If anyone has any money to throw toward that, then great, I say we do it. We probably should have done it a long time ago. But I have my girls to think about and a bank account sucked dry by my husband's unfortunate habit of flushing money down the toilet. So tell me what you want and let me be." I heard my voice then and felt ridiculous. Who was speaking? The feathery fringe of post-pregnancy hair at my forehead had come loose from my ponytail and floated around my face with every jerky movement I made. Rose was squinting up at me, preparing to cry. I took her from Sylvia a little too roughly and gestured to Betty, who was holding a cheap stuffed bunny by the throat and looking dangerously close to tears.

"Oookay," said Fred after a long, terrible pause. "I think this has gone well."

I stormed out then, inasmuch as one can storm out when one has to settle two small children into a double-decker stroller, arrange pacis and sunhats, and struggle out a heavy door that of course no one helped with. "Goodbye, Juniper," I called behind me. "Be good." The door slammed shut. "Or don't."

fifteen

No matter how many times I tried to tell myself that Fred and Sylvia were sad and scared, too, by late afternoon, leftover Lipkin irritation still fizzled behind my eyes. It rendered me extra-sociopathic as Laura and I watched a waifish mom-or-grandma? candidate fuss over her Guatemalan toddler, who appeared to have obtained a splinter during ill-advised activities on the playground. You could tell by looking at her that she was one of those "Are you making good choices?" parents, that the kid was enrolled in six or seven classes all throughout the borough—bilingual music lessons, introduction to baby math, toddler tai chi—that she probably had researched charter schools and chosen one to volunteer at before sending in her adoption application. Poor woman, she was trying to do everything right, and here we were, sitting on our bench sucking down iced coffees and ignoring our effortlessly obtained offspring. But what could we do? Our favorite pastime, after all, our shared passion, was sitting around and judging people. It was like high school but on less sleep and more self-esteem.

"Wait, isn't that the kid who was running in circles and shrieking at story time yesterday?"

Laura squinted. "Yep. That was him."

"Oh, that was awful. Total parenting nightmare. And she sat there saying, 'No, no. We're going to have to leave if you keep doing that' the whole time, in that super-nice mom voice that's thinly veiled hysteria, but they never left, and then by the end, *all* the kids were screaming. Except Emma." I paused at the conversational fork in the road. Maybe now I would ask Laura how she got Emma to be so infuriatingly well behaved all the time—special vitamins? secret beatings?—in a tone that would attempt lightness only to stumble clumsily toward accusation. I decided on "How does someone even end up with that haircut?"

Laura pursed her lips as if to chide me. *Little Miss Perfect. Doesn't she think she has any flaws? She kind of gets to me sometimes.*

Oh, stop. Laura's basically my husband now. She's certainly more dependable.

But I could tell even Laura was impressed by the don't-ness of the do. Despite being alarmingly thin, the woman had a face that was mostly neck, and her nearly hip tortoiseshell glasses were framed by a mullety arrangement of mouse-colored hair, topped off with a short, spiky fringe of bangs. It almost could have been trendy in a so-bad-it's-good way, sported by a Williamsburg hipster in leg warmers, but wasn't on her, pushing fifty and wearing pleated shorts.

Laura tilted her head. "Maybe it looks better curled. Maybe she curls it sometimes?"

"Maybe her hairdresser was mad at her?"

"Maybe some gum got stuck in it and had to be chopped out."

"A lot of gum." We paused, enrapt, like wildlife photographers. Then I fingered my own ratty mop of a ponytail and said, "I should talk. I hardly have a 'fashion point of view,' like they say on all those makeover shows."

"Psh. You're fine. Look at your sandals. What are they, alligator?"

I channeled the East Coast Valley Girl drawl of my former co-workers. "I like to think of my look as 'post-style.' Like, my look remembers being stylish but has decided against it." Laura put a finger to her chin and nodded in mock concentration.

"Oh, Miguel," the woman was saying mournfully to the little boy. "Oh, *dear*." I wondered if she was aware of being such a parenting type, like the crazy TMI mom we avoided on the playground, or the professional parents who belonged to every neighborhood institution you could belong to—co-ops and gardens and block-greening committees. Maybe I was just another parenting type: the pissed off and possessed.

"So I've been thinking," said Laura. "About what you said."

"Uh-oh," I said. "What did I say?"

"You know, about the recordings. The midnight recordings at the diner."

"Oh. Oh, yeah. How is that going? That's a good title for them. 'Midnight at the Diner.'"

"Hey, I like that. That or maybe 'Laura Needs a Normal Hobby.' Anyway, I listened to some of them, and you know what? Some of them are actually kind of good. I mean, parts of them. People say some really interesting things. I think there could be something. A story of the neighborhood. The way people make a neighborhood, the way a neighborhood is a kind of a family. That sounds so cheesy—"

"No, no, not at all," I said. "Go on."

Laura looked flustered. It was an unfortunate side effect of our shared passion for pooh-poohing everything that we were preemptively dismissive about anything we might try to accomplish ourselves. We moved through our lives prepared to be told no, ready to shrug and pretend that we'd never expected anything else. "When you don't know a place, or you're new to it or visiting, you do all these things to try to live how the locals live. You get coffee at the place the guidebook says normal people get coffee, or you shop at a local market or something, and you walk around and look at things, and you think you've gotten an idea of a place."

I nodded. I could remember, vaguely, such concerns. How to maximize a travel experience: what a childless person's quandary. I thought of my mother and the awful tourist traps she would gush over when she returned from her Egypt trip.

"If I try hard, I can sort of remember how this neighborhood struck me before I lived here. I remember thinking it was so beautiful—all the rows of brownstones and trees and little shops—and how it would be impossible to ever find a parking spot—"

"Which is true."

"But I also remember thinking it seemed kind of fake, *too* pretty, and like everyone else in Manhattan—we were living in Murray Hill then—I thought it was all annoying self-righteous moms shopping at the Food Coop and judging everyone."

"Also true."

"But no, you see—that's what I think these recordings are turning out to be about. The life of this neighborhood that's been going on for decades and keeps going on despite everything else. The real reason why we love it here. It's getting forced out—people getting priced out of their apartments and white yuppies moving in, you know, *us*—but also people are finding ways to make space for themselves, if not actual space, then mental space. The privacy of the nocturnal world of the neighborhood. You know?"

"I think I do. You're saying it's about the double life of Brooklyn."

"I guess. Oh, I like that. That makes it sound all smart."

"I *did* go to graduate school once upon a time. Have you started editing it down?"

"No, not yet. I don't know where to begin or who to think of as the audience. Oh, that sounds so ridiculous. I mean, what audience! Right?"

"I think you're being too hard on yourself. Just enjoy the process."

"Listen to you. Since when are you the Zen master of creativity? Speaking of which, how's the sewing?"

"Honestly? I have more business than I know what to do with. I made five dresses last week. And Laura, I think maybe I've never been happier."

That was what I had not yet admitted to anyone, what I figured Fred and Sylvia suspected, what I tried to tamp down because it seemed so wrong. Because shouldn't I be miserable?

You're alive. You're young, and healthy, and attractive. Why shouldn't you be happy? Why shouldn't you have everything you want?

Everything? Well. There are plenty of reasons why I shouldn't have everything I want. Where to start?

Life's too short, Jenny Lipkin. Life's too short.

Laura and I stopped talking, a little embarrassed by the earnestness of the conversation we'd been having. Betty and Emma bounded over begging for snacks, and we dosed them with graham crackers and sent them back to the swings, Emma angling her cast out like a pro. Rose was getting restless, so I got up to plop her in a baby swing. She kicked her fat legs and squealed, and I checked my cell phone for texts while simultaneously judging a nearby nanny doing the same.

I should have known—it was as if she had a homing device alerting her to bubbles of peace she might swoop in and pop—Nell appeared by the fence, waving her flabless arm like Princess freaking Diana. She looked fresh as ever, supermodel legs in tiny seersucker shorts, sandals displaying a perfect pedicure. Her copper-colored hair was effortlessly swirled up in a silk scarf. Whenever I tried that it made me look Hasidic. I squinted to see Nell's daughter, Sophia, join Betty and Emma in collecting the sprinkler water into filthy plastic cups they'd swiped from the wreckage of a nearby barbeque.

"Oh, hi, Nell," I said without enthusiasm.

"Hi, Jenny! Hi, Rosie-posie!" I guessed I would be idiotically happy, too, if I were Nell. I sucked in my breath and mentally added fifty dollars to the price of her dress. "How's my frock coming along?" she asked. She leaned against the fence as if posing for a summer-fun fashion shoot in a parenting magazine.

I bared my teeth. "Great!" I hadn't started it. "How's my cash coming along?"

She giggled. "You're too *funny*." It sounded like an accusation. I could just hear her asking Mr. Nell to take out the trash. *Could you do me a teensy-weensy favor, sweetie? Since I've been on my feet absolutely all day, do you mind terribly? It's not too heavy for you, is it, lovey-dove?* But who was I kidding? She was Nell, after all, and Mr. Nell was probably just as irritatingly perfect. He probably got up at four a.m. every morning and cleaned the whole house and entertained Sophia and made breakfast for the whole family while Nell took a leisurely shower. He probably loved taking down the trash.

This woman is terrible. Why do you care?

I don't care. She just bothers me, is all.

You need to stop worrying about other people. Let it go already.

You sound like a self-help guru.

I am *a self-help guru, in case you haven't noticed, your own personal version. But no, really, we do need to keep an eye on her.*

Wait, what? I thought you were telling me not to worry about her.

Oy, my dear girl. Don't be such a fool. She wants to be the happiest one, don't you see? She wants to win. And you can't let her. I'm saying there's nothing to be jealous about. Don't envy her; watch her. She's watching you.

I don't have any idea what you mean.

Of course you do.

Then: Cute Dad. Riding his bike down the path that skirted the playground, Maude and George pedaling along beside him. It must have been later in the afternoon than I thought. No wonder it was so hot and stagnant. No wonder Rose was looking wilted. He raised an arm in greeting, and I waved back, trying not to blush. Nell wiggled her fingers at him, then turned back to me. "Isn't he adorable?" she cooed.

You're fucking kidding me.

I told *you.*

"Don't you think?" Nell pressed. Everything she said was a trap in some way, though I didn't always know which way. I was bad at this sort of thing, which explained my lack of social success in both high school and the magazine industry. I didn't get it. Did she also have a crush on Sam? She couldn't possibly, could she? I imagined she could love only a broker with a crew cut. No, she seemed to me more like a professional yenta, like the propriety princess of the neighborhood. She didn't want the order of things to be interrupted. Maybe it was silly of me to imagine no one would notice what I was still pretending was an innocent flirtation. After all, I did live in the biggest small town in the world.

I shrugged, pushing Rose in the swing and clapping my hands at her when she swung toward me. Even I could sense the overcompensation in my animated swing pushing, the wigged-out enthusiasm, like a working parent on a summer Friday off.

"You two have gotten really close, haven't you?" Nell continued.

"Uh, what? No. I mean, you know. We just see each other around a lot."

"Do you!"

"What? I mean, you know, here. At the park."

Nell arched her eyebrows, smiling. "Any word from Harry?"

Betty raced over just in time, saving me from the trouble of strangling Nell with a swing-set chain. "Mommy, Emma said 'doody'!" I gave a Nell a "whatcanyado?" shrug and lifted Rose from the swing.

"It's time for us to go home, kiddo. We need to start thinking about dinner."

Betty headed toward the stroller. "Okay, but Emma said 'doody'!"

"I heard you."

"Doody!"

"But now you're saying it." The unassailable logic of this statement stopped Betty in her tracks. She looked up at me wonderingly. I wrestled Rose into the bottom bunk of the new stroller, which I hadn't totally figured out yet, and shackled a goggle-eyed toy to the strap. I never got used to that action, which seemed hilariously unfun, as in *Play with this toy! Or else!* "Get in, Betty." She knit her brow as she climbed into her seat, whispering, "Doody," and chuckling to herself.

Nell, who had followed our procession from the swing enclosure to the shady benches where Laura was parked, leafing through a magazine, winked—*winked!*—at me. What an asshole. "Bye-bye, Betty! Bye-bye, Rosie!"

"See you around, Nell."

"Can't wait to see the frock!" *I think we should add $25 to the price every time she says "frock."*

Agreed.

"Okey-dokey!"

Nell perched on the bench beside Laura, who sent me a despairing look. "Bye-eee!" I trilled in my best Nell.

I spent the following evening hours in a funk, everything tinged with a dull wash of dread.

She knows. But it doesn't matter.

She knows what? *There's nothing to know. I haven't done a thing.*

Jenny. Stop. You can't fool me. You can fool everyone else, maybe even yourself, but not me.

What do you want from me, anyway?

I want you to be honest with yourself. With yourself. You want him. He wants you. Anyone can see it. No one will say it. That's what you don't realize, that's the beauty of it. No one will ever say a thing.

But they'll know.

But it doesn't matter.

Did it? Would everyone continue to pretend not to notice our heated flirting? We lived in an only slightly updated Puritan colony, *The Scarlet Letter* with cell phones and contraceptives. I didn't want to be *that* girl, the Hester Prynne of Park Slope, the one who crossed the line everyone had agreed not to cross, from playground flirtation to— To what? I hardly knew myself what I meant, where I thought this was headed. The rusalka purred in my head, in my chest, in my gut. *Look, Harry is gone. That's the choice he made. You are here, and you are alive, and you and Sam, you want each other. It's summer. You're both here and lonely. Why not? Why not take some comfort in a kindred spirit?*

I was starting to realize the rusalka wasn't the best person to listen to. What did I know about her? Who *was* she, this new self of mine, this recently arrived Siamese twin? It was beginning to strike me, in moments of sickening dread, that I might be just another sailor coiled in her hair, seduced by her promises of impossible passions, believing I was being buoyed up as she slowly strengthened her squeeze, dragging me down to the ocean floor.

I know this will seem strange, but it was only then, a month after I died, once she had transformed me from a cowering weepy mess to the self-assured woman in cute shoes and unapologetically wild hair who flirted with men and told off my obnoxious in-laws, performing her supernatural makeover tricks when I was least prepared to protest, once I found myself becoming the most sought-after seamstress of Seventh Ave., that I began to wonder about her. About who she was or once had been.

I found myself flipping through the old tomes of Russian folklore that had somehow survived our many small-space-necessitated book purges, tattooed with my grad-school self's embarrassing notes, looking for, I don't know, something. A clue. It seemed like decades since I'd concentrated on anything, though, and I never got to read an entire passage before being interrupted by one kid or another, or remembering some crucial household chore. It was like conversations I had with other moms, the only people I seemed to know anymore—I'd get home from a playdate or a day in the park and, hours later, wonder where that strand about so-and-so's husband had been going, or the thread concerning her antidepressant dosage, but no, the conversations were blown this way and that, never anchoring anywhere.

But how *did you die? But* why *wasn't your spirit at rest?*

She resisted my questions like a mental tennis player. *You sound like your toddler. Why, why, why? I'll tell you one thing, if I'd lived to be as old as you are now, I wouldn't have spent my time shilly-shallying around the damn park all day, feeling sorry for myself.*

Ah, so you died young.

A reluctant pause. *Yes.*

Did you kill yourself? Is that why you became a rusalka? Were you a spurned lover? Unwed and pregnant? And you jumped into the water? That's what it always is in the old stories.

Another pause. I kept waiting for her reply, but there was nothing. Just the coldest, emptiest silence I'd ever felt.

sixteen

Cute Dad and I kept pretending it was an accident that we ran into each other in the park by the Picnic House every afternoon at three on the dot. I told myself there was nothing unseemly about our daily volleys of flirty text messages. Which was how you knew, wasn't it, when there was something wrong with what you were doing? We hadn't said anything that lacked propriety, done nothing officially against any rules, and yet I didn't tell Laura about it and he didn't tell Juliet about it and we insisted on pretending it was an accident every time. "Oh, HI!" I'd cry, waving and waving like he was a grade school chum I was unexpectedly encountering in Helsinki. "Oh! Jenny! Hi!" Sam would say. Sometimes we got as corny as "Fancy meeting you here!" or "Mr. Kralik!," our awkwardly cutesy nickname for each other. It became a game—pushing the carriage over the hill, scanning the field dotted with picnics and summer-camp mobs and the occasional unleashed dog. One time I didn't see him right away and was surprised by how heavy my heart felt. He hadn't come. Okay. Okay! What was I, twelve? But there was no escaping that leaden weight. I spread out our juice-besmirched picnic blanket, and then I heard him call, "Oh, hey, Jenny!" And it's ridiculous how my heart slopped against my ribs. How I loved the way he said my name.

"Oh! Well!" I grinned idiotically. "Fancy meeting you here!"

He looked tired. Maude handed him her helmet—she'd gotten a scooter and rode it everywhere, which fascinated Betty—and marched right over and flopped down. "*Now* can I have my snack?" She glared at me before turning back to her daddy.

She knows. She knows everything.

Don't be ridiculous. She's a child. *He obviously told her to wait for her snack.*

Until they found us? Do you think he said that? He wouldn't be so obvious, would he?

And exactly what difference would it make? You're neighborhood friends, meeting in the park. No one can say you're doing anything wrong. You haven't done anything wrong.

But we want to.

I know you do.

Everyone knows we do.

What do you care, "everyone"? Grow up. This isn't high school.

Of course it is.

Just—shh.

Maude and Betty quickly engrossed themselves in a game that seemed to involve mostly collecting sticks and then fighting over them. Rose sat at attention, gnawing on the wipes case. I lazily waved a rattle, which she ignored. My phone buzzed. Laura. Where were we, and did we want to play? They missed us. I closed my phone, turned to Sam. "You look tired," I said sympathetically. It was a hard habit to break, the wifeliness.

Sam smiled but didn't say anything. He extracted from his pocket a mangled wildflower. "Maude and I found this in the meadow."

"A Johnny-jump-up," I said.

He raised his eyebrows. "Heartsease."

"Same thing," I said, probably blushing. I couldn't help it. "Thanks. No one's given me flowers in ages."

"Flo*wer*," he corrected.

"Ah, yes. No one's given me flo*wer* in ages."

"What can I say? I give good flower," he said, and my smile felt arch and knowing to me but probably looked pinched. He leaned back so that, it seemed, I could see the length of him. He was a largeish guy and soft-seeming, but when his T-shirt strained against his front, it revealed a musculature that made my suddenly teenage blood heat up. I wanted to strip off his shirt and press my face against his hot, sweaty chest. I wanted to smell his scalp and poke at his belly button and touch the smooth skin beneath his belt. *Stop stop stop,* I told my stupid brain. But it wasn't listening, not to me, not anymore.

"Juliet wants to move," he said.

I suffered a mild cardiac arrest, recovered, and smiled. "Oh? Where?"

He lay back on the blanket and shielded his face with his arms. "Queens. Or Staten Island. Or maybe Jersey." Any of those places, we both knew, may as well have been the opposite end of the earth. We'd been through it before. Betty was at the age where her babyhood friends were starting to scatter as their families outgrew their expensive and tiny Park Slope setups. It was all fine and good to stow a newborn in a corner of your bedroom or a toddler in a cutely wallpapered closet, but at a certain point you started to crave a door. So people would shrug and explain that they'd found this great house in the suburbs but would be in the neighborhood to visit all the time, and you'd see them one last time, maybe twice if you were motivated to schlep out on the LIRR or New Jersey Transit to their housewarming party. And Queens, forget it, that was just as bad. Worse, even, depending what train line they'd stranded themselves on. It was better if someone moved to Chicago or L.A., where there were at least direct flights. Someone in a cute row house out on the J-M-Z line might as well have gone to outer Mongolia for all you'd ever see them. And you'd tell yourself they were fools, that while their children languished alone in their unnecessarily large bedrooms, yours would be reaping the benefits of all that city culture and diversity that they never really did because you were usually too exhausted to take them anywhere at all.

"Oh!" I said, trying to sound cheery. "Well, not far away, then."

There was no response.

"But Maude got into pre-K at St. Ann's," I said. "People would kill for that. They might. They might kill you for it. Wait, is that why? Don't worry, Sam, I'll protect you!" Rose was starting to scoot off the edge of the blanket. "Rosie, we've got to protect Sam!" I lifted her up and whirled her around in the air, a chubby helicopter. She giggled and drooled on my head. "Ah, thank you. How refreshing."

Sam forced a smile. "I know. It will take us a while to find a place, anyway."

"But. So. Why?"

You, I was afraid he'd say. But of course not, it was ridiculous. "You know. Same old thing. We need more space. I mean, we do. We definitely do."

"Do you? Can't you, like, have a stoop sale?"

"We're beyond that. I mean, Jenny, we live in a studio. Juliet and I sleep in the walk-in closet."

They did? "You do? I always thought— Why did I think you had a fabulous three-bedroom?"

"There are fabulous three-bedrooms in the building. We just don't happen to live in one. And the kids are getting too old for it. They need their own space. We all do. It just—sorry to be babbling on like this at you"—I shook my head vigorously, like a bobblehead in a fender bender—"but it makes me so mad. We love this neighborhood. It's pretty, it's safe, it's easy. And it's so goddamned expensive, it makes me mad. I feel like the city is slighting us. No one can live here in any civilized way unless they're millionaires, and soon it will be them and the completely poverty-stricken, no room for normal families like us or, God forbid, artists. My in-laws are paying for private school, and thank God for that. It's humiliating, but still. I don't know. I used to feel such love for this city, and now I feel like it's this huge evil Fritz Lang machine and it's spitting me out. God, sorry, end of rant." He laughed self-consciously and shook his head.

"I know," I said. Really, I was thinking, *Ohhhh, your in-laws pay for it. Okay, there's one mystery solved.* "It's crazy how poor you can feel here without being actually poor. My relatives in the Midwest think we're total morons. They're like, 'Wait, we don't get it, why do you live in such a tiny apartment?' As if it hasn't occurred to us to live somewhere decent. My mother basically thinks it's tantamount to child abuse, the way the girls share a room and don't have huge plastic toys."

"Well, it *is* prosecutable by law."

"True. And it *is* actually only because I don't really love them."

We shared a bitter laugh. Then I said, momentarily possessed by my mother, "You guys really live in a studio?"

Sam rolled his eyes. "It was never meant to be anything other than temporary, and then somehow, suddenly, it's our life. You know? You reach that point where you realize that this is it, we're in it, that real life isn't about to begin but has begun and here you are with no career or accomplishments to speak of, nothing in the bank, two kids, a wife who's fed up with you . . . jeez, sorry. Listen to me."

How much more of an invitation do you need? He needs you. He wants you. You coward.

She jerked my hand like a cranky puppeteer. I reached out then and squeezed his leg. His leg! Had I ever touched a leg? In the cloudless sky, a pair of bright kites tangled together.

"I know. Believe me."

He didn't open his eyes. "Is there anyone who doesn't feel this way? Is there anyone who is really living? Do you know what I mean?"

"I do know. I keep wondering when I'm going to feel like an adult and not just the same goofy me."

He looked at me now and smiled, resting his large paw of a hand on mine. He sat up. And who knows what it might have been about, because Rose crawled into his lap. He held her comfortably, let her reach her fingers into his mouth and examine his teeth. I watched her, weirdly jealous. *I* wanted to touch his lips. *God, how sick is that? She's a baby. My baby with my husband.*

You are remarkably boring, you know that, don't you? What year is it, anyway? I thought people did whatever they wanted anymore.

Maybe they do.

You *don't.*

Well. Maybe I do.

Leaving the neighborhood. We'd talked about it a million times, Harry and I, like everyone else. When I was first pregnant, we'd viewed sprawling apartments in distant reaches of each borough and calculated the commute times into Manhattan. We'd tiptoed through "marginal" and "up-and-coming" neighborhoods, telling ourselves it wouldn't work not because we were racist—of course not! who was racist anymore?—but because of the schools, oh, the schools, the schools were no good. We'd driven out to the suburbs and made fun of all the chain restaurants and drooled over the square footage at open houses. Though all the bitching about the cost and the space and the yuppies and the lunatics and the stink of the city lent the scaffolding to a good percentage of my interactions with other adult humans (what did people who lived in other places talk about? the weather? politics? advances in astrophysics? I honestly didn't remember), it's true that I probably would have been even more miserable had we left.

One of my problems had always been that when I started to feel sad, I went into hiding. In college I would go for days barely speaking to anyone, avoiding even my roommate's cat, as if an obese furball purring against my leg were too much of an emotional drain. The worst part was that I knew an interaction of some kind would cheer me up. It just seemed too hard. Ignoring my antisocial fits and dragging me out of my gloomy shell was one of the ways Harry had won me over. It was how the city had won me over, too.

Whatever else you could say about the part of Brooklyn where I'd landed, it was pretty much guaranteed that every time I left the building, I'd encounter a Mr. Rogersy barrage of neighborliness. Sometimes it was the nosy Puerto Rican lady who lived on the first floor and stuck her head out the window all day, pretending not to speak English until she wanted to tell me it was too hot to take the girls out or else to accuse me of stealing the *Post* she'd left on the stoop. Sometimes it was a mom I knew or sort of knew from around the neighborhood, and we'd find ourselves matching our gaits to discuss some parenthood minutiae, and a few blocks later, I'd wave goodbye feeling somehow less alone and maybe armed with a helpful project idea or tantrum tamer. It might be the friendly proprietors of the butcher shop or cheese store or fruit stand chucking Betty on the chin, or a flock of birders fluttering toward the park, or a young couple much too pleased with the new puppy that they'd be considering abandoning as soon as they procreated a few years down the road but in the meantime asking for directions to the dog beach; there was always someone around, trying to engage you, if in the most superficial of ways. It kept me on my melancholy toes.

This business of making dresses had deepened the way I saw my corner of Brooklyn, adding another dimension to the familiar streets and shops. The neighborhood had been a part of me for some time, and now I'd become a part of the neighborhood. Like with Evelyn. After I'd measured her, fondled her inseam, come to know the damp smell of her body as she undressed in my kitchen, after I'd glimpsed the soft expanse of her back, the tiger stripe on her belly from her most recent baby, now that I knew she got bikini waxes and wore weirdly sexy underwear—silken lacy things that looked expensive, tucked beneath her creased khaki shorts; who knew?—and after I'd seen how lovely she could be in a well-tailored (if I do say so myself) shift, and after I'd seen her mood lighten, her whole body seem to lengthen, in a few moments away from her kids, from her life as the scatterbrained mom, it was different when I saw her on the playground or, like now, in line at the bank. I knew there was a secret Evelyn in there, that I'd caught a glimpse of the Evelyn she imagined herself to be, her platonically ideal self.

My kids squirmed in their stroller—but at least Rose wasn't screaming, that was an exciting new development—as I fished out of the diaper bag a personal check from my landlord's daughter. I'd hemmed an armful of suit pants for her at half of what the dry cleaners charged. Or rather, the rusalka had. Whatever.

"Jenny!" Evelyn waved as if we'd found each other by strange chance and she couldn't believe the serendipity. "Hi!" And then in a baby voice, "Hi, Betty! Hi, Rosie!" Betty hurled a raisin at her. The pickle-faced man between us in line scowled. I shrugged. I'd stopped apologizing for other people's behavior a while ago. I closed my eyes. It felt wonderful in the bank, so air-conditioned and quiet.

The tellers all looked scrubbed clean, brand-new, as if they'd just popped off a bank-teller conveyer belt. We'd been in the park all morning, and I was Pompeiied in a gritty paste of apple juice, dirt, and sandbox. When I opened my eyes, Evelyn had replaced pickle-face in front of me. "Ack," I said, like a bedraggled character from the funny pages. "Where are the little guys?" I asked, not because I cared but because it was what you said when you saw a mom friend without her tiny entourage.

"Today's one of my nanny days. Oh, thank you for the raisin, Bets!"

Betty started talking, and we both ignored her. "I didn't realize you were back at work."

Evelyn waved her hand. "Oh, I'm not, I just—you know, you need some time to do errands and things. You know? And the housekeeper comes today, so we all have to be out, anyway. Tabitha's taking the kids to Music Together right now. Are you guys taking that?"

I mumbled some excuse, swatted away a swarm of mom guilt, and smiled. "How'd the dress work out, Ev?"

She leaned forward and touched my arm. "Oh my GOD. Huge hit. Huge. And I told everyone how you made it. People love the idea of a handmade dress, they really do! So couture. But budgety. People love that."

I bent over to pop Rose's paci back in her mouth. "Oh, good. I aim to please."

The line inched forward. Evelyn was next. "I hope you can handle some more business, because I am sending tons your way. Long story short—too late, I know!—my former boss's daughter is getting married, and she wants you to make her a wedding dress! Isn't that a scream! She's prepared to pay hundreds and hundreds, it's not that, but she's— Oh, okay, I'm up. Listen, I gave her your number, hope that's okay?" She scooted toward the open teller. I felt like everyone in the bank was staring at us—we were the only ones talking—and thinking what idiotic Brooklyn moms we were, what stereotypical shallow yuppies. I hated when people talked loudly to me in public spaces. I'd always hated the sounds of public spaces, the dings and Muzak and phone rings fizzed like water spots in my vision, cross-sensory blips crowding out the ordinary thoughts. I willed myself to smile and nod at her, and mouthed, "Okay!" I heard her say, "I need to get a necklace from my safe-deposit box" before the next teller called me. I heaved the stroller forward, slapped down my slimy check and, swallowing the mucousy embarrassment, the sackful of coins I'd toted along to be exchanged into bills. "I'd like to trade you these things for some actual money," I told the teller's mask of a face. She didn't blink throughout our entire transaction.

Sure enough, Evelyn's acquaintance, a bubbly twenty-seven-year-old named Anne, called me that night. I sat at the kitchen table with a mismanaged skirt lying limply beneath the sewing machine's idle foot, hoping that if I squinted long enough at the dump of dishes in the sink, they'd transform into something pleasant. It had not been an easy bedtime. I was exhausted, prone to visual hallucinations flitting around the corners of things. "So I'm getting married!" cried the girl, as if anyone cared.

"I was excited about getting married, too," I told her. "A long, long time ago."

"Oh! How great! How long have you been married?"

"Three and a half years."

A pause. "Oh! Ha-ha!"

"So you need a dress," I prompted.

She gushed on and on about how she couldn't find *anything*, and oh, she'd tried on every dress in the world, but *nothing* was the dress of her *dreams,* everything was too frilly and lacy or else too sheathy, and she had some *curves,* for heaven's sake, so she needed some *structure* but not a "big beautiful bride" situation, if I knew what she meant. I did. They had this whole garden kind of theme to the invitations and favors and everything, and it was going to be at the Brooklyn Botanic Garden in early autumn, and they had everything set from the photographer to the place settings, but she needed a darn dress, didn't she! She did. The problem was she didn't know exactly what she wanted it to look like, but she did know how she wanted to feel in it; she wanted to feel how she imagined a bride would feel when she was a little girl marrying off Barbie and Ken in the backyard; she wanted to feel beautiful and flowery and earthy and ethereal, and she wanted it to be hers, all hers, and oh, she knew that didn't make sense, but she'd tried on every dress in the world and the wedding was coming up and she was starting to feel desperate and did I know what she meant? Even a little bit?

I did. I knew exactly what she meant. Despite myself, I felt a seed of excitement sprouting. A wedding dress. It would be a challenge in so many ways, not the least preventing myself from making bitter asides about the state of marriage. A fairy tale! Right! With enchanted in-laws and an angelic elfin offspring and a fantastical 401(k). Good luck, sister.

It has nothing to do with marriage. It's a wedding dress. The rusalka was acting funny these days. She'd disappear for hours or days at a time only to buoy back up to the surface at weird moments. Sometimes I physically jerked when I felt her return, as if possessed by a B-movie demon.

For her wedding. To her future husband.

That's what I'm saying. It's called a wedding *dress, not a* marriage *dress. It has nothing to do with* your *marriage. You get to make someone into a princess for a day. You can't say that doesn't sound fun.*

Princess. Where did girls get the idea that being a bride was anything like a fairy tale? And how on earth did this idea stick with us through all the toad-dating and premarital cohabitation, the path to wedding bells littered as it was with odiferous tube socks and empty beer bottles that never managed to get thrown out? The rusalka scoffed, shook my hair, stood me up. I tried to resist, which never worked. *I need to finish this skirt.*

I need a soak.

Her needs, as always, came first. Otherwise, it was nag, nag, nag, and then inexplicable cases of heartburn I'm sure she stirred up somehow. So I ran us a bath, poured in the envelope of brackish powders she'd prepared one night when I was coaxing Betty to eat and not paying close attention to either thing. Within moments I was asleep. When I awoke, I was flung across the unmade bed, dry but not feeling especially clean. According to the dusty alarm clock, six hours had passed.

Okay. What just happened?

Oh, well, golly, we danced all night at an enchanted ball until our slippers were worn through! What do you think? We took a bath and then went to bed. Exciting times.

No, seriously. I passed out. I don't even remember getting out of the bath. Did you date-rape-drug-bathe me?

Ha-ha.

That wasn't a joke.

Why do you worry so much? I know what I'm doing.

I couldn't help feeling uneasy. And I dreaded seeing Sam, as if I might discover something in his look that proved the rusalka was up to no good and, in losing patience with me, might start taking things into her own scaly hands.

seventeen

In the morning I was back to normal, by which I mean that I was so depressed, I couldn't get out of bed. It was as if I'd never died, as if I'd never met the rusalka at all. Rose nursed and then crawled around, playing with pillows. Betty loitered, begging for breakfast. "I know, I know, I know. One second," I said to her, my face muffled beneath bedsheets. (I knew I said this too much when Betty's dolls started constantly telling one another, "One second! One second!")

I couldn't, I just couldn't, and it was heartbreaking to be like this again. I'd thought the rusalka had fixed me, that now I was one of those normal people for whom the word "depression" meant an economic downturn, a person who cried only when she had a reason, or onions to chop. Maybe the rusalka had been not a tonic but a Band-Aid. Maybe trying so hard not to think about Harry had been too exhausting for my subconscious, and something had worn through, broken irrevocably. Maybe I was the same as ever. Because leaving the building seemed impossible, staying in all day even worse. I had this weird feeling that the rusalka had done something the night before, had taken me somewhere, to see Sam, maybe. What did I know about the laws of this habitation, anyway? Had

I been sleepwalking around Park Slope all summer without even suspecting? I couldn't bear the thought of seeing Sam. I couldn't bear the thought of not seeing Sam. My head, usually humming with the rusalka's nattering narrative, felt hollow and far too quiet. As if in answer, the phone rang. Could it be she'd left me, taken up residence in someone more sassy and fun, and was calling to gloat?

Don't be ridiculous. Get out of bed.

Oh! There you are!

My dear Jenny, you almost sound actually happy to see me!

I can't do this alone. You know I can't.

A secret for you, dear—you can. And eventually, you will. But for now you will pick up the damn phone. That ringing is driving me mad.

The rusalka took hold of my limbs, launched me out of bed. The phone stopped ringing. She moved me into the kitchen, reminded me, like a spectral physical therapist, how to drink a glass of water, how to begin breakfast, how to answer the phone when it rang again. It was my mother. I sighed, pinched the phone between my ear and shoulder, and started toasting Betty's waffles, then raced from one air conditioner to the next, turning them off so the toaster didn't blow a fuse. "Hi, Mom, still hot, still no Harry, how are you." I felt myself settling back in my body, the depressed heaviness starting to dissolve.

"Oh, fine! Getting ready to leave for Egypt tomorrow!"

I deposited Rose onto the changing table, where she immediately began to writhe onto her side so that I had to pin her down with one arm while fastening the puffy generic disposable. "Oh, *yeah.* Mom, that's insane. Don't you think you're going to miss Dad?"

There was a pause. "Eh, between you and me, kiddo, not so much. Yesterday I was starting to think I really would miss him, and then he asked me what he was supposed to eat for dinner while I was gone, and sweetie, I just about lost my mind."

I knew what she meant, and I knew that my husband (assuming I still had one) doing something like that would make me crazy, too, but it seemed different when it was my dad. I mean, the poor man hadn't fixed a dinner in forty years. True, that was annoying and ridiculous. It was also true that he hadn't because she always had, so she hardly had the right to be so huffy. It's not like she ever offered to mow the lawn so he didn't have to. I wondered about my parents' marriage sometimes, I really did. Though I know everyone thinks this, in my case it seemed not just unlikely that they'd ever had sex but entirely impossible. Had they ever felt driven mad by passion? Had my mother ever flirted on the playground, made out with another man—Dr. Olson!—in our living room while we slept upstairs and Dad was away at a conference somewhere? The thought turned my stomach.

"Did you leave him some frozen dinners or anything?"

"Jennifer! No! He's a grown man. Let him figure it out."

"Okay, okay."

"I'm sorry. It's just that—I'm so darn excited. I can't remember the last time I was so excited. I feel like I'm about twenty years old. Yesterday Beverly and I went to buy fanny packs—"

"Mom. Fanny packs?"

"Of course, dear, we have to put our passports there so they don't get stolen by scam artists."

"You're supposed to— Oh, never mind. What were you saying?"

The toaster dinged. I deposited Rose into the pre-crusted high chair, which she was finally able to sit in, albeit a bit unsteadily. I arranged a landscape of measuring cups in front of her, fished the waffle out of the toaster with a fork, and extracted the margarine from the fridge. "Betty! Breakfast!" I called toward her room, holding the phone away from my face.

"So Beverly told me that the Wilsons got mugged in the airport in Rome . . ." I tuned her out, staring blankly at the coffee machine, hoping to be struck by inspiration. The steps involved in making coffee seemed so complicated that I imagined I'd be able to complete them only after I'd had some coffee, which I couldn't have without making it, an impossible logical loop that clicked through my head like one of my dad's ludicrous train sets Möbius-stripping its way throughout the attic. I held the phone away again. "BETTY!" Not having heard a peep from Betty, I went to poke my head into their room. "Oh my God. Mom, I gotta go," I said, clicking the phone off. "Betty! What on earth are you doing?"

"Nuffing, Mommy," she said, standing in the middle of the destroyed room, her dark eyes open wide. She had unearthed from somewhere a few of my fancy handbags, and they sat on her bed, gaping open, stuffed with unwholesome meals of markers, dolls, pajamas, a tiara, what looked like my cell phone. The dresser drawers all hung open goonily, the sheets were pulled off the bed, the rug was dampened with a sordid stain of semi-recent chocolate milk. The room looked like it had been gutted. I slumped down onto the floor. "Betty. What did you do?"

She burst into tears and threw her arms around my neck. I patted her back. "It's okay, sweetie. It's fine. But what happened?"

"Going to see Daddy," Betty said into my hair.

"Oh, Betty. Oh, Betty, Betty, Betty." I pressed my eyes into her shoulder so she wouldn't see me cry.

A few hours later, Sylvia showed up to watch the girls, looking like she'd won the lottery. There had been news from Harry. "News?" Not news, exactly, but a clue. "Like a postcard?"

"What? No, why would— No, Jenny, something from the detective."

"The who?"

She plopped down in a kitchen chair, stabbing her hair with her nails before welcoming a hug from Betty. I rocked Rose on my hip, swaying back and forth. "The private investigator we hired, Jenny. Remember?"

"Well, no. What? Was I even consulted?"

She shot me a withering glance. "You would have been, but if you'll recall, you stormed out of our family meeting in a huff. And then you skipped our meeting with the detective. Which made him very suspicious, of course! Very suspicious!"

"What! I hope you told him—I don't remember this at all, by the way—"

Sylvia cocked an eyebrow. "Fred said he left you a message about the meeting."

"I never got any message. I hope you told him that I am a single mother to two little kids right now and don't exactly—"

"He knows that. Obviously, he knows that, dear. He's looking for your husband."

"I hope you told him I wasn't a suspect."

Sylvia drew an invisible line on the table and examined her fingertip. "Suspect in what? The going theory is that he left of his own accord. Isn't it? Didn't he?"

I'll handle this.

Please, no, be polite—

"I don't know where he went or why, Sylvia. That's the whole problem. Remember?"

Sylvia sighed. "The point is, there's good news. Do you want to hear it or not?"

Betty was sitting in her lap and watching us both expectantly. "Little pitchers have big ears," my father's voice echoed in my head, or maybe it was Pa from *Little House on the Prairie*. "Go play," I said to her. She looked at me like I was speaking Chinese. Which she didn't understand. Because I didn't sign her up for toddler Mandarin. Because I sucked. "Go watch *Dora,*" I said, because I really sucked.

"Yippee!" Betty said, springing up and racing past me. She knew how to turn on my laptop and find the *Dora* DVD, because I really, really sucked.

"He's been able to track Harry as far west as Reno." Reno! Not even Vegas but Reno, dust bowl of decayed grandeur. Classy. Still, it was a relief to have confirmed what we'd suspected—that he was okay, he was out there, it was all another gambling binge. An epic gambling binge, but still. This was the Harry I knew. The wave of relief was followed at once by eddies of dread. I wondered how much he had lost—that had to be why he'd stayed away so long—and, dear God, what sort of unsavory characters he'd mixed himself up with. It was terrible to think about, terrible. But, Sylvia went on to say, that was months ago. Harry seemed to be dealing in cash and not leaving much of a trail, until the car had broken down outside of Reno—it served him right, didn't it—and he'd had it fixed. He'd paid in cash—okay, so he was doing pretty well, all things considered—but had given his name. A sloppy mistake for someone determined to stay hidden, the detective had told Sylvia and Fred, suggesting maybe on some level, Harry wanted to be found. Since then the detective had lost the trail. I imagined him as a cartoon fox in a Sherlock Holmes outfit, smoking a pipe and slinking up a tree after a bluebird with Harry's face. Clearly, I was spending too much time with small children.

Rose subtly and politely requested a diaper change, which was one of those situations that requires an outfit change as well. Then my phone buzzed in my shorts pocket: a text from Sam. The park was boring without me. Life was boring without me. I slipped my phone back into my pocket, unable to answer. What did he think he was doing? Didn't his wife ever look at his phone? Rose and I rejoined Sylvia in the kitchen, where she was examining the dress form for Anne's gown, draped on the mannequin in the corner like a patient ghost. "Hey," she said to me softly, softer than I'd ever heard her speak. "Hey, this is darling. This is just darling."

I pushed my hair out of my flushed face, plopped Rose down on her play mat. She started screaming. I scooped her up again and bounced. "This is very educational, this play mat," I told her. "It's extremely developmentally appropriate." The baby ignored me. To Sylvia: "Oh. I mean, it's nothing yet."

"You're making a wedding dress?"

"Yeah. It's for this woman— I don't know. A friend of a friend, sort of. She's paying me a shitload."

"Oh, how vivid." But she smiled a little.

"What do you think?" I said. I looked over her shoulder. We'd finally cracked it, I think, the bride and I. It was going to be modern, sculptural, a form-fitting, Jackie O-esque sheath, but with a peacocky flounce in the back. Unusual but not insane, flowery but not *quinceañera* material, and flattering to her curvy figure without being apologetic about it. I was surprised by how into the process I was getting. And it *did* make me remember my own wedding, and how it had been exciting, how I had felt like something out of a fairy tale. A good part of a fairy tale. The rusalka had been helping, she must have been, because I would sit down sleepily and stare off into space, and then when I awoke in the still-dark morning, an astounding amount of work would be sitting there, neatly folded or draped on the mannequin.

Sylvia looked at me, her eyes cataracted with dreaminess. "It's beautiful! I knew you could sew, but this is really marvelous."

"Well, thank you. You don't have to sound surprised to learn that

I'm capable of something, but—thank you." I was trying to make a joke, only it came out sounding defensive.

"Oh, no, it's not that. It's just— You know what this reminds me of?" I could have sworn that Sylvia was transforming before my eyes. Her painted eyebrows softened, impressionistically. She drew her forefinger across the fabric and leaned toward me. "It reminds me of dancing. Did you know I used to dance? I did. I used to dance before I was married. I was in a traveling ballet for one season, in the chorus. I was never any better than that, but oh, I loved it. Especially the costumes. The princess dresses, the frothy tutus. And I loved to dance."

I was almost speechless. Almost. Sylvia! A dancer! It seemed so . . . sensuous. I wandered around the kitchen, looking for something to occupy myself. Dora sang ecstatically in the background, Betty humming along and sometimes singing mostly nonsense words. "You're kidding. Why didn't I know that? And then you just—stopped?"

She smiled bitterly. "Stopped. Just like that. I married and became a housewife, and once Ever So Fresh started, I worked there. And we never so much as went out to a disco. I can't believe it, when I think of how much I loved it." It's not that it didn't make sense. She'd been older when she'd married Harry's dad, and she must have been doing something before that. It also explained her stalky posture. "Do Harry and Fred know?"

"Of course. There's a picture of me dancing up at the house. They grew up with it there. And I'd drag them to see *The Nutcracker* until they were old enough to protest, which wasn't very old. They never really asked. Boys, you know. I think they know."

"That picture is *you*?" I knew the photograph she was describing. It hung at the top of the stairwell, its sepia-toned finish lending it a look more antique than it was, as it turned out. So that hard-bodied ballerina with the arched back, toes en pointe, arms outstretched like wings, was my crabby mother-in-law, Sylvia? I'd always thought it was a cheesy stock photo, maybe the one that came in the ornate frame. What a jerk I was.

Sylvia and I ended up having the nicest morning we'd ever spent together. It was strange that just remembering the self of her youth seemed to melt some of her elemental hardness, but it did. We were buddies, almost, a little, sharing stories about our fanciful dreams and how we had shelved them and conveniently blamed the shelving on someone else, our husbands, for example. "He didn't make me give up dancing. But the way I tell the story in my head is that it's his fault I never made more of myself, that I never became a principal at the New York City Ballet. It was easier than admitting that I was never that good."

"Wow, Sylvia. You've figured it all out."

"I'm old. And half of my family has disappeared. I've had a lot of time to think."

It all seemed to be of a piece—my mother's wanderlust, Sylvia's dancing, Laura's midnight recordings. Everyone and their others. The next day Laura was positively glowing at the swing set. I plopped Rose in a baby swing and shouted at Betty to be careful as she scowled her way along the perimeter of the swing enclosure, clutching the black comb she'd unearthed from an old suitcase of Harry's. I'd seen plenty of kids get clocked in the head by errant swinging feet, and the last thing this family needed was head trauma. She didn't acknowledge that she'd heard—she'd been especially glowery lately—but clung to the chain link like a mini juvenile delinquent, watching a shirtless man do pull-ups on the exercise equipment that was placed (oddly, as if to shrug in the face of creepy peepers everywhere) directly facing the baby swings. Finally, Betty skulked off to the sandbox, where she sat raking the comb through the diseased sand, creating a crooked Zen garden.

"Well, look at you," I said to Laura. "Did Will try something fancy last night or what?" It came out sounding meaner than I'd meant. I hadn't seen or heard from Sam in two days—the girls and I had sat on the damn hill for hours, encountering no one more significant than a friendly pug named Lola—and it was making me exceedingly crabby. Pregnancy hormones, baby blues, spousal abandonment: As any teenager could tell you, none of this was anything compared to a crush.

Laura puckered her eyebrows at me and gave Emma another gentle push. "No, Looney Tunes. I finally talked to Julie's husband. Remember? About the recordings? They came over for dinner and Will made this amazing feast and the kids watched a video and I played Ed the recordings and . . . he thought they were great! He really did! At least he said he did. He wouldn't say it if he didn't mean it, right? There wouldn't be any point. Right?"

I shook my head, giving Rose a push with a little too much velocity. She knocked the back of her head on the rubber swing and looked at me, offended, puffing out her bottom lip. "Shh, shh," I said, trying to locate Betty out of the corner of my eye at the same time. They needed to outfit playgrounds with periscopes, they really did. Rose started to snuffle. "No, I'm sure he likes it, if that's what he said."

Unless he just wants to jump her bones.

Oh, please don't say that. Even I'm not feeling mean enough for that.

Why do you all insist on pretending not to notice that you're all eyeing each other, testing each other out, trying to see who's game . . .

Why do you *insist on pretending this is some exciting soap opera and not just a neighborhood full of stressed-out parents? You know, before you came along, my most fervent desire was for a few extra hours of sleep. My guess is it's the same for most everyone else.*

But don't you think my version is more interesting?

I don't know. Maybe.

"So anyway," Laura said, lifting Emma from the slightly too small swing, "he said I could use his editing equipment to turn it into a demo to play for NPR! He said that!" I ignored my initial riot of jealousy and allowed myself to experience a surge of pride in my talented friend. Here we were, doing the things we'd said we would do! I wasn't sure why something that sounded so easy felt like such an unlikely triumph, but it did, and I reached out to squeeze Laura's arm in congratulations.

"That's great, Laura! So promising! When do I get to hear them?"

"Mama. Mama. Mama." Emma tugged at the bottom of Laura's shorts. Laura had cute shorts, cuffed linen with silver specks, shorts that were never other pants sheared on a hot afternoon. Another reason to love her. And hate her sometimes, a little. "Mama. Mama. Mama!"

"Oh, whenever you want—I know you don't have time, but I'd love your help—what, sweetie? I'm talking to Jenny. What is it."

Emma gestured around frantically, a tiny Richard Lewis. "I want to play with Betty, but where is she?" Emma was so much more articulate than Betty, a fact I tried unsuccessfully not to worry too much about. Was it my fault? Too many cartoons? Not enough classes? Had my parenting skills decreased that dramatically since Rose had been born? I seemed to remember reading many more books to Betty before Rose. I was so busy running down my own failings and extracting an increasingly fussy Rose from the swing—it was so hot that the swing rubber seemed to have gone slightly gummy—that it took me a moment to process what Emma had said.

"Oh, sweetie, Betty's right—" I spun around. "Oh, man. BETTY!"

We exited the swing enclosure and stood sentry by the playground entrance, scanning the bouncing dots for signs of Betty. "Do you see her?" Laura shook her head, squinting. As soon as a kid could walk, you had these awful moments, though they were usually over after a few heart-racing seconds when you spotted your own dear dot leaping through the sprinkler or hawking imaginary ice cream beneath the slide. Unless the kid was running into the street, or getting kidnapped by aliens or, worse, a religious cult, or maybe falling, like Emma, accruing an injury other playground moms would surely, if silently, hold you accountable for. Betty had been so naughty lately, probably acting out, probably missing her father . . . there, I had landed on a way that this, too, like everything, was Harry's fault. If anything happened between me and Cute Dad, it would be Harry's fault for leaving. If anything happened to the kids, it would be Harry's fault . . . though it was more satisfying to feel this way when there was a Harry to bicker with about it.

There was a dark-headed girl in a yellow tank top. Not Betty, too tall. There was a curly little head—a boy. She'd probably wandered off and was halfway to the street because people were too idiotic to close the goddamn playground gate. She'd probably been abducted by some shirtless creepo who pretended to exercise so he could leer at the children. She—

Stop. Stop. You're getting hysterical.

Prove me wrong, then. Make it right.

A little faith, child. Just a little faith.

"Laura," I said.

"There she is," said Laura.

I squeezed Rose in relief. "Really?" I followed Laura's pointing finger. There, in the clutch of benches by the sprinklers, darkened by shade, was Betty's tiny figure, holding the hand of a man. Sam. We raced over.

"Betty! You scared me to death! Don't ever wander off like that! Never, you hear me?" Betty looked at me, surprised by the velocity of my hug. I cupped her face in my hands, stared in her eyes as if performing a retina scan, squeezed her close again.

"Hi, Mama!" she answered brightly. "Sam!" She pointed to Sam.

"I see that, sweetheart."

"Hi, Sam," said Laura, with what struck me as exaggerated normality.

"Hello," said Sam. "Sorry to scare you, Mr. Kralik. I wasn't going to steal your child to eat for my lunch, I promise." Then he cackled villainously and lifted Betty up into the air, holding her and play-biting her tummy. Betty shrieked. "Down! Down! No wunch!"

I was afraid to look up. I knew I was gleaming with sweat and that curls had escaped from my ponytail and were snaking around my red face in non-pretty-tendrilly ways. My heart pounded against my chest, my knees weirdly wobbly.

"Still, Betty, you scared Mommy," I said, flustered. It was all so confused in my mangled mind, as if my wanting Sam had caused Betty's potential playground harm. I deserved to have terrible things happen to me, but my kids didn't. I was sure I was the bloody hue of a juiced beet.

Sam let Betty down, and she hugged my leg, and then she and Emma puttered over toward the sprinklers, Emma's cast entombed in a makeshift cover fashioned from a plastic THANK YOU THANK YOU THANK YOU bag. We stood at the perimeter, getting spritzed now and then by the icy water. I ungracefully shoved Rose into the carrier, and she pasted her sweaty head to my sweaty chest. Seriously, this summer had to end eventually, didn't it? Everything would feel easier at a brisk eighty degrees. Wouldn't it?

Adrenaline still coursed through me. I could feel Sam studying my face, waiting for something, and Laura watching him watching me.

She knows something's up.

You're the most paranoid non-adulteress I've ever met.

"So, have you heard that Laura is going to be a radio star?" I said numbly, for lack of anything else to say.

They exchanged a look.

"Wait. What?"

"I know," said Sam. "She's recorded me."

Laura was avoiding my eyes, watching the girls with what struck me as exaggerated care designed to point out my earlier negligence. Or maybe that was completely paranoid. I thought of the Chinatown T-shirt: JUST BECAUSE I'M PARANOID DOESN'T MEAN THEY AREN'T OUT TO GET ME.

"What! Laura? *Him?*"

He laughed. "Yeah, did you know I was a donut-craving insomniac?"

"I did not. And?"

"What do you mean, *and*?" He bumped my hip playfully with his. I quickly scanned the playground to defiantly evil-eye all the scandalized observers (none, seemingly).

"What did you talk about?"

"He can't tell you that," Laura said.

"Oh?" Fear prickled across my chest. What had he said? What did Laura know?

Look at her. Nothing. She knows nothing. Bubeleh, *please.*

I'm not so sure.

"I said you could listen to it and help me edit, if you want. Or you can wait to hear it on WNYC!"

It was later, after Laura and I had bribed the kids into their strollers with snack traps of Cheerios and begun walking slowly home through the shade, that she said, "Could you guys flirt a little more, please?"

Oh, look who's jealous!

"Who?"

"You know who. You and Cute Dad. Jeez Louise."

Luckily, I didn't have a heart anymore but a misshapen lump of coal, or this might have really gotten to me.

Jeez Louise, indeed. What is with this Little Miss Perfectface, anyway?

"Oh, please. You're exaggerating."

"Am I?"

I decided to change the subject before my head exploded. Who needed that sort of mess? "Well, I think the whole radio project is just wonderful. Good for you." I almost added, *It's amazing the things you have time for when you only have one kid,* but thankfully managed not to. A rock lodged itself between my silver sandal and dead-skinned foot. Or maybe a piece of glass. Or crystallized bile.

Laura blinked. "Yes, I guess so."

I hopped along, shaking my foot like a lunatic. It was really sharp, whatever it was. "Do you guys ever think about having another?" I was desperate to move things away from me and Sam, even though we'd had this conversation a hundred times. Laura was an only child and had told me she didn't want Emma to feel as lonely as she had. This was what I told myself when it looked like my own toddler was really, actually planning to murder her baby sister: *They will be friends someday; they will be friends someday; best best best best friends.* But Laura was so organized and patient, and would probably wait until Emma was five, and have another perfect little baby, and their spacious apartment would never be gummy from floor to ceiling with various unidentified baby tars. Laura was the type not to find out what gender the baby was before it was born. This made me insane. It was like someone being vegan near you—you could feel the self-restraint oozing toward you like sanctimonious secondhand smoke. I'm sure it's normal to hate your best friend so much at times. It must be. Anyway, I said, "Time's a-wasting." It was an especially cruel thing to say because Laura was older than I was, pushing forty. Time really was a-wasting. Not in a New York way—you were considered a teenage mother here if you procreated before thirty-five—but in a rest-of-the-world way, in a biological way, yes.

Laura seemed to be deep in contemplation of a squirrel performing Cirque du Soleil–style acrobatics on a low-hanging branch. "Um, ha," she said. "Actually. Can I tell you something?"

Uh-oh.

"Of course, anything. Sorry, I was just teasing."

"No, it's okay." She stole a glance toward Emma, who was already snoozing, her head at a horrible angle. "I actually—um. I had a miscarriage." She looked at me, and her eyes were welling up. I felt awesome. I felt like a really wonderful person and a fantastic friend. Why had I ever felt self-loathing when I was so sensitive and kindhearted?

"Oh, Laura. Oh, no. When?"

"A couple months ago. Actually, right around the time Harry left. I figured you had enough on your mind, so I didn't tell you."

I tried to remember her acting sad or weird around that time, and awfully, I could remember only how I had felt. How I had been acting sad and weird. How it had occluded everything, blinded me to everyone. "Excuse me one moment, would you? I'm going to throw myself in front of this bus."

Laura smiled. "Oh, stop. Don't feel bad."

We crossed the street, leaving the shade of the park. "Why are *you* telling *me* not to feel bad? Stop being so fucking sensitive and kind all the time! It's making me crazy! Jesus, are you okay? I'm so sorry! What happened? How far along was it? Were you, I mean."

Laura looked teary. "Uh, twelve weeks. We were about to start telling people. We were being cautious about it because I'd had so much trouble with Emma. But we went in for the sonogram, and they said—ah—sorry, I guess I'm still sad about it." She took a minute to compose herself. I reached out and squeezed her arm clumsily, horribly, like a teenage boy trying to console the girl he's just deflowered. Laura even looked pretty when she cried. She cleared her throat. "He— It just wasn't moving. It— You know. No heartbeat."

"Oh God. God, I'm so sorry."

We turned the corner, almost at my building. My kids were quiet, I realized. Weird. Napping or heatstroke? A couple of large bedraggled-looking women from the shelter down the block barreled toward us, one pursuing the other in an O. J. Simpson speed chase. "Get back here, you crackhead bitch!" screamed the pursuer. The other woman, closest to us, sporting a matted wig and an ill-fitting tube top, stopped and spun around. She pointed a finger and cried, offended, "I ain't a bitch!" They huffed past us.

"And people in the neighborhood want to have that shelter moved," I said. "Why? It makes things so colorful around here, don't you think?"

Laura smiled obediently at my attempt at comic relief. "Anyway, sorry to dump that on you. I feel like I'm not over it yet."

"Of course, of course! Why would you be? I'm so sorry. That must have been awful, and I'm sorry I wasn't there for you."

We stopped in front of my building. I couldn't even look at the stairs to the door. I poked Betty. "Wake up, bunny. Time to walk." She shifted and murmured, "Nofankyou." I looked at Laura and shrugged. "We'll walk you home." Sometimes I felt like a perpetual motion machine. It was easier to keep moving forward than to stop, so I continued on but only out of laziness and lack of drive.

Anyway, let's be honest, I owed Laura. We walked slowly to her gorgeous limestone building, four long blocks away, and when we got there, we kept going past, bumping our strollers aimlessly over the rutted city sidewalks. I asked her questions about the miscarriage, about her project, about her lack of desire to go back to work, about Will. I let her talk and I listened instead of thinking about how I had everything harder. She told me how she'd started the midnight recordings around the time of the miscarriage because she kept waking up in the night with weird cravings, which made her even sadder—the pregnancy symptoms had outlasted the pregnancy—and so one night she'd gotten dressed and gone to the diner and eavesdropped while she sipped her mint tea, and then she had started to record, on her phone at first. Laura! I wanted to cry. I wanted to cradle her in my arms, to be able to make everything okay with a hug and a kiss, the way I could with my children. She told me she had this need to collect something, to hold on to something, to remember what it was like to be alive. "It's like you and your sewing," she said.

"What? No. I just started sewing again to make some money," I said.

She and the rusalka scoffed in unison. "Right, but you need something like that. You'd need something like that even if you didn't need money." Though I couldn't imagine not needing money, I didn't say anything. "Sometimes you just need something that's yours."

Or someone, added the rusalka, unhelpfully.

eighteen

At around three p.m. on Labor Day, summer convulsing in its muggy death throes, the city began to repopulate. Double-parked SUVs clogged the narrow streets while everyone who'd summered at the shore unloaded their duffels before heading off to battle for parking spots. Even the dust caking their luggage reeked of privilege—these were people whose children had gotten to munch all summer on good clean country dirt, not the glass-studded amuse-bouches of city park gravel. Now that they were back, there were more white-people picnics, distinguished as they were by pretty blankets, fancy cheeses, and guys with guitars, scattered in among the salsa-thumping pig roasts that had colonized the park every skin-scorching summer weekend until now. For the first time that whole stultifying summer, the air began to cool and sweeten. It felt miraculous. You could walk up the stairs without sweat trickling between your shoulder blades. At night I would open the windows, car alarms and sirens and summer concerts in the park be damned, and let a cool breeze sift through the apartment.

This time of year always reminded me of when Harry and I first met, so, predictably, I was moping around. Worst of all, or maybe best of all, things continued to get weirder with Sam. He and Juliet and the kids had gone away to visit his parents, and he'd come back hungry—hungry for space, hungry to misbehave, hungry for me. I admit I was happy to see him when he reappeared with the kids one day on the playground. Too happy. I leaped up from the bench and waved and shouted, jostling poor Rosie, calling, "Sam! Sam!" He located me and smiled. It was like the moment in a stupid teen romance where they spot each other at the prom and the edges all go soft focus and everyone else fades away—it really fucking was. Can I add that I was still breast-feeding Rose? What on earth do you do if you get close to the object of desire while you happen to be lactating to feed another man's child? Shouldn't some primitive law of the jungle make that physically impossible? Like, if we were to get together, you know, *together,* and he was kissing my neck, his hands moving gently down my sides (in this fantasy, these are sculptural lines free of mottled bits or stretch marks or sticky scabs of strawberry jelly, obviously), and he leaned down to lick my breasts, to nibble a nipple, I mean, I'm sorry, but milk would come out, and— It was no good to think this way, no good at all, very unhelpful, particularly on a dazzlingly sunny morning on a playground teeming with children.

Sam and I had been driving each other crazy over the past few weeks with these texts we were trading, like amorous teenagers, or robots, or married people daring themselves to get caught. Then there was that missing night during which anything might have happened. And then there had been this absence. And so, I don't know, when I saw him, I couldn't shut it down. I'd been so unhappy for days and days, and then my entire body flushed hot pink. I nestled Rose into the stroller and turned to Laura—"Could you keep an eye on her for a second?"—and ignoring their shared look of incredulity, I jogged over to Sam and he jogged over to me. We might as well have hired a skywriter to pass over Prospect Park scribbling SAM AND JENNY ARE GOING TO DO IT in neon-orange clouds.

Maude looked up at me and frowned. "I have to go to the bathroom," she said to her dad's hip.

"Me, too!" I squealed. "Let's all go! Laura's watching my kids for a second."

I was rewarded for this idiocy by a perfect specimen of the Cute Dad smile, the intense eye contact, the slight shyness pursing the edges of the mouth. We slipped around the corner of the parks department building against which the shadiest benches, my best friend, and my baby were all lined up, and Maude ducked into the bathroom. She poked her head out to say, "I have to do a number two, but I'll wipe myself and everything. I'm a really good wiper."

"Sounds good," Sam said, raising his eyebrows at me.

I looked around quickly and then—it was stupid, maybe the stupidest thing I'd ever done, and obviously, I'd done my share—there, on the fringes of the playground where innocent children—*my* innocent children—romped around, where all the adults I knew were loitering, bored, vaguely but voraciously anticipatory—I leaned forward and kissed him, lingering to breathe the musky perfume of his neck. He smelled so different from Harry. Woodsier, somehow. Darker. Delicious and impossible, like someone else's meal. He looked at me, squeezed my hand, let it drop. "You're crazy," he said, laughing.

"I *know,*" I said. "I really missed you."

"There's nothing so crazy about *that*. I'm very charming."

"It's true!"

He rubbed his hands over his face. I wished I were his hands. "Jenny. You're making me nuts, you know that? I can't stop thinking about you—I mean, all week—"

"Oh!" Nell jumped in from nowhere, and as if someone had shaken out the pavement like a crumby bedsheet, Sam and I jumped apart, and Maude popped out of the bathroom and jumped, too. We'd been standing too close, and that, I had to reassure myself a thousand times, was all Nell could possibly have seen. And what did that prove? Nothing! Not a thing! Body language, whatever! Maybe we were slightly European or something, for all anyone knew. So what? Nell had nothing on us, nothing nothing nothing, so we weren't at all troubled or the slightest bit perturbed in the least when she said, "Oh, *hi,* kids. I didn't realize it was that kind of party!"

Fucking Nell. She fluttered her manicure at us—a deeper pink than usual, I noticed, for the coming of autumn, must have been—and winked. Betty stood unblinking at her side like a creepy life-size doll. "Found this little lady making a break for the running path!" Nell trilled. "Thought you might want her apprehended."

I stared at Betty, her sweaty curls matted to her head, the black comb clutched in her fist. "Oh," I said. "Oh, yeah. Thanks."

Nell shook her head. "No problem, neighbor! I mean, what is this neighborhood if not one big family all looking out for each other! Right?" She tousled Betty's hair. I automatically tensed, waiting for a swat or bite that, thankfully, didn't come. Betty only scowled up at her without coming any closer to me.

"Right," I said. "Betty, don't run off like that."

"So," said Nell, looking from me to Sam and back. "So."

"I—" I said eloquently.

"You—" Sam added brilliantly.

She shushed us and winked again and made that awful locking-lips-and-throwing-away-key gesture, dear God, if only, and shimmered into the concrete cave of the public restroom.

We probably should have known then that we were done for. We should have been able to tell that, like the summer, our whatever-it-was had an expiration date, that we'd dithered too long without acting, that too many people were starting to examine us, a pair of molding specimens in the local petri dish, and to suspect before there was anything that interesting to suspect. As I guess everyone else already knew, it was stupid to believe that rules didn't apply to you just because you weren't paying attention to them.

Sometimes I wish this were some other kind of story. That there weren't the humid realities to trudge through. That Sam and I run off to Paris together and drink fine wine and have mind-blowing sex and live thrilling, sophisticated, lusty lives happily ever after, the rusalka happily bossing me from one adventure to another from her whirring homestead amid my internal organs. While we're at it, I lose ten pounds without even trying, my hair always looks good, I find lucrative and satisfying work at a charming dressmaker's shop, my kids go to French boarding school and turn out well behaved, bilingual, bereted. Believe that, if you like. End here. *Salut.* Enjoy.

nineteen

At least the wedding dress—for which I really was going to be paid a shitload, thank you very much—was coming along swimmingly. I would sit down each night feeling exhausted and utterly daunted. But every morning when I awoke, there was a gorgeous new stretch of satin embellished with almost invisible freshwater pearls. I could understand why people loved what I was making these days. Whatever my process was, it somehow changed the fabric, which came out more luminescent and responsive than you'd think ordinary cloth could be. My seams were dainty, the fittings impeccable—all this in a world where everyone was used to shuffling into ill-fitting, cheaply constructed garments born on conveyer belts in countries with lax labor laws. Had I always been so skilled? Had it always come so easily? Of course not. It had little to do with me. Still, it felt good to be—or to act, for now—an expert in something. I'd always considered myself a bit of an interloper, a dabbler in many things but expert in none, and when you got to a certain point in your life, this began to feel distinctly depressing.

Anne came over one evening for a second-to-last fitting before I finished the seams and hem. I was mildly humiliated at the thought of her seeing our home, with its plague of puzzle pieces and cuddly lupine mobs, but it was easier than coordinating with Sylvia and lugging all the dress bits on the train. I also figured she would feel better about paying me so much once she'd seen firsthand our middle-class squalor. The first fitting of the muslin had been at her spotless apartment in Brooklyn Heights one steamy August afternoon while Sylvia had the girls. Her coffee table sported a glass bowl full of fragile metallic orbs that I couldn't keep my eyes off of. It was like something from another planet. I literally could not process it. My hands itched to cradle one of the globes and smash it against the wall, if only to show her why it was a bad idea to display such hazards. Someday Miss Anne would have kids and would look back in wonder at the days when she'd owned such an object. Or maybe she would have the kind of kids who listened when told not to touch Mommy's things, who played in their tidy rooms where they alphabetized their own toys.

Obviously, her parents had money or her husband did, because she was a social worker or something and seemed to work about three hours a week, yet the wedding that was being planned was completely out of control. The evening she came over for the fitting, she was frazzled because, as she explained, there was a problem with the calligrapher they'd hired to address the invitations—something about how the gold ink they wanted wouldn't work. Anne was beside herself. "I don't mean to sound like a total bridezilla or anything"—she'd said this one too many times for me to believe her; who even used that word? bridezillas, that's who—"but is it so much to ask to just have the ink match the invitations, which match the table settings, which have already been ordered and paid for? I'm not being a lunatic here, am I?"

"Of course you're not," I said, pouring her some iced tea. It was a balmy eight hundred degrees degrees in the apartment. I felt bad.

"My friend had a total nervous breakdown when her florist said she couldn't have tulips in August. Total nervous breakdown. She literally slapped the florist!"

"Oh, my," I said. I was trying hard to keep sarcasm out of my voice.

Anne lifted her white-blond hair from her neck and sipped the tea. I noticed a full Betty handprint on the side of the glass that I hoped Anne didn't. She was obviously a lunatic. Who knew what she was capable of? As she continued on about all the perfect weddings she'd been to and how it didn't seem too much to ask to have one of her own, just one perfect day, I tried to imagine the clean-cut banker she was about to wed. What did he think as he watched his blushing bride having conniptions over table runners and song lists? Did he think, *Yes, good, what terrific attention to detail*? Or was he filled with a sinking, sickly dread, knowing his life was about to be micromanaged with the same frenetic fervor? Were they hopelessly in love? I suspected they were more of the "planned to be married before thirty, and here is a suitable mate" school, but that was probably an unfair assumption I had about people with very neat hair.

Anne stood in the kitchen continuing to talk while I measured her. She'd added an inch to her waist since our first measurement—I checked and double-checked—but I wasn't about to mention it. I was sure she'd had a lot of stress eating to accomplish, what with the whole horrendous calligrapher ordeal she'd somehow survived. I wrapped my tape measure around her, as I'd learned to, snugly but without touching the actual torso at all, murmuring, pins porcupining my mouth, like a masochistic lady-in-waiting, "Mmm-hmm. Mmm! Mmm? Mmm-hmm."

"I can't for the life of me see why Josh is insisting on having five groomsmen when he knows I only have four bridesmaids! You know? It's going to look completely ridiculous. All the photos will be lopsided! What could he be thinking? And it's just so awkward, you know, what, do I ask some random sort-of-good friend to be a bridesmaid? My four best friends are, you know, we're all best friends—we shared a house in college—and the fifth would be some random cousin or, like, a friend who's not as good a friend, you know?"

Something about this last little rant broke through the haze in my head. I stopped my inspection of the hem-to-be and peered up at her, a skeptical supplicant. "Anne," I said. "If I may."

She blinked. "Is there a problem with the dress?"

I stood up and, in a completely uncharacteristic gesture, took her hands in mine. We stood closely enough that I could see the tiny blackheads peppering her pert nose. Brave blackheads, to infiltrate the perfection of white-fingered Anne! "No. The dress is going to be perfect, and you are going to look beautiful and feel like a princess." She smiled gratefully. "But I have to tell you something. I know you didn't ask. But I've been married for a while now, and I want to tell you something. A man can be a wonderful thing. A man can make you happy, like a beautiful day can make you happy, or your favorite song, or finding a dollar on the street. But no one can make you okay. You have to make yourself okay. Your husband may love you and he may be great, but he can't get inside your brain and rearrange it for you. No one can." I was glad these things were being said to this pale and fretful girl, standing in my kitchen wearing a cream-colored armor of unseamed dress planks. This girl who was staring at me like I'd put a dish towel on my head and belted out a number from *The Sound of Music*.

I continued. "What you have to do is let him let you be happy. He won't be able to guess what would do it. For example, have you told him why you don't want him to have five groomsmen?"

Anne bit her coral-glossed lip. "Well, no. But honestly, don't you think he can figure it out?"

"Probably not. Don't make him guess. Don't do that to him, and don't do it to you. Do you know what he's thinking all the time? Of course not. He probably just wants his best buddies to be his groomsmen and is thinking of nothing other than that. I don't want to say men are stupid, of course they're not, not all of them, but they're not fucking mind readers."

She flushed, starting at the neck.

"Here's the thing about being married. You're still just two people living in the world. You know? It's not going to make him any more sensitive or you any less sensitive. And you're both going to be animals gnashing through life, driven by your same old appetites, thinking of yourselves first even when you think you're not. And it's like, I mean, we try to be better than that, and to be more evolved and everything, but I guess what I'm saying is—no one can make you truly okay but you."

As the words tumbled out of my mouth, I realized they were true and that I had not known them in time. I was grouchy and sad and difficult to be around a lot of the time, and I'd blamed Harry for not making me into a different kind of person. And when Harry got grouchy and sad and difficult to be around—as I'd always known he was, and it was probably part of what had attracted me to him in the first place, because there was some of me in him, because I thought he might understand me—I felt wronged and put upon, and maybe, just maybe, I'd done my part to drive him away despite myself.

The next day I felt a bit woozy, as if with honesty hangover. I had said too much too openly to my poor little bride who had wanted only, after all, to live a fairy tale. And who could blame her?

She's not even going to want me to do her dress now. Who wants such a cynic behind your bridal veil?

Don't be silly. She needed to hear those things. Every gown fitting should come with such good advice.

She didn't need to hear those things from me, though.

Why not? Haven't you ever gotten great advice from a beautician?

I guess if I went to beauticians, I would. And I would probably have better hair, too. Wait.

Hmm?

Did she hear those things from me?

Why, whatever do you mean, my pet?

Or did she hear them from you?

You're being silly. What's the difference?

I'm starting not to know. Is there a difference? Is there a me left in there without you?

What an exhausting question. It's too early in the morning for this kind of thing.

It *was* early in the morning. The apartment was dark, Betty still snoozing, when Rose and I colonized the living room. Anne's dress hung on the wall, its hems optimistically basted. Outside the living room windows, trucks idled in the street, making deliveries to the block's bodegas and bars. I wished for an Inspector Gadget arm to erupt from my shoulder socket, snake robotically down into the street, click off each roaring motor. Rose squirmed on her belly on the play mat. I left her there to go make coffee. And then there it was, one of the many moments parents have when they simultaneously think *Yay!* and *Oh, no!* The baby started to crawl. By which I mean she'd pushed up onto her hands and inched her way forward, sort of dragging her legs like a very adorable war veteran. "Wow, Rosie! You're doing it!" I said, toasting her with my mug. "Fucking hell!" I put my steaming coffee on a high shelf and made a quick sweep of the room, gathering up Betty's cherished choking hazards into my shirt like a child picking blueberries. Rose squealed with excitement. I guess I should have, too. I would have, maybe, if I hadn't been thinking about Harry and how he was missing it.

Later, Sylvia came over, looking about ten years older than usual. It was unsettling to see her without makeup on, like seeing a bespectacled friend on the first day after Lasik, or a fleshy coworker at a pool party. *Compose yourself, Sylvia,* I wanted to say. *Get your shit together!* Her hair even seemed to be obeying the theory of gravity. I thought of my own unstylish mother, wondered how she was faring on the dark continent.

I handed Sylvia a cup of coffee. Betty immediately bounded toward her, as if magnetically drawn to the steaming burn risk. "Gwamma! Uppa uppa!" Sylvia put her coffee down and let Betty scramble into her lap, enduring the tutorial that followed on the grimy My Little Pony we'd recently acquired at a stoop sale and how you combed its hair with her special black comb. During the lecture, I scooped up Rose and arranged her in the high chair with a couple of wooden spoons and a casserole of water. She splashed, grinning toothlessly.

"Well?" I said when Betty had scooted off to bury the plastic pony in a grave of throw pillows. "You seem like you have something to say."

Sylvia nodded, pressing her fingertips to her forehead in a way that managed to lay the talons flat. Her face had a deflated look, and I had a brief and terrifying vision of her plunging her nails into her forehead, where they would sink as if in a Jell-O mold. For some reason, her anxiety made me feel impatient with her instead of sympathetic. "Talk fast. Betty's on a tear today."

"You let her control things too much," Sylvia snapped. "She decides everything around here."

"What? What are you talking about?" Just how, I wondered,

could I make things be any other way? It wasn't like if I told Betty to sit down and wait quietly while the grown-ups were talking, she would. It wasn't like I hadn't tried. I was getting pretty tired of Sylvia acting like she had done everything I was doing but better, when she'd had a husband at home, and money, and the support of an entire extended family, and a fucking yard. Of course things seemed easier then. Anyway, why was Sylvia being so grouchy with me when we'd just had such a breakthrough? Hello, the dancing? The dress? I wanted my conversational money back.

She shook her head. "I'm sorry. I didn't mean— That's not what I meant to say. I'm sorry." She cleared her throat. "Hey, you don't think there's any chance Harry's in New Orleans, do you?"

"New Orleans? Uh, the thought hadn't occurred to me, no. Why, that storm?"

"Have you been watching the news? It looks like the apocalypse down there."

"Sylvia. You didn't come here to talk to me about Hurricane Katrina, I know you didn't. Spit it out."

Sylvia couldn't seem to make eye contact with me. Never a good sign. "Fred and I had a meeting with our accountant, and last night we had a long talk and went over everything."

Rose slammed a fist into the water, splashing me full in the face. "Okay," I said, alarm starting to simmer in my belly.

"It's just—it's a lot worse than we thought. The money. It's been obvious that we weren't doing so great for some time. It's so sad, when I think of my husband starting this business, of how excited he was. I remember the night he came home from a bar and said to me, 'Sylvie my sweet,' that's what he always called me, he said, 'The boys and me, we were all drinking beer, and I thought, Gosh, I'd like a salty snack.' He'd asked the boys, what if they were selling bags of peanuts and things there, wouldn't they buy one right now, and they all said sure they would, sure, that would go great with beer. And so we started that very weekend, tying up cellophane bags of mixed nuts, and he went around with them in Fred's toy wagon, no kidding, selling them to bars. And that's how it all started. You believe that? He had a good idea, a very good idea." She tapped a nail on the table for emphasis. Rose watched and tapped her spoon tentatively on her high-chair tray in the same rhythm. "And he believed in his idea. And look, that was forty-five years ago already. He raised a family on that idea."

Betty had disappeared into one of the bedrooms, and it was quiet in that bone-chilling way every parent of a toddler knows and dreads, but I'd never seen Sylvia in such a quivery state, even after Harry left, when she just seemed mad, so despite my better judgment, I let her continue without investigating. Sylvia looked me in the eye, and I was glad I'd let her go on. She was looking at me as if I were another adult in the situation for once. Though I knew a decision had been made that would affect me and that I had not been consulted, I still appreciated the look. "It's just not working anymore. And with Harry gone—and— Our accountant thinks we should file for bankruptcy. I mean, he says we are. Bankrupt. Really."

Even though I'd seen it coming, I felt sucker-punched. "Really?"

"Really. We've tried calling all our vendors' loans, and you know we've reduced our operating costs to the bare bones. And there's just—there's nothing else to do, I guess. That's what Morty says."

No more Ever So Fresh? No more bags of stale candy and nuts as holiday presents? No more ghost-town office? No more family business? No more family business. No more *money*.

"But what about Harry?" I said, panicked. Harry! I'd never gotten used to not worrying about him, fretting over his daily well-being, and maybe I never would, no matter how angry with him I got. Thinking about Harry in this way, when he'd become in so many ways an abstract absence, made me almost double over with guilt. What *about* Harry? He was still a person out there somewhere. He was still a person I had married. How on earth could I ever explain to him the thing with Sam? The thing with the rusalka? I had kissed another man. I had tried to die. These were not nice things to do. It hurt, physically, sharp as a gut ache, as simultaneously compressing and expanding as a labor pain.

He should be the one worrying, not you. How does he explain to you why he left you alone with your two children, with his two children? He is the one who is wrong.

He's going to be devastated. Have a heart.

You already have been devastated. And I do have a heart, thank you. Yours.

"What about when he comes back? You just tell him, what, 'Sorry we closed the business while you were gone'? Don't you need him to sign off on these things? What is he supposed to do?"

Sylvia looked pained. She said quietly, "We're starting to think of that as 'if.' If he comes back. Not when."

"Since when? Says who? The detective? The police? Fred? What was this, a family committee decision at another mysterious family meeting? What if I'm still saying 'when'?"

"Of course, honey. Of course you are. We all are. But in terms of the business, he's part of why we're in this mess in the first place. We assume— There's a lot of money missing— Don't make me say it."

I slumped down in my chair. It had been too long since Betty had appeared. I would have to go see what horrors she'd inflicted on our security deposit this time. "What am I supposed to do? About money, I mean?"

Sylvia reached out and patted my arm. "I don't know. I'm so sorry, dear. We'll figure it out. We'll all pitch in and help, of course we will. And now that I won't be working, if you find a full-time job, I can watch the girls, you know I'd be happy to do that. My house is paid for. If it ever came down to it, you know that you and the girls would be welcome to come live with me."

Sweet Jesus. "Could you hold on for a second?" I said, unsuccessful at masking the tremor in my voice. "Could you just hold on for just one second?" I got up and peeked into the girls' room. Nothing. Peeked into our room. Er, my room. Betty was facing the full-length mirror, wearing a shirt and pretied tie of Harry's and a pair of my fanciest flats, with Anne's perfect, just completed veil, now defiled by menstrual smears of red and purple marker. "Betty!" I cried, and when she turned around, I startled at her gruesome clown's-mask face, done up in old-lady unguents. "Oh my God! No, no! Where did you even find so much makeup?" The war-paint smudges of eye shadow, the lifeguard nose of whitish concealer, the loop-the-loops of crimson lipstick. She looked terrifying, and even more so when she cackled. "I wook pretty!" she insisted. Sylvia's purse gaped open on the floor.

"That veil! Do you have any idea— Agh, Betty! No! Bad! What is *wrong* with you?"

Sylvia appeared behind me, balancing a soggy Rose on her hip. She took one look at Betty and started laughing. Really cracking up, hyena gasping, yukking it up. I took Rose from her. "It's not— Betty, it's not funny. Not okay." But Betty's pleased smile widened as she watched Grandma double over with giggles, and I had to leave the room before beating them both to an intergenerational pulp. The fucking veil. I felt so shuddery with guilt and fury that even smiling turned my stomach, the way you feel the first time you laugh after someone close to you dies. *Betty, sweetheart, I am trying to love you unconditionally, but you are making it difficult.*

Sylvia cleaned Betty up and even forgave her smashing of the department-store lipstick, and the next time she came over, horribly, she handed my innocent toddler a pink plush purse stocked with a plastic compact, lipstick, and mirror. Not exactly the sort of forward thinking I wanted to instill in my daughter and, more important (as I was beginning to realize), rewarding bad behavior.

In the meantime, I redoubled my efforts to drum up new sewing jobs, as if I could stave off the hounds at the door—Jesus, bankruptcy!—with good old American hard work. It was one thing to have a disappeared husband but another thing altogether to have a disappeared jobless husband too off the grid to even apply for unemployment. I entertained melodramatic visions of burning furniture for warmth, of the electricity being shut off, of eating condiment sandwiches on fetid Dumpster bread, of having to cancel our Y membership. I did the math. At the rate I was going, I could support the girls with my sewing so long as no one ever got sick. Or wanted dessert.

What made it worse was my nagging sense that the rusalka was getting bored with me. It was like realizing that a man is falling out of love with you. I was terrified of being alone again, unprotected against the pall of depression, with no watery presence between me and the abyss; I felt desperate to keep her happy. We weren't gallivanting around the city and trying new things and flirting and feeling full of possibility. I wondered if she felt like she'd been hoodwinked. Here she was, stuck in my sweatshop of an apartment, sewing each night until dawn, worrying about money. What probably seemed to her a chance for ribald New York City adventure had turned out to be a glorified indentured servitude. It probably was a lot more pleasant in the sea. But I knew what she wanted. I knew, I thought, how to keep her.

twenty

I hadn't seen him since that ill-advised playground kiss despite dragging the girls on languorous strolls around the neighborhood, slinking along under awnings, strategizing across game boards of shade, moving slower and slower the later it got, until I was shuffling along like a tourist in a museum or a dying person. Rose squirmed fretfully in the bottom of the double stroller. She rode so close to the ground down there that I would often unearth her at the end of a walk to find her cheeks darkened with a city-dirt facial. I was shamed at these times by my desire for someplace clean and air-conditioned, the shopping malls I'd thought I hated as a kid. What I wouldn't do for a day in the antiseptic cavern of the Mall of America, where first-graders birthday-partied in a vomitiously pink storefront, having makeup applied until their faces were immobile as baby Joan Riverses, where everything to eat was fried and no one cared. It would be easier elsewhere, I was always telling myself, without regard to whether or not this was true.

Why did I have it in my head so unrelentingly that mine had been a more wholesome upbringing than the one I was giving my girls? So summer smelled to them not of cut grass but of rotting trash, sounded not of locusts but of the buses and bar crowds you could hear when the windows were open. So I had been on the subway with them once when a drunk woman activated her pepper spray, so they had seen the flaccid wiener of a homeless man peeing in the park. So there were things I couldn't protect them from. So what. Suburban kids may have had their own backyards, but they also loitered in large structures devoted to commerce and tumid with formaldehyde, spent their teenage years driving around stoned. Most of my summer memories involved making lanyards at day camp and then watching untold hours of television in our carpeted basement, sometimes catching a titillating flicker of staticky Skinemax. It hadn't exactly been Shangri-la. Still, as many times as my fishy fairy godmother hissed *Don't be such a fucking bore,* the midwestern part of me spent these hot, sticky afternoons craving an Orange Julius in someone's dim rec room.

Instead, we strolled. We ran into people we knew, waved to the firemen and their dog at the storybook firehouse, invented errands that could be completed entirely at shops with propped-open doors and aisles wide enough for our monstrous stroller. We stopped at the bookstore and the health-food store and the wine shop and the Italian meat-and-cheese market, so by the time I finally did see Sam, the stroller was ponderous with packages, Rose was passed out in a heatstrokey nap, Betty was a whining wreck refusing to be entertained by even the Holy Grail of my cell phone, and I had a net bag of bloody meat slung jauntily over my shoulder.

"Well, hello," he said. He said it proprietarily, as if our relationship had progressed without me, as if he'd always known he would have me and now he did. Was I reading too much into his tone? Nah. He was without his kids. I didn't even ask.

"Oh, *hi,*" I said, or she said. Batting my sweaty eyelashes.

We were on the busy, unforgivingly exposed corner of Seventh Avenue and Ninth Street. In another lifetime, I would have pulled to the side in consideration of pedestrian traffic, but I couldn't find it in me to care about such things anymore. A line of tired-looking middle-aged women, each holding too many plastic bags, waited for the bus. I felt automatically that Sam and I were performing for them, even though none of them showed any sign of paying attention. Betty arched her back in the stroller and expressed her feelings about this last stop in a sound that resembled a dinosaur toy running out of batteries. My beloved child, I ignored her.

"Have you been getting any sleep?" Sam said. He shot me a meltingly sweet look before leaning over to offer Betty a complicated series of high fives that distracted her from her overheated crabbiness. What was a question like that? I unconsciously smoothed my too tight tank top, my skirt, checked quickly my golden thongs. A question like that meant we had been seeing each other at night. Did it? No, ridiculous—it meant I had young children and looked tired. My heart pounded against engorged breasts (we really had to get home to nurse soon). *What have you done? We've never left the girls alone, right? Oh God, has he come over? The neighbors! The mess!*

You would do well to relax every once in a while, you know that?

"I don't know," I said finally. "Um, why? Have you?"

He laughed. Whatever that meant.

I was aware, maybe only in my own invention, of the bus-stop ladies glaring at us in disapproval. Julie, one of the playground moms, walked by and waved. I might have imagined the askance once-over. My ground chuck moldered at my side. I took a breath to speak, only to whip my head around at what I thought was another wave but was really the broken wing of a smashed pigeon adhered to the road, flapping in a breeze. "Sam," I said. *I feel terrible,* I was going to say. *I didn't mean to kiss you, and I am sorry about that. That is very awkward, is what that is.* She wouldn't let the words out. She held them like a selfish child clutching a bunch of balloons. *I shouldn't have kissed you. And we shouldn't be sending all these texts to each other. And we shouldn't—*

He had to lean in to hear me through the clamor of the street. "Jenny," he said.

The rusalka was fighting me. She was trying to say, and I was trying to stop her, *Come by tonight. Come over.*

"What is it, Jenny?"

Come, come to me, after the kids are asleep.

He smiled uncertainly. "I do have to go pick up Maude from ballet."

I waved at him. "Oh, nothing, nothing! I forgot what I was going to say!" Brilliant. He raised his eyebrows and nodded. "Okay, Bet, my pet, be good for your mama."

"No!" screamed Betty.

We exchanged shrugs—oh, toddlers! oh, parenthood!—and went our separate ways. I walked home as quickly as I could, sweating a heart shape on the back of my shirt. But a few hours later, I took out my phone while the girls were distracted and tapped out an inviting text I hoped no one but Sam ever read. I couldn't take it anymore, or maybe *she* couldn't take it anymore. I was sure I would explode into a million fleshy chunks if I didn't see him soon. I wavered before pressing "OK" to send. The rusalka tamped down my finger. In a suspense-filled instant came the reply, the most thrilling line in the history of romance. John Keats never wrote anything more eloquent in a letter to Fanny Brawne, Tom Hanks couldn't have said it better to Meg Ryan: "C U AT 9."

I spent the afternoon in a confused tizzy, microwaving Betty's spinach patty into a rubbery puck, skipping everyone's bath time and speed-reading bedtime stories. Betty came up to me and held my face in her hands and said, "Is Mommy sick?" But the heat of the day had sufficiently melted her so that I could bury her in an avalanche of stuffed animals, and she was soon snoozing. One down. Rose nursed and nursed and nursed until I was sore, and then she dozed off, and after bargaining with the clock (five more minutes and she will really be asleep), I oh so gently placed her in the crib, and the instant her back touched the mattress, it arched and her eyes popped open like a plastic doll's. She had forgotten all about being sleep-trained. This went on for over an hour. My shoulders twinged with each careful lowering. When she finally relented, it was nearly nine. I accidentally chose to hurl some toys toward the bin rather than shower in the few moments I had before my phone lit up. I'M HERE.

Harry and I once rented a movie about a suburban stay-at-home mom who had a torrid affair with a stay-at-home dad. Harry had teased me about it: "So that's what you fantasize about, huh?" I'd laughed. "The real fantasy here is that their children both nap at the same time and long enough to allow for any kind of illicit encounter," I'd told him, and it was true. Between the kids' activities and naps and colds and errands, who could ever coordinate such liaisons? I could barely make playdates. Sam was sneaking out tonight, but then what? Maybe I simply wasn't cut out for having an affair. Here we were, allegedly getting together to chat, and I was a nervous wreck, hearing him tromp up the stairs and worrying the whole time about the neighbors listening, seeing, suspecting. We hadn't gotten to second base, and already I was obsessing over the ninety people on our street who surely had seen him slip out of his front door with his gym bag, walk the long way around the block, and reappear on my stoop. Maybe, like everything else, sneaking around was easier in the suburbs. To have an affair in Brooklyn, you had to be organized. You needed a discreet babysitter and the patience to ride the subway to some other neighborhood in order to meet. Or you had to be rich enough for livery cars and hotel rooms, and who could afford that on top of rent?

Then I was calm. The rusalka spread down through my limbs, like the creeping warmth of a comfortable, one-too-many-with-dinner drunk. I didn't think. This was the great joy of my life as a dead person. The old Jenny Lipkin had been prone to fretfulness, forever running through logistics. The new me threw on a diaphanous shift I'd painstakingly pieced together for my local coffee-shop owner and was supposed to deliver tomorrow; somehow one irresponsibility bred another. Feeling like the evil sexpot in a cheesy eighties video—I could almost see the smoke-machine mist, feel my hair crimp and coil like a hair-sprayed Medusa's—I slipped my feet into my shoes, *the* shoes, those beautiful lifesaving slippers from the bridge, as alien on my crumb-studded floor as a frog in a royal castle.

He opened and closed the door quietly, an expert in tiptoeing around sleeping babies. Seeing him in my tiny home made me realize how large he was, how ridiculously tall. I thought of the time a whale had found its way into the Gowanus Canal. The whale died, I remembered, dismayed.

Sam smiled. "Hi."

My heart raced. I knew this feeling, kind of—the unhinged sensation of a moment more like a movie than real life. I'd felt it the day I gave birth to Betty; I'd felt it, awfully, on September 11, standing shoulder to shoulder with silent others in a bar to watch the gruesome coverage; I'd felt it on the day I died. I'd felt it, I was sure, when Harry proposed, although I was having trouble remembering that right now. My handful of dramatic instants. And all this man had to do was walk through my door, and it was so wrong and so right and so deliciously unbearable that it took on the tenor of a national catastrophe.

So there I was in the kitchen, in my kitchen, my children's kitchen, Harry's kitchen, pouring wine into mismatched juice glasses. "Fancy meeting you here."

What is that, a catchphrase? I would never really say that. This is just some bad romance novel to you, isn't it?

Oh, hush. If it's anything, it's a good romance novel.

I couldn't bear to look at him, turning to rummage nervously through the cupboards instead. "Are you hungry? Want a snack?" I sounded like such a, well, mom. "Goldfish? Cheerios? I can offer you some decaf instant coffee and biscotti. Well, teething biscuits, but they honestly taste just like biscotti."

He didn't smile. Maybe it had been too much, like starting off talking about our kids or mentioning the names of our spouses. He was looking around. I swallowed the urge to apologize for the mess, gestured toward the couch, and brought the wine over. "Sit, sit!" I cried, patting the cushion like the deranged hostess at a failing party.

Sam perched on the edge of the sofa, hands splayed on his knees. "What am I doing here?" he said, as if to himself. At some point in the day, his flirty bravado from the street had left him. I, I would have crumpled at this, at this poor hapless man, at Cute Dad of all people drawn into my living room of iniquity. But she had taken over, and she was in no mood to appeal to his guilty conscience, which was boring, and ordinary, and not worth her time, so she leaned in and smiled and offered, "Well? What *are* you doing here?"

He smiled unhappily. "I don't know. You tell me. You're

supposed to be the one with all the answers." I just nodded like a therapist, which I knew was an annoying response. He shook his head, unloosing an unfairly adorable coil of hair. "I told Juliet I was going to the gym. I can't stay long."

You could tell he didn't mean it, that it was only what he felt like he should say. You could tell he would stay all night if I made it worth his while, but that he thought he should let himself be talked into or out of it, that he was feeling reluctant to make the decision because he was unwilling to shoulder the consequences, the way men always were about everything. And I have to say here that this wasn't me, this woman who leaned closer in such a way as to smoosh together some cleavage at him. It wasn't even any part of me. I had never been that girl. I followed the rules! I loved the rules! It was one of the ways I maintained the moral upper hand over Harry, my ne'er-do-well husband—he was the one who did illegal things, he was the one who overindulged while I was home minding the children. So who was this? This was not me. This was just some mermaid.

Which was why my hair moved in a nonexistent breeze as if we were chatting underwater. Which was why I could have sworn I was emitting a seaweedy odor, why I found myself inching toward him like a large hunk of driftwood.

"Jenny," said Sam. "You—you're. I, I—"

I laughed. "I was just going to say that!"

"I think about you all the time."

"I think about you, too," I said. My insides performed an undignified happy dance.

"I wish—it were some other way." He was having difficulty, looking at his hands, flushing beneath his stubble. I was gripped with a confused, cannibalistic urge to unearth his eyeballs from his head and swallow them whole. Also, it sounded like someone was squeaking in the other room. *Oh, no, no. No, babies, you sleep, damn you!*

"Look, I'm not trying to make you do anything you don't want to do. I just thought that it would be nice to hang out and chat without all the kids around for once," I said idiotically. "I like you, you know? We're friends, aren't we? It's so hard around here—there are so many assholes." The squeaking was making me tense, occupying a growing sector of my consciousness.

He smiled. He was just too nice, he really was. The way his eyes crinkled when he smiled—*I could love that forever,* I thought, *I know I could. I would never get tired of that.* "I don't want to chat," he said.

"Yeah, me, neither," I admitted.

He leaned forward, or maybe I did. We both did. We all did. The rusalka, she pushed my chest out. The heat between Sam and me was palpable. I hadn't been so worked up about a kiss since Dennis Hellman at sleepover camp reached his friendship-braceleted hand toward mine, his smile semi-precious with orthodontia. I felt as though I might pass out, as if mashing my lips against this other person's lips could change my life, could heal every hurt I'd ever had. *Yesyesyesyes* said my brain, or the rusalka, or someone. *Yesyesyeskissme.*

I wish I could report that here I turned away, or he did. That one of us said, *No, I'm sorry, I really couldn't. The whole marriage thing, you know.* Or *This won't really solve anything for either of us, now, will it?* I don't know what his excuse was. All I know is that kissing felt too delicious not to, like falling asleep when you shouldn't but you're so exhausted that it takes over, a bandit in your body. And also, my mermaid, she wanted it. We kissed. It was an excruciating pleasure. We kissed for a hundred years. We did.

And Sam! Cute Dad! Who would have thought? His hands were

everywhere, on my breasts (*Don't leak, don't leak,* I pleaded), up my skirt, squeezing my thighs so urgently that I found a map of ardent bruises in the morning. My legs wound around his waist, my hands tangled in his hair. This was not the kind of thing I had ever done in my whole entire life. It definitely wasn't me inching off my underwear, whispering into his ear, teasing him, no, begging him, to fuck me. No, plain old Jenny had always made men wait, had been reserved in bed, had turned the lights off every time, and more recently, mom Jenny reserved her body for her babies, for gestating and nursing and comforting, transformed her carnal self into just another friendly mammal. This rusalka, I am telling you, she was crazy. Was this how you seduced a man? It felt like such a violence.

Yet I didn't want to pull away, I wanted to be pressed against him in that instant forever. He smelled so good, like plain soap and coffee, and his body was surprisingly firm beneath his soft gray T-shirt. He paused for a moment, rested his chin on the top of my head. My face was rubbed raw from his stubble. We sat there for a long time, kissing and stopping and then kissing again and running our hands over each other's bodies and every once in a while looking into each other's eyes and laughing, because we were just so happy, and so nervous, and so disbelieving. After years with the same man, it was tremblingly novel to have this whole new terrain, not to know the exact thing he liked in order to get it all done in the most efficient way, to have everything ahead of us. All I could think already was *Goddammit. This could be really good. We really could have a lot of fun together.*

Suddenly, he pulled away and studied me with those large dark eyes. He brushed a curl out of my face with one finger. Something about this action undid me completely. *Fuck it! Let's go! Don't you want to know what it's like, at least? Don't you think this could really be something?* It could, that was the whole problem. There was this ease between us, a web connecting our brains. It was weird how it happened. Sometimes I'd be riding the subway or ordering coffee somewhere and there it would be, a small shared moment with someone, a tiny flicker of recognition—of what? of something—and I'd know that were our lives to run parallel a few instants longer, I could be in love with this stranger, that we shared—what was it?—*something*. I'd always felt this about Sam, and now here he was and here I was. "Sam, Sam, Sam," I whispered into his chest. I wanted him. Maybe that's all it really was. I just wanted him. And I wanted him to want me. And I wanted, I allowed a tiny part of myself to admit, Harry to know that I wanted someone and that someone wanted me, that he couldn't just leave me alone and expect me to wait. I know. I know. I know it wasn't a nice thing to do. But what can I say? We did it.

Afterward, like everyone everywhere, we lay together, breathing, sweating, my head on his chest, his hands in my hair. Sleeping with someone else's husband, I now know, is very much like jumping off a bridge. The ineluctable urge, the incomparable pleasure of relenting, the moment of bliss, pure as a raindrop. And then, post-release, the immediate, dizzying, eternal regret. *What. Oh. What. Have. I. Done.* From the rusalka, that bitch: silence.

"This is good," Cute Dad whispered into my hair. "We deserve a little bit of happiness." Which distracted me. Worse, it popped the bubble, transformed the shimmery surface into just soap for a depressing instant before it disappeared completely. We were two people again. It was awful.

I squirmed away, sat up, began to dress. *We deserve a little bit of happiness.* What the hell was that? We were always saying things like this to ourselves and each other, as if our everyday lives were wrought with struggle. So our spouses were tired and cranky, so our families expected a lot from us. So what? I'd found that people who said things like "I have to start thinking about myself" tended to be people who were very good at thinking about themselves. And Sam and I were always saying things to each other like "We have to think about ourselves." Did we really? Was there anything so valuable in thinking about ourselves more than we already did, which was almost constantly? But it was tempting to agree. *It happens every day. People do it every day. Why not you? It will be so good. It could be so good. Let's do this again tomorrow and the next day and the next. Let's have fun.*

He pulled me close again, his hands in my hair. Was this really how easy it was? I told him we wanted each other, and then we did? Up close his eyelashes were darker and curlier and prettier than I had ever known. I heard one of children stir. Apartment dwellers really couldn't have trysts. Maybe there was a way to find out how it was done. Maybe you could you dial 311—"Hi, I need a place to meet a lover? 11215 zip code, preferably?" Maybe it was an in-demand service I could start if the sewing thing ever dried up. I accidentally thought of Harry, of all the times we'd done it on that couch because one kid or another was sleeping in our bed. You couldn't ever have a moment alone, could you?

"Jenny, Jenny," Sam said, nuzzling my neck, holding my face in his ursine hands. The nuzzling tickled, so I giggled, which he took as encouragement, pressing closer. I again pictured Harry's face—"Sam? As in Sam and Juliet? You're kidding me."

I stood up suddenly. "You should go." Looking into Sam's eyes unhinged my brain, so I looked away, toward the windows, where the orangey undark of the street reflected us back to us. I should have at least thought to close the shades. I was no good at this. "We probably shouldn't have done that."

"But I really wanted to," he said, like a boy.

"I know." My chest felt as if it had been dipped in concrete and dropped into the ocean, my heart disposed of by gangsters it had done wrong. "Me, too."

Sam straightened his ponytail. His ponytail! How could I have been so absurd? It was difficult to believe a few moments earlier, he'd been inside of me, unmetaphorically, that the dampness leaking out of me was— Oh God. I pressed at my face as if I could mold myself back into myself. Sam was saying, "You're right. No, you're right. Of course you are. I'm—I'm so sorry. We don't—"

"I mean, really. We— You have such a nice family. Such a nice—wife." It was difficult to say the word, like a foreign idiom I hadn't mastered.

"I know, I know." He shook his head. "Let's not talk about this now. Just—don't say it. That was— I want to see you again." It was a silly thing to say. Like it or not, we would of course see each other again, probably every day. And now we'd have to pretend we hadn't, you know. Fucked. Fuck.

His body looked different to me, as if I could see his skeleton. He didn't look at me as he dressed, patted for his keys like any disheveled dad.

Well, mermaid? Was it good for you? Are you happy now?

You know I don't like when you call me that.

Excuse me, but I just gave you what you've been wanting all summer, at great personal risk. I've probably just ruined our lives. Or at least our marriages. All for you.

For me? Don't make me laugh! You know who that was for. And by the way, you're welcome.

I see. I see how it is. Hey, guess what, actually. There's something I've been meaning to tell you.

And what's that, you fool?

You have to go.

I have to WHAT?

"You know, this probably isn't the time or place, but there is something I've been meaning to tell you," Sam said. He was at the door, a giant in the jamb. It had been all of fifteen minutes, and already the sex was starting to feel like a highly improbable, misremembered dream. "Ah, we're moving. She found an apartment in Astoria. Well, get this—Nell found it and said she knew it was perfect for us."

After all I've done for you. You were nothing. Nothing. You were dying! I saved your life!

"Astoria! Jesus! That's so far!"

Don't you ignore me! You think I'll just dissolve? What, you think you can pick and choose? When you want me, when you don't?

"I know. I know," he moaned.

Nell. Nell! It took all my concentration to block out the rusalka's muttering, to think things through. Why did Nell care enough to take him away? I'd have imagined she'd be just as happy to watch us destroy ourselves while she sipped an iced green tea and oozed superiority, which was her specialty, after all. But there was something else unsettling in all this, something difficult to define and even more difficult to locate, like a hair coiled in an eye socket. The forces of the city, the code of the town, pushing him away from me, to protect him, or me, or somebody, or everybody. Too late, as it turned out.

"I won't tell anyone," I said, not looking at him. "I promise. Listen, Sam. It's not you. It's perfectly obvious to everyone, I'm afraid, that I'm crazy about you. Too crazy about you. I've wanted you forever. And that was—great, really. It really was amazing. But I think— This wouldn't fix anything. You know? I think I need fixing. And it needs to be me doing the fixing. Not you. Not anyone else." That sounded good, I thought, like something from a smart article. I hoped I could remember it.

He looked at me as if I were speaking another language. Maybe I was. I felt so damn sorry for him, I thought I might cry, but I also was really, really tired of crying. I realize how that sounds. It wasn't that he'd, like, gotten a taste of my *Kama Sutra*–style moves and now would have no more, boo-hoo for him. Hardly. It was more that I was sorry I'd dragged him into the whole mess, that I'd, I don't know. Seduced him. Seduced him in order to prove a point to myself. Now he would always have to know in his heart that he was a man who would cheat on his wife, that, given the chance, he was that kind of guy. He wasn't, I really believed he wasn't, until I made him.

Harry would have leaned in and kissed me, hard, would have taken my hand and said he would give me time to think but we would see each other again. Or no, he would have pressed me to the couch and taken me again right then and there. But Sam, poor Sam. He was too fucking nice. It was exactly what I liked about him, but it was annoying, a little, too. *Don't listen to me!* I wanted to say. *Take me in your arms, show me how it could be, make me love you.* But he was reasonable. He was adult. He was going to let my family sort out our own particular mess, and he was going to the gym now, to responsibly establish his alibi. Poor Juliet. Poor all of us.

Sam smiled, took a breath, about to say—something. Something life-changing, I'm sure. But what happened next was straight out of a romantic comedy, one of the goofy studio numbers in black and white that I'd spent my evenings in front of before I remembered sewing. Not a good romantic comedy, either, but one that had been thrown together hastily on a back lot, the scenery showing its seams. We didn't kiss sweetly and talk it over, we didn't throw caution to the wind and get all hot and heavy again. No, we didn't do anything, because my baby started to scream. We leaped apart.

I buried my face in my hands before apologizing and running in to grab her before she woke Betty, and when I came back out, my nipples leaking coins of milk through my dress, he had gone. Here was the reality of my life—illicit sex to breast-feeding in five minutes flat. The rusalka raged, but what could I do? I left the dress on the couch, kicked off my heels, and, babe in arms, retired to the boudoir.

twenty-one

In the same way that it highlights a nose's ruinous blemish, or lays bare the black under-eyes of a hangover, the light of morning renders all our animal appetites ridiculous. The next day my rusalka delighted in the physical ache of the aftermath, how it hurt to sit, stung to stand. What she loved even more, now that I'd pissed her off by ordering her away, was how miserable the rest of me felt, guilt scintillating around the edges of my vision like a moral migraine. Come on. This was bad. It was the worst thing I'd ever done. It was done and could not be undone. Because this was me, my chosen commandment breaking turned out to be one entirely without lasting rewards. Couldn't I have stolen a large sum of money instead? Guilt-inducing but at least helpful?

It didn't help matters to have a rusalka storming around inside me. *After everything I've done for you. I've saved your life ten times over. And now you try to evict me? That's not how these things work, little girl. And just how do you expect to get rid of me, anyway? Throw me off a bridge?* Her words sent a cold chill down my spine, or maybe that was her clammy caress. Here was something I had never considered: that I would be like this forever, harboring my spectral fugitive until I died again, for the last time. That I would be fielding her demands as we wheeled around our futuristic nursing home, like any other Dame of Dementia (*No, I'm not stealing extra Splenda packets for you, leave me alone!*), or that if she were to untangle herself from me, the rest of me might die without her. Maybe she was all that propped me up, and my whole post-bridge life had been nothing more than a mythology-infused *Weekend at Bernie's*. I shuddered. I hadn't been thinking carefully enough about the consequences of my trysts lately, or possibly ever.

I was in such a state that it was almost—*almost*—impossible to enjoy the e-mail I got that morning from a reporter (okay, a mom I knew from the playground who happened to freelance) proposing a profile in *The Brooklyn Paper*. Of me. She'd heard about my fantastic dresses and thought that readers might enjoy hearing about a local mom's burgeoning new business. After all, she told me, people loved that throwbacky-crafty stuff (so hip-grandma-y!), and I had such a talent—she was a friend of Evelyn's and had seen my work—and would I mind having my photograph and an interview run in the paper? Relief spored over my guilt. *Oh, that's right!* I was just a local mom, just a lady who liked to sew, an ordinary person with a charming hobby, not a supernaturally possessed sexual predator *at all*.

I read over the e-mail about eighty times, certain it was meant for someone else. Who would give a shit about me and my pointless stitchery? But there were too many details that checked out. She must mean me. I spun Rose around the living room, gave Betty a high five. Maybe it would bring more business! Maybe everything would work out after all! And maybe, just maybe, I wouldn't need the rusalka's dexterous interference to make it work! It meant a lot of running around—the reporter mom promised linkage to my nonexistent website, wanted some sample prices I'd have to dream up, and needed photos and an interview by next week—but it also made my sewing feel real, made my "business" feel like a no-quotes-necessary business, and, best of all, distracted me from the Sam situation. By the end of the day, my only question was why I hadn't thought to throw myself into my sewing instead of off a bridge in the first place.

Funny how, after a part of your life is over, it all seems to fit into place, as if it couldn't have turned out any other way, as if fact equaled destiny. First there was Sam, then there was the sewing thing, and then, with strange serendipity, my dad called me. "Dad? Oh God, who died?" My father never called. And yet I had been thinking about him, about him and my mother and their impressively long, remarkably anodyne marriage. They had lived without passion for at least the past thirty years, so why shouldn't I?

"What? No, no one died."

"Why are you calling in the middle of the night?"

There was a pause. "It's eight thirty."

"We can't all be party animals like you, you know. Besides, it's later here."

Another pause. "So, nine thirty."

"Like I said. What's up, Pop?" I settled back into my sewing. I was working double time, staying up as late as I could stand it, my fingers cramped and creaking. To my surprise, the idea of having to go back to a real job, as suggested by Sylvia, had not come as a relief, as a return to real life, the way I'd always pictured it. Instead, I found myself taking on as many pieces of sewing as humanly possible, hustling for hem jobs, pushing Anne to tell her betrothed friends about my great work and free advice, throwing each scrap of money on the sad pile, hoping each time for a miracle of multiplication to occur.

My father cleared his throat. "Yes."

"How's the weather there?" I prompted him. How did this man not know how to have a conversation? What did he do at work? In a social setting, assuming he ever encountered those?

"The weather? Oh, fine, I guess."

"Great. How's Mom? Readjusting to American life?" She had returned from Cairo, triumphant, rattling with souvenir scarabs and pointless stories that even an exotic backdrop could not redeem, mostly about "hilarious" misunderstandings that she and her bovine buddy Bev had with the locals. I was happy for her. I was. I also looked forward to a time when every sentence wouldn't be answered with, "Oh, well in *Egypt* you know what they do . . ." She was worse than a college junior after a semester abroad.

He cleared his throat again. I wondered where he was in their big empty house. In the basement rec room, I guessed, by the dormant pinball games and teetotalers' wet bar stocked with store-brand cola, while my mother watched *ER* upstairs, holding a tangle of yarn in her lap as if at any moment it might begin to knit itself. "Yes, your mother. She's fine. She had a real nice time on her vacation."

"Yes, so I heard. That's great, Dad. Isn't that great? Don't you think that's great?"

"Well. Yeah. I think she and Beverly were real pleased with themselves."

"Sure. Of course. They had an adventure." I tried to keep the eye rolling out of my voice.

"So now she wants to go again."

"To Egypt?"

"What? No, no. Somewhere else. I forget. India, I think."

"Really. Wow! Guess she really got the travel bug, huh?"

"Well, she had a little diarrhea, she said, but mostly, she was okay."

"No, Dad, I— Never mind. I mean, she liked traveling."

"Oh. Yes, I guess so."

"Well? Is she going with Beverly again? How do you feel about all this?"

"She has to wait a year or so to save up enough vacation days again. But the thing is, she wants me to go." A tremor crept into my dad's voice. Fear? Excitement? Nausea?

"That's good. She wants you to have an adventure like she just had." *And she wants to stay married,* I didn't say. *She wants to spice things up and make it work.* Who knew?

"We've taken lots of nice trips. Last spring we went to visit my cousin Herb in North Dakota."

"That doesn't count, Dad. That's not a nice trip. That's a shitty, boring trip. I'm sorry, but it is. That's just—shitty." My cheeks flushed. I'd *sworn* at my *father*. I was turning into a bad girl after all.

My dad paused. "Herb got a new pickup."

"Yeah, see, no one cares. Mom doesn't care. Mom wants to go to India, or wherever, and see interesting people and something famous, the Taj Mahal, I bet, and—"

"—get diarrhea again?" The poor man sounded positively furious. I hadn't heard him so kerfuffled since I'd told him I was marrying a Jew. In a park. The interfaith issue was one thing, but the threat of bugs and rain was too much for him to handle.

"Maybe! I guess so! Why not, Dad? What's the worst that could happen? You spend a few days on an air-conditioned bus, you take some snapshots, Mom embarrasses you by talking to strangers in a tourist market somewhere . . . So what? Live a little!"

He sighed meaningfully. Finally, he said, "I've never met anyone who's been to India."

"It's really going to be okay. Why don't you guys go out for Indian food in the Cities one night and discuss it?"

There was a long silence.

"Indian food, Dad. It's like . . . rice. Potatoes. And, you know, curry. It's . . . like ketchup. You'll like it."

"I don't like curry."

"You've never had curry."

"Because I don't like it."

"Dad, you don't know that. For chrissakes, you're worse than Betty. Look, I have to go. Tell Mom I love her. You should agree to the trip. It would mean a lot to her."

"It's very expensive." He was stalling. This was rivaling the longest conversation I'd ever had with him in my whole life. "We were going to refinish the deck."

"Fuck the deck. Say yes. It's weird for me to say this to you, but I think your marriage needs this. Mom's going to jump out of her skin if you guys don't start, you know, living." *And shagging,* I couldn't say.

"Huh."

"Why don't you go upstairs and talk to her?"

"Hmm."

"Good night, Dad."

"Hmm."

"Bye."

"All right, then."

"Hanging up now."

I could just see him sitting there with the phone in his hand, looking around the room. This was the marriage I'd grown up observing without realizing I was observing it. I'd derived half my DNA from a man who thought a nice vacation was a weekend in North Dakota admiring Herb Wilson's Ford. Every night I could remember, my parents had slept with their door open. Nothing fancy going on in there! I knew it was unfair to blame them, but I also knew that they had done it to themselves, they had let shyness become silence, distance turn into disdain. The chilliness of their marriage was not any more inevitable than it was irreversible.

So there was something hopeful in this unexpected future for them as tour-bus world travelers. I just wanted my parents to go to India or wherever they were going (never mind the fact that I could hardly leave the borough) and e-mail some grainy pictures of them grinning in moon-white sneakers in front of the Taj Mahal and have sex with each other or whatever they needed to do and leave me out of it. I wanted them to be happy with each other, as I realized they'd probably never been before.

It was as if my family somehow got my psychic distress signals months too late, only now dispatching themselves to check in on crazy, abandoned Jenny in Brooklyn. Because the next thing that happened was that Sarah and her hyperactive son, Max, came for an impromptu weekend. To stay with us. In our minuscule, packed-to-the-gills apartment. I wanted to murder her. Literally. As in I planned it, right down to how to produce the least blood.

Somehow I was able to swallow my anger, tamp down the raging rusalka, pretend I hadn't just slept with my neighbor, and grit my teeth into an angry-gorilla grin for two whole days. I maneuvered my guests through brunch, the park, the nightmarish riot of the children's museum on a Saturday, endured the constant squabbling between Max and Betty (their typical repartee went a little something like this: "No!" "NO!" "Mine!" "MINE!" In unison: "MOMMMMYYYYY!"), and absorbed Sarah's annoying analyst's pestering. How was I feeling? No, but how was I *feeling*?

Finally, after twenty-plus hours of conversations in which I left out everything that was really happening, Sunday night arrived and found Sarah and me sharing a bottle of wine on my grimy couch, whispering to avoid waking Max, who lacked my city kids' ability to sleep through sirens. Now that she was about to leave, I was able to view her with kindness. She was prettier than I was, which had always been annoying, like looking into a magic mirror capable of showing you how you might look if your features were slightly different—the eyes more almond, the hair shining blond and naturally straight (seriously, how was it fair?), the lips fuller, the demeanor calmer. What made it worse was she always dressed as if she hadn't noticed that she might be beautiful, where I—not recently but traditionally—had made an effort, probably too much of an effort, probably managing to look like a slightly pretty girl who was really trying, whose lips were shellacked with red and feet were encased in shoes that begged for attention of any kind, like the chatterbox the teacher's always chiding about having something to share with the rest of the class. But Sarah wore blue jeans in the effortless manner of the long-legged (okay, relatively speaking—she was five-four), and faded T-shirts, and her hair actually looked pretty in a ponytail. She was the most annoying kind of sister one could possibly have, and of course she was mine.

"Well," I said, "thanks for coming. Now it's back to your perfect life, ugh, poor thing!"

Sarah stared into her wineglass. "Yeah. Actually, you know, I came here because I wanted to tell you something in person, and I think I almost chickened out."

"Oh?" I was already punishing myself for resenting her. Dear God, she had cancer, Max had cancer, Mom had cancer, I had cancer, we all had cancer.

"This is so hard, especially with everything you're going through, and you've been so strong and amazing, and I'm so proud of you, and I don't want to add to your stress . . ."

She'd somehow found Harry, and he had cancer, too. Harry was hiding out with them, no, Harry was having an affair with her, no, she *was* Harry's secret other family, Max was their love child, that was why I found him so annoying and yet familiar—

"John and I are splitting up."

John? I momentarily drew a blank. Oh, John? Her husband? *Oh, who cares.*

"Oh my God. Really?" I managed to pull myself together and act, I hoped, like a semi-normal human being. I even reached out and patted her hand, something she was always doing to me. No wonder she hadn't noticed I was on the verge of a complete psychotic break. John had always struck me as sort of a douchebag, though Harry liked to tell me that was only because I was at heart so evil that I couldn't trust someone who was as blandly good-looking, polite, successful, *and* good at baking as my brother-in-law. That was why I had loved Harry, I think. He somehow always knew things like that about me, things that wouldn't have made sense to anyone else, things like how I could always distrust my sister's sweet husband because he once served us foie gras while playing a Dave Matthews CD, the combination of which had left me eternally nauseated. "My God, Sarah. Are you sure? Like for good or a trial thing?"

She wasn't looking me in the eye, a bad sign. "I'm pretty sure it's for good. He's moving out this weekend, while we're here."

"Really? Does Max know?"

"We're going to tell Max when we get home. We're taking him to Chuck E. Cheese's. It's probably the worst idea ever. He'll be so confused and grow up hating mice and not know why. But it's the way John wanted to do it—I don't know, to make it fun or something?—and I'd already vetoed too many things from him. I figured I owe him."

"You owe him? Wait, Sarah, why? What happened?"

She made a little tent out of her fingers—I could just see her doing this with her patients, it looked so shrinky, and I distracted myself momentarily by wondering if this was the kind of thing they taught at whatever school you had to go to in order to become an analyst. And if a couples therapist got divorced, was she still allowed to be a couples therapist? Could she be disbarred or something? She said, "Ah, well. This is so hard to say. To you. So weird. To admit."

"Don't even say it. I know. He had an affair. Sarah, that's so awful—I'm so sorry—"

Sarah laughed, which I hadn't expected. I stopped short. "He? No, no—John is just as perfect as he seems. That's the problem! Jenny, it was me. I had an affair. With a patient." She buried her face in her hands for an instant and then sat straight up, as if someone had pressed a reset button on her spine. The look on her face was not one I had seen before. Frank and embarrassed and shamed and . . . happy? Happy. "It's awful. I know it's awful. Do you hate me? I know everyone hates me. But I'm so—happy. I'm happy. He left his wife already, but there were no children, so it was simpler. Not that it was easy for him, but—we both want this. And it's just— Life is too short, you know?" People were always saying this, it occurred to me, but that wasn't the problem at all. The problem was that life was long, far too long. I felt a hundred years old suddenly, a thousand years old, and as if all I wanted to do was sink to the bottom of some cool dark river somewhere and sift through bits of seashells and glass shards and never see another human again. I had to talk to Sam. I had to make sure he didn't leave his wife, that I hadn't done something worse than all the other crummy everyday things. Also, I wanted to go to sleep without Sarah beside me.

I sat there, chewing on the inside of my cheek, trying to figure out what a nice, normal human would do in such a circumstance. Part of me wanted to rage at her—how could she be so selfish? Think of Max! If everything had been unthrilling but fine with

John, then why break it all to bits? But what did I know about marriage? I had not seen or heard from my own prince in shining armor for months and much of the time I'd spent attempting to seduce someone else's spouse. Sarah had studied the subject. Maybe she knew something I didn't.

Instead, I rallied some force inside me—well, we know what force—and applied a smile that was somewhere between sympathetic and joyful and said, "Oh, Sarah. Well, if you're happy, then I'm happy for you." As I said the words, I realized how true they were, how this new whoever-he-was was making her happy, and that with Sarah, there was a chance the happiness would stick. That for her, it could be the single transgression that began a new, even more perfect life. That with me and Cute Dad, it was a different situation altogether.

As usual, the bright light of Sarah's life revealed what was so flawed in mine. So, I'd been unhappy, then Harry had left, then I was still unhappy. He was gone, so I was unhappy, presumably because I missed him and was upset that he was gone. But I *had* been unhappy before, I knew I had been, and before, it had always been for a vague miasma of reasons and nonreasons and chemicals and such. Sometimes there had been a man to blame it on, and sometimes I'd had to get more creative with my justifications. It didn't quite hold that if I was unhappy now because Harry had left, then the unhappiness would go away when he came back, if he came back. Of course it wouldn't, because there would be all the anger and feelings of betrayal that he had left in the first place, not to mention how I'd been unhappy before, so it wasn't like his leaving was the cause of the unhappiness. Maybe it was even a result.

So, Sam. If we dared to follow this through, let's see: Maybe in the best-case scenario, Sam and I keep fucking. Let's be honest, it wouldn't be tender lovemaking or the efficiently pleasant sex of the married. It would be groping, grasping, desperate, secretive fucking. And it would be exciting for a while, very very exciting, and actually pretty great. And then what? He would stay with his wife and we would stop eventually and I would find someone else or something. I would become *that* woman, the neighborhood prowler. Or he would leave his wife and we would be together and there would be angry exes and scheduled visits from confused children and we would be *those* people. And then I would probably, because I was me, still be unhappy, and he'd feel ripped off, and we'd fight, and he would leave soggy food bits in the drain trap or deposit besmirched Kleenexes in the bed when he had a cold or some other annoying thing, and soon I'd be slinking to bed at night begging off sex because I was so tired. In my free time, I'd want to sit by myself and sew, and I'd have to entertain him instead or, even worse, his kids when it was his weekend with them . . . and there would be the same old problem, like a jawbreaker lodged in the sweetness of wanting to remember who Jenny was, who Jenny is, of being Jenny while still being everything to everyone. Every mother's same old boring problem. In other words, I was reasonably sure Sam would change nothing. That what needed to change was me, not any of the men around me. But this sounded *hard*. And I was *tired*.

I wanted to tell Sarah about Sam, about my whole fucked-up summer. But like I said, I was tired. Instead, I said, "I think this could be really good for you. It could be what was missing in your life, whether you knew it or not. I think it's all going to work out somehow."

She hugged me, eyes brimming with tears. "Oh, thank you, thank you, that's exactly what I was hoping you would say."

I poured her more wine and spent the evening being as sympathetic as I could muster. It seemed easiest to be nice to her—we avoided any difficult conversations, she didn't feel the need to turn the questioning back to me, and she was so relieved by my reaction that she snuggled up to me and gushed about her new love and their planned new life together, and everything stayed peaceful. I did want her to be happy, I did. It was cowardly, I knew, to trade a difficult but important conversation for a peaceful evening. But pleasant. Maybe that was the real story of my life: cowardly but pleasant. Maybe that was what taking Harry back would be. Well, I reminded myself, the question of taking Harry back hadn't exactly presented itself yet. It was possible I'd never get the option.

The next morning they left, and our apartment seemed habitable again. Sarah! I felt like I needed an exorcism. Then came a couple days of what passed these days for normal life—the kids, the small uneventful events of our day, evenings spent sewing before collapsing into exhausted sleep. I avoided Sam, except that I also thought about him constantly. Was this how it had been with Sarah's new man (I had forgotten to ask his name), an obstinate haunting? *I wonder if Sam likes green curry or red,* I'd think while scanning a take-out menu; *I wonder if Sam wakes up early or late,* my brain offered first thing in the grayish morning; *I wonder if Sam and his wife have sex*—the thought floated up as I squeezed a lumpy pillow to my chest. I did want it to stop, I just didn't know how.

I'd thought sleeping with him might get it out of my system, like a Cute Dad vaccine. Turned out I was more infected than ever. Turned out that despite my vow to be done with Sam, to have ended our whatever-it-was, I found myself creepily stalking him in the park one day when I saw him walking alongside our mutual neighborhood acquaintance, a blandly pretty mom named Karen. We hadn't talked about what had happened that night in my apartment. In fact, we hadn't talked at all. I had ignored his texts and calls, once pretended not to see him on the street. Every move (or non-move) was a battle against the rusalka, but I couldn't face him, face what I'd done, what we'd done, what we would do next. Turned out I made a crummy mistress but an excellent coward. And now here he was with Karen. A flare of jealousy singed my hair roots.

That should have been awful enough, but the rusalka inched me forward. *Follow. Go. We need to see what they are doing, where they are going. He is yours now.*

He is not. I don't want him to be.

It's a bit too late for that, bubeleh. *March! Onward!*

Sam and Karen were joining a picnic with, of all people, Nell and Evelyn. I pretended I'd happened to be passing by—"Oh, hi, you guys! Hi, Sam!"—and invited myself to join, texting Laura to come by if she could. Sam avoided my gaze. We played along like the others, patting down blankets and kicking off shoes and arranging cups of Cheerios, each of us halfheartedly chiding our children to share and use nice, soft touches instead of swiping at each other ferociously. Add that one to the list of things children dread and adults love, along with sleeping and bathing: nice, soft touches. I sent a psychic message to Betty—if she was going to bite someone, let it be Sophia.

Sam and I sat on opposite sides of the spread. I grinned nonsensically, laughed uproariously at everything, as if to prove how happy and normal and unruined and nonthreatening and totally not having sex with Cute Dad I was. I stretched out my legs, pressing my body down toward the slightly damp earth as if I might otherwise sail off into space. Betty and Emma disappeared behind a nearby oak. Rose crawled toward Sam, as usual. I should have at least tried, but I couldn't stop staring at him. His hands reached for the sunscreen, and I felt them on my skin. He sipped from a water bottle, and his lips were touching mine. He continued to avoid eye contact with me, probably embarrassed by my goony staring. I was confusing him. I was confusing myself. Or else the rusalka was. (Even as I started to find her presence ominous, I did enjoy blaming all misdeeds on her. A built-in scapegoat is, in its way, a wonderful gift.)

The sun fingered down through the tree branches. When Karen leaned toward Sam, light spangled the tips of her hair. All the dozy, sunny, lazy happiness was making me feel a surge of generosity toward Karen, toward all these moms I knew. How I loved them in that weird moment! These women whom I had, if not loved, at least seen a lot of all summer; who had known my children, if not well, for their whole lives, at least. How lovely it was to find these friends in the park and picnic an afternoon away—what other way could it possibly be? Why should I feel bitterly toward any other woman when we were all just doing what we could, trying to navigate the rapids of our strange new lives, exhausted from the demands on us and clawing toward how to be good mothers and wives, toward ways we could still be ourselves? I'll tell you why. Because in the next moment Karen purred something under her breath to Sam, and he laughed. I mean the special Sam laugh, the laugh I'd *thought* was special, the way he had of holding your gaze and seeing only you. She touched his arm—oh, ha-ha!—and leaned back, annoyingly well lit in the dappled shade.

It sounds like just an instant, and it was. Maybe it was the first time in a while that I'd been far enough from Sam—it took a bed-sized picnic blanket to lend you some perspective sometimes—to see him, really *see* him. It wasn't me he was in love with. It was ridiculous of me to think what he felt toward me was love at all (and only now did I realize I'd assumed all along that it was, that he couldn't live without me, that what we'd done was my fault and would break his heart forever). Cute Dad, like anyone, wanted some *attention*. He wanted to feel wanted. And who knew why Karen was all in his face like a kid with someone else's toy, but when she giggled at something he'd said, his whole self lit up—it's possible he was trying to make me jealous, but it's also possible that he had moved on already—and, fucking fuck, that was what I had been doing, too. From across the blanket, the flirty back-and-forth looked desperate and sad. It looked ridiculous. It looked *obvious*.

I flopped back on the blanket, ignoring the twig that impaled my spine. Rose crawled over and started working my hair into cornrows with her mysteriously sticky hands. I knew Laura was watching me and that Nell and Evelyn probably were, too, wondering why I would cede my flirting rights to Cute Dad so summarily. It seemed obvious that everyone knew everything, that it had been clear to everyone we knew that due to a convenient confluence of circumstances, Sam and I had found ourselves that summer just that much more susceptible to the emotional equivalent of the common cold. We wanted to be noticed. We wanted to be sexy and desirable and more than someone's spouse or parent. We wanted to be wanted, and it made us stupid.

The more I thought about it, the more I realized that I didn't even know what it was I liked about Sam. He was nice. He had lovely brown eyes. We both liked lame movies. He was available in that unavailable way. There was the thrill of the illicit. I now knew he was good in bed. So *what*? We were just like any idiots drawn to hotel-room trysts. If we'd met in a bar somewhere when we were both single, I was willing to bet my nonexistent life savings that I'd never have thought twice about him. His screenplay! His ponytail! Jesus Christ!

And poor Harry. After all, he was still alive, still a person, still my husband. Even though we hadn't spoken in months, there was this tether connecting us, and even though he was wrong to be doing whatever it was he was doing, an insistent adult voice in my head pointed out that it didn't give me permission to act badly, too. If anything, I had to be the good one, the example for our children, the moral Elmer's that would keep this scrap heap of a family together.

Oh, STOP. You really must be the most boring woman in the world, you know this? This is your LIFE, Jenny Lipkin. This is the only one!

Listen. You had your life. You threw it away. Why don't you just shut up?

Me shut up? Maybe I should have let you drown.

What kind of thing is that to say to me? I thought we were friends, kind of, a little. You are a real crab sometimes, you know that?

I had no way to explain it to her. This summer had shown me how difficult it was to go it alone, how soul-sucking. If I hadn't had the rusalka, I wouldn't have survived it. I found myself missing Harry and our old life so badly, it hurt. I could do both, I was pretty sure I could. I could be this new version of myself, making dresses, making money, happier and lighter, while also being his wife, their mother. It had to be possible. Didn't it? Couldn't it? I ignored the rusalka's rueful laugh. What cynics these spirits were.

There I lay on the ground in the forest in the city, staring into the too bright sky, listening to Sam's husky laugh. I may not have been perfect or extraordinary or even normal, but in that moment it felt okay to be lying there having my children climb all over me, their grubby fingers coiling in my hair. Had I noticed them all summer? Poor Betty and Rose had become like tiny coworkers—always there, barely known.

Betty peered curiously into my face. "What *doing*?"

"Um, I'm looking at the clouds," I told her, scooting a little ways out from under the tree's shade so that this might be true. "Looking for shapes."

"Awesome," said Betty, having obtained the word from somewhere and now happy to show it off, like a traded-for sticker. "Me, too." She lay down beside me, and we touched our heads together and stared into the largely cloudless sky. Rose inched in between us, laughing at something. "Mermaid," Betty said.

"Where?" I squinted. I didn't see the mermaid, and wonderfully, I didn't feel the rusalka. I reached out and squeezed Betty's hand. "I see a heart," I said. "All full of gooey, marshmallowy love."

"Where?" she asked.

I pointed.

twenty-two

I left the picnic without really speaking to Sam. I wasn't sure what I was supposed to say to him at this point. Maybe I should have called to say, *I'm terribly sorry for sleeping with you, but if it's all the same, let's not actually have an affair. Cool? And for what it's worth, good luck with Karen, she seems up for anything. Hey, you guys wanna go to the pool next week?* Everything was so murky here in the etiquetteless existence of the post-adultery world.

And then it happened on an ordinary whatever it was—Thursday, I think—yes, because it was after yoga and then toddler ballet (my bad little ballerina, decked out in her tutu and light-up sneakers, had been threatened with expulsion after having bitten two classmates) and a stop at the overpriced but convenient grocery store and then an overburdened schlep up the stairs with Rose squirming on my hip and Betty chanting, "SpongeBob! SpongeBob!" and me chanting, "No way, Jose, no way, Jose"—and then our grouchy next-door neighbor brushing past us on his way down and making a face as if we were a surfeit of skunks stinking our way into the building—and when I stuck the key into the lock, it opened too easily and I thought, *Shit, I left it unlocked?,* but no.

I almost didn't recognize him, froze, heart racing. The rusalka—I'd forgotten about her for a minute—surged like adrenaline. *My God. Are you kidding me? Jenny, whatever he says, don't listen. No excuse could excuse this.* She made good points, that spectral friend of mine, I was just getting tired of hearing them. *I mean it now, mermaid. Go away.*

I needed to think. I needed to think a thought of my own. A thought like: *Harry? But I'm not ready yet.* Because there he was, husband of mine, sitting at the kitchen table, his back to the door, his newly unfamiliar shoulder blades working beneath his T-shirt like vestigial wing bones. He was fingering a length of silk chiffon, and I had to stifle my instinct to scream, *Put that down! I need that for a skirt!*

He stood up and turned around. I had expected some big reveal here, a half-burned face, a missing eye. I think I was hoping for a bedraggled knight home from the Crusades, or a virtuous youngest son who had completed his trials and proved his worth to the witch. But he looked, when he warily met my eyes, the same as always. A little tired, maybe, but the same, as if a rough night at the track had passed and not an entire summer. All the tender thoughts I'd been having for him in the wake of sleeping with Sam, talking to Sarah, all the guilty daydreams about how I would do anything to restore our sweetly nuclear family, leaked out of me in some psychic water-breaking. I wanted to kill him.

Betty, as if channeling my rage, collapsed onto the floor in an instantly top-velocity tantrum. "NO DADDY! NO DADDY! NO DADDY!"

Harry raised his eyebrows at me. I was not conscious of making any expression at all. I stroked Rose's back proprietarily. She craned her neck with mild interest toward the newcomer. It broke my heart to think that even though she would never remember it, on some cellular level Rose had already lost her father, had absorbed his absence as she grew.

And then there was Betty, a dervish of tears, showing off how her tantrumming skills had improved in the past few months. Betty, who had been clutching Harry's black comb as a talisman, sleeping with it tucked beneath her pillow like a warning to any errant tooth fairies. Betty, who had (I couldn't have recognized this only now, could I?) transformed in response to his absence, who'd gone from a typical happy-go-lucky if mischievous two-year-old to a glowering menace who attacked other children. Betty, who had taken to responding to everything I said with a charming "Go away, Mommy"—this Betty now clung to my leg, her face shiny from crying-fit snot, screaming, "That's not Daddy! Not my daddy! I want Mommy!"

I knelt down and squished her against a corner of my chest not occupied by the baby. "Shhhhh" was all I could think to say. "Shhhhhh." I was not in the least bit happy to see my child so heartbroken and confused and sad—I'm not *that* bad—but I admit that a part of me smirked. *So there, Harry. You thought you could just drop back into our lives like nothing happened? What did you think, we'd throw you a welcome-home parade? Of course Betty hates you right now. We all do.*

Even so, I experienced an unwelcome flicker of sympathy for the man who stood there with his arms futilely outstretched, his mouth open. He obviously couldn't figure out what to say or do, and he seemed to just now realize what he had broken by leaving the way he did. I knew he wanted to step back into his family, to collect the ecstatic post-work greeting to which he had become accustomed, to be the revered relief pitcher who swooped in each evening and made everything okay again. Every time he stepped forward, Betty flinched, as if being approached by a noisy birthday-party clown, and howled louder.

We moved the scream show into the living room, and within a few minutes I'd somehow calmed her down, and sooner than I would have expected, she was even smiling. Then Harry said, "I have something for you in my suitcase, half-pint." The tiny traitor lit up, having forgiven, for the moment, everything. Kids.

"I want it! I want it!" Betty did her best impression of a pogo stick while Harry presented her with an elaborate baby doll. She shrieked, "It pees! Mommy, the dolly PEES!"

"Is that so," I said, trying to stop Harry's heart with my glare. It didn't work. I tried harder. I watched Harry whirl Betty around in the air, now that she was allowing him to touch her, kissing her cheeks and smoothing her dark curls. "I missed you," he said into her scalp, looking over her at me.

I raised my eyebrows. "I hope you brought me something better than that," I said, nodding toward the doll.

He smiled apologetically, the expression of someone who'd forgotten to pick up milk on the way home. Or cigarettes. "I didn't."

I was seething. In all the time he'd been gone, all the times I'd imagined how or when he might return, I had never decided what I would say to him, and now that he was here, finally really actually here, I wanted not, as I would have guessed, as I had imagined so many times, to beat at his chest and scream at him and demand an explanation, but to cry, to collapse into his arms and cry. This too was his fault. Everything was his fault.

Harry stood up, Betty's legs slung around his waist, her body pressed to his chest like a pink polka-dotted shield. "Jenny," he said finally. "You're looking well."

"You think?" I was trembling all over, I couldn't help it, and I released Rose onto the rug. She sat there blinking at Harry and smiled, showing off her big hillbilly tooth. "Surely you remember the baby?" I said over my shoulder as I hung up the diaper bag and tossed a couple of rattly plush toys toward Rose.

Harry looked genuinely wounded. He gently let Betty down and got onto all fours, crawling toward Rose, who giggled and swatted her hands, doughy as tiny pork buns. "Rosie, my sweet," he murmured, nestling his nose into her belly before scooping her up. She squealed in panic, tensing her back into a feline arch.

"She doesn't let strangers hold her," I said.

"Jenny," Harry said as I took her from him.

Betty smashed a rag doll into his face. "Don't wook at her! Wook at me! This is my dolly her name is Samantha I named her after Sam"—I winced—"and Emma broke her arm and she got a dolly named Dolly and there is a new slide at the playground and Gwamma got a swing set at her house and—"

"Go wash up for dinner," I interrupted. I put Rose down again and went into the kitchen, shoved my fabric off the table to the floor, started flooding a large pot with water, taking a package of spaghetti from the cabinet and slamming it onto the counter. "Will you be joining us?" I said to Harry.

Rose was touching his face like a blind man. He looked up, his eyes sagging gruesomely from her tugging. "If I'm welcome."

If he was welcome! As if I'd kicked him out, as if he'd been trying to come back all along. I slammed a jar of spaghetti sauce onto the counter. A crack shot up the side. Good. I wanted to break everything in sight, dissolve into a true toddlery tantrum. My kind and gentle family-oriented thoughts from the picnic revealed themselves to be the mental ramblings of an idiot. Now that he was back, I hated his fucking guts. Excuse me, but he was not allowed to do that! Just take off because he needed some time to himself? Didn't he think I wanted some time to myself now and then? Would I ever disappear for months at a time? I'd poison his dinner, I decided. I'd stab him in his sleep.

"Come on, Bets," he said, taking Betty into the bathroom. "Mommy said time to wash up." I could hear them playing in the sink, splashing water around, Betty continuing to ramble on. I looked at Rose, who was about to topple over—how would he know she wasn't that steady at sitting? How would he know anything about any of us? Even if he'd been here all along, I thought bitterly, scooping up Rose and slipping her into the high chair, he wouldn't know anything about us at all. Anything about me.

My phone buzzed in my jeans pocket. I handed Rose a wooden spoon and turned toward the stove, taking my phone out to check the text. "Need to see you. Told J I'm going to the gym at 8." Sam. *Don't cry,* I warned myself.

Reading his text there in my kitchen, with normal happy family sounds restored to the apartment, hearing Betty giggle and protest, "DADdy!" I felt as if I'd encountered a movie star on the street, and I realized that without the makeup and the lights and costume, the star's beauty vanished, she was just a normal person with bad skin and goofy sunglasses. What the *fuck*. I couldn't imagine what I could have been thinking. Sam? Cute Dad? And me? Really? That would be something you could never take back, something that would change our lives, certainly his life, maybe the lives of our whole neighborhood, our spouses, our children, and for what? For a moment or two of feeling slightly better than we did before?

My eyes brimmed hotly as I tapped out a message with my thumbs: "Don't come. I'll explain later." Apparently Sam had not gotten my psychic message that we were through. I was aware that Harry was standing behind me but that we were still in the sort of wonderful, terrible in-betweenness, like when you're driving across state lines and find yourself in between a "Thanks for visiting" and a "Welcome to" and picture your car traversing the map's black line, and that he couldn't yet ask whom I was texting, that I didn't yet owe him even the mildest of civility. We were strangers; he was a dinner guest at a single mom's apartment. By the next night, if he managed to stay that long, everything would be different. We'd be stiff with each other, a little sore, like human scabs, but by then we would be beginning to know whether we were a married couple or not. Maybe after the girls were in bed, he would tell me he wanted a divorce. Maybe I would tell him I wanted one. Maybe I would kick him out, tell him never to come back. I muttered the word "divorcée" in my head, trying it on for size. What an interesting thought. "My ex-husband." Huh.

But for now we had to get through dinner and put the kids to bed so that we could talk. I thought of Sarah and John shouting their plans for divorce at Max above the Chuck E. Cheese's din. I'd never called to find out how it went.

As much as I wanted to hear whatever it was Harry was going to say to defend himself, and as curious as I was to find out just where he had been, how he would explain this one, whether we'd come out winners or losers, at the same time, it was a relief to be quietly traveling through the black line. I bit my lip a little too hard.

"What is Rosie eating these days?" Harry said, pulling up a chair.

My chest twanged like a banjo string. "Ah, yes," I said, "how would you know? Well, *dear,* there is a jar of sweet potatoes in the cabinet. She's been eating solids for a couple of months. Her first was rice cereal. She liked it."

"Jenny," he said softly. He looked pained. There was some small satisfaction in knowing it hurt him to realize how much he'd missed.

I whirled around, the pasta scoop in my hand. "Yes?" Betty was perched on her booster seat, studying us. I smiled, thinking of gorillas bearing their teeth in anger. "Betty, sweetheart, would you like milk or water?"

Betty cocked her head at her daddy. "Juuuuuuicy?"

"No," I said quickly. "Just because your father's home doesn't mean all hell can break loose. We still have some laws in this land." Hell. Oops. It would be fun to hear that one get repeated in some public setting.

Harry popped open the baby-food jar and started spooning it into Rose's mouth. I wordlessly slipped a bib on her, glaring at him over her head. Instead of calming down throughout dinner, I managed to get angrier and angrier, my heart racing like in a near-miss car accident. My voice tasted sour in my mouth. Every time he attempted to ask a question, my answers got snippier and snippier—"Yeah, I've been sewing a lot. What did you imagine I was doing this whole time? Catching up on *American Idol*?"—until he stopped asking, looking chastened. At least that was something. It made me feel mean to acknowledge it, but it was true: I wanted him to seem unhappy. And I wanted him to think that I was fine, just fine, that everything had been just fine. Fun, even! Great! Never been better! Wait, no—I wanted him to think we had suffered, to know that he had damaged his family, that he had dissolved my trust. Wait. I guess I didn't know what I wanted.

Betty demanded the Total Daddy Treatment all night, ordering him to bathe her and showing off her new rubber ducky—"From Sam!" she crowed, and again I cringed, listening from the hallway. I nursed Rose to sleep and deposited her gently into her crib, while Betty melted into Harry's arms as he whispered her bedtime stories. Aliens could have sliced open our building like a dollhouse to study our behavior, and even their advanced, space-travel-capable brains would have seen only a happy family, a sweet bedtime scene. I wanted to cry. I did cry.

By the time Harry tiptoed out of the girls' bedroom, easing the door shut, I had already cleaned up after dinner and was sitting on the couch slugging down the wine I'd bought for—dear God, it felt beyond pathetic, remembering how, as I'd selected it, I'd hummed Betty's favorite princess song, "I know you, you danced with me once upon a dream"—me and Sam. I closed my eyes. I could almost feel him, almost taste him. Sam, I mean. Or maybe Harry. I opened one eye, like a timid woodland creature. "Oh," I said. "It's you."

He smiled as if he got the joke. He perched on the far end of the couch, cautiously, as if I might bite. Which I might have. I handed him my juice glass of wine. He took a hearty gulp, looked around. "So," he said.

I was almost able, in that moment, to see him the way I once saw him. It was weird to imagine that I was meeting him for the first time. Maybe I was. It had always been a problem, how fucking good-looking he was. It had always meant he'd gotten away with a lot. He had precise, pointed features—the beaky nose that Betty had inherited, Rose's sharp chin—and mocking almond-shaped eyes. He had great hair. He really did. It was thick and bristly and stuck up in the front, effortlessly cute, like a little boy's. He had gotten it cut since he'd been gone. If I tried to imagine how this had happened—a foreign barber, a tender woman—I would fall apart completely. So I didn't. I thought about Sam's hair and the wild way it framed his face when it came out of its ponytail, the lion's mane of curls, extravagantly threaded with red and gold, heroine hair, far too pretty for a man.

"So," said Harry, when neither of us had spoken in a while. I sucked down some more wine, feeling its warmth eke throughout my limbs. "Where's the dog?"

I stared at him. "The *dog*?"

He looked around the room, held out his palms as if testing for rain, and looked at me again. "Yeah. Where is she?"

I collapsed back into the couch and rubbed my face. "Where is the *dog,* Harry? You go out for cigarettes and come back *months* later with no word, no note, no calls, one measly postcard—you let me and your mother and your brother worry ourselves sick, not knowing if you're *dead* or *what,* you asshole, you miss *half* of your baby's entire *life,* you steal money from the company, which has gone bankrupt in case you hadn't heard, and then you just reappear one day and that's what you have to say for yourself? Where is the goddamn *dog*?" I was getting loud, despite my efforts. He looked stricken. He was struggling to be the new Harry, I could tell—swallowing a tide of rage, resisting the urge to make a bitchy remark that would send everything spinning into argument.

"You didn't— Just tell me you didn't put her down." Harry raked his hands through his hair. He was the only person I'd ever met who actually made his hair look better like this, by accident. I poured another glass of wine. A bad idea, I knew, but I'd been sort of into bad ideas lately.

"Harry. Are you really more concerned with the dog's well-being than your family business going bankrupt? Did you hear that part? Your family going broke? You and I have some things to sort out. We need to *talk,* my friend. You tell me where on God's green fucking earth you have been, and then I will tell you what's become of that half-witted mutt. Deal?" I was pointing my finger at his chest like an angry Uncle Sam. The wine did nothing to soothe my thumping heart. My phone vibrated in my pocket again. I ached to read the text. Part of me hoped Sam hadn't gotten my message, that he would burst through the door and gather me into his arms, just so I could see the look on Harry's face.

Harry knitted his brow. "I understand. You deserve that, you do, of course you do. But it's a really long story." He tried to gather my hand into his. I jerked it away, sloshing my cup, and stood up.

"Don't touch me," I said.

"Okay."

"Talk."

He sighed. "Okay."

What followed, I am sorry to report, was not especially satisfying. He'd never meant to stay away so long. He never would have done that to me and the girls and his mother. Except that he did. Yadda yadda yadda. It had started, as we'd all suspected, as just another gambling binge. Yes, he took company money. Yes, he took his overnight bag. He went to Atlantic City. He drank too much and played a lot of poker. "I don't know if I've ever really tried to explain it to you, but Jenny, it's so weird, this thing that happens to me. I feel like I'm in control for once. And it's exciting. People—when you're winning—they gather around and cheer and want to be a part of it. You're a rock star. You're on top of the world. Strangers are suddenly your pals. It's a different world from, you know, the office, boring life—"

"Your wife and kids," I supplied. I was getting impatient and annoyed that my anger was dissipating, that soon I would be feeling sympathetic—he did seem so *sad*—and the months of saved-up anger would no longer be useful to me. "Harry, you disappeared. You deserted me. I have been alone with two babies all summer! And it's been so fucking *hot*! I've been going *crazy*! I didn't know how we were going to pay all our bills, or what to tell people, or what to tell Betty or myself. I didn't know if my girls would ever have a father again. For all I knew, you could have been dead! Or with some other woman!"

"I would never," he protested too quickly. "I swear to you, there's no one else. I know this must be hard for you, believe me, I— Jenny, will you at least sit down?" His words sounded stilted, as if he'd memorized what a decent human being might say. It was annoying that he didn't seem to have considered the possibility that I'd been with another man. I felt perversely proud of my secret, of how bad I had been, of how shocked he would be, how hurt.

I shook my head, backing away. "Just—talk. Just talk."

He stared at his hands while he told me the whole nonstory. He'd been feeling cooped up and irritable and like he was going to bust. As usual. I couldn't help it, burst out, "Oh! And I'd been feeling like the bee's knees! Because having two little kids and no money is supposed to be a fucking walk in the park, everyone knows that! You know what I do when I'm feeling cooped up, Harry? I take a goddamn bath. I do some goddamn yoga." He let me finish, apologized again, took a deep breath, and continued. He'd gone to the tables. He'd lost. Then he'd won. Then he'd won big. Then he'd lost big. Bigger. Really big. And then he was too ashamed to come home.

"Jesus Christ!" I sputtered. "That would have been a lot better than just disappearing, don't you think? Disappointing me a little?"

But he had disappointed himself. And he'd driven from Atlantic City, indebted, broke, broken, discouraged, really discouraged, seriously discouraged, suicidally discouraged. Thinking we would all be better off without him. Getting all *It's a Wonderful Life,* minus the guardian angel. He needed to get better, to be a better person, before he could face me and the girls again. And so he drove on, out into the dessert, on some sort of freaking vision quest, where he had a spiritual epiphany while hiking on the red rocks in Sedona, Arizona—

"Are you kidding?" I had to interrupt again. "Who *are* you? Did you wear crystals and feathers, too? And talk to the spirit of a long-dead Indian chief? Harry, it's just not fair. Parents don't have time for vision quests. Parents have to suck it up and hang in there until college, or at least pre-K. What the *fuck,* man?" The look on his face was enough to shut me up, or it should have been. "Okay, okay, I'm sorry. Continue." But I couldn't help it—I'd had too much wine—and when he confessed the power that the mountain's energy vortexes had held over him, I snorted with laughter.

Unexpectedly, he smiled. "I know how it sounds." Something flickered across his face. A hint of the old Harry. He was trying. He really, really was.

"It sounds bonkers, Harry," I said between sobs of laughter. "It sounds *stupid.*" I held a hand out, as if to provide a "stop" signal for my hysteria. "I'm sorry, I just—vortexes?"

Harry chuckled. "I *know*! I know. I would have said the same thing a few months ago." Laughing together opened something up between us, exercised my muscle memory, made us feel suddenly like a husband and a wife again. Vortexes! Wait, vortices! "Okay, okay, so what was this epiphany?"

"Don't make fun of me," he said sheepishly. "It's hard to talk about."

"She's at Fred's," I said. "Juniper. Is at Fred and Cynthia's. She's brought them back together, if you can believe it."

Harry looked relieved, and thanked me for telling him, and continued. So he'd realized that, duh, he needed to stop gambling, that he would lose everything, that maybe he already had, and that there were programs that would help this happen, and that he'd always thought rehab programs were total jokes, and that gambling wasn't *like that,* but then again maybe it was, and so he found one and admitted himself and stayed there until they pronounced him healed. And then he had come back. And here he was.

"Mm-hmm," I said. "And here you are." I got up, paused to ride out a bout of light-headedness, and went to the kitchen, where I poured myself a glass of water and stood on one leg like a stork and drank it.

"I know that's not all you have to say," Harry said after a minute.

"Mm," I said, shaking my head and holding out a hand, like I was too terribly busy sipping this water to respond just yet. I rummaged around in the cabinet, returned to the couch with a sleeve of saltines, sat down, spent a long time opening the crinkly plastic, ate a cracker, chewed it until it turned to paste, then swallowed. When I looked up, Harry was peering into my face. "Mm, you're right. It's not," I said finally. I ate another cracker. Chew, chew, chew, chew. Swallow. Like a meditation. Chew. Chew. Chew. "Well, hmm. So, how did you pay for the rehab?"

"Oh. This is going to sound bad."

"You won money playing poker."

"Yes. At an Indian casino."

"Oh, wow. That's what they call irony, my friend. And they didn't need to contact your family? You didn't need to apologize in the whole twelve-step thingy? That wasn't part of the whole deal at the rehab place? You didn't think, 'You know, I'll just call the wife, let her know what's going on. I'll shoot my mother an e-mail. I could take a sec to text my brother.' Nothing like that occurred to you?"

"Ah. No. I mean, it did. I just—couldn't."

I held up a cracker to my face, looking at my husband through one of the salty peepholes. "Is that so?" I paused. His eyes flickered around the room. "No more lies. Just give me that much." I took the cracker away from myself and picked a fleck of salt off the small bland pane.

"I told them I didn't have any. Family. At the rehab place."

"Nice."

"No, I know it wasn't right, but I didn't want to talk about it. About you. And, well—I made this deal with myself. I was going to get better, get ahold of myself, and I wasn't going to bother you until I was better."

I aimed a saltine at his neck. "How noble! You know, it would have been no bother at all. 'Hey, you know, I'm doing this thing, I'll be back in September, don't worry.' Would that have been so difficult?" I hurled the cracker, a tiny, savory Frisbee. I could see the headlines now. KILLED IN FREAK CRACKER ACCIDENT, HARRY LIPKIN, 40. "How was your birthday?"

"Oh." Harry looked embarrassed. "Fine. They had cake. At the place."

"You told them your birthday? Not about your family but about your birthday?"

"It's hard to explain, Jenny."

"You don't even like cake."

"Okay, it's impossible to explain. I understand. And I want you to know, I understand if you want nothing to do with me anymore. I do. I'll go spend the night at my mother's or something. I'll leave you alone. I just— I just wanted to come back to you better. Healed. And if I didn't think I could be better, I wanted to not come back. To disappear. I was—I am—so ashamed. All the times I've lost money or taken off. I thought you would all be better off without me." Then he did the least Harry-ish thing I'd ever seen him do. He buried his face in his hands. I reached out and, from old habit, patted his back.

"I wish I could say I didn't understand," I told him. "But the thing is? Actually? I do."

I never got to have a satisfying shouting fit. I never got to make Harry fall onto his knees and beg my forgiveness. It was not how I would have imagined his homecoming. I would never have thought I'd feel, after a few hours, a belated surge of wifely relief that he was okay, that he was alive, that he was back. It didn't mean I was making room for his stuff in the closet, but it did mean I could focus my emotions. Now I could be angry or forgiving; I could self-consciously style my response to what had happened. At least it had stopped happening; the unknowns were back to being the same old unknowns. Believe me, had the rusalka been running the shop, she would have been pissed, churning around inside of me, wailing, *Nonononono! Make him paaaaaayyyyyy!* Harry and I drank some more wine, and I filled him in on what the girls had been up to, some of it, and around eleven I told him he could sleep on the couch. He was acting so . . . *nice.* I was across the room, heading for bed, when he stood up. "Jenny," he said. The way he said my boring old name, it sounded as rare and precious as a foreign coin. He had grown thin, I noticed. "Can I hug you? I—I've really missed you."

"I don't think so," I said. My voice broke. "You know, Harry, I died for you."

He looked, unsurprisingly, surprised. "What?"

"I died for you." I sat down in the middle of the floor. It felt good to say it aloud, to be able to admit the truth. He eased off the couch and sat down next to me. We sat there for a while without touching. I hefted Rose's tooth-marked rattle in one hand, Betty's balding princess doll in the other, to help me keep my balance. "I don't mean, like, metaphorically, in case that's what you're thinking."

Now it was his turn to say, "Hmm," and I heard in the murmured syllable a hint of the old condescending Harry. I sucked in a deep breath. "I jumped off the Brooklyn Bridge. I did. I thought about doing it, and then I turned around and saw my shoes and I didn't want to leave them, and I didn't want to leave my life, you know, I changed my mind, but I tripped and fell, and then I drowned." I couldn't tell him the whole story. I wasn't sure I could ever tell anyone the whole story. Not even my sister, who believed in fortune-tellers and that kind of wacky shit, not even my college roommate who had claimed to be a witch. A mermaid. A possession. It wasn't the kind of thing you said out loud. "I mean, I went in the water, and I almost drowned. But I didn't. I survived. It was a miracle, it really was, and— Well, I just haven't been the same since. So you should know that."

Harry knitted his brow, again reached for my hand. I got up as if it were important to put away the children's toys right at that moment, and I moved around the room gathering friendly hunks of chiming plastic, feeling Harry's stare. "Are you serious?" He was going to say something else but swallowed and started again. "You seriously jumped?"

"I fell," I corrected him. "I think. You know, I don't even know if this is really Betty's book. I think it might be Emma's." The grinning fairies didn't look that familiar.

Harry paused for a long time, considering. He had just been telling me about his vision quest. It was hard to say whose story was less likely.

"Are you making fun of me?" he finally said.

"Excuse me?" I held an orphaned jigsaw piece in the air, looking for its puzzle. "You know, I haven't told anyone about what happened, and now I confide in you, and look how sympathetic you are. Really nice. Do you understand what I am telling you?"

"I just mean— Jenny. I would have heard about something like this. Everyone would have heard about it." He was saying it gently, he was.

"What's that supposed to mean?"

"It's a big story when someone jumps off the bridge and survives. It's in the news. You would have been fished out by the Coast Guard. You would have been interviewed by that awkward guy from NY1. You would have been on the cover of the *Post* with some awful punny headline. 'Fish Tale.' 'Real-Life Mermaid.' 'A Watery Save.'"

"I like that last one. That's a good one."

"I know it was awful, what I did. I know you must have hated me. You must hate me now. But don't make up stories."

"Make up stories? What am I, three years old? Harry, I am telling you the truth. I died that day."

He stood up and grabbed me by the arms. It was all very Clark Gable as Rhett Butler. I closed my eyes. *Sam would never do this. Sam is gentle. Sam is so—* "Look at me," Harry was saying. There he was, the furious old Harry, the violence in him that had, let's admit it, drawn me to him. The Harry who got rough during sex, the Harry who was full of passion. I remembered, out of nowhere, an old friend of his saying upon meeting me, "So here's the girl who tamed Harry Lipkin." Who were we kidding, he hadn't been tamed, but the idea of someone who needed to be tamed had lit a flare beneath my breastbone, between my legs, and something about the way he grabbed me, the fire in his eyes, it woke up a long-dormant part of me, a hibernating sliver of the old Jenny, the really old Jenny, the pre-marriage-and-kids Jenny, as if I had received a letter from the girl from Minnesota who listened to sad music and dreamed of big-city romance. "Jenny, look at me," Harry hissed again. "You're scaring me now. Tell me the truth."

"I am. I died," I said, and hearing my blubbery voice was the first clue that I was crying. It was a good cry, a deep-tissue-release cry, the kind of cry I'd heard of happening when people got intense massages. It came from my muscles, released like a scent. "I did. I'm not lying. I remember it."

"You said you would never think about it again. You promised—"

Crying loosened something within and made it hard to keep the reins on her. She shoved her way to the surface, propping my mouth open like a puppet's: "What? I promised I wouldn't think about suicide anymore? What about you? How could you leave me alone with the children? How could you trust someone like me? You made a mistake, Harry. You were thinking of yourself, and you should have been thinking of us."

He released me, as if slapped. "I *was* thinking of you."

"You knew I had to go off my depression meds while I was nursing Rose." There. I had said it. I collapsed onto the couch, tears gone. I felt as dried out as an autumn leaf. Harry studied his hands, finally speechless.

"Do you have any idea how hard it has been for me? No pills, all those insane pregnancy and nursing hormones? You didn't think abandoning us would be upsetting to me? You weren't at all worried that I might—"

Harry knelt on the floor before me. The supplicant posture infuriated me. He had never even properly proposed! My brain piled up protests. "Listen. I— What I did wasn't right. I know it wasn't. But I knew I could trust you with the children. You're a great mother, Jenny. You're a perfect mother. You are. And I knew that you wouldn't hurt them or yourself."

But he was wrong. Because I had. I had tried to hurt myself. And if it hadn't been for the rusalka inhabiting my body, whispering ideas for coping, helping me along step by step, if it hadn't been for Sam, who knew what might have happened? "I think—" I started, and then cleared my throat, "I think you should spend the night at your mother's."

Harry studied me. Had I even remembered him correctly? It occurred to me that in the months he'd been gone, I'd remembered all the bad times, all of his flaws, conveniently leaving out the things about him that I loved, and only now that he was here, when I should have been most furious, did it all come flooding back. I loved him. Fuck. I did, I loved him. What a stupid brain I had.

What a stupid heart. He stood up. "I understand," he said. "I really do. Thank you for talking to me. Thank you for letting me stay for dinner. I really— I missed the girls so much. I know how that sounds, but I did."

"That's nice." I poured the last dregs of wine into the cup. I was thirsty.

"Can I see you again?"

"I don't know. Maybe. Maybe not. I'll think about it."

"Can I call tomorrow?"

"I guess you'd better. Betty will want to see you."

Harry paused before leaving. "Jenny?"

"Hmm?"

"I—I'm sorry."

"I know," I said. I didn't look at him. Then I said, "Harry?" I could smell the hope wafting off of him. He stood stock-still.

"Yes?"

"Did you ever get those cigarettes?"

"Oh. Nope."

In a moment the door closed.

twenty-three

It was as though every few minutes I was waking up, and every waking was accompanied by a throat-lumpy thud, a dull gut-sinking. I was pregnant with pain, like a third baby.

I thought of a notebook I'd kept as a child, full of floor plans and sketches of my future home. I was going to live in a huge Victorian house on a wooded lot with a creek and a rope swing. I snipped furniture out of catalogs. Back then my tastes tended toward the romantic, with a heaping helping of batty old lady: lots of fat chintz sofas and grand pianos and crushed velvet curtains. I was going to have three children—they existed in the notebooks as a girl, a boy, and a sexless eternal baby—and we were all going to sing together every night while my husband played the piano. But people were only hazy presences in this imagined life. It was mostly about the beautiful house, the sense of peace. There was a weeping willow and a field of daffodils in the spring. Actually, it was always spring. I would have a pack of tame cats that followed me across the meadow. Life was nothing like that. I'd known this for a while.

Nor was I living the life I'd expected when I moved to New York, thinking I'd finally found my place. I did not breeze from pitch meeting to Midtown lunch date and then home to cook the dinner

I'd prepped in the morning; I did not have the sexy marriage that was the envy of my friends; I did not have a haircut that flattered my face; I did not have ingeniously organized shelves; I did not have a perfect black dress. I didn't have a perfect anything. Just me, still the same Jenny I'd always been, transplanted to Brooklyn in the hopes that some coolness or something would soak in by osmosis, propped into some fancy shoes and hoping for the best. I hadn't even been able to have a torrid affair the way modern people were supposed to. Ugh. Life.

Over the next few days, I let Harry visit the girls in tense, supervised living room playdates—Betty was overjoyed, more like her old bubbly self and less like her recent tantrummy *Exorcist* incarnation—but we never had any sort of adult conversation. Maybe we were just never going to talk about it. Maybe we would never speak to each other again, never meet each other's eyes except by accident. Maybe this was how a long marriage worked.

All week Sylvia kept her distance from me, as if Harry's return had eliminated the need for the two of us to speak directly, as if it would be a relief for us to revert to our previous chilly coexistence. Then on Friday she showed up unannounced around nine a.m. When I answered the door, she threw her hands up as if in surrender. "I don't even know what to say," she said.

"Me, neither," I said.

"He looks tired."

"Yes."

She shrugged, eyes wide, as if we were commiserating about just another hapless husband mishap, putting the baby's diaper on backward, maybe, or sending an anniversary card on Mother's Day. How silly men were! Despite everything, I was happy to see her. "I hope you're here to babysit," I said. Then, because that sounded so demanding, I added, "The girls really miss you."

"I'm here," she said. "I'd like to see the girls. You do what you want. I guess you probably have errands or something." But what I really, really had to do was to go over to Laura's.

I hadn't spoken to Laura since Harry's return, hadn't seen her since the Sam-and-Karen picnic. It wasn't until I was on my way to her building that I realized how much I'd missed her, how I couldn't wait to see her, as if I'd just returned from some long voyage alone.

I strode past an office's reflective windows, experienced the dislocating jolt of seeing a familiar-seeming lady only to realize it was me. I'd gotten lean from my summer of wandering around in the heat and never cooking grown-up dinners. I could feel that I was stronger and quicker, and I had the strange impression as I trotted along that, left alone, I had begun to transform into some sort of sinewy forest animal. I found myself moving faster and faster. Past the bar and grill that had once been our fallback married-person-date-night locale, past the bakery where Sam and I had flirted so laboriously, past the coffee shop where, in another life, Laura and I had met to soak in the air-conditioning. There was a picture book Betty loved in which the illustrations were made from mosaics of tissue paper and newsprint, and as I hurried through the familiar streets, they, too, seemed composed of translucent layers—scraps of narratives, remembered images—gummed together to create a whole.

Laura looked surprised to see me—I hadn't called first, knowing I was intersecting with the nap time of organized Emma (who had finally gotten her pink cast off) and so would find them at home—but she welcomed me in with a hug so ferocious, I knew I must have looked aggrieved. "Come in, come in," she said, presenting me with an iced coffee and a chilled dish of raspberries before I could even catch my breath. We sat at her dining room table, where a mason jar of sunny ranunculus held court amid a gathering of puzzle pieces. I pressed my hands to the sides of the jar, hoping the goodness of the flowers could heal me.

"So he's back!" she said, taking obvious pains to sound casual.

I nodded. "What am I going to do?" It wasn't what I'd meant to say.

"What do you mean?"

"I don't even know. Do I take him back? He's such a shit." I plucked an ice cube from my coffee and watched it melt in my palm.

"What did he have to say for himself?"

I bridled at the question, indefensibly defensive. "It's a long story. You know, he was troubled." I explained as simply as I could.

"How do you feel? What do you want to do?" she asked.

"I want none of this to ever have happened," I said. "I want us to be different people."

Laura smiled. "Listen, I love you. I just want to help."

"I know," I said, unable to say any more.

"Can I ask you something?"

"Oh, dear. What."

"Cute Dad?"

It was funny to hear our old nickname for him. I missed the days at the beginning of the summer when he was just plain Cute Dad, without all the fret and complication of a real person. What a drag people were, in reality. So . . . real. I shook my head. "Yeah. I don't really want to talk about it. It was bad. I mean, it was good, but in a bad way. We— It went too far. Just—yeah. It was a big mistake."

"Okay."

"And it's all over now."

"Okay."

"I think he's putting the moves on Karen, actually. Who knew he was such a predator? He seemed so innocent!"

Laura allowed a tiny checkmark of a smile. "I think he's just flirty. I mean, that's always been my impression."

"God. I feel so stupid. I just really feel so stupid."

She stood up. "Can I play something for you?" She went into the other room to get her laptop. We pulled our chairs closer together to huddle in front of the computer screen, like old-timey kids excited for a radio drama.

"I was wondering if you were ever going to play me your midnight recordings," I said. "You secretive thing."

"Me, secretive? Ha. Here, I think it's . . . here?"

The part she wanted to play for me was prefaced by a nutty old man mumbling about how there was a conspiracy between all the bisexuals and the squirrels and you could tell because of the bisexuals' hairstyles, or something like that. The bisexuals! As if they were an organized force, sexual communists or something. He sounded terribly, terribly sad, and confused, and angry over his nonsensical theory, angry at himself, maybe. It brought to mind my first months in the city, when, like every newcomer, I'd marveled at the gnomic wisdom of subway ramblers and proselytizing hobos, wondering why everyone else was ignoring them. What a smaller New York I inhabited now.

But the next voice on the recording was familiar, so familiar it might have been my own. He didn't say his name, none of the speakers did. I couldn't look at Laura. She didn't say anything, just let it play. Of course he'd been having trouble sleeping. It was a weird thing to hear his voice without him. It sounded lower than in person, or maybe he'd been tired. Or drunk. Or trying to be discreet. "Something's been weighing on my mind," he was saying. "And I can't sleep. So I come here and eat donuts and drink coffee.

I don't know what my problem is! It's like I'm on a mission to never sleep again."

I could hear the recording Laura ask a question softly. Sam took a moment to answer. I pictured him sitting there at a booth, opening and closing his large hands the way he did sometimes. I didn't even know what kind of donuts he liked. Harry only liked plain, but I was willing to bet Sam went for something like strawberry iced. I swallowed the urge to ask Laura what he'd ordered.

"There's a woman I know." As he continued, I stared at the screen's EKG-like zigzags fluctuating with his vocal patterns and imagined it was a heart monitor tracing my own flipping, flapping muscle. "She's turning my whole life inside out. I don't know what she wants from me." He paused. "That's not quite true. Of course I do. I'm just afraid to accept, I guess, what I want from her." He paused again, and we could hear the matter-of-fact clatter of the diner in the background, spoons and coffee cups and a to-go order being screamed from cashier to cook. *No! I said CORNED BEEF! Cut in HALF!* "I don't even know if I like her that much, I guess, but who doesn't want a woman throwing herself at you, you know?" At this I felt a terrible pang, as if I'd been stabbed in the stomach. Like so many relationships, ours had been largely theoretical, based on a neediness algorithm. "I mean, I know people do this kind of thing all the time. You hear about it."

Every time he paused, the diner sounds welled up like water in a hole dug by a child on the beach. You could see how these things needed clever editing to make them listener-friendly. "But *I* don't do this kind of thing. Except that I am. And—I don't know—the more unlike-myself things I do, who is the self I'm thinking I'm unlike? Sorry. I'm not making sense. I hope my wife never hears this. She'll definitely kill me." He paused. "You know who I'm talking about." The recording Laura said, almost imperceptibly, "I do."

Laura clicked the recording off. "It goes on like that for a while."

"Oh," I said. I felt feverish. Another revelation: He was *boring*.

"I won't include it. In the documentary. But I thought you might like to hear it." She looked guilty. "I hope that didn't make you feel worse."

"I don't know what would make me feel better right now, so no harm done," I said, trying to sound lighthearted.

Emma's voice crackled over the baby monitor. I was unused to the sound—we'd never needed such a contraption in our Rubik's cube of an apartment—and jumped. "Mommmmmy," she said sleepily. "Hello, Mommmmmmyyyyyyy?"

"That's how she wakes up?" I said, watching Laura close the laptop and stow it away. "She sounds so sweet. Betty always comes out of her naps like a bag lady who thinks someone's touching her cart."

Laura reached out to touch my hand. "You're going to figure this all out, and it's going to be okay. You're a really good mom. And a really good person."

"Oh, please," I said automatically. I felt like I had when I was nine years old and my best friend informed me, awfully, that no one played with dolls anymore and that we had to stop. I didn't want anything, no grown-up responsibilities and certainly no men at all, nothing but the small world of this friendship. "Please let's change the subject," I said, my eyes welling up. "I'm about to get all *Anne of Green Gables* 'bosom friend' on you, and then we'll throw up from the saccharine, and what a mess it'll make." Then I said, trying harder, "But, uh, thanks. I mean it. Thank you." I stood up, my mind already shifting back to mother mode, tracking through the things I needed to pick up on my way home. "I should go. Give Emma a big hug for me."

"Raissssinnnnns," Emma was quietly requesting over the monitor. "Emma want some raissssinnsss."

"Hey, guess what else," Laura said before I reached the door. I turned around. "I'm pregnant."

"What! Laura! Why didn't you say that to begin with? Oh, congratulations! Oh, good, good, good." I hugged her, sure I could hear the little minnow humming inside her, sure I'd known all along.

"And I feel miserable, which my doctor said is a good sign."

"I'm so glad, Laura. I hope you continue to feel utterly miserable."

She laughed. "Me, too."

I told her to let me know what I could do to help with Emma, promised her all our baby stuff, and hugged her again. As soon as I hit the street, I called her, and when she answered, I said, "Hey, I forgot to ask you something. When we're old, want to go on a trip to Egypt with me?" She laughed. "Of course! Can we wear fanny packs?" "Future fanny packs," I said. "They will hold our future passports but also get future Internet and allow us to breathe underwater." "Done." "Okay, good. Later." "Yes."

Somehow her news made me feel like we were all going to be all right. The babies didn't care about our weird petty things. They just wanted to be born and to grow toward the light. An unaccountable happiness loosened my limbs. I stopped on the way home to buy a bright armful of blooms at the bodega, as if I could capture the feeling of lightness and make it zing around my home, reflecting off the children's crowns like the sun.

twenty-four

Somehow I got talked into a Lipkin family picnic at the end of September to celebrate, of all things, my thirty-fifth birthday. It was a perfect Indian summer, if anyone called it that anymore. The heat that had leaned against us since spring, like a tumor displacing organs, had dissolved, dissipated. Betty frolicked around the meadow, bringing us poisonous bouquets of berries, feathers, the first changed leaves. By now the baby allowed Harry to hold her, and Fred and Cynthia chased around Juniper, who miraculously minded them, though she did pause to lunch on a desiccated squirrel carcass. Sylvia presided from an unraveling folding chair at the edge of the blanket. After we'd eaten our sandwiches and watermelon slices and bean salad and pickles and the last of the Ever So Fresh candy stock, Harry and I went for a stroll along the edges of the woods and down to the boathouse. It was a day when I felt less furious at him than usual, maybe only because the weather was so nice. We walked by the lake, scummed solid with green algae that a few resigned swans mucked their way through. Harry reached out to hold my hand. For the first time since he'd been back, I let him.

It was annoying to admit to myself, but it felt good, being with Harry. I'd missed the me I was with him in our best moments.

Certainly, things would have to be different. Because I also liked the me I had unearthed—that the rusalka had dredged up—and it was weird for me to feel this way, to feel that there was a kernel of myself that was undespicable, that I was capable of life, of living, of being whole. So I didn't protest when he took me in his arms and, to the lewd hooting of a passing flock of summer-fat geese, he kissed me.

It's a curious feeling to have a second first kiss with your own husband. Though I wouldn't recommend the months of abandonment and anger and loneliness, it was a lot more exciting than the welcome-home peck on the lips we'd gotten into the habit of before he left, complete with stomach quivers and tooth clashing and flesh flushing. Everything about Harry seemed as simultaneously new and familiar as it had that first time. Maybe, in a way, it was a true first kiss. After all, I had died and come back to life and learned to live a whole new way since he'd been gone, and the new me was kissing the new him, and thankfully, since we had those kids and all our books and stuff were mixed together and everything, we fit.

You know how, in certain kinds of stories, a kiss can awaken a slumbering maiden, transform a creature into another kind of creature? I can't say I ever thought much of that sort of scene until the whole thing with Harry happened. When you think about it, the idea that pressing your mouth against someone else's mouth can be romantic, can be something your body desperately wants you to do, is weird enough—all that saliva and plaque! Then to think that by kissing this man, I could turn myself inside out? I know it's strange. But that's just what happened. What I mean to say is that I could feel the rusalka, my dear old mermaid, who in recent weeks had all but evaporated, emptying out of me like an exhale of smoke. For a moment it hurt. For a moment I was terrified, convinced that without her, I would collapse like a sleeve of snakeskin. Then, though I know this can't be true, I could have sworn I heard a watery plunk, as if something had dropped into the pond beside us.

I can only imagine she was pretty pissed once she realized what she'd done, finding herself flattened out in a shallow divot of weed-choked water, more likely to be razor-burned by paddle boats' bottoms than to encounter any fallen sailors to seduce or wanton women to inhabit. I don't imagine she ended up staying very long. No, I see her hitching a ride with some poor lost soul as far as the river, and then traveling out to sea.

Acknowledgments

My eternal thanks are due:

to the intrepid PJ Mark, Cecile Barendsma, and the whole team at Janklow & Nesbit;

to Sally Kim, my kind-hearted, big-brained visionary of an editor, from whom I've learned so much, and to her wonderful crew at Touchstone, including Allegra Ben-Amotz, Cherlynne Li, and Beth Thomas, who helped make these words into a book;

to the sagacious Jenny Geras, who really *gets* it (and not just because she's a Jenny), and the good people at PanMacmillan;

to my forever first-readers, Lauren Haldeman and Amanda Fields;

to my mom-friends, particularly Sarah Holden, font of sewing expertise; Gilly Berenson, fancy shoe consultant; and the woman at the playground who said, "I just want a book for moms like me";

to all the women who watched my children so that I could write, and especially my mother, who once flew across the country so that I could have a moment to concentrate;

to the original Jenny Lipkin, my great-grandmother, who had a ne'er-do-well husband she divorced and remarried, who supported her girls with her virtuoso sewing, and who, according to my grandmother, once had her life saved by a pair of shoes;

to my amazing children, for never being colicky, and for reminding me daily what it is to see the world with scrubbed-clean eyes;

and above all to my husband, Adam, who has supported me in every way throughout my writing life, and who has, kind soul, allowed me to sneak away from my perfect family again and again so that I could write about a disgruntled mother. The life of a writer's spouse, I imagine, is a tiring one. My apologies, and my thanks.

About the Author

Amy Shearn is the author of the novel *How Far Is the Ocean from Here*. She lives in Brooklyn with her husband and two children.

TOUCHSTONE READING GROUP GUIDE

The Mermaid of Brooklyn

FOR DISCUSSION

1. What do you think Jenny learns from her time with her mermaid? How does she change from the beginning of the novel to the end? What are her strengths and her weaknesses? How are your perceptions of these altered throughout the story?

2. How do Jenny's ideas about what constitutes a "good" or "successful" mother change from the beginning of the novel to the end? Consider the revelations she has about herself, as well as about Sylvia and her own mother.

3. Discuss Jenny's attraction to Sam, aka Cute Dad, before the rusalka comes into her life. Do you think she would've acted on her feelings if there weren't a mermaid in her head urging her to? Why or why not?

4. What do you feel Sam's motivations were in his pursuit of Jenny? Did your opinion of him shift throughout the novel? Toward the end, Laura plays Jenny Sam's diner recording. Were you surprised by anything he said?

5. After sleeping with Sam, Jenny thinks: "I'd found that people who said things like 'I have to start thinking about myself' tended to be people who were very good at thinking about themselves. And Sam and I were always saying things to each other like 'We have to think about ourselves.' Did we really? Was there anything so valuable in thinking about ourselves more than we already did, which was almost constantly?" (page 286). Do you think there is a difference between thinking

about yourself and caring for yourself? Do you think sleeping with Sam was ultimately helpful for Jenny?

6. Jenny seems to have something of a love-hate relationship with New York; though she and the other Park Slope moms complain about the unique difficulties of raising children in the city, they continue to stay. What do you think it is that keeps them from moving? Do you think they see their frustrations as something of a badge of honor? Do you find that's true in your life as well?

7. Think about all the different women who influence Jenny's life. What does she learn from each of them at various points throughout the novel?

8. There are a multitude of characters—from Jenny to Sam to Laura—in the book who are constantly struggling to appear as though their lives match this grand, group-perpetuated fantasy of what family-dom in Park Slope should feel like. How does this affect them? What does this say about the power of belonging versus our intrinsic desire to stand out? Why do you think people put such stock in appearances, when the truth is that everyone has problems, often the same ones?

9. Most fairy-tale heroines are rescued by magic in their darkest moments, just as Jenny is. But often they realize that the magic isn't enough to save them, just as Jenny does. If you could have a magic, what would you want yours to be? What would you do with the type of second chance Jenny receives?

10. At several points Jenny considers that no matter how dramatic personal problems feel, they are shared experiences, part of a larger narrative. The rusalka, too, points out that Jenny's every-

day struggles are nothing new, that "maybe if mothers had time to write, all the old epic poems would be about trips to the grocery store instead of wars" (page 113). Do you agree?

11. Laura and Jenny go from having a fun, if somewhat shallow, friendship to something much more lasting by the end of the novel. What do you think causes the shift? Does their friendship remind you of any relationships in your life?

12. Where did you think Harry had gone? Were you surprised when he returned? What do you foresee for Jenny and Harry?

13. Jenny recalls her magazine days as having a haze of perfection about them, though she knows in reality she had an equal number of frustrations then. Do you think this grass-is-greener trap is one we all fall into during difficult times in our lives? Has it ever happened to you?

14. Similarly, she also reflects (about her daily life as a stay-at-home mom): "I hated that I felt like I had to be unhappy in order for it to count as important" (page 57). What do you think about her statement? Do you feel that today we equate stress with importance and contentment with a lack of ambition? Why or why not?

15. Jenny finds that sitting down at her sewing machine is one of her only ways to find a minute of peace and express herself. For Laura, her late-night interviews offer the same type of outlet. What hobby or talent allows you to reveal yourself more clearly to others? Is there something specific about you or something you are good at that you feel draws others to you?

A CONVERSATION WITH AMY SHEARN

You note on your blog that the book is (very!) loosely based on the life of your great-grandmother. What elements did you draw from her story?

Well! My paternal great-grandmother's name was Jenny Lipkin, and she was married to a ne'er-do-well named Harry who supposedly had ties to the Chicago mob—but you didn't hear that from me. He was notorious for leaving to buy cigarettes and not coming home for months or years, which I would think would be a very annoying habit in a husband. They actually divorced once and later remarried. (When I asked my grandmother why she thought Jenny would take Harry back so many times, she shrugged and said, "She loved him." This, from the least romantic woman in the world.) Jenny and Harry had three daughters, Rose, Betty, and my grandmother May; and when Harry was gone Jenny supported the family with her sewing. According to family lore, Jenny became famous in their corner of Chicago for being able to perfectly copy department store dresses. She was also very small in stature, with tiny feet, and particularly in her later years, given to grouchiness.

Everything I know about her has been dispensed in dribs and drabs by my grandmother May, who is now in her late nineties and not much given to reminiscing about the past. About nine years ago we were shopping for shoes for my wedding and May rather casually said, "Did I ever tell you about how a pair of shoes saved my mother's life?" This was a story that only the women in the family had been told—my father had never heard it. But according to May, back when Jenny was still in the old country (some unspecified region of Lithuania) and Harry had gone to America and not yet sent for her (probably they were married, possibly she was pregnant), Jenny was feeling low. She climbed onto a bridge and considered jumping. But then she looked back and saw her shoes, a fancy pair of lace-up boots of which she was very fond. Remember that she had tiny feet and Zappos didn't exist yet, so good shoes in her size were hard to come by. Jenny thought about how she didn't want anyone to take her shoes. And then, she didn't jump.

When I asked my grandmother why Jenny considered throwing it all away, she shrugged and said, "She was depressed!"

There are other bits of family history dispersed through this novel somewhat at random, with very little attention given to chronology. For example, Ever So Fresh was a candy company run by my grandparents and great-uncle and aunt in midcentury Chicago. I just loved the name and always wanted to use it for something. It sounds so sweet and lovely, but as a child I always heard it mentioned with a shudder of bitterness—the company had long since dissolved, and had not exactly caused feelings of family togetherness.

Are there any moments in the book taken from your own life as well?
Oh, dear. Much to my (very good, decent, devoted) husband's mortification, Jenny's life on the surface does resemble mine, or at least at the time when I was writing the first drafts. When I started writing this I had a four-month-old baby. She grew and acquired a baby brother, so by the time I was doing my final revisions I had a two-year-old and a new four-month-old baby (which led to some last-minute rewriting of child-related scenes, as you can imagine). We were living in what I affectionately called "our Park Slope tenement," one of those oddly configured walk-ups in a cut-up brownstone that seems so charming until your children start moving around. Like Jenny, I found a community of parents in Park Slope that helped me deal with the weirdness of new parenthood. And like Jenny, my

background is bookish. I also worked briefly at a magazine, though I was not nearly as devoted to it as Jenny is—I was a freelance web editor and therefore kind of an interloper mostly there to spy and get book ideas. Oh, yeah, and I also have a poorly behaved mutt.

But I'd like to add that I DO NOT HAVE A CUTE DAD (that's for my husband, but it's true) and also that I was lucky not to have to deal with the issues Jenny faces, namely, depression and postpartum depression. I did know many mothers who felt adrift after the birth of their babies and who had really dark feelings they felt guilty about addressing. It seems ingrained in our culture that good mothers should be loving every moment of child rearing, and also that it should all come naturally. So in many ways when I started writing this I was talking to these freaked-out mothers I knew, and of course to me, in that 1 percent of the time when I felt totally crazy. I actually think all mothers of small children feel like Jenny does about 1 percent of the time. She just has the misfortune to feel that way 99 percent of the time.

What inspired you to add a supernatural twist to the book? Was there anything particular about mermaid mythology that fascinated you? Were there any other creatures you considered before deciding on the rusalka?

When I first heard the story of the original Jenny Lipkin and her life-saving shoes, I was in graduate school studying literature and writing. I'd been reading a lot of fairy tales for this other (now nonexistent) novel I was working on and had come across the rusalka, that menacing mermaid of Slavic lore. Somehow these two ideas mingled in my head immediately—the rusalka being the soul of a lost woman, and the Slavic Jenny Lipkin almost losing herself, maybe losing herself anyway, who was to say—but I didn't know what to do with them yet. For some reason I thought it was a personal essay. I remember going for a walk in the woods with my friend the excellent writer

Amanda Fields and telling her about it and having her say, "Shearn, that's not an essay, that's a novel," and looking up at the sky through the leaves and thinking, *Shit. She's right. But that sounds hard.*

What was your favorite fairy tale or myth growing up?

I was enraptured with Thumbelina, particularly Tasha Tudor's dreamy illustrated version of her, and really any story that involved small creatures appropriating everyday objects as beds, boats, and the like. I don't know if this counts, but for a long time I was obsessed with all the Oz books and L. Frank Baum's particular brand of witty magic. And, I'm sorry to report, I recall a sustained delight at watching the dress changing colors in Disney's *Sleeping Beauty*.

The rusalka's background remains something of a mystery. Did you imagine a story for her while you were writing? What do you think the rusalka did during the six hours Jenny can't remember?

I did. I actually wrote out her whole story and it is in an early draft, but my insightful first readers pointed out that it became distracting. I think it was important for me to know, because like anyone, the rusalka's actions are shaped by her past, but in the end I like the idea that the readers can create it for themselves if they are so inclined. I also feel that leaving it out gives readers more room to consider the possibility that the rusalka is not actually a discrete consciousness but instead a figment of Jenny's mind.

I can't reveal any of the rusalka's secrets. Mostly because I am afraid of her.

It is said that authors write themselves into their characters. Did you find this to be true? Are any of the characters in *The Mermaid of Brooklyn* based on people you know?

I'm sure, probably more than I realize. I used to love Carl Jung's idea that every character in a novel stands in for an aspect of the author's consciousness. Then I looked it up one day and realized I'd retrofitted his idea for my own purposes, and that he was actually talking about dreams. Oh, well. At any rate, while I vehemently deny that Jenny is me, I'm sure aspects of myself and other mothers I know show up in her.

Laura is kind of an amalgam of mom friends. Weirdly, after I wrote this, I had several friends mention that they'd had miscarriages, like Laura does, in between their first and second babies. (Each time I was tempted to say, "FYI, if you ever read my novel, I already put something about a miscarriage in there, but it's not yours," but somehow it just didn't seem appropriate.) I feel like this miscarriage symbolizes the many things women know and experience but don't talk about except with each other. There's this whole dark and difficult side to motherhood you don't have access to until you're in that world.

There are other people in the book who are caricatured versions of Park Slope playground archetypes; Nell, the annoyingly perfect mom; Evelyn, the hot mess; the frazzled late-middle-aged mother of an adopted Guatemalan kid; even the nannies screaming into their cell phones. I love Park Slope, I really do, but sometimes you have to poke fun. I mean, I'm fully aware that the novelist-parent is just another Park Slope type. What can you do?

This is your second novel. Was the writing process any different from that of your first book, *How Far Is the Ocean from Here*?

In some ways it was very much the same. Like most humans, I always have something time-consuming going on—with the first book it was a nine-to-five job, with this book it was motherhood—so necessarily I have a workmanlike approach to writing. I carve out some time, reserve it for writing, and use every second of that time to work, work, work. If you do this every day or every week, eventually you have a draft of something.

Besides the logistics, the main difference was probably my ideal reader. With my first book, I was fairly certain no one would ever read it and so I had this weird freedom to write something that pleased me and only me. With this book, I had a specific, if imagined, non-me reader in mind. Here's what happened: I'd just had this conversation with my wise, tells-it-like-it-is agent which had made it clear to me that it was time for the Jenny Lipkin story, which I'd been too afraid to write because it seemed so intense and dark and maybe too close for comfort (i.e., I didn't want my grandmother to be mad at me). Later that day I found myself at the playground as usual, pushing my baby on the swings. A somewhat frazzled mother I knew was talking about how she couldn't find any novels she wanted to read and also about how frightening she found parenting a baby, particularly in Brooklyn. She said she just wanted to find a book for moms like her, not glamorous rich moms who were constantly having hot sex with their gardeners or whatever, but middle-class educated women who felt a little adrift, who weren't sure if it was okay to raise kids in the city or if they were doing their families wrong by staying here. I knew I had my ideal reader. The next step was to start the book, which I did later that day (that's probably a lie, but that's how I remember it), as my baby slept in the carrier on my chest, because newborn babies are awesome.

Would you share a little about your writing methods? For example, do you plan your stories first with an outline or do they come to you as you write them? Did you know the end of the story when you first started writing, or did it evolve as you went?
I've always been one to set aside blocks of time for writing, but with this book I had even less time of my own, as in none, so I had to be more efficient. With my first book I started with an image and a character and kind of dreamily wrote my way through. This time I started

with an outline, had the end in mind, tried to write toward that end. I'm sure if you looked at the two books side by side you'd be able to tell which was written in long, uninterrupted, muse-consulting sessions by an open window in my home office and which was pounded out in frantic stolen hours in noisy coffee shops. It worked out, though—this book is quicker and leaner and more direct, I think.

That's not to say there weren't lots of revisions. There were. In an early draft that I don't even think anyone read, Betty runs away the night Harry comes home, and it's when Harry finds her and brings her home safe that Jenny realizes how much she loves him and the family needs him. I quickly deleted this, felt too much like a device: The action was being dropped onto Jenny, as usual, rather than her creating or deciding something out of her own will. I realized it was important that Jenny is thinking for herself, after all this time trying to please others or being dictated to by the rusalka. Also, as my own daughter reached the age of two, I thought, *There is no way a kid that age would get all the way down those stairs and out the door by herself.*

How has being a columnist, a blogger, and a mother affected your fiction writing? Do you ever find it difficult to wear both the mom hat and the writer hat at the same time?

Oh, of course. Besides the logistical issues, being a mother means that you have all these things to say about motherhood that aren't necessarily pleasant, but also that you want to shield your babies from all the unpleasantness in the world. A blog feels ephemeral, but with a book, you start to worry about your kids reading it someday and going, "Uh, Mom? Are you okay? Did you hate me when I was a baby?" I feel like I don't want them to read this book until they have children of their own, when they'll understand that the angst in the book is nothing personal.

I also think that my blog is lighter and funnier and goofier than my fiction, because in my real life, I'm not depressed, my kids aren't colicky, I have a great husband who's incredibly devoted to his family, and I've never had to deal with the really awful things Jenny encounters like spousal abandonment and non-sleeping babies—so the blog has much more about, you know, fun outings and art projects, funny things my adorable kids say, and books we like to read. But, as I always tell my daughter when she gets anxious about the parts of picture books where things actually happen, "You have to have some trouble in a story or it's not a story."

I am lucky to have this part-time job writing blog posts and short essays for oprah.com, which means that I get some hours every week to devote to seeking and creating subject matter that is life-affirming, uplifting, and focused on happiness—which I have to say was a truly lovely antidote to spending so much mental time with Jenny Lipkin.

Who are your writing influences? What are you currently reading? I've always been a catholic (with a small *c,* of course) reader, and I'm influenced by everything. My early literature loves were the Modernists, especially Virginia Woolf, who could write absolutely everything, from clarion essays to psychologically complex novels to totally crazy formal experiments. I'm continually awed and inspired and nourished by Vladimir Nabokov, J. D. Salinger, Kathryn Davis, Joy Williams, James Salter, Marilynne Robinson, Lydia Davis, Miranda July, Lorrie Moore, and I could go on and on.

In thinking about writing this book, I looked to writers who tell difficult stories beautifully, like Elizabeth Strout, Alice Hoffman, Alice Munro, and Charles Baxter. More recently, my slow readers book group read Katie Ward's *Girl Reading,* which I adored, and a book-blogger friend pressed into my hand a copy of Tove Jansson's *The Summer Book,* which is the perfect, quiet summer book. And on my bedside table, along with a stack of my kids' picture books (really) are Sheila Heti's *How Should a Person Be?,* Karen Russell's *Swamplandia!,* Cheryl Strayed's *Torch,* Carol Rifka Brunt's *Tell the Wolves I'm Home,* and Amanda Coplin's *The Orchardist,* and I wish I could read all of them at once right now. I have a constant hunger for novels, clearly.

What do you hope readers remember and carry with them after reading your novel?

My greatest hope for this book is that it might help one mother somewhere feel less alone and less freaked out, or at least to know that it's okay to have complicated feelings about motherhood and marriage. I wanted to write about the secret lives that women lead, the stories that women only tell other women, the creative potential so many women squelch because of the circumstances of their lives. My mother's painting always took a backseat to raising us kids, same for her mother who was a life-long aspiring writer, same for *her* mother who wrote at least one never-published novel—I think there is some story like this in every woman's life.

But mostly I just wanted it to be entertaining.

What are you working on next?

Well, I try not to talk about projects in progress because I start to feel superstitious, but I will share that it's a ghost story, which is ridiculous because I never read ghost stories and have certainly never written one. I was inspired by Patrick DeWitt, the author of this amazing, gorgeous, funny, sad Western novel called *The Sisters Brothers,* who said in interviews that he was totally unfamiliar with the whole Western genre and just made things up as he went along. My hope is that my ignorance will set me free. Or at least not hinder me *too* much.

ENHANCE YOUR BOOK CLUB

1. We learn bits and pieces of the rusalka's story, but never the whole truth. Have each member of the group write a short origin story for her, then share them.
2. Alternatively, have each member pick a country and research its folklore on mermaids or water spirits to share with the group. Or read a classic mermaid tale, like Hans Christian Andersen's "The Little Mermaid," and discuss how it differs from the popular Disney retelling.
3. Compare this novel to another book that share themes of motherhood and self-discovery such as *The Peach Keeper* or *Prospect Park West*. How are they similar? How are they different? If *The Mermaid of Brooklyn* was made into a movie, who would you cast?
4. Visit author Amy Shearn's blog, householdwords.wordpress.com, and her website, amyshearnwrites.com, to follow her real-life adventures as an author, mother, and Brooklyn resident.